Praise for
the action-adventure novels
by Captain David E. Meadows

"An absorbing, compelling look at America's future place in the world. It's visionary and scary."

—Joe Buff, author of *Seas of Crisis*,
Straits of Power, and *Tidal Rip*

"If you enjoy a well-told tale of action and adventure, you will love David Meadows's series *The Sixth Fleet*. Not only does the author know his subject but [his] fiction could readily become fact. These books should be read by every senator and congressman in our government so that the scenarios therein do not become history."

—John Tegler, syndicated talk show
host of *Capital Conversation*

"Meadows will have you turning pages and thinking new thoughts." —Newt Gingrich

"Meadows takes us right to the bridge, in the cockpit, and into the thick of battle. Meadows is a military adventure writer who's been there, done it all, and knows the territory. This is as real as it gets." —Robert Gandt

"Meadows delivers one heck of a fast-paced, roller-coaster ride with this exhilarating military thriller."

—*Midwest Book Review*

CHARLIE CLASS

DAVID E. MEADOWS

BERKLEY BOOKS, NEW YORK

THE BERKLEY PUBLISHING GROUP
Published by the Penguin Group
Penguin Group (USA) Inc.
375 Hudson Street, New York, New York 10014, USA

Penguin Group (Canada), 90 Eglinton Avenue East, Suite 700, Toronto, Ontario M4P 2Y3, Canada
(a division of Pearson Penguin Canada Inc.)
Penguin Books Ltd., 80 Strand, London WC2R 0RL, England
Penguin Group Ireland, 25 St. Stephen's Green, Dublin 2, Ireland (a division of Penguin Books Ltd.)
Penguin Group (Australia), 250 Camberwell Road, Camberwell, Victoria 3124, Australia
(a division of Pearson Australia Group Pty. Ltd.)
Penguin Books India Pvt. Ltd., 11 Community Centre, Panchsheel Park, New Delhi—110 017, India
Penguin Group (NZ), 67 Apollo Drive, Rosedale, North Shore 0632, New Zealand
(a division of Pearson New Zealand Ltd.)
Penguin Books (South Africa) (Pty.) Ltd., 24 Sturdee Avenue, Rosebank, Johannesburg 2196,
South Africa

Penguin Books Ltd., Registered Offices: 80 Strand, London WC2R 0RL, England

This is a work of fiction. Names, characters, places, and incidents either are the product of the author's imagination or are used fictitiously, and any resemblance to actual persons, living or dead, business establishments, events, or locales is entirely coincidental. The publisher does not have any control over and does not assume any responsibility for author or third-party websites or their content.

CHARLIE CLASS

A Berkley Book / published by arrangement with the author

PRINTING HISTORY
Berkley edition / November 2009

Copyright © 2009 by Penguin Group (USA) Inc.
Cover illustration by Anthony Russo.
Cover design by Roman Pietrs.
Interior text design by Kristin Del Rosario.

ISBN: 978-0-425-23109-8

BERKLEY®
Berkley Books are published by The Berkley Publishing Group,
a division of Penguin Group (USA) Inc.,
375 Hudson Street, New York, New York 10014.
BERKLEY® is a registered trademark of Penguin Group (USA) Inc.
The "B" design is a trademark of Penguin Group (USA) Inc.

PRINTED IN THE UNITED STATES OF AMERICA

10 9 8 7 6 5 4 3 2 1

Foreword

This book chronicles the beginning days of the Middle East war best known as the Yom Kippur War, when Egypt and Syria, with a surprise attack, drove Israeli forces back from the Suez Canal and the foothills of the Golan Heights. It was a war that catapulted the United States and the Soviet Union to the brink of war, where nuclear gamesmanship eventually drove both to back down.

During the history of the Cold War, three years marked the ascendancy of a chase by the Soviet Navy to best the United States Navy on the high seas and to achieve the age-old dream of Russia to be an ocean going Navy power.

My first book, *Final Run*, released in May 2007, revolved around the year 1956. In 1956, there was only one nuclear submarine in the world (the USS *Nautilus*) and America had it. The Soviet Union wanted one also, and the action-adventure novel *Final Run* had an American diesel submarine infiltrating the Soviet Northern Fleet to find out how far along the Soviet Navy was in developing one.

The second book in this trilogy, *Echo Class*, released in February 2009, took place in 1967. In 1967, America was mired in Vietnam and Rickover had driven the American submarine force to become a near-total nuclear force. The Soviet Navy was achieving the same and was beginning to flex its growing Navy might in the oceans of the world.

The events of the Cuban Missile Crisis were never forgotten by the Soviet Navy or its Admiral of the Fleet and the father of the Soviet Navy, Admiral Sergey Georgyevich Gorshkov. Gorshkov dominated the Soviet Navy in his quest to achieve Russia's dream of being an ocean going Navy force. And, after the humiliation of the Soviet Union in 1962 during the Cuban Missile Crisis, he wanted to achieve parity or superiority, to meet the U.S. Navy on equal terms on the highways of the oceans. He was a sly old fox, having been born in 1910, joined the Navy as a youth, fought in World War II, and, in 1956, the pivotal year for the fledgling Navy, become the head of it.

He used the events of the Cuban Missile Crisis to convince the Kremlin to accelerate the submarine force to a nuclear one. But he was unable to use the arguments to convince them of the need for aircraft carriers. Even in 1967, the Soviet Union was suffering economic ills because of its military race with the West.

On October 5, 1973, Egypt and Syria, against the advice of the Soviet Union, had already moved its forces into place. The Soviet Union ordered its fleet to sail from its friendly ports in Egypt and Syria, so as to distance itself from what it considered an ill-conceived idea. When the Arab armies launched their surprise attack at noon on October 6, 1973, they caught the Israeli military asleep.

Israel was forced to fight pitched battles against the advancing Arab armies as this small Jewish nation, set amid a sea of hostile nations, rushed to call up its reserves. The success of the Arab armies surprised even the Arabs, as it surprised their patron the Soviet Union.

The largest airlift of supplies since the Berlin Airlift was started by the United States: Operation Nickel Grass. I flew with Fleet Air Reconnaissance Squadron Two out of Rota, Spain, during this period, providing early warning protection for the massive United States Air Force logistic effort.

With the Israeli military forces reconstituted and military supplies being transported directly to the battlefront from off-loading USAF transports, the tide turned against the Arab armies. The Israeli military started driving back the Syrian Army, which quickly evaporated, leaving nothing between Israel and Damascus. On the western front, the Egyptian Second Army was routed and the Third Army was surrounded.

The Soviet Union threatened to intervene with its Army and Air Force deploying to engage the Israelis directly. Things went downhill rapidly between the United States and the Soviet Union.

This book, *Charlie Class*, does not intend to capture the entire scenario of this war, which brought the United States and the Soviet Union to the brink of nuclear war, closer than anything that occurred during the Cuban Missile Crisis. It centers on the beginning days of the war, when the Israeli forces were being turned back and their supplies of war-fighting materials were quickly being depleted. It incorporates the historic personalities of the event along with an action-adventure story of undersea warfare between two submarine captains of the United States Navy and the Soviet Navy, as they try to prove to themselves, to their crews, and to their superiors the value of their service. I hope you enjoy it, and I hope it stimulates you to find out more about the events of October 1973, for in that month and that year, the Soviet Navy did not back down as it did in 1962, and if not for the political and nuclear gamesmanship of the Nixon administration, World War III would have been a distinct probability.

Acknowledgments

After fourteen military action-adventure novels, *Charlie Class* will be my last for the foreseeable future.

I want to thank Tom Colgan of The Berkley Publishing Group for his kind advice, support, and for providing the opportunities Penguin Group gave me in writing these fourteen works of military action-adventure. I would also have been lost wothout his able assistants, Sandra Harding and Niti Bagchi, who worked with me to bring these books from gestation to publication. I would also like to thank my agent, John Talbot, for his encouragement and dialogues while writing these last two series.

And I would never have published the first book if my wife, Felicity, had not encouraged me to write about what I knew: the Navy. Her inspiration and the support from my daughter, Sara, and son, Nicholas, always gave me the energy and enthusiasm to write.

Many of my shipmates and friends provided me technical advice and assistance through the years of writing these military action-adventure novels. To all of them, who are too many to name without accidentally missing someone, my hearty thanks and appreciation for your help in this literary ride.

Even with all of this encouragement and guidance, I would never have written these books without you, the reader. I want to thank the thousands of loyal readers who honored me by reading my books. I have enjoyed writing them and I have been honored by your patronage. I always looked forward to the e-mail reviews chronicled in the online bookstores as well as the feedback sent to my website at www.sixthfleet.com. I also made contact with former ship-mates whom I had lost contact with over the years of a U.S. Navy career, and those instances were great rewards for writing.

May Davy Jones provide calm seas and following winds to each and every one of you.

Cheers,
David

ONE

HE slowed the car at the front gate to Norfolk Naval Base, pulling behind the two in front of him. The sailor manning the entrance waved the first through with a perfunctory glance inside the car. The one directly in front of him was driven by a military wife and had a couple of children dancing around in the backseat. The sailor held up his hand and leaned inside the car. He imagined the woman in a short skirt with a few inches of skin showing above the knee. A moment later the sailor waved her through, his eyes following the car for a moment before he turned back to him.

"G'morning, Warrant," the sailor said as he slowed at the gate.

"Looks like a nice day, Petty Officer Lawrence," he replied, reading the man's name tag. The sailor looked familiar, but they changed so often on the gate—only those shit-canned off the ships or having medical problems ever earned long-term assignment as gate guards.

"It is. I like Sundays. You don't have a lot of traffic. Just those folks heading to the base exchange for a little shopping, or some tourists who want to motor along the piers and look at the ships."

The warrant officer forced a smile. "I know what you mean. Well, I have to get going."

"Oh, sorry, Warrant," the gate guard replied, rendering a half hearted salute as the warrant officer drove by him onto the base. If they ever caught the guard and asked, he would say one reason had to do with lack of respect. Warrant officers and limited duty officers—LDOs—were treated a little beneath the level of respect accorded normal officers, who were mostly graduates of "Boat U" up in Annapolis.

He drove straight until the road ended near the eastern end of the base. Across the channel was historic Fort Monroe, famous for having been the best site from which to watch the battle of the *Merrimac* and *Monitor* during the Civil War and then for incarcerating Jefferson Davis afterward. A cargo ship was coming through the channel, shipping crates that were boxcars stacked four high across the main deck. The sound of seagulls rode the light morning breeze carrying the smell of the sea along with their hostile cries.

He turned left and followed the S curve around to the first pier. Four aircraft carriers were tied up at the pier, two on each side of it. He made a mental note of their names. Parking was plentiful this morning. Only the watch crews were on board. He looked at the clock on the dashboard. Once the churches let out around noon, more would show up. Families would come down to spend the afternoon with their husbands and fathers who were stuck on the gray behemoths until Monday afternoon. Weekend duty was the bane to the married fellows. Then, again, there were some like Joe . . . oh what was his name? He forgot the last name, but Joe had six kids. If he had had six kids, he would have volunteered for weekend duty every weekend.

He passed the aircraft carriers. No aircraft were on them, which indicated that none were planning on getting under way anytime soon. Besides, the aircraft from Oceana Naval Air Station would fly on board them once they were out to sea, so the absence of aircraft meant little, but his handlers wanted to know.

The sound of bells being struck carried through the open window of the car as the clock on the dash showed ten o'clock. He reached down and turned on the radio. The talk show host of WHRV was talking with someone about the history of jazz. He turned it down where it quickly became background noise as he drove.

He wondered why his handlers wanted this information.

He slowed as he neared the set of wide piers so he could count the large amphibious helicopter carriers tied up alongside. How small they looked alongside the aircraft carriers—and how huge they looked when they were operating alone. Five years he had been doing this, and when he retired from the Navy, his Navy pension would be pocket change compared to what he was being paid now. While the money had meant something when he started doing this, the excitement of doing it now outweighed the money.

He sped up after passing the four tied-up amphibious ships and mentally noting their names. The cruisers and destroyers he was not interested in. They were warships, but his handlers wanted the aircraft carriers, amphibious ships, and the classes of auxiliary ships in port.

The warrant reached over and rolled down the opposite window to let some of the near springlike September breeze flow through the car. He drove quickly and came to where the submarines and auxiliary ships were docked. There was no movement other than the American flag from their bridges and a couple of sailors standing watch near the brow.

Movement at the auxiliary piers caught his attention. It seemed a lot of activity compared to what he had noticed on other Sundays. Tractor-trailers were lined up with their back doors opened. Lines of sailors ran from the trucks, up the brow, and into the ships as they hand-over-hand moved boxes from the land to the ships. It had to be food and "lights," as they called anything that could be lifted by hand. Ammunition, weapons, large items needed the crane, and none of the cranes were manned or operating from the ships.

As he passed the last ship, the USS *Concord*, AFS-5, he saw three gray Navy tractor-trailers with the words "Earle Weapons Station" painted on their gray doors. None of the doors were opened, and armed sailors walked around them. Two of the trucks were enclosed, but a gigantic tarp covered the third one and the outline of the "things" beneath it was long and slender. He figured they were torpedoes—Mark 45 variants—though nowadays they could be Harpoon cruise missiles. It was harder to tell. He did a quick calculation— fifteen canisters, he estimated. Another tidbit for his paymaster.

From where the trucks were parked, he guessed they were going to off-load onto the USS *Concord,* which had a huge "5" painted on both sides of her bow. He recalled when he saw the *Concord* in 1967, how new the auxiliary ship was. Movement along the side of the ship caught his attention. Here in 1973, six years later, boatswain mates hung over the side sitting on a plank of wood suspended from the main deck, chopping away specs of rust.

"Shit, man. I've been there and done that," he said aloud, chuckling. "I don't envy your job, but at least it's a nice sunny day for breathing iron." He laughed and then with a sneer mumbled, "Stupid shits."

Concord must be making ready to sally forth to do the nation's work. He smiled. If they only knew that because of him, his . . .

What should he call them? Sometimes he thought of them as handlers, based on some spy novels he'd read, and other times he referred to them as the paymaster, for the money was the metric for his success. He smiled. He sure as hell did not think of them as his bosses and definitely not partners. He was the one in charge. Not only did he know it, but they knew it, too. The smile faded. The only thing that eventually would be a problem was that he was going to retire from the Navy. When he did, he didn't see much he could provide them. But he'd think of something.

A burst of steam shrilled across the pier from the *Concord*, drawing his attention for a moment.

"If you only knew what I knew, you'd know they know every damn thing that is going to happen." He wondered if the Navy would ever catch him. "Not a snowball's chance in hell," he told himself.

A base police car was parked at the end of the logistics

pier, between the last tractor-trailer and the pierside road. The two officers glanced his way as he passed them. He threw up his hand and one of them returned the wave.

Near the end of the piers he passed the offices of Cruiser Destroyer Group Eight. The two-star admiral that commanded that Group was responsible for war-fighting readiness of the cruisers and destroyers stationed in Norfolk. This admiral's peers in Charleston, South Carolina, at Commander Cruiser Destroyer Group Two, and in Jacksonville, Florida— Commander Cruiser Destroyer Group Twelve—had similar responsibilities, but nowhere the size of the fleet that Eight commanded.

The warrant cocked his head. He had to admit that being a member of this superpower Navy gave him a lot of earning power. Being a communications specialist gave him a lot of access. Some retired and made a few hundred as a contractor. He smiled. In his closet were boxes stacked full of hundred-dollar bills.

The road curved to the left slightly as he reached the end of the first set of piers. He followed it around the small curvature to the second set. The USS *Mount Whitney,* with the white bow number "20," was the first ship, at the first pier. Antenna clusters crowded the top of the command and control vessel that Commander U.S. Second Fleet called home. It would be this ship that would sail forth with the Second Fleet if the United States ever had to fight the Soviets in the Atlantic or the North Atlantic.

Lots of good friends on these ships with whom he had served over the years. Most of whom would go down fighting with their ships if such a confrontation ever occurred. But in his heart he knew his Navy—*he still thought of the U.S. Navy as his Navy, even as he did what he did*—would never fight the Soviets. The Soviets were too weak to ever take on America's powerhouse fleets.

As he slowed near the first pier, the voices of several sailors, who were grab-assing near the end of the pier, drinking beer and hanging with cigarettes, rode the slight September breeze. He caught the words "Building 20" and knew they were referring to the *Mount Whitney*. A Navy slur about the ship was that she so seldom got under way she might as well be a building.

Several destroyers blocked the next few piers. Piers his "masters"—nope, wrong name for them. "In this game I am the master." He glanced at the speedometer and saw he was doing five miles an hour. Nice, leisurely drive in the morning.

More submarines came into sight. He counted eight at the two piers. Last week, there had been twelve. Four were gone. This would be useful information for them and worth a little bit more revenue, in his mind. Carriers and submarines, submarines and carriers. If he could get the cryptographic keying material for the submarines, he'd be sitting on some beach somewhere hoisting those drinks with umbrellas and having little señoritas filing the fungus from his toes. But, he didn't work at Submarine Forces Atlantic, and even if he had, their security would be dangerous to circumvent.

Submariners had no sense of humor, in his book. Everything was black-and-white with them. Either you did it this way or you didn't do it at all. Rickover had really screwed the pooch on them, forcing them to do things one way and one way only. It was this nuclear "thing" that cost them their laxness. SUBLANT made him think of an anthill with everyone doing his own little job and only his job.

The last pier had the vintage USS *Yellowstone* with the number "27" painted on its bow. The destroyer tender was older than dirt. Built during World War II, the tender got under way about once a month, which was twice the number for the *Mount Whitney*. *Yellowstone* spent most of her time tied pierside fixing the ships tied up alongside her.

His forehead wrinkled. He wondered if the *Yellowstone* ever worked on submarines, but then shook his head. "Those bubbleheads would never, ever allow anything with the word 'destroyer' associated with it to touch a screw on board their hallowed boats." He had done his time on 'destroyers' and he had pulled liberty with bubbleheads—those vainglorious dolphin-owners.

Dolphins were the gold-and-silver chest devices awarded

when a submariner successfully qualified on board a submarine.

At the end of piers, the warrant officer backed into a nearby parking space, took out a pack of cigarettes, and lit one. The smoke filtered out the opened driver's window as he watched the submarines. He hated those black boats and all who rode them. He laughed at the thought.

A base police car drove down the pier, and seeing him parked there, it pulled into the empty parking space alongside his car.

"G'morning, sir. Is everything all right?"

"Morning, Officer. Everything is fine. Just out for a drive." He pointed at the ships. "Never thought I'd see the day that I miss being at sea."

The two policemen exchanged glances.

"Well, have a nice one, sir," the driver said as he put the Norfolk Naval Base cruiser into reverse and turned around.

"And today isn't the day either," he said aloud as he tossed a wave at them. The one on the shotgun side returned it. "If you only knew what I knew."

He finished his cigarette and looked at his watch. He had two hours to do the same thing at Little Creek, though why anyone would be concerned about the smaller amphibious ships there, he had no idea. If an amphibious task force was going to deploy, it would start here with the "big guys" such as the *Iwo Jima* and *Guam*.

Also, the Marines would have to embark, and that was done at Morehead City, North Carolina. To get the Marines ready, Commander, U.S. Marine Force Atlantic, over at the Atlantic Fleet Compound, would have been burning the lights brightly and pizza delivery trucks would have been burning rubber through the gate all last night.

He had driven through there the night before and seen nothing that indicated anything other than normal routine for a Saturday. Today showed him that Norfolk Naval Base was asleep as usual on the weekend, so why were his clients—that was a good name for them: clients—insisting he do this drive-by surveillance.

He turned right at the intersection between the two sets of

piers and was quickly out the gate and heading toward the Naval Amphibious Base at Little Creek in Virginia Beach. Forty-five minutes later he was finished there and on the expressway heading north, passing through the tunnel, heading toward Williamsburg. He glanced at his watch. He'd make the rendezvous easily, with time to spare.

October 3, 1973—Wednesday

ADMIRAL Sergey Georgyevich Gorshkov folded the message carefully and laid it on his desk. Sitting across from him in his Kremlin office were two of his aides and Admiral Anton Zegouniov, an aide to Chairman Brezhnev.

"What do you think, Bear?" Gorshkov asked.

"It is a precarious situation, Admiral."

Both men were famous for different reasons. Gorshkov had assumed the mantle of Admiral of the Soviet Fleet in 1956, the same year that Admiral Zegouniov had become the commander of the first Soviet nuclear submarine. The difference was that Gorshkov was known throughout the Soviet Union and Zegouniov's prestige was limited to insiders within the Kremlin and the Soviet Navy. Another difference was that the influence Gorshkov peddled permeated throughout the Kremlin, but Zegouniov was primarily limited to Brezhnev—and to himself.

"What are your suggestions, Admiral?" Zegouniov asked.

Gorshkov shook his head. "I have already started actions, Bear. I have alerted Admiral Volobuyev, who is the commander of our Fifth Eskandra in the Mediterranean. By dusk on Thursday, October 4, every Soviet warship in Egypt and Syria will be at sea. They will sail from Port Said, Alexandria, and Lattakia. Those in the anchorages east and west of Crete will remain at anchor for the time being."

"And the submarine force."

Gorshkov grunted and smiled. "We are fortunate in that we have over twenty submarines in the Mediterranean right now. Largest number we have had for some time. Serendipitous, really." He let out a deep breath. "We will have over eighty warships in the Mediterranean. Most are warships capable of launching anticarrier cruise missiles at the Americans. For the first time in a very, very long time, Bear, we are in a position of superiority."

"That is good news. Would you mind if I shared that with the chairman?"

Gorshkov laughed. Did he mind if Zegouniov shared this with the chairman? What did Zegouniov expect him to say? No, Bear, we must keep this from the chairman. We must never tell him anything. Instead, he looked at the younger submariner and bearer of the Hero of the Soviet Union medal and said, "Of course not. I think the chairman will be pleased with his Navy."

"There will be challenges with the Americans."

Gorshkov nodded. "When have there not been?" He pushed his chair away from the desk and walked around it. "They will sortie their Sixth Fleet to the Eastern Mediterranean, and then from their bastions along the East Coast they will send additional Navy forces. We will have six to ten days before the Americans will achieve parity. I do not want them to achieve dominance."

Zegouniov agreed. "Then we must do something to slow that down."

"I have already started Stallion."

Zegouniov's eyebrows furrowed. "I don't think I am familiar with Stallion."

"Stallion, or Steadfast as it was first known, is the cover term for when we have little option but to take on the American Navy."

Zegouniov bit his lower lip for a moment. "I am not sure if the chairman wants to do this, Admiral."

Gorshkov sat down in the empty cushioned chair near Zegouniov. "It is a precautionary measure, my friend. On Friday, October 5, if our Arab allies—and I use the term very loosely—go against our recommendations, they will set off a chain of events that will catapult the Soviet Union and America into another confrontation." Gorshkov rested his chin for a moment on clasped hands. Then he looked at Zegouniov. "I am not going to suffer another Cuba."

"I understand, sir. I do not think this chairman would allow us to—"

Gorshkov laughed as he interrupted Zegouniov's thought. "It is ironic, isn't it, my esteemed friend?"

"How is that, Admiral?"

"The Americans have as little control over their ally as we do ours. I believe our third world partners—as we and the Americans like to think of them—know how to play us against each other. They are like beggars in the street pestering you until you give them something. You get a few minutes of respite and then discover their hands are in your pockets again."

Zegouniov nodded, but said nothing.

"At least the Americans have no idea what is going to happen in forty-eight hours."

"I don't think the chairman shares that belief, Admiral."

"He will."

"How can you be sure?"

Gorshkov grinned. One of his aides set a cup of hot tea in front of him. "Are you sure you won't have another cup, Admiral?"

Zegouniov waved the suggestion away. "I would never sleep tonight if I have one more cup of this strong tea."

"The reason we know the Americans are unaware of Sadat's adventurism is we have a friend in Norfolk. His last report showed no signs of the Americans hastening to deploy another carrier. The submarines are tied pierside. The amphibious ships are in their port a few miles down the coast, in Little Creek. There have been no late night deliveries of pizza there, and our other friend at the Pentagon confirms the same in Washington." He smiled. "But, most of all, our friend in Norfolk has access to their most secret communications. He is able to read their intelligence warnings and there is nothing there."

"And he knows what is going to happen on Friday?"

Gorshkov shook his head. "I would never trust a traitor, even when he works for us. All he does is provide weekly reports on the status of the American fleet, along with copies of their daily intelligence messages." He sipped his tea. "We are negotiating with the American for copies of their crypto-graphic material," he lied. Two years ago the Glavnoe Raz-vedyvatel'noe Upravlenie (GRU), which stood for the Main Intelligence Directorate of the Soviet Navy, had already acquired access to the U.S. Navy's cryptographic material and were exploiting much of the Navy's encyphered messages. The one place they had had no success had been the tactical messages of the warships at sea. Their contact had been unsuccessful in providing them. There were some things best kept within the Soviet Navy.

"I would submit, Admiral Gorshkov, that on Friday when our ships begin to sortie, the Americans will realize some-thing is up."

"I would agree. We cannot stop them from sending addi-tional warships to the Mediterranean, but we can slow them down."

"Submarines."

"My thoughts also, but I cannot afford any of my subma-rines that are with Admiral Volobuyev's fleet in the Mediterranean." Gorshkov paused for another sip of the tea. He nodded at the aide. "Very good." Turning back to Zegouniov, he continued by holding up one finger. "Number one, Volobuyev will need them because the Americans will try to enter the Eastern Mediterranean en masse." He held up a second finger. "And, number two, you know how Admiral Volobuyev is. He would send a squad of Spetsnaz to discuss with me why in the hell I would take his boats away at a time when I want him to confront the Americans."

"How about Admiral Yegorov?"

"I see our great minds work alike, Admiral Zegouniov," Gorshkov said, tapping the side of his head. He set the cup on the coffee table in front of the two men and leaned sideways toward Zegouniov. "Admiral Yegorov has offered five Project 670 boats operating near the Iceland–United Kingdom gap. I have told him what we have discussed, ordered him to slow the Americans from augmenting their force in the Mediterranean. I expect a plan from him before midnight."

Both men looked at the mounted clock behind Gorshkov's

desk. It showed a few minutes before nine o'clock. Street and building lights on the other side of Red Square flickered through the two huge windows that flanked the narrow wall between them and where the clock was mounted. Directly beneath the clock hung the framed Gorshkov quote: "Better is the enemy of Good Enough."

"I suspect he has his men bent over the charts even as we speak," Zegouniov said.

"I suspect you are right, Comrade Admiral. I have also told him that covertness is paramount in getting his boats into position."

"You mean?"

"I mean they are not to be detected. They are to reach their destination and there must be no witnesses to this change—to this deployment. The American Navy is no one's fool. It will not take them long to associate our emergent deployment from Egypt and Syria with imminent military action, but there is a chance they may intepret it for what it is: our desire to distance ourselves from being associated with this madness on the part of the Arabs."

"If that is our intent and the Americans realize it, Admiral Gorshkov, then there is a chance that we will not have a confrontation."

Gorshkov leaned back in his chair and nodded. "But, if they detect the Project 670–class boats moving into the Atlantic, which the boats will have to do if they are going to be in position to slow down any augmenting of the Sixth Fleet, then they may reevaluate the real reason for our deployment as being our moving into position to keep them from helping Israel."

"Then we would have a confrontation."

Gorshkov agreed. "Oh, we are going to have a confrontation. This is our moment to avenge Cuba. This is a moment for the United States to realize that our Navy is more than capable of meeting the American Navy at sea and holding our own."

"Many may die and it could escalate quickly, Admiral," Zegouniov cautioned. "I am not sure the chairman would go that far."

"Confrontation does not mean we have to go to war. Confrontation means standing eyeball-to-eyeball and making sure your opponent knows that if necessary you will fight. Once that occurs, our relationship with the Americans—and with their NATO allies—will change forever."

"And if the Americans don't blink?"

"We don't either. Then it will be up to our politicians to reach agreement."

"I think the chairman is prepared to stand eyeball-to-eyeball also."

Gorshkov laughed. "I know he is. You know he is, too, Bear. The chairman is very smart. He also knows we are at the pinnacle of our military might, and what is the good of having a strong military if you are never going to use it? Give it pretty uniforms, make it strut-march through Red Square every May? No, eventually you have to show that you are more than a show toy in a shop window."

TWO

"WHERE is it?" Beckenbauer asked the first mate as he stepped out onto the bridge wing of the German freighter SS *Silesia*. A night gust of moist Arctic wind caught the hatch. He blinked his eyes as ice formed on the lashes. Beckenbauer pulled the hatch shut behind him and latched it. His nose hairs were also freezing, but you never squeezed the nose when the hairs were hard-frozen—they could cut the tissue and cause bleeding.

"Good thing," Hans said, his teeth clattering as he nodded toward the hatch. "Too much heat being lost on a night like this even with them locked down."

"Where is this submarine our Irishman says he saw?"

"Not one, sir," the overweight first mate replied, holding up two fingers. "He said he saw two."

Hans handed the binoculars to the master and pointed off the starboard bow. "About two thousand yards—a nautical mile, Captain. The radar painted it. Two of them for sure, sir. I caught a glimpse before they disappeared from the surface. I thought they looked like submarines; could make out something that looked like masts in the moonlight, but I cannot be sure."

"Submarines? For sure?" he asked in disbelief as he lifted the binoculars to his eyes.

"Two of them."

"Why would submarines be on the surface? Out here they have to be Soviet, American, British, or French. And they are all nuclear-powered now. They spend their entire lives beneath the ocean. Why would any of them want to surface in the Arctic? Especially with a sea state that would rock their boats."

"Eventually, Master, even a German submarine runs out of beer."

Beckenbauer lifted the binoculars and scanned the area. "I don't see anything. And by the way, Hans, the few submarines we have are diesel-powered. Three days max they can stay down, and I doubt they have even been out of sight of land since World War II," he said. Then in a soft voice he mumbled, "Only diesels." If Germany had nuclear submarines, it could be another superpower, he thought, but that would never happen.

"You were in the German Navy, weren't you?" Hans asked.

"I did my service."

"Submarines?"

Beckenbauer shook his head. "Destroyers and coastal antisubmarine patrols. Did my three years of active duty." His thoughts turned to the antisubmarine exercises he had participated in as the underwater weapons officer for his warship. When the watch-standers reported a submarine, he knew immediately if they had truly seen a submarine, or a migrating whale, or once they reported a stick floating upright in the water as a periscope. The sea could play tricks with your eyes so you did not know what you were looking at.

"Someday we will have our own nuclear-powered submarines," Hans said with a hint of ire. He slapped his heavy gloves together and then slapped them against his chest.

"Not as long as anyone remembers World War II," Beckenbauer snapped. "Not as long as the world fears today's Germany would turn into something like yesteryear's."

"Someday, then, Captain." Hans pointed off the starboard

bow. "Seaman Ferguson saw them. My glimpse of them was not sufficient to call them submarines, but they looked like submarines."

Beckenbauer handed the glasses back to the first mate. "I can't see anything. No running lights. The waves are too high. How could either of you have seen submarines on a night like this?"

He leaned against the outer railing and looked up at the signal bridge. A sailor stood there, the main mast light outlining his silhouette. A sliver of spray rained between the sailor and him.

"Ferguson, have you ever seen a submarine before?" Beckenbauer shouted in his deep German-accented English.

He saw the outline of the head shake. "No, sir, but I know they were submarines."

The man's English with its heavy Irish brogue made Ferguson hard to understand. "Two submarines together is very unusual, don't you think?"

"I think one submarine on the surface is unusual," Hans added.

"Sir, I just know what I saw."

"Very well," Beckenbauer acknowledged, turning again to the first mate and switching back into German. "Whales are probably what he saw. Since you said they had masts." He shrugged, "then they could have been narwhals." Narwhal whales had long horns on their snouts that made many call them the unicorns of the sea. "This is their time for running to the Arctic."

Hans's lips pursed out as he nodded, the double chin almost bouncing off the man's foul-weather jacket. "Most likely you are correct, Captain. Most likely what the Irishman saw were a couple of narwhal whales on the surface giving each other handjobs."

"I think they must be Americans," Ferguson shouted in German.

Beckenbauer looked up at the watch. "American?"

"Only country that has submarines out here, sir," Ferguson replied in English.

A fresh series of sharp northerly breezes caused Beckenbauer and Hans to reach up and check the zippers on their jackets. Ferguson never moved.

The bow of the *Silesia* dipped as a wave broke over it. Beckenbauer and Hans grabbed the railing, Beckenbauer's curiosity over the comment forgotten as he shivered.

"Brrrrr," Beckenbauer laughed. "I hate going through the Iceland-UK gap—this cold channel of the North Atlantic. It funnels the wind. It causes even a wind with little power to whip through you, almost as if Iceland and Scotland are laughing at the puny ships as we transit between them."

"And Ferguson's report, sir?"

Beckenbauer shrugged. "We have little choice. Draft a possible sighting report, and when the radioman comes up, have him send it to German Naval Headquarters."

"Aye, sir."

"Now let's get our asses back inside before they freeze to the metal."

Beckenbauer was first back into the relative warmth of the bridge.

"What is our course and speed?" he asked the helmsman.

Hans followed, closing the hatch behind them.

"Course two-zero-zero, speed ten knots, Captain."

Beckenbauer worked his way to the radar repeater, putting his face against the rubber face-piece that filtered out any surrounding light so the viewer could see the radar without visual interference. It could be taken off at night, but most times it remained attached.

When the sweeping hand of the radar reflected land, it smeared the radar returns much like a child running his hand through wet watercolors. Beckenbauer knew this land smear to the north marked the coastline of Iceland. There were more to the west and south showing the outer ring of the Scottish islands that marked the farthermost edge of the Great Britain territory. Satisfied he had no ships near the *Silesia*, he moved to the navigation table, spread his fingers on the chart, and twisted it around so he could read it under the red light. "Hans, is this accurate?"

"Yes, sir, it is."

"That north wind is pushing us ahead of schedule. At this

rate we should be able to turn onto the southern leg of our journey about sunrise." He looked through the forward window and let out a deep sigh. "This is bad enough passage, but it could be a lot worse."

"I know, Captain. It could be better, too."

"The trip between Ireland and England will be a little better, but I'll be glad when we are through these channels and into the Atlantic. I have seen—"

Hans laughed. "I know, Captain, you have seen waves higher than the bridge wash across the beams."

"Hans, if you were not so fat I would have thrown you overboard years ago."

"I would not be fat if you had not hired the German cook."

Both men smiled.

"Tomorrow morning, go ahead and make the turn when we reach our turning point. Tell the watches to keep a good lookout for other traffic. A lot of the traffic coming from the Americas, the Mediterranean—"

"And going toward Germany."

"Prefer the channel between Ireland and England rather than face the English Channel. I know I do."

"When we off-load this shipment at Barcelona, how long do you think we will be in port?"

"We have to stop at Liverpool first. Off-load a couple of pallets of imports and pick up some additional cargo. We'll be there a couple of days."

Hans grimaced, "Liverpool! They can have their Beatles and tasteless food. Give me Spain any day. So how long will we be in Barcelona?"

"Long enough for you to wipe the city clean of tapas."

Hans guffawed. "Tapas!" he exclaimed, holding his right thumb and finger an inch apart. "Not enough food to keep a man alive. No wonder the Spanish are still in the third world. They have no strength eating nothing but tapas and drinking local rotgut beer."

"I do like Barcelona."

Hans put his thumb and forefinger together, held them to his lips, and smacked them with a kiss. "But the Spanish woman is something to behold. Tight dresses, inviting eyes . . . It is their eyes, you know. They can catch you with their eyes, mentally undress you, take you to new heights of ecstasy before they walk past you, and you are left a weak-kneed man, collapsing to the sidewalks." Hans paused, and then with a serious look asked, "How do they do that?"

"I don't know, Hans," Beckenbauer answered with a chuckle. "But it is tapas most likely you will have with your San Miguel beer." Before the first mate could respond, Beckenbauer said, "I'm going back to my quarters."

He glanced at the clock over the forward windows of the bridge. "Give me a call in the morning when it is time for the turn." He pointed upward. "And don't wake me if Ferguson sees any more mating whales."

"You still want a sighting message to the Navy?"

Beckenbauer bit his lower lip thinking about it. He had already said he did. He sighed loudly again and waved his hand as he headed toward the starboard door leading off the bridge. "Yes, yes, yes. Do it as we discussed."

"Should I mention the whales?"

Beckenbauer shook his head. "He didn't report seeing whales; he reported seeing two submarines." He pointed at Hans. "And you said they were submarines. Report two separate sightings of the submarines." He nodded. "Besides, it will give our Navy something to do while they wait for their nuclear submarines." He shut the hatch behind him, wondering if Hans would do as he ordered.

"EMERGENCY dive, emergency dive!" Captain Second Rank Deniska Bagirli shouted from the bridge. The Arctic wind whipped over the curved edges of the conning tower railing, but adrenaline racing through his body for the moment drove the wind chill away.

He stood on tiptoe as he leaned across the railing to check the forward escape hatch. The shoes of the topside watches up on the main mast clanged as they hit the deck behind him. He mentally counted the four sets as they hit. Though he knew it was supposed to be closed, he still turned and checked the after escape scuttle. Behind him he heard the fourth and final starshina scramble through the scuttle, sliding down through the bridge access trunk toward the control room below.

He squinted in the dark, trying to see if the dark spot he was looking at was closed or not, then a wave washed across the aft portion as the sub started submerging. If it had been open, the wave would have curved down into the hatch; not to mention the screaming and shouting he would have heard from the control room below.

"They are all accounted for, Captain!" Lieutenant Vasily Kiselyov, the boat's torpedo officer, reported. The young officer leaned up from the voice tube.

The wind whipped across the conning tower, drowning out the last few words of Kiselyov's report, but Bagirli knew what he'd said.

Kiselyov leaned down again and then straightened. "Sir, control room reports panel is all green with exception of the bridge."

"Very well." The conning tower was also known as the bridge.

Bagirli squinted off in the direction of the contact as the Arctic wind whipped across the two men again. A faint green light highlighted the contact's starboard side, and since he could not make out the white stern light, he knew the K-321 was off the merchant's forward right bow. The number of mast lights told him the size of the ship. He could see how sonar could mistake the vessel for the Soviet submarine tender *Volga*, but he could not forgive it. Sonar had again put him in an awkward position.

Bagirli glanced over at Kiselyov. Light from the small bulb beneath the railing of the conning tower highlighted the small openings in Kiselyov's makeshift face mask for the eyes. The nose and lips appeared ghostly, as if almost floating apart from the body. "Very well, Lieutenant Kiselyov, get below!"

He waited until Kiselyov was through the hatch before glancing forward. The bow was completely submerged. In seconds the sea would wash across the conning tower. He grabbed the rung on the deck and in a second was below.

He stopped on the ladder long enough to secure the scuttle. Then he continued through the bridge access trunk into the control room. A starshina from the topside watch rushed back up the ladder and double-checked the scuttle. Only need one open hatch, scuttle, or quick-acting water tight door to sink a submarine.

"Make your depth fifteen meters!" Bagirli shouted. "Up periscope!" came the second shout. That was supposed to be the Soviet support ship *Volga* who was bringing needed supplies. After all, his boat and the K-301 had been patrolling this area for over forty-five days. Only two things limited a nuclear-powered submarine's ability to do its wartime mission: food and weapons. He had weapons. Of course on Soviet nuclear-powered submarines, water was also a problem, but don't ever tell the powerful Navy ministers.

"Tell K-301 to take position one thousand meters off my starboard beam!"

"Aye, sir," Lieutenant Commander Pyotr Lepechin replied, grabbing a nearby handset for the internal communications, hitting the *Boyevaya Chast*'s channel four button, and relaying the order to the communicators forward. Lepechin was the operations officer for the K-321. This was his second voyage with Bagirli.

Bagirli squatted, planting his eyes against the eyepiece as the periscope rose upward. How could his sonar technicians mistake a western merchant ship for the *Volga*? The hydraulics clicked loudly as the periscope reached maximum height, bringing a cringe to Bagirli's face. He spun the periscope while in the background the announcements of depth, course, and speed echoed through the control room.

When Moscow heard about this, they would blame him. It was the fault of the useless sonar technicians. His breathing picked up as he thought of the impact this was going to have on him.

"Making my depth fifteen meters!" Lieutenant Commander Pyotr Lepechin shouted. Bagirli always made the operations officer the officer of the deck whenever the boat surfaced while on patrol. Doctrine called for the sonar officer to be the OOD when at battle stations. But he had changed this. The sonar officer barely knew how to wipe his butt on board a submarine, much less act as the officer of the deck in anything but the most routine of activities.

Bagirli mentally chalked up another against the young officer. Two fuckups were enough. No more.

Lepechin, on the other hand, was a fantastic officer. Did his job well, with exactness, and was quick to point out how Bagirli was an inspiration to all on board the K-321. No, Lepechin was too valuable to be at the OOD position for long. Bagirli didn't believe in keeping the services of such a valued officer on the watch for the entire time, but if they had to emergency dive, such as now, he wanted someone he could trust. He looked around the red-lighted control room and saw no one looking at him. He breathed a sigh of relief.

Pressing his eyes back against the eyepiece, Bagirli spun the periscope slowly the second time around. The waves made it hard to see much from the low height of the periscope eye, but off his bow between the swells he saw the mast lights of the contact.

"Sonar reports they have passive noise coming from the contact."

Sonars worked two ways. One was active, where it shot out a burst of what could be thought of as underwater radar signals. This was the most accurate way of detecting and locating a target, whether it was on the surface or below the water. Unfortunately, an active sonar also gave away your own location to the target, thereby destroying the most important tactical feature of a submarine: its stealth.

The predominent way submarines and surface ships used their sonar was passive. A passive sonar mode detected underwater noises and translated them into lines of bearings. A team of trained specialists in the control room took those timed lines of bearings, and whipping around a plotting table with pencils, rulers, and metal compasses, the antisubmarine team developed a course, speed, and estimated range to the contact. It was inexact in comparison to active sonar, but it worked, and torpedo exercises from passive sonar calculations sank targets.

"Very well, Commander Lepechin. Tell Sonar to continue with their reports." Bagirli leaned back and looked at the unmanned plotting table. "Where is the target-motion-analysis team?" he shouted. "Man the TMA table immediately!"

"Aye, sir," Lepechin replied. The operations officer jerked down the handset and started giving the orders.

Over the speaker from Sonar came the voice of Lieutenant Jasha Iltchenko, the sonar officer and deputy weapons officer. The sound of the officer's voice caused Bagirli to cringe. The sonar officer he did not trust. The man could run aground in the middle of the Atlantic Ocean with no land visible for a thousand miles. Some are destined to be Jonahs for their entire lives, and those he did not need nor want on board his boat.

"Recommend course two-seven-zero!" Lieutenant Commander Alik Obukhov shouted from his position as the navigator.

Bagirli was not surprised. Obukhov always picked one of the four main points of the compass for his initial course, whichever was nearer the original course. It would take the Georgian another ten to fifteen minutes to recommend a more refined course and speed depending on their destination.

"Make your speed ten knots!" Bagirli shouted without ever removing his eyes from the scope. He spun the scope along the line of direction where the merchant vessel was located and waited until the swells cleared sufficiently for him to see it again.

He spun the dials alongside the handles of the scope until the contact came into focus. "Mark!" The bridge area of the merchant was amidships. The contact had a raised bow, and the main mast was halfway between the bridge and the bow. It was a cargo ship; therefore it most likely had a curved stern.

Swells obscured his vision again. He waited, and several seconds later the silhouette of the contact reappeared. A funnel jutted from the center of the merchant bridge area, with a smaller mast nearer the stern. One crane system was aft of the main forward mast. Definitely a dry-goods cargo ship. In the dark it was impossible to tell the nationality of the ship, but his sonar team should have known the difference between a civilian merchant and a Soviet submarine tender.

From the mast lights and what he could see, the ship was over one hundred meters in length. He clicked the photograph button even as he doubted the picture would take in this poor light, but tactical doctrine called for it. Then he wished he had not taken the photograph. It could be used as evidence when they questioned him as to why he allowed not only his boat but the junior submarine K-301 to be seen. *But it was night! We don't care; you were the captain! Off with his head. Off with his head.*

"Contact bears one-seven-seven degrees!" the executive officer, Captain Third Rank Yerik Demirchan, announced from the other side of the scope.

"Range two thousand meters and opening," Bagirli snapped as he leaned away from the scope. Where was the XO when this mistake was happening? He had not heard the man come into the control room. It was then he noticed that both the fore and aft watertight doors to the control room were undogged. "Contact is on a left bearing drift. He is opening from us," Bagirli added.

"Were you able to tell anything about it, sir?"

"Dry goods merchant. Probably heading toward the English-Ireland channel." He leaned away, shaking his head. "No way in the dark to tell nationality. Could even be one of ours, but for the fact its course will take it near the western side of Scotland sometime tomorrow. Probably heading into the waters separating Ireland and England." His voice was calm. He prided himself on hiding his emotions behind a façade of calmness. *Where were you, XO? Why did you not double-check Sonar? Do you secretly covet my job? Of course, you do, as I did when I was XO. Well, you can go with Lieutenant Iltchenko when he goes.*

"Do you think he saw us?"

Bagirli shrugged. "Who knows, XO? Merchant seamen are such an undisciplined, scurvy lot. I would be surprised if the helmsman was awake at this early hour of the morning." *Just as you and Iltchenko are a scurvy lot, trying to sabotage my career for your own.*

Demirchan shook his head. "We should have known."

Bagirli nodded. *You should have known,* he thought. *While I was on the bridge freezing my balls off and you were down here sipping your hot tea, you lost the bubble on what was going on?* His eyes widened against the eyepiece. Maybe Demirchan did know what was going on and kept quiet? *What in the hell happened?* was what he wanted to say, but he didn't. Instead, quietly so others would not hear, he replied, "That is three times that Iltchenko's team has screwed up. Isn't it? What was it this time? Equipment? Environmentals of the sea? And secure those two watertight doors. We are targeting this ship and we are acting as if it was an exercise."

Demirchan's eyes widened. "Yes, sir. I don't know how Sonar mistook this contact for the *Volga,* sir, but I will find out."

"Do that, but while we are waiting, invite Iltchenko to the control room."

Demirchan stepped away, and within seconds both watertight doors were dogged down tight.

Almost immediately, the sonar officer undogged the forward watertight door and raced into the control room. He was panting as he stood in front of Bagirli and Demirchan.

"Sir, Lieutenant Iltchenko reporting as ordered, sir."

"What happened, Lieutenant? That was not the *Volga* that saw us," Bagirli growled. "Most likely it was a NATO merchant who is already reporting our presence to NATO. By morning, we are going to have American antisubmarine warfare aircraft all over the area. So what in the hell happened?"

The man visibly shook. "Sir, I do not know. The equipment was working well. My men were excited over properly identifying it as the *Volga*—"

"But it was not the *Volga.* It was a dry-goods merchant vessel heading southwest. It had its running and deck lights on. For all we know, it could be an American vessel reporting our position."

"But, sir, it had all the attributes of the *Volga.* It had the twin propellers. It was in the spot we were told to expect the *Volga,* and it was coming toward us."

Neither Bagirli nor Demirchan said anything.

Bagirli sighed and in a fake softer voice, continued, "Lieutenant, you have only given me one sonar factor: the two screws. The other two factors are navigational and operational factors. Sonar must have three," he held up three fingers, "sonar-related factors such as screw rotations, frequency hertz readout, sound detection of a pump or something that helps classify it. Not just that they had two screws. Ninety percent of the ships at sea have two screws. Do you know why?"

"No, sir."

"Because if one fails, they still have the other to get them back to port. Even we have two screws," Bagirli said, his voice growing louder with each word. It never hurt for a captain to show his superior knowledge, even when it was of minor things such as number of shafts.

"Yes, sir."

"Now, you tell me the contact was coming toward us? Right?"

"Yes, sir; it was on a constant bearing, decreasing range. Everything fit for it to be the—"

"Coming toward us? It was on a constant bearing, decreasing range toward the K-321? Did you notify the officer of the deck?"

"Yes, sir," Iltchenko stuttered. "I called on the intercom and told Lieutenant Commander Lepechin that we had the *Volga*—"

"But it wasn't the *Volga,* and because of your assessment, I surfaced?"

"No, sir— I mean yes, sir. But we thought it was," Iltchenko replied, his words coming in short, choppy bursts.

Bagirli knew the man had reached his own conclusion that he was about to be relieved from his duties as the sonar officer. It would mean the end of the man's career, but the safety of the boat was more important than one man's feelings, intentions, or career. Then again, Bagirli had no spare officers to give the duty. He looked at the XO. Here was the man whom he could give it to. Where was his XO in all of this? He looked back at Iltchenko.

"Give me a full written report on this incident by breakfast, Lieutenant."

"Yes, sir," Iltchenko said. He turned to go, and then thought of something and turned around. "Sir, if I may."

Bagirli nodded.

"My men are good sound technicians. Detecting and recognizing ships by the sounds they put into the water is not an exact science." As Iltchenko talked, his voice seemed to take on passion. "I know we have some challenges in not being one hundred percent accurate, but we are good, sir. Whatever mistakes are made by Sonar are mine and mine alone."

"You are very right, Lieutenant," he snapped. "You are dismissed to return to Sonar. Have that report on my desk tomorrow morning." As Iltchenko turned, Bagirli added, "And I want the names of all who were involved."

Iltchenko nodded and quickly departed the control room, heading forward toward the small sonar compartment.

"Maybe the lieutenant can be groomed and trained, Captain. You have to admire him rising to accept responsibility as a positive trait."

"Positive traits do not make an excellent officer if he has no professional skills, XO," Bagirli said softly, feeling the blood racing into his neck and face. He should make his first star from this voyage, and no one and no incident was going to stop his upward mobility. Maybe the XO and Iltchenko had served together elsewhere. Maybe they planned on the XO fleeting up to relieve him as captain. He was the senior officer of a two-boat wolf pack.

Working in tandem with another Project 670 submarine was not time for a shabby performance. Regardless of how good the officers and men were, he knew Soviet Naval Headquarters would attribute their mistakes to him. He shivered with the hidden surge of anger over his failure to double-check the information before surfacing.

"Steady on course two-seven-zero!" Lepechin announced.

Bagirli returned to the periscope and tweaked the departing merchant vessel once again. "Distance to contact two thousand meters," he reported.

"What do you think?" Demirchan asked cautiously.

"About what?"

"About Iltchenko? Do we want to leave him in place as the sonar officer or replace him?"

"We will sleep on it, XO." He glanced at the gauges along the port side of the control room.

"He is scared of you and me, you know."

"Good. If he keeps screwing up, he will be more than scared. He will be petrified." *I don't think he is scared of you, XO.* "Let's discuss it tomorrow."

"I like his passion for the job. He truly believes in his sonar team, and believing many times can create its own reality."

"You are probably right, Yerik," Bagirli lied. He was going to nail the sonsofbitches to the bulkhead. He knew what they were doing because he had done it to his first skipper. "Such as identifying an unidentified merchant as our submarine tender."

"It is a mistake. Thankfully, we are not at war," Demirchan said.

Bagirli looked up at the XO, "This man is a fuckup."

"He is right about underwater sound. I disagree with him about it being an inexact science. It is both a science and an art. Only years of experience and mistakes turn out the true experts in underwater warfare. Today, he is a young officer, but if he remains in the field of sonar, tomorrow he might well become one of our best."

"If he doesn't sink us first." He was going to hear the wails and cries of the man when he finished with him.

Lepechin announced the final trim of the boat at sixteen meters.

Bagirli bit his lower lip, for he had been thinking the same thing. He looked at the XO. "Tomorrow, bring Iltchenko's record and let's review it. Have Weapons, Lieutenant Commander Nehoda, with you. If I decide to relieve one of Nehoda's division officers for incompetence, then someone will have to take over Iltchenko's duties and responsibilities. If this was wartime, I would have relieved him tonight."

"But we are gearing for war," Demirchan said.

"We have been falling forward toward war since 1962, when Khrushchev led us away from our opportunity to prove—"

"Comrade Brezhnev will lead us to this opportunity," Demirchan interrupted.

"Let's hope our allies in the Middle East stay in their place and don't lead us there too soon." He leaned away from the periscope as it slid down. "I would like to be there when it happens."

"Captain, something is happening. Something that will place us face-to-face with the Americans. And I think we are moving into position now. We have too many submarines in the Mediterranean for this to be considered normal. I would be very surprised if the Americans are not aware of the unusual number of submarines."

"The *Pravda* clippings the communicator brought to my cabin this morning said the Egyptians are conducting their annual command post exercise. Today marks Yom Kippur for the Israelis. Unless Moscow knows something we don't, I would submit that we will continue to have business as usual," Bagirli said.

"We have been told to expect an emergency change of orders," Demirchan offered.

"Probably extending our patrol."

"An emergency change of orders is unusual, Captain."

Bagirli sighed. "You may be right, XO, but until we receive orders differently, then we will rendezvous with the *Volga*, and continue our extended patrol in this area."

Demirchan nodded. "And about Iltchenko?"

"I don't want to discuss him anymore, Yerik!" Bagirli snapped; then, in what he thought of as a calm voice, he continued, "We'll discuss it tomorrow when you bring his record with you. It may be that we should place Iltchenko in another position. One where his talents would better serve."

"Like maybe the Party-political officer, the *zampolit*?" Demirchan smiled.

As if hearing his title, Lieutenant Mikhail Volkov entered through the aft watertight door to the control room. He was munching on a chicken leg wrapped in a napkin. He smiled when he saw Bagirli and Demirchan and waved the chicken leg at them.

"Ah, Captain Bagirli and Captain Demirchan," the *zampolit* said, spitting out bits of bread and chicken as he made his way toward the periscope.

Volkov was loved by everyone on the crew, which was unusual for someone put on board specifically to ensure the officers and crew walked the Communist Party line. Volkov could be found everywhere on the boat. He was unlike any *zampolit* Bagirli had ever sailed with, and for that one reason he tolerated the man's insatiable appetite and the bulging waistline that was creeping over his belt. One moment Volkov would be in Engineering sitting down with the crew sharing cookies and the next moment in the torpedo room giving out anchovy-stuffed olives he had pilfered from the mess. Bagirli had yet to have one snide comment or negative report reach him about the *zampolit*.

Zampolits were the politically correct conscience of the Party on board warships of the Soviet Union. Most times they were tolerated, because the crew had little choice. Volkov was not the run-of-the-mill *zampolit*. But he was still a *zampolit*, and Bagirli had no intention of upsetting the officer. Neither did he intend to trust him as everyone else seemed to.

"Lieutenant Volkov," Bagirli said, shaking his head. "I have some very bad news."

The *zampolit* stopped chewing. "Is it very bad?" he asked, the heavy cheeks rippling as he forced himself to swallow the half-chewed food.

One of these days the man was going to choke to death. Bagirli sighed. "Yes, it is. We are supposed to rendezvous with our tender, the *Volga*. Unfortunately, it was the wrong vessel, so we are now waiting to see if it comes."

Volkov smiled. "It is an easy name to confuse with mine . . . Volga-Volkov, Volga-Volkov," he repeated several times, holding his pudgy hand out and tilting it right to left with each repetition. Then he stopped and looked at Bagirli. "Has almost the poetic rhythm for the start of a good nursery rhyme, don't you think?" The *zampolit's* deep blue eyes twinkled and his jowls bounced slightly as he laughed. "Besides, the *Volga* will show up, Captain. Soviet ships always show up."

"Unfortunately, this one has the food we need to continue toward our new mission. Without it . . . "

"Food?"

"Yes," the XO added. "Without the food, I will be forced to lock the pantry and ration everything until we meet them. This will be very hard on the crew, and we will need your support as the *zampolit* to show the crew how this strengthens Soviet—"

"Everything," Volkov said, aghast.

"Soviet Navy discipline," Bagirli jumped in. "That is what it will strengthen. Maybe I should institute a rationing exercise for a couple of days to give the crew the feel of what it would be like?"

The smile left the *zampolit's* face. "That is truly bad news, Captain, XO. We must find the tender. Maybe a search pattern?" Volkov offered, one hand making a circling pattern. "Widen it up until we find it."

Even Bagirli smiled at the obvious angst on the political officer's face.

"No, Lieutenant Volkov. We will rendezvous when the tender arrives," Bagirli said. "Now, why are you in my control room at this critical time?" He was serious, but tried to ask it with humor. Even for the man's jovial nature, he was still the *zampolit,* and to risk the ire of the *zampolit* was to bring the Party noose around your neck. They never stayed around your neck long. Just long enough to make sure you were strangled effectively.

Volkov looked around the control room. "I thought we were at normal depth and cruising, sir."

"Didn't you feel us surface and then do an emergency dive?"

"I felt the rise and fall," Volkov said, his pudgy hand, palm out, going up once and then down once before he dropped it.

"That was it."

"My apologies, Captain and XO. I thought we were maybe searching for a layer in which to hide the boat."

"That is perfectly all right," Bagirli said, trying to keep his words from sounding curt.

"Why are you here?" Demirchan asked.

"I need to conduct some Party-political discussions tomorrow, sirs. I would like to have the off-going watch first; then I can do the on-going watch next. Then, to ensure I have covered everyone, I will do the third watch, which should be finishing their four hours by then."

"And the officers?"

"I was thinking after dinner . . . if it is an early dinner."

Bagirli nodded. "I believe we can accommodate you. Anything for the *zampolit*."

Volkov smiled. "Thank you, sir. That is very kind."

"Where will you have the discussions?" Demirchan asked, already knowing the answer.

"I was thinking in the crew's mess for the men and in the wardroom for the officers."

"Make it so, Lieutenant Volkov."

"Thank you, sir." He turned to go, and then turned back to Bagirli. "You are not serious are you, Captain, about having a rationing exercise? For such an exercise might have grave impact on the ability of the crew to pay attention to the their Party-political work."

Bagirli shook his head. "No, Lieutenant Volkov, I don't see a reason at this time. Your insight into impact on crew morale is more than enough for me to forget any such exercise." He hoped the man observed that comment of his in the secret personnel logs *zampolits* kept.

Volkov grinned. "Then I have done my duty." Volkov thanked him, but instead of heading toward the aft door, he diverted toward the navigator. The zampolit stood above Obukhov, wàving the chicken leg and talking with the man.

"Guess Volkov has not given up on getting Obukhov to join the Party-political work," Demirchan said, watching the *zampolit* and navigator talk.

"It must be a *zampolit* thing," Bagirli offered. "Each submarine has two navigators and that is all they do: navigate. They are the only ones on Soviet submarines who are exempt from attending Party-political work."

"Everyone should have some benefit from his assignment." Demirchan looked at Bagirli. "I wonder if Obukhov will cave in as Zaharovich has."

"I do not know, XO. Tell me later how Volkov managed to convince a navigator to give up the one big perk he has."

Seconds later the hefty Russian *zampolit* was out the aft watertight door, sticking the remnants of the chicken between his teeth to free his hands to secure it behind him.

"He will choke someday."

"Maybe, XO, but he is one of the best *zampolits* I have served with," Bagirli said. You never knew who was a spy for the Party and who was not.

Demirchan agreed. "He takes his work seriously enough without trying to interject himself into operations. Do you think he keeps individual records on everyone as *zampolits* are supposed to do?"

"Just keep feeding him," Bagirli replied, not answering the question. If Volkov did not keep individual records and failed to bring back his own subjective interpretation of individual Party loyalty, then the *zampolit* himself would be suspect. Best to keep the man fed and happy.

"At this rate, we may be unable to get him through the topside scuttle when we dock back in Severomorsk."

"Steady on course two-seven-zero, speed ten knots!" Lepechin announced.

"Very well!" Bagirli replied.

The internal communications system rang. Lepechin picked up the handset, spoke a few words, and turned to Bagirli. "Sir, that was Communications. They have contact with the *Volga*."

"Did they get a location?"

The IC rang near the navigator, who lifted the handset and answered it.

"XO, talk with Lieutenant Commander Obukhov and try to get him to answer the handsets properly. 'Control room,' not 'Hello.'"

"Aye, sir."

Lieutenant Commander Alik Obukhov hung up the handset and scanned the notes in front of him. He slid the ruler along the chart and then looked up at the captain. "Captain Bagirli! The *Volga* bears zero-six-five from us, distance fifty-five kilometers.

"Very well, tell the K-301 to break off and make for the *Volga*."

A moment later the order had been passed and acknowledged by the sister submarine. K-321 was on its own.

"Officer of the Deck, make your course zero-six-five; bring her up to fifteen knots." Bagirli glanced at the clock on the aft bulkhead. He still had plenty of time. The clock on the bulkhead showed midnight. Dawn was a good eight hours away. They would rendezvous with the Soviet submarine tender in less than two hours, small-boat transfer the increased rations, and he would be beneath the waves before the American P-3C antisubmarine patrol aircraft were overhead. Seldom did they fly at night. Four hours at most on the surface.

"Commander Lepechin, tell Sonar the location of the *Volga* and tell them to provide an intercept course on the tender. Tell them I want an estimated course and speed on *Volga*."

"Sir, I have that," Lieutenant Commander Lepechin replied.

"Good. Then you will know if they are accurate or not."

"Yes, sir."

The forward watertight door opened, bouncing once off the metal prongs designed to keep it from hitting the bulkhead. "Captain!" Lieutenant Mauduna Karimov shouted as he hurried toward Bagirli.

"Shut the hatch!" Lepechin growled.

Bagirli shut his eyes for a moment. Uzbeks were emotional lots. Why in the hell they let them on board Soviet submarines was beyond him. *Look at the man,* he thought, *his body is designed for the back of a horse, galloping across the plains, not sulking away deep down beneath the ocean surface.*

Karimov swirled around and quickly twirled the wheel on the watertight door, the dogs tightening around the edges and sealing the control room from the forward portion of the submarine.

A moment later Karimov stood ramrod straight in front of

Bagirli and Demirchan, one hand in a salute while the other held out a message.

"As you were, Lieutenant." At least the overabundance of respect the man showed was admirable ... even for an Uzbek. Bagirli wished his other officers could take a lesson from the Uzbek on this one thing.

Bagirli read the message, his eyes widening. "Officer of the deck, where is the contact?"

Lepechin turned toward Bagirli with a questioning look.

Bagirli gave the message to Demirchan, who read it quickly.

"The status on the contact, Lieutenant Commander Lepechin, if you please!"

Lepechin grabbed the internal communications handset and hit the *Boyevaya Chast*'s three button, connecting him with the underwater weapons post. Sonar was located just outside the forward hatch, before the communications compartment.

"They can't be serious, can they?" Demirchan asked, slapping the message.

Bagirli turned to the Uzbek. "Lieutenant, contact Rear Admiral Ramishvili and confirm the order."

Like a sprinter at the sound of a gunshot, Karimov was charging toward the hatch. One day the wheel was not going to turn fast enough to stop Karimov from slamming into it. Bagirli would have smiled on a normal mission, but Ramishvili's message was earth-shattering, and if true, then it meant the Soviet Navy was for the first time flexing its muscle.

"Sir!" Lepechin announced from near the plotting table in the center of the control room. "Jasha—I mean Lieutenant Iltchenko has the unidentified merchant ship bearing one-nine-zero degrees, right bearing drift. It's a fast bearing drift, but she is not far from us."

Bagirli had not authorized active sonar, which operated much like radar, but instead of radio frequencies, sound was shot out into the water, and when it bounced back from a contact, the sonar operator had both direction and range to the target. Contacts quickly became targets when active sonar was employed.

"Make your speed ten knots, Officer of the Deck. Come to course two-one-zero." The course and speed should put him off the port beam of the contact. "She was only two thousand meters thirty minutes ago."

"Are you going to do this before we have confirmation?" Demirchan asked in a soft voice.

"It is a valid order."

"It may not have originated from the admiral."

Bagirli thought for a moment. The admiral's chief of staff was known for his hotheadedness. The XO might be right. He shook his head. Orders were orders. Submariners did not question orders. They questioned nothing! That was what made the submarine force the front line of defense in any Navy. This would help mitigate being caught on the surface. And it was a valid order. He knew it. The XO knew it.

"We are going to move into position to execute the orders, XO." He sighed. "By then, we should know." He turned to Lepechin. "Lieutenant Commander Lepechin, sound battle stations."

"Battle stations?"

"What is wrong? You have lost your hearing, my operations officer? Sound battle stations and quit repeating everything I say!" Bagirli snapped. He wondered for a moment if the American Navy suffered this questioning from their subordinates. Of course, they did not. The American Navy had been around long enough to breed it out of their bubbleheads.

A soft, repetitive sound of gongs echoed within the skin of the boat. Throughout the K-321, sailors rushed to their battle stations, even as officers knocked them against the bulkhead as they, too, hurried to theirs. Most figured it was another of the captain's unheralded training exercises, but this time there had been no whispered warnings to the crew.

Status reports echoed through the control room from the engineering spaces, torpedo room, and other stations throughout the boat as the K-321 became ready to fight.

HANS looked up as the starboard door opened to the bridge. "Ah, Eugen, it is good to see you."

"You wouldn't have seen me if you hadn't sent for me," the man growled, reaching up and rubbing the stubble on his chin.

Hans laughed. Such a skinny man. Even though the radioman stood near the door, not coming closer to the front of the bridge, Hans knew the smell of stale beer enveloped the man.

Hans grunted. "You drink too much."

"I drink as much as I want to when I am off duty," Eugen replied, scratching his neck now.

"Well, you are back on duty for a while."

"Why don't you just tell me what it is you want me to do, let me do it, and then I can get down to my rack again?"

Hans sighed. "I have a message you must send to German Navy Headquarters."

Eugen stopped scratching. "German Navy Headquarters?" he asked, his eyes wide.

Hans nodded curtly. "Yes."

"Wow, First Mate. I didn't even know we had a Navy."

"Fuck you. Germany has always had a Navy. If you Austrians had had a sea instead of being surrounded on all sides by land, you'd know—"

"I am not Austrian," Eugen snarled. "Just give me the message and I'll go send it. I don't know why it could not have waited until morning."

"Just what I told the captain, but he insisted," Hans said, transferring the onus for waking the snarling radioman from his sleep to the skipper. He did not need a complaint filed with the union. He walked over to the radioman and handed him the message form. It was filled out.

Eugen read it. "Submarines." He laughed. "What bullshit." The man walked to the window on the starboard side of the bridge and looked out of it. "And who saw the submarines?" He pointed to the young helmsman behind the ship's wheel in the center of the bridge. "Him?"

"Don't involve me in your arguments," the helmsman said. "I didn't see the submarines. All I saw was the compass in front of me and the captain's orders displayed here," he said, slapping the sheet of paper secured to the side of the helm console. "It says eight knots, course one-niner-zero unless told otherwise. I haven't been told otherwise."

"Listen, Eugen, would you go send the message? Then you can go have another ten or twelve beers and go back to bed."

Eugen's eyes narrowed. Without another word, the radioman left the bridge, slamming the door behind him.

"TARGET bears one-nine-zero, range four thousand meters and closing, Captain," Lieutenant Commander Lepechin said.

"We still have not received confirmation, Captain," Demirchan said.

"XO, when you get confirmation, tell me," Bagirli snapped, his voice still low. What in the hell was wrong with his XO? Didn't he understand how every screwup must be compensated with something good—no!—something extraordinary that outweighs any indiscretion.

"Yes, sir," Demirchan replied in a voice that suggested he knew that to argue further would not only be useless, but might result in him finding himself confined to his stateroom. "I understand. I am only offering you a different opinion—"

"When I want a different opinion, I will talk to my wife. Now we are going to carry out the order. When we rendezvous with the *Volga*, we will see Admiral Ramishvili and then we can confirm it."

"Aye, sir."

"XO, please man the weapons control station. After all, we are at battle stations."

Bagirli looked at the back of Demirchan as the XO moved toward the weapons control panel. The K-321 was his boat and it was going to remain his boat.

"Up periscope!" Bagirli commanded.

The hydraulics kicked in. The silver-hewed periscope started up. As the eyepiece emerged from the storage chamber below the control room, Bagirli squatted and put his head against it as he flipped the handholds out. A moment later the lens broke the surface.

He spun the scope, watching the compass image inside it.

He lined it up with one-nine-zero. The stern running light of the target was visible for a moment before a wave hid it.

"I have the target." He leaned away. "Do we have a course and speed on it?"

No one answered.

"Officer of the Deck, Commander Lepechin! I asked if we have a course and speed?"

"Sir, I am waiting for Sonar—"

"Then ask the well-trained sonar team again."

Lepechin pushed the channel three button. Bagirli went back to the periscope as he listened to the officer of the deck quiz the sonar team. He spun the periscope completely around twice, checking for other contacts in the area. "Do we have other contacts?" he asked without moving his head.

"No, sir, just the target," Demirchan answered.

Bagirli leaned away from the periscope. "Then tell Sonar to use a single ping to refine the course and range to target."

EUGEN stumbled into the radio shack located behind the bridge. They could have waited until morning for this bull- shit. He flipped on the light and pushed the energy switch up, listening to the electronic buzz as the radio transmitter warmed up. But no, the first mate enjoyed tormenting him.

He flopped his thin frame into the chair, nearly causing it to tumble over. "And I am going to tell the union rep that they should replace this chair," he snapped, adding it to the long list of grievances he intended to file when they returned to Hamburg.

He nodded his head, waiting for the equipment to warm up, finish its analog diagnostics, and then he would have to do a couple of checks to make sure it was working. His lids fluttered a couple of times and then Eugen slept.

THE single active sonar ping rippled through the underwater world, expanding outward in a three-hundred-sixty-degree near-perfect circle. Each temperature gradient in the water slowed or sped up the sound as it expanded, but with such a minute change it would be indistinguishable to the sonar technicians on the K-321.

The ping hit the starboard aft quarter of the *Silesia*, and then started its near instant return to the K-321.

"Range two thousand three hundred meters; bearing one-nine-zero, sir!" Lepechin announced.

"It is opening from us," Bagirli said. "Make your speed fifteen knots."

"Sir, we are close enough to fire," Demirchan offered.

"I want to be close enough to make sure our torpedoes do not miss or have a chance to return to us."

BECKENBAUER'S eyes flew open. Was he dreaming? That was a sonar pulse. A single pulse. He had lain down in his uniform, thinking to check on the course turn in a few hours. He jumped out of the rack, grabbed his coat, and in seconds was heading toward the bridge. His stateroom was on the other side of the radio shack. He slammed his door on the way out.

Eugen's eyes flew open when the captain's door shut. The captain was on the move. He leaned forward and started his transmission checks.

Beckenbauer dashed onto the bridge. "Hans! Did you hear that?"

"Hear what?"

"A single pulse—a ping?"

"I heard it," the helmsman said. "What was it?"

"What was it?" Beckenbauer asked. "What do you think it was?" He wanted someone else to confirm what he already knew.

The helmsman shrugged. "I don't know, sir. I've never heard it before. Thought it might be Eugen in his compartment playing with his radio stuff."

"Eugen is in Radio?" Beckenbauer asked.

"He's in his shack. He is transmitting the submarine sighting."

For once Beckenbauer was happy Hans had not followed his orders, to wait until morning. He hurried through the same watertight door through which he had entered the bridge moments ago. Two steps down the passageway and he jerked the radio shack door open.

Eugen nearly fell out of his chair.

"What are you doing?"

"Sending this submarine sighted report, sir," Eugen said, his voice shaking slightly. He started to stand up.

"Stay seated. Have you sent it yet?"

"No, sir. Just finishing the—"

"Add to it that we have heard one sonar pulse hit the *Silesia*."

Eugen nodded.

Beckenbauer could tell the idea of a single sonar pulse meant nothing to the radioman. It meant a lot to Beckenbauer. Destroyers and submarines used a single pulse to refine the location of a target.

"Tell Naval Headquarters that the submarine may be using the *Silesia* as a target of opportunity."

Eugen felt his mouth go dry. "Target, Captain? As in going to fire a torpedo at us? They can't do that."

Beckenbauer's initial grimace turned into an awkward smile. "You are right. Submarine captains like to train. Sometimes they train on merchant ships such as ours." He didn't say that this was the first time he had heard of them using active sonar to do it. "But it is against maritime law to do that."

Eugen pulled the message sheet toward him, bending over it. "So how should I tell them—"

Beckenbauer grabbed the message in front of Eugen, the smell of stale beer enveloping him as he bent near the radioman.

"Captain?"

The man's breath smelled of rot. Beckenbauer's lips curled in disgust at the sight of the black spots along the man's teeth, from years of not caring.

He took the sheet to the nearby table and quickly scribbled another line onto the message. "Now send this. Mark it as urgent."

"ANOTHER pulse?"

"Wait one, Lieutenant Commander Lepechin," Bagirli said. "His stern light is emerging." He paused. "And the starboard running light is still visible.

"Weapons! Ready?"

"Aye, sir," Demirchan said from the weapons control panel. His fingers were poised above the clear plastic coverings over the torpedo firing buttons.

"Bearing, mark: one-eight-three!"

"Target bearing one-eight-three!" Demirchan echoed.

"Angle on stern thirty-degree port," Bagirli said, listening to the targeting information ripple through the control room. He licked his lips. They were awfully dry.

At the weapons control panel Demirchan punched in the data Bagirli was relaying. Down in the torpedo rooms, the information was being electronically translated into firing data.

"Range?" Demirchan asked.

Bagirli leaned back. "Tell Sonar I want another pulse," he said, holding up one finger. "One pulse and only one pulse." No way would the merchant know what the sound hitting his bottom meant. After all, they were just merchant seamen.

BECKENBAUER was fully awake now when the second pulse hit them. He slapped the paper. "Send this now!"

Eugen started to shake, looking around the compartment, his eyes staring at the file cabinet.

Beckenbauer turned quickly, opened the top drawer, jerked out the bottle of whiskey, and just as quickly unscrewed it. "Here, take a drink!"

Eugen jerked the bottle from the outstretched hand, turned it up, and quickly took a deep drink. Then he handed it back to Beckenbauer.

Neither man said anything.

Eugen put his hand on the slight pad in front of the transmit key and started the series of Morse calls identifying the ship. After several seconds, the parent company in Hamburg acknowledged the *Silesia*. Thank God for German efficiency. Eugen started a series of key strokes without looking at the message.

Beckenbauer knew his Morse code, as most merchant officers did. "What are you doing?"

Eugen looked up, his eyes going to the bottle on the edge of the nearby desk. He licked his lips. "Telling them I am trying to raise German Navy watch desk, sir," he stuttered.

"Have you told them?"

"Yes, sir. They are relaying latest shipping weather—"

"Tell them to clear the channel. Then I want you to start calling Naval Headquarters." He held up three fingers. "Do three calls and then start sending the message." At least the company would have the message.

THREE

LIEUTENANT Harwell stepped out of the duty vehicle and looked up at the entrance of the officers club. He patted the security pouch tucked under his left arm and wondered what the reaction of the *Manta Ray* captain would be toward the message. He wasn't sure about his own reaction when he read it, but he was the admiral's aide. His job was to deliver the message, not defend or define it.

The Arctic air whipping through Keflavik was freezing his exposed cheeks. He just knew he was going to be in Medical by morning with some ill-trained military doctor dragging a scalpel through dead skin, all the while mumbling platitudes about not dressing properly for nights such as this. The doctor didn't work for Admiral Clifton.

Harwell flipped the collar of the heavy wool bridge coat up against the bitter Arctic wind. God, he hated Iceland. Take him back to Rota, Spain, or Naples, Italy, any day. He grabbed the railing with his gloved hand and went up the stairs, expecting any moment to hit a patch of ice and break a leg. Same doctor appeared in his vision. *Ought to be more careful.*

Successful in reaching the top without having his face fall off or breaking a leg, he pulled open the huge door, and a moment later he was standing in front of the concierge asking for directions to Commander "Mickey" Brandon. The clock behind the Icelandic blond showed twenty minutes after nine.

"You can't miss them. They are upstairs in the Fleet Bar," the concierge said, her English twirling seductively in the deep Icelandic accent. She put the pencil down on the table, stood up, and walked toward the stairwell.

Lieutenant Harwell nodded as he watched her hips sway. Then again, while Spanish and Italian women had their allure, Iceland had tall Nordic blondes with a sensuous gait that would have left a man drooling if it wasn't for the fact that it'd freeze and he'd stand there looking like some frozen waterfall.

Damn, he loved Iceland. Probably because he was inside and she was not outside, hidden beneath one of those coats designed to make everyone look like a walking whale. Maybe that was it. Inside—out of the weather, with their women present—Iceland was the place to be. Outside—in the weather, their women hidden beneath fur and masks— Iceland failed to compare with Spain and Italy as places to be. Why couldn't God combine the best of both and slap it somewhere near Connecticut?

He undid the top button on the bridge coat, glanced at a nearby shelf with rows of haphazard officer hats thrown on it, and laid his white hat on top of the pile.

When he turned, she was standing at the base of the stairwell, pointing upstairs. "Second door on the left. You'll find Commander Brandon in there." Her forehead wrinkled. "I'd be careful if I was you," she said with a hint of disgust. "They are—how you say? Chugging? Brennivín." She smiled, "Chugging. I don't think we have a word for it in Icelandic."

He smiled. Brennivín was the Icelandic version of schnapps. It was never meant to be "chugged." Some called it "black death." You only had to wake up after a night of Brennivín to understand why. Even Greek ouzo was easier to drink. He shivered. Not that he would ever do that again either. Brennivín burned going down—brutal stuff—and created a human volcano once inside. Rumor was if you stayed there long enough, you developed a taste for it.

"They are rewarding an officer for finishing something." She shrugged.

Harwell nodded. These were fellow submariners he was going among. He sighed. Drinking to celebrate earning one's dolphins was something you wanted to start with the wardroom, not come into at the end. Lord forbid, you should come in the middle of it such as he was.

From the direction of the stairwell, several garbled shouts followed by loud laughter drew the attention of both of them.

He smiled. "Thanks."

She shrugged and turned back to the small desk with its telephone and schedule book. Any interest in him evaporated after she'd provided the asked information. She was the third concierge hired to work evenings in six months.

Lieutenant Harwell tucked the security pouch tighter under his left arm and mumbled thanks again as his eyes took in the curvaceous figure walking away from him. Legs stretched to heaven, or so he had been told.

She looked back at him. Rippling blond hair fell across her shoulders, framing mischievous blue eyes and inviting lips.

"Is there something else, Lieutenant?"

He shook his head. "Just warming up from the outside." He jerked his thumb over his shoulder toward the door.

She laughed. A deep throaty laugh with a twinkle in the eyes that made him fall in love for the few seconds it lasted. "This is nothing, Lieutenant," she said. "You should be here when we have a true Arctic blast roar over our country. Then you would know cold weather." With that she sat down and returned to the papers she had been working on when he came in.

He sighed as he headed toward the staircase. Like most Americans stationed here, he would never get to meet any of the local women socially much less date one, unless they worked on the base. Even if he should be so lucky, he could not afford the cost of lunch and drinks on the Keflavik market.

Harwell stepped on the bottom rung and bolted up the red carpeted stairs. His mind returned to the message he was carrying.

Huge white doors paralleled both sides of the wide hallway. Framed cheap prints of famous U.S. Naval battles lined the hallway between the doors. The red carpet curved from the stairs and continued down the center of the hallway.

Harwell walked briskly toward the wide-opened doors on his left. Laughter, clinking glasses, and male voices from that direction told him this was where he would find the skipper of the Permit-class submarine USS *Manta Ray*—SSN-597.

The USS *Thresher* (SSN-593) was the first of this class of submarine, but her ill fate during sea trials on April 9, 1963, had resulted in her loss, and the Navy renamed the submarine class after the number two submarine, the USS *Permit* (SSN-594). The *Manta Ray* was the experimental platform for next-generation modifications, such as moving the near-amidships torpedo room back to be more conventional fore and aft torpedo rooms. Seemed the submarine force wanted its submarines capable of fighting whether they were charging or running, instead of only when they were bow-on.

He turned the corner and looked into the half-lit crowded room. A motley march of white shirts, each with a pair of blue shoulder epaulets with gold stripes identifying rank, ebbed and flowed through a yellow haze of cigarette and cigar smoke. Those at the bar were replenishing their drinks while others crowded around the buffet "pooh-poohs" against the far wall. The wardroom tide ebbed and flowed between the bar and the buffet.

Unusual for dress blue uniforms to be worn on a Friday night, but this was a celebration. Harwell glanced at his watch. Nine-thirty.

"Drink, chug-a-lug! Drink, chug-a-lug!" started a chant near the far end of the bar. Around the young officer who was holding the gigantic mug, the *Manta Ray*'s wardroom hoisted their beer as the tempo of the chant picked up.

The junior officer tilted up a huge mug of beer, holding the monstrosity with both hands. Beer leaked around the edges as he drank. A floor light near a couple of lounge chairs lit up a submarine dolphin device bobbing in the beer.

Just as Harwell suspected. He was right. He pulled his gloves off and touched his cheeks. They felt all right. If you could feel them, then you still had them. He fought the quick urge to check his balls.

He recalled when he made his dolphins on another Permit-class submarine, the USS *Plunger* out of Pearl Harbor. He shivered. From the sunny beaches of Pearl to the sensuous warmth of Spain to the ice-encrusted pumice beaches and bundled women of Iceland.

The sound faded as individuals dropped out of the chant, but all eyes continued to watch the young officer. More beer spilled around the edges of the mug. More spilled out of others' mugs also.

"You can do it, Dickie!" a voice from the back shouted.

"Yeah, Dickie! He's our man, if he can't do it, no one can!"

"Except every one of us in the wardroom! Hey, Dickie! Can I have your wife if you don't make it?"

Everyone laughed.

The last of the beer spilled down the officer's throat; the collar of his white shirt was soaked. Everyone clapped and cheered as the man held the dolphins by his teeth.

"First time! What an achievement," the gentleman in the center of the wardroom said.

Three gold stripes ran across both of his epaulets. This had to be Commander Brandon.

"Everyone give 'Big Dickie' Orville a hand!" Brandon commanded.

"With a nickname like that, I don't think I can satisfy your wife. You can have her back!"

"Cut that shit. We're here to congratulate the lieutenant on earning his dolphins, not on his fine taste in women."

Everyone laughed.

Harwell stood just inside the door, observing the commanding officer of the USS *Manta Ray*. Two bushy paths of hair ran along the top sides of the head, with a shiny bald spot in the center. A too small neck jutted from the buttoned white shirt. He looked like a "gone-wrong" Einstein.

The round of applause and catcall cheers about spilling drink echoed through the room again.

"But he did catch his dolphins in the first beer."

Another round of catcalls, whistling, and applause.

"It is not easy to earn the submariner's dolphins, as every one of us knows. Big Dickie Orville has accomplished this in two years. Not a record, but a respectable return." Brandon stopped, held his stomach, and let out a belch that echoed in the room. "And it took me three beers to catch my dolphins. Could have done it in one like you, Big Dickie, but then I would have missed the other two beers." Brandon reached up and shook the huge shoulder of his damage control assistant.

The wardroom cheered and applauded.

"Damn good thing the other two junior officers still have a ways to go in earning theirs. Don't know if the bar has enough beer."

Everyone reached out, touched, jerked the shoulders, and gave light slaps to the back of the heads of two officers standing in their midst, followed by hoots of catcalls and cheers.

Everyone tried to congratulate Orville, punching his shoulder or shoving another beer toward him.

Brandon reached up and took the pin from the officer's lips. "First rule to learn after catching your dolphins is getting them out of your mouth as soon as possible. Don't want to lose you to a choking incident." He shook his head, the hair on both sides of the bald spot moving. "No, siree. Too much paperwork."

Commander "Mickey" Brandon. Korean War and Vietnam War veteran. Harwell started working his way to the bar, where "the" Brandon stood. The Navy was full of characters. Characters made the legends of the sea and the heroics they brought with them. Brandon was one of the best the submarine service had. Rumor had it he would always be a commander, though, because he preferred to be at sea and had turned down senior warfare college as well as orders to the Pentagon. It was a mistake Harwell had no intention of making.

Harwell moved toward Brandon. While the partying conversation never stopped, he knew, as he bumped and mumbled "excuse me's," that the officers of the *Manta Ray* noticed him much like an established herd of elephants eye a strange bull moving into their midst. Watched warily and with hidden curiosity.

"This is a private party," a lieutenant commander said, touching Harwell on the shoulder.

"Yes, sir. I have a message for Commander Brandon."

"I'm Lieutenant Commander Dev Elliot, the XO of the *Manta Ray*." Elliot nodded toward the front of the room. "Why don't we go over there and you can give me the message. I'll see the skipper gets it."

Harwell faced the XO, making a quick assessment. Tall, with the lean physique of a jogger. XOs were the bane of junior officers. When they weren't chewing your ass out, they were assigning new tasks on top of old tasks, as if seeing how much weight that mule could carry before it sat down or quit. He smiled.

"I'm sorry, XO, but the admiral asked I deliver this," he said, patting the security pouch, "as soon as possible to Commander Brandon and bring him a reply."

The faint smile left the XO's face. "Consider me the same as the skipper. On board the *Manta Ray* I am his twin."

Harwell wanted to pop off that they weren't on the *Manta Ray*, but the man was still one pay grade senior to him. Plus, he had enough to worry about with his cheeks without worrying about a pissed-off XO.

"I wish I could, Commander Elliot, but the admiral would have all of our hides if I went back and told him you ordered me to turn his personal message over to you."

Elliot backed away. The smile reappeared. "My misunderstanding, Lieutenant. When you said message, I thought it was a Navy message—kind of like a logistic request."

"No, sir; it's not a LOGREQ. Fact is, XO, I don't know what the admiral has sent the commander," he lied. "I'm just his aide and for tonight the duty watch officer for Keflavik."

"What's going on, XO?"

Harwell turned. Commander Brandon stood to his left.

"Nothing, sir. We were just heading your way. This is the

duty watch officer and he has a message from Admiral Clifton."

"Well, I'm here, son. Give me the message."

"I'm the admiral's *personal* aide, sir," Harwell said.

"You have my heartfelt admiration, Lieutenant. Now let me see the message."

Harwell looked around. Other members of the wardroom were gathering around them. "Sir, it is top secret," he said nervously.

Brandon laughed. "Son, if you had been concerned about the classification of this, you wouldn't have brought it to the officers club. Besides," Brandon continued, "I can personally vouch for all these officers as having top secret clearances."

A voice from the back of the crowd chimed, "Except for Rafael."

"Rafael?" Harwell asked, quickly wishing he had kept quiet.

Brandon laughed and jerked his thumb at an officer wearing the sleeve bands of a lieutenant commander. "Except for Lieutenant Commander Rafael McMahon, my chief engineer, who they tell me had a top secret clearance before his conviction . . . "

Everyone snickered, punching each other in the side with an elbow and exchanging winks.

"But I think he's trustworthy as long as I only take him out of the reactor room when we can all be with him."

"They never found me guilty."

"Only because you killed the witnesses," someone shouted from the back.

"It was because I was Irish . . . or maybe it was because I was Latino?"

The same voice from the back added, "But he has given up drinking and smoking."

"Eat shit and die," the chief engineer snarled, taking his beer and drinking it down. He slapped the mug on the bar, motioning for the bartender to refill it.

"Only his wife knows if he enjoys sex."

"Hey! My wife knows I enjoy sex!"

"Why? Did you wake her up to ask?"

"Okay," Brandon said, "cut the crap." He looked back at Harwell. "The message?" he snapped his fingers.

"But, sir, if we could have some private area, more secure . . ."

Brandon sighed, took a deep breath, and then straightened. "Hey, Barkeep!" he shouted.

The Icelandic bartender looked up.

"Turn around and face the mirror until I tell you to turn around again."

The man smiled, tossed up a hand with a drying towel in it, and turned his back to the wardroom.

"There you are, Lieutenant; now we've turned this room into a classified reading joint. XO, you and OPS come up here. The rest of you go on with your professional discussions. We wouldn't want our newest dolphin holder to think we are ignoring his great accomplishment."

The wardroom started to split apart, with some heading back to the bar and the others toward the buffet, as the three officers moved near the far wall of the room.

A tall, thin officer, with heavy eyebrows and right front shirttail hanging out, joined Brandon, Harwell, and Elliot.

"This is Lieutenant Commander Mike Fitzgerald. He's my operations officer."

Within seconds the volume increased as the wardroom attention returned to fun, games, and badly told jokes.

"Let's read this message you came all the way across the base in the dead of a cold Icelandic night to give me."

"Sir, I feel uncomfortable—"

He looked back at Harwell. "You a skimmer?"

"No, sir," Harwell replied sharply. "I'm a submariner just—"

Brandon laughed. "A bubblehead assigned to a Naval Air Station? Well, why didn't you say so? Now, give me the message," he ordered, the smile disappearing.

Harwell hesitated until he saw the look in Brandon's eyes. He quickly opened the briefcase and brought out the folder.

Brandon took it from him, quickly opened it, read it—and then handed it to Elliot. "Well, XO, looks as if our partying time in Keflavik is going to be short-lived."

"This is great!" Elliot handed the message to Fitzgerald.

"Mike, you'll have to update your charts and your operation plans."

Fitzgerald scan-read the message. "This is great news, sir," he said, handing it back to the XO.

Brandon laughed. He stood on a chair and whistled, causing all the chatter to stop. "Well, everyone, it looks as if our North Atlantic cruise has been canceled. Hope all of you have your suntan lotion."

"Where we going, Skipper?"

"Can't tell you; it's top secret!"

"Sir, did you read the intelligence blurb at the bottom of the page?" Fitzgerald asked.

Brandon nodded. "I did, OPS."

Elliot took the folder back, flipped the message to the second page, and quickly scanned the intelligence glimpse that told the *Manta Ray* why they were heading to the Mediterranean.

"There goes our liberty," Elliot mumbled.

Harwell licked his lips and reached for the message.

Brandon took it from Elliot, folded it, and put it in his shirt pocket. "I think I'll keep this, Lieutenant. After all, it is to me."

"Sir, would you prefer the security pouch for the message?"

"Mr. Harwell, this is my 'top secret' pocket." Brandon touched the other pocket, on the right-hand side. "This pocket is for lesser classified messages."

Harwell looked at Brandon. He didn't know what to do. He wanted to put the message back in the security pouch and return to the operations center. He also wanted to read the message again. He knew it changed their mission, but the intelligence page he'd only scanned. What was it they saw that he'd missed? "Sir, it is top secret," he mumbled.

Brandon nodded. "You're right, Lieutenant." He pulled the message from his pocket. "Hand me your security pouch."

Harwell breathed a sigh of relief. He was going to get the message back where it belonged. He handed the dark black leather pouch to Brandon.

Brandon took the message and shoved it inside the pouch. Then he folded over the flap, clipping it shut. He handed the pouch to Elliot. "Here, XO. You're responsible for keeping this until we get back to the boat."

Harwell's eyes widened. "But, sir—"

"Son, there are no buts on my boat."

"But I signed for the pouch."

Brandon grinned, reached forward, and patted him on the shoulder. "You're right. I got in trouble once for not returning something I signed for." He looked around, found a napkin on a nearby table, and quickly wrote a receipt for the pouch before handing it to Harwell. "That should take you off the hook."

Harwell read the note. In places the ink had run, making it nearly undecipherable.

"I think you have done your duty, Lieutenant," Brandon said.

Harwell straightened, gave a quick nod, and departed. He patted the napkin note in his pocket on the way down the stairs.

"HE'S gone. Nervous sort, wasn't he?" Elliot said. "Looks as if our liberty time in Rota, Naples, Palma—"

"May still get it, XO," Brandon said. He ran his hand across the bald spot on the center of his head. "What worries me is, Why all of a sudden does the Soviet Union put all its submarines to sea in the Mediterranean?"

"Fleet Ocean Surveillance Information Facility message out of Rota, Spain, said that there were at least twenty-two Soviet submarines in the Mediterranean. Largest number FOSIF says they have ever seen."

"FOSIF must have offered an opinion as to why so many?" Elliot asked.

Fitzgerald shook his head. "No, sir. Everything's calm in the Middle East. Commander, Fifth Eskandra, the Soviet equivalent to our Sixth Fleet—"

"Quit trying to impress us, OPS," Brandon said. "We know what FOSIF is and where it's located, and we know the commander of the Soviet Fifth Squadron is the same as our Sixth Fleet." He looked at Elliot. "Don't we, XO?" He looked back at Fitzgerald. "And we know the Russian word *eskandra* is translated into the English word squadron."

Elliot nodded curtly. "I may have forgotten since this morning, but I thank our intellectual operations officer for reminding me."

"Touché," Fitzgerald said. "I was just trying . . . "

Brandon smiled. "Just busting your chops, OPS. Go ahead."

"FOSIF also said that the Soviets had some submarines up here, Charlie-class. There may be at least two, and one of them may even have a flag officer on board."

"Wow!" Brandon said, shaking his head. "I wish I knew which boat had the admiral on it. I'd send the skipper a condolence card." He chuckled. "Let's hope Clifton never decides to ride with us."

Several officers wandered over from the bar.

"What's going on, Skipper?" a voice asked.

Brandon picked his beer up and turned to the question. It was Lieutenant Dave Label, his navigator and administrative officer. Beside Label stood the supply officer, Lieutenant Cliff Jones.

"Well, as you probably heard the XO say, we are heading to the warmer climate of the Mediterranean tomorrow morning, but we may only get a quick stop for refueling at Rota. No liberty envisioned, which should make the officers and sailors of VQ-2 and the Naval Communications Station happy."

"It is hard to compete with a hundred gentlemen submariners on liberty."

"With their wallets full of American dollars," Jones said.

"Is the Middle East heating up?" Label asked.

Brandon and Elliot shook their heads.

"I don't think so. Egypt's doing some annual exercises, but I understand they are always doing something," Fitzgerald offered.

Elliot pulled the message out of the pouch and handed it to Label, who quickly read it and then passed it to Jones.

The supply officer mumbled as he read, as supply officers are prone to do. A trait that makes them remember what they are reading, so the boat never sails without the proper outfit for the mission. The four officers listened as the quiet voice of Jones read the message aloud. The first couple of short paragraphs ordered the *Manta Ray* to deploy to the Mediterranean, where it would report for duty under Commander, U.S. Sixth Fleet, for duty as may be assigned. It had the departure date and the mandatory arrival date. It was the last paragraph their attention focused on, because there lay the true purpose of their diversion—the intelligence picture.

Naval Intelligence was concerned about the huge number of Soviet submarines and surface forces moving into the Eastern Mediterranean. Enough so that Sixth Fleet had ordered both aircraft carriers out of port and to move toward the area. While there was nothing going on to indicate a Middle East war as far as the intelligence people could tell, the buildup of Soviet Naval forces made the U.S. Navy uncomfortable. Jones folded the message and handed it back to Elliot.

"What do you think, Supply?" Elliot asked.

"I think the Soviets know something that we don't," Jones answered, his deep bass Georgia drawl riding above the chatter.

"And what might that be?"

"Don't know, XO. But right now we have nothing going on that would cause the Soviets' ordering their fleet to sea. Vietnam is winding down. All of the small wars have been that way for a while. The Middle East is quiet and has been since Nasser died." Jones shook his head. "But what do I know? I'm just your supply officer who you enjoy making fun of."

Everyone laughed. Jones smiled, revealing bright white teeth against his dark skin.

"The truth, I think," Brandon offered, raising his hand, "has something to do with the fact that the Soviets have over twenty-two submarines in the Eastern Mediterranean. They outnumber us about five-to-one right now. What you don't see in the message from my 'reporting for duty' meeting with Admiral Clifton this morning is that Naval Intelligence thinks there may be more submarines on their way to the Mediterranean. Chief of Naval Operations has drawn a line in the proverbial sand; no more Soviet submarines in the Mediterranean. We may have company on our own trip to the Med since they have to go through the Strait of Gibraltar like us."

"You think we're going to fight them? Maybe this is the time—their time," McMahon said.

Brandon paused for a drink. Every old-timer in the Navy believed one day the United States Navy and the Soviets were going to have that short burst of Navy chest-beating to see who the best was. There was no doubt the U.S. would win, but the Soviet tactical doctrine of overwhelming missiles and might would take a lot of men to their deaths on both sides so America could keep its mantle of the world's Navy superpower.

Elliot tucked the pouch under his arm and walked toward the bar. Over his shoulder, the XO said, "Of course, we're going to fight them, Lieutenant. Anyone who doesn't think that is in the wrong century. Nations like the Soviet Union are sprinkled throughout history. Strong military and willingness to use it. Not only to strengthen their position in the world, expand their national borders, but also it is how they keep their civilian population in chains."

Before he reached the bar, one of the officers handed him a tray with a couple of beers and two shots of Brennivín on it. Elliot gave the officer the security pouch and headed back toward Brandon.

The XO walked up. Brandon took one of the beers and a Brennivín from the tray. He looked around the group forming. "Big Dickie, this is for you," he said, handing the Brennivín to the junior officer.

"It would be a nuclear holocaust," the supply officer, Jones, said.

Brandon shook his head. "I don't think we'll ever have a global rain of nukes between us and them." He shook it more. "Nope; don't see it happening." He took a sip and set the glass down.

"But, you said—"

"I said that one day the Soviet and U.S. Navies are going to slam our chests against each other to see who the world's

most powerful Navy is. That's not going to catapult us into
World War III. All it'll do is give fodder for politicians, and
after a few weeks of saber rattling, front page news, and a
slew of "we're-walking-into-another-Vietnam" editorials, the
world will settle down to new facts of life."

"Facts of life?"

"Yep, one of us is going to be the top dog. And the
other—well," he paused, "the other is going to be waiting for
his chance to reverse the result. You know what's going to be
ironic about that confrontation when it comes?"

The three officers shook their heads. "No, sir."

"The winner just might be the one who loses the most
ships and has the most dead men floating. Bottom line—
whoever wins, we all lose."

The telephone rang at the end of the bar. The bartender
picked it up, and then looked toward Elliot and Brandon.
"Captain! Captain! It is for you."

Brandon nodded at Elliot.

Elliot made the few steps to the bar and took the telephone. He spoke into the handset for a few seconds and then
hung up.

"Wonder what that was about," Brandon said aloud as Elliot made his way to the four officers.

"Well, whatever it is," he continued, "the XO isn't smiling. Know what I know about XOs, gentlemen?"

"No, sir."

"If they're not smiling, then it is either bad news or they
are happy. What you got, XO?"

"That was Base Operations, sir. Admiral Clifton wants
you at his office tomorrow morning at zero six hundred."

Brandon shook his head. "Looks as if his aide didn't like
you taking his top secret message, XO."

"Me?"

"That's what XOs are for: to take the blame off the shoulders of the skipper. I promise I will do everything I can for
you."

"Let's hope that is all it is about."

"I would not be too concerned except for one thing."

"What's that, sir?" McMahon asked.

"They knew where to find us. That young lieutenant didn't even go to the boat. He came right here, and they even had the right telephone number for the room we are in." He shook his head. "The days are changing for the U.S. Navy. Next thing you know we'll have women on board the boats."

"That would give new meaning to hot-racking," Label added.

No one laughed at the old joke.

"Also, they said expect to receive a message changing your orders."

Brandon laughed and with the back of his hand slapped the leather security pouch. "Already got it."

"GOT them!" Eugen said. He wiped spittle off his chin with the back of his coat sleeve.

"Send it!" Beckenbauer shouted.

The radioman started transmitting the message, which was interrupted a few times by the German Navy operator on the other end.

Beckenbauer glared at the top of the radioman's head. This would be Eugen's last trip with him, he thought. He did not know how right he was.

"OPEN forward torpedo doors one, two, and three," Bagirli ordered. With his hands still on the handles, he leaned around the tube of the periscope, watching Demirchan on the weapons control panel. He nodded once when he saw the three green lights turn red.

"Range?" he asked.

"One thousand nine hundred meters," Lepechin replied.

Bagirli acknowledged the officer of the deck. He took a deep breath and looked at the XO.

They both nodded at each other. Words weren't needed. Both knew what they were about to do. The Soviet Union had not done this since World War II.

He returned to the periscope. "Bearing!"

"One-eight-five!" Lepechin shouted from near the helmsman, holding the handset away from his ear for a moment. "Sonar says one-eight-five!"

"Angle on the stern, thirty-five degrees. Range one thousand five hundred. "XO," Bagirli said in a low voice, his eyes still glued to the eyepiece.

"Yes, sir."

"Have them check for contacts in the area."

He listened as Demirchan asked for the information. Nearly a half minute passed before the answer came back of no contacts in the area other than the target. At least no witnesses were around.

Bagirli stepped from the periscope to the narrow railing that encircled the small periscope platform. "Listen up. We are going to fire a salvo of three torpedoes. I want them set for shallow run. We are going to do this by the book. And we are going to do it right. After we see how much damage we have inflicted on the target, then we will decide whether to fire additional torpedoes. Does everyone understand?"

The enlisted men nodded their heads. Demirchan and Lepechin answered together, "Yes, sir."

Once again he locked eyes with Demirchan for a moment. "Guess this is it."

Bagirli nodded. "We have not heard anything from Admiral Ramishvili changing the orders?"

"No, sir. But we could delay. We could continue to get closer. The closer we get, the better our odds of hitting it."

Bagirli nodded. "Thank you, XO. That has been my intention. I think anything around one thousand meters is close enough for our torpedoes." Would this overshadow being caught on the surface by a merchant vessel? Sinking the same merchant might mitigate the transgression. He shut his eyes for a moment wishing it to be so, even as he knew it would take more than executing orders.

"Target bears one-eight-three," Lepechin said.

"Another pulse and then prepare to fire."

"Aye, sir."

The vibration of the sonar pulse reverberated through the control room.

A second later, Lepechin reported, "Sonar reports nine hundred fifty meters."

They were still closing. He wanted to be closer, but considering the explosive power of the torpedoes, it might be unacceptable. Doctrine called for long-range firings and nine hundred fifty meters was well within the maximum range. *No,* he told himself. *This is the window of opportunity to sink the target or let it go.* He had too much riding on the success of this order to tactically ignore it.

He returned to the periscope. "Tell Sonar to keep those passive bearings coming!"

"Bearing one-eight-five!" Lepechin replied. "Range nine hundred meters!"

"Angle on stern twenty-degree port. Stand by!"

"Standing by!" Nehoda replied.

"Fire one!"

A couple of seconds passed. "One away!"

In the forward torpedo room, a starshina stood between the torpedo tubes. His lone job was to manually fire the torpedoes in the event the electronic command from the control room failed. Behind him was the chief starshina torpedoman who had earlier opened the outer doors, a job that someday the enlisted sailor straddling the tubes might reach the rank to do.

"Fire two!"

"Number two fired electrically!"

"Fire three!"

"Number three fired electrically!"

A few seconds passed before Demirchan reported, "Sir, forward torpedo room chief reports all torpedoes fired electrically. Torpedoes running true on base course one-eight-five. Time to impact . . . "

"Give me a countdown!"

" . . . two minutes!"

Bagirli waited with a mix of excitement over what he was doing and the concern if he was correct in doing it. Sometimes orders were misunderstood. Especially if your senior changed his mind. He wanted to reread the message right now. Right this instant, even as the torpedoes sped toward their target. Would this—

"Torpedoes merging toward target, continuing to run true!" Demirchan announced, interrupting Bagirli's thoughts.

BECKENBAUER straightened. "They have acknowledged receipt," he stated.

"Yes, sir."

The third sonar pulse echoed through the metal skin of the *Silesia*. It was stronger than the last two. Eugen looked up, his eyes wide.

"Sir, what was that?"

"Sonar," Beckenbauer whispered. He shut his eyes. Years of German Navy destroyer experience came back. Three sonar pulses were a sure sign of an imminent torpedo launch. He knew. He had done them. Maybe in exercises, but he knew the tactics. He also knew instinctively that the submarines were Soviet. American submarines never did this. With freedom came too many loose lips.

"Get on your life vest!" he shouted to the radioman.

Beckenbauer left the door open behind him as he raced into the passageway, took two steps to the left, and shoved open the door to the bridge.

"Ah, Captain," Hans said. "I have now heard the sound twice—"

"Helmsman, right full rudder, all ahead full!"

"Sir?" the helmsman asked, still holding steady on the original course.

"What is the matter, Captain?" Hans asked, crossing the bridge toward him.

"I said," he shouted, "right full rudder, all ahead full! Fuck it! Right now! Right now! Right now!"

The helmsman spun the wheel, watching the rudder indicator in front of him until it pegged to the right. Then he reached over for the annunciator and rang up bells for full speed.

The *Silesia* heeled slightly to starboard as hydraulic motors moved the massive rudders in response to the helm. The speed was coming up slowly from the steam engines in the bowels of the merchant vessel.

Beckenbauer saw the sharp looks from the helmsman and from Hans.

"Captain?" Hans asked through his confusion. "What are you doing?"

"That may have been submarines Ferguson saw earlier. Those three pings—or pulses as we call them—were probably targeting sonar pulses."

Hans laughed. "So they are using us as a target of opportunity. We both know they do that. Probably Americans."

The first torpedo spun down the port side of the *Silesia*. No one saw it. It made no noise. It just continued alongside the turning merchant and disappeared off in the direction fired.

Beckenbauer shook his head. "No. I think they are Russian. Soviet submarines."

The second barely hit the port side of the turning vessel, but it exploded, knocking Beckenbauer and Hans off their feet. The helmsman was catapulted backward against the bulkhead, his head bursting on impact with the metal. The merchant seaman slid down the bulkhead. A streak of blood marked his journey to a sitting position on the deck.

"Grab the helm!" Beckenbauer shouted. He grabbed the telephone and rang the radio shack.

RADIO was vacant. Eugen had done his duty. He and his bottle were nearly second deck down when the explosion hit, causing him to lose his balance on the ladder. The bottle shattered against the metal railing of the ladder as Eugen tumbled, his head hitting a jutting lever on a nearby pipe. He was dead before he hit the deck.

The third torpedo caught the *Silesia* between its two propellers, exploding when the blades caught it. Directly beneath the aft engine room, the explosion created a gigantic hole, and freezing North Atlantic waters rushed into the compartment. Within seconds the water and the steam engine plant at its superheated temperature collided.

Beckenbauer and Hans perished with the gigantic explosion that ripped through the aging German steamer.

FLAMES lit up the night sky from the oil on the sea. Something wallowing ahead of him caught his attention and he stretched his arms out, swimming toward it. The water was already draining the heat from his body, and unless he found something to pull himself onto, he would die shortly. His right hand hit the edge in the middle of a stroke. The left grabbed the rough edges of it, and Ferguson pulled himself onto the makeshift raft. He shivered, but curled up into a fetal ball to help conserve his body heat. The heavy foul-weather jacket and gloves helped protect him somewhat, but the North Atlantic was a cold lover.

Ferguson shivered, reached up, and pulled the watch cap down across his face, already feeling the embrace of the icy fingers of the sea. Protect the main part of the body and you had a chance. After a couple of minutes, he reached up and pulled the watch cap off, squeezed out the salt water as best he could, and then put the cap back on, stretching it down as far as it would go. Then he slipped off into the darkness of sleep; exhausted, cold, wet, but out of the freezing water, riding atop whatever he was on, wrapped in the heavy foul-weather garb of a topside watch.

THREE and a half hours later the K-321 wallowed lightly in the lee of the huge submarine tender *Volga*. The captain of the *Volga* had guided the Project 670 submarine to its starboard side so the Arctic wind whipping down from the north was shielded somewhat off the low-riding submarine. K-301 had arrived an hour before Bagirli did, which was good because they were nearly finished with their replenishment by the time K-321 came alongside *Volga*.

It took another hour and a half for the tender to miraculously transfer sufficient food to keep the K-321 going for another thirty days. The skipper sent six bottles of good vodka to Bagirli along with his compliments. Within the small gift was a security pouch, which Bagirli knew would contain correspondences that could not be trusted to the communications system. Personally, the skipper of the *Volga* thought it was a waste of time and energy to hand-deliver anything that was critical, because by the time you got it, whatever it was you were supposed to do would most likely be too late.

Bagirli instructed the starshina chief to have both delivered to his stateroom.

Dawn was breaking as the K-321 cleared the submarine tender, and the decks of the K-321 were empty. Bagirli was once again the last man through the topside scuttle as the boat submerged. He had been beginning to feel a little nausea from the rocking and rolling on the surface. A submariner's place was beneath the ocean, where all you had to worry about was other submarines, underwater mountains, the occasional mentally deranged sailor, and toilets exploding upward while you were seated on them.

IT was thirty minutes after submerging before Bagirli walked down the passageway to his stateroom. The case of vodka was there, but the security pouch was missing. He picked up the handset, dialed the communicator, and told him to bring him the pouch.

Whenever Bagirli saw his communicator, Karimov, he always wondered, *How in the hell did a Uzbek end up in the Soviet submarine service?*

Most of them were Moslem, which was enough to make all of them suspect, and most did their service in the Soviet Army. He had yet to meet another Uzbek in the submarine service. "Come to think of it," he said aloud as he started unbuttoning the heavy foul-weather jacket, "I haven't seen another one anywhere in the Navy."

A few seconds later Karimov knocked on the frame of the doorway. "Captain, I have your pouch."

"Tell me, Lieutenant Karimov, how did you know there

was a security pouch?" He hung the foul-weather jacket up near the sink and away from his rack. Water still dripped, so he slid the trash can beneath it.

"But, sir, they always send you a security pouch. It is easier for me to have a cup of tea in the wardroom and wait for them to deliver it to your stateroom than to try to intercept it when it first arrives."

Bagirli forced a smile. "You are a strange communications officer, Mauduna Karimov." He looked in the mirror as he unbuttoned the top buttons of his shirt. He could see the reflection of the squat man with broad arms and imagined Karimov easily on a stout pony riding forth with the Huns, chopping off heads, stacking skulls into pyramids, and leaving his seed in innocent Russian maidens across the steppes.

"You can lay it on my rack, if you would, Mauduna. I have a few more things I need to do before I open it."

"I will wait in the wardroom, sir."

"I will call you." He saw the change of expression flicker across the Uzbek.

"If you would not mind, Captain, I would prefer to wait until you are finished. That way I can ensure it is secured."

Bagirli took his shirt off. The hair on his chest was matted from the sweat. Dress warmly for the Arctic, but don't sweat, as it will freeze to you. It was a fine art to stay warm and not sweat.

"If that is what you prefer, Lieutenant." He knew Karimov was more concerned that he was going to leave the stateroom and not call him. He smiled. He had done it once, but the communicator had never forgotten because Uzbeks never forget, or forgive, though they may never mention the incident.

"Thank you, sir."

Bagirli turned to say something, but the man was gone. He stepped to the door and looked toward the wardroom at the far end of the passageway and nothing was there. He grunted. "Amazing."

Several minutes later, he sat down on the edge of his rack, opened the pouch, and dumped the contents on his blanket. He raked his hand through the few dispatches in there until he found one marked for his eyes only. He opened it. Read it quickly. And within minutes he was rushing back toward the control room. Why in the hell didn't they send this via enciphered communications? There were other things he was going to need and he could have gotten them from the *Volga*.

FOUR

BRANDON held the cup of coffee between both hands as he watched the activity pierside.

The voice of Lieutenant Junior Grade Dickie Orville overseeing the working parties on the pier drew his attention. The line of sailors faced the *Manta Ray*, shoulders nearly touching the sailor beside them, passing box after box from one sailor to the other. The line curved across the brow before making another sharp turn along the port side of the boat toward the bow. Seconds separated the boxes from one another as they passed hand-over-hand to the forward escape hatch, where the supplies disappeared down into the boat.

Most of it was food. But in the area of logistics and supplies, the war fighters depended on the supply officers, so Brandon was unsurprised when he saw Lieutenant Jones standing at the forward escape hatch with his clipboard, notating each box as it went below.

Brandon sipped the hot coffee, relishing the warmth as it traveled downward. He held the coffee to both cheeks. Leaving Iceland. What more could a sailor ask for than the warmth of the boat once it was beneath the ocean surface?

He had been on a diesel submarine once in his junior officer years. Nearly froze his balls off. Nukes such as the *Manta Ray* had an unlimited supply of heat, and no, it did not cause bubbleheads to glow green.

"Careful with that!"

He smiled, recognizing the Filipino accent. It was the storekeeper Chief Emano, Lieutenant Jones's number two. He looked up. The short, stoutly built Filipino was in the face of a sailor nearly twice his size, the chief's head practically buried in the young man's chest. The sailor was number four in the line from the rear of the supply truck.

"I tell you and I tell you. These important supplies for *Manta Ray*. You listen? No, you don't listen. You jerk them from his hand and toss them to this one's hands as if they trash. You wanna eat trash? What you name?"

"Seaman Snoggins, sir."

"Don't call me sir! What you think I am?"

"A chief."

"Chiefs ain't sirs. Our parents are married. You understand?"

Brandon's eyes widened for a moment.

"No, Chief—I mean yes, Chief."

"Okay, you understand? You gonna screw up anymore?"

"No, Chief," the sailor replied, backing up slightly.

"Don't run from me when I talk you." Emano put his index finger on his chest. "I gonna have problem with you anymore today?"

"No, Chief."

The first sailor in the line bent over putting both hands on his knees, taking a break while the chief and the sailor were having their discussion.

"Good. No more problem, Snoggins," Emano said as the stocky chief walked away, his hands on his hips. "I want no more problems." He looked up at the sailors and shouted, "You hear me, sailors? No more problems!"

"Yes, Chief," they said in unison, then laughed once.

Emano smiled. "What a bunch of shitheads! Where most powerful Navy in world get such shitheads?"

The first sailor straightened, reached up, took the next box passed down from the truck, and started the line functioning again. Emano turned for a moment to watch, seemed satisfied, and started his round on the pier between the brow and the truck.

The other chief, Chief Norman, watched with his hands crossed against his chest. Two chiefs and one working party. Seemed like overkill to Brandon, but as in sea and anchor details when the boat was replenishing, everyone had a duty station. His was the conning tower.

Brandon smiled. He touched the right pocket of his foul-weather jacket. His pipe, tobacco, and the accouterments necessary to light it were there. Before they set sail, he wanted to have one last smoke. While he allowed cigarettes in the berthing compartments, he did not allow pipes and cigars.

I should call Louise before we sail, but she would understand, he told himself. *Should have done it last night, but had a dolphin to drink down.*

Brandon epitomized the fable of the man at sea—in love with the sea. If the Navy had wanted him to have a wife, they would have issued him one, as the joke went. Louise was his second. The first one issued had failed to work out.

With his first, Pauline, he had had two sons—Mitchell "Mickey" Junior and Timothy O'Connor Brandon, named after his mother's father. They still lived in New London, where Pauline worked as a bookkeeper in her father's pub. After ten years of marriage, she split. He never truly understood why; after all, Navy life was being at sea and being gone for months. The pub he missed.

Louise he had met in Savannah, Georgia, six years ago, during a port call for the city's famed St. Patrick's Day celebrations. He could never quite recall at which pub they had met. A whirlwind romance of a week in port, a month of exchanging letters, a quick visit by her to Norfolk, and they were married, with Harrison Leroy on the way.

Six years later and she was firmly entombed in Norfolk, Virginia, homeport of the *Manta Ray*. Five-year-old Harrison Leroy had a three-year-old sister, Elvira, who was Brandon's princess, though if he had his way, she would have been named something else, but Louise had put her Southern belle foot down and given him a choice: Elvira or Maud. It had been an easy choice, plus the wardroom had been waiting at the Norfolk Officers Club to celebrate the birth.

Brandon took a deep breath. This was what he lived for: the smell of getting under way. Land was a place to get laid, have some beers, and, when the money ran out, to up anchor and head out to sea.

A horn from the end of the pier caught his attention as a car came toward the *Manta Ray*.

The six o'clock briefing this morning with Admiral Clifton had gone like other briefings that other admirals had had with him after first nights ashore. The incident with the classified message had reached Clifton's ears by the time Brandon had showed up at six. Being an airdale admiral, Clifton understood the "drinking of the dolphins" ritual, which was similar to pinning on one's wings. He congratulated Brandon on having another wardroom member earn the coveted submariner's device.

Brandon knew there was a "but" somewhere in the admiral's start. Every officer knew how to "pat on the back" before shoving the inevitable "but" up the butt. The admiral must have been really upset, because the "but" was there a couple of sentences after the ass-reaming.

And it was a huge "but" judging from the tenor, tone, and volume. Admiral Clifton blasted into him about mishandling the top secret message and possibly compromising it to the non-Americans in the officers club.

There was only one and he was a bartender.

Brandon did the obligatory two-foot shuffle with apologies, but it failed to work with this flag.

It then turned into a one-sided conversation with the taller, older airdale admiral letting Brandon know how happy Keflavik Naval Air Station would feel once he—Admiral Clifton—was able to see the stern of *Manta Ray* on its way out to sea. And, Clifton said—slamming his fist down on his desk—they expected to see the stern of the boat no later than fourteen hundred local time.

Brandon had saluted smartly, done an about-face, and was nearly at the door when the admiral shouted, "And don't ever do that bullshit bubblehead dance and apology with me again, Commander Brandon. I am not Admiral Hyman G. Rickover!"

But everyone knows who Admiral Hyman G. Rickover is, Brandon wanted to say, but even with unknown two-stars, they were still two-stars.

The sailor whom Emano had been chewing out only minutes ago dropped a box; the sound of cans knocking against one another rode the still air.

"Snoggins, you stupid shit!" Chief Norman shouted from behind the line.

Chief Emano came running from near the brow. "What happen, what happen?" Emano demanded in his clipped Filipino accent.

"He dropped the box," Norman said. Norman was a throttleman on the *Manta Ray. Poor sailor,* Brandon thought. *Bad enough with just Emano, but now you got two chiefs on your ass. Better you than me, son.*

"He keeps dropping boxes and trying to pass them along before the next guy is ready for them."

Emano walked up to the sailor, his face directly in the man's chest again. "I told you. Did'n I tell you? Did'n I say I no want no more problems with the load?"

"Yes, Chief, and I only did it this one time since you talked to me."

"One time? I only talk to you one minute ago!" Emano stepped back. "No," he said, waving his finger back and forth. "Every time you do it, you slow up the line."

"Chief!" Lieutenant Jones shouted from the deck immediately below Brandon. "Let's get the line moving. We got a full truck."

Emano turned and saluted. "Aye, aye, sir." He turned back to the sailor. "No more shit from you. Okay?"

"Okay, Chief."

With that, Norman and Emano walked away, satisfied that they had, in their infinite chiefdom wisdom, resolved another Navy problem. Something officers would never understand, as they would tell each other in the goat locker.

Brandon fingered the pipe in his pocket as he watched the

two chiefs walk away. Norman was fairly new on board *Manta Ray*. Didn't seem too bad of a sort. He bore watching though. Had a quick temper, as evidenced by the fiasco in Holy Loch the night before the boat departed for Iceland. Brandon had the letter from the four-striper at Holy Loch he had to answer. Wasn't the first one.

The long line of sailors passing the boxes from one to the other picked up the pace as Snoggins hefted the dropped box and passed it along. A second later the manual loading of the *Manta Ray* was continuing. Now, there was a good example of a two-foot shuffle and an apology. Brandon smiled. That Snoggins was admiral material in any man's Navy.

He pulled back the heavy sleeve of the faded green foul-weather jacket and looked at his watch. It showed ten-twenty in the morning. He took a deep breath. Except for the usual oily smell of an active pier, the air would have been fresh. The wind was mild from the north. *Isn't it always from the north in Iceland?* Clear sky with a splattering of clouds. Quite the nice day for Keflavik. He took a sip of coffee. Cold. He forced it down and hoped someone brought him another one soon. He could ask, but wasn't the same.

The sound of the car horn pulled his attention back to the car inching its way through the maze of pier-stacked supplies toward the *Manta Ray*.

It looked like the admiral's car that had taken him to the "briefing" this morning. The lights were on, but there was no flag flying from the right bumper.

"What's a matter?" he mumbled aloud. *Was there part of the ass-chewing the admiral forgot this morning?*

Behind him the sound of someone climbing through the scuttle drew his attention. It was Lieutenant Commander Devlin "Dev" Elliot. "So how is Engineering, XO? They fix that sump pump?"

Elliot wiped the back of his hand against his forehead, leaving a dark smudge. "They had a little help." He pulled his gloves from the foul-weather jacket pockets and slipped them on. Nodding at the car that had come to a stop behind the working party, Elliot asked, "What's going on?"

"After this morning, maybe the admiral decided some

whip-and-chains might convey his dissatisfaction with our performance last night."

"Ours?"

"Well, you are right, XO. It was your fault. As the executive officer, I expect you to stop the skipper from doing stupid things."

"Aye, sir; I will remember that next time."

"Too late," he mumbled as both of them stared at the car. "I've already made a note for your fitness report."

The left rear car door opened and Lieutenant Harwell stepped out.

"Looks as if our young Harwell is paying a visit this time."

Elliot nodded. "Like a young toy poodle paying a visit to the Dobermans."

"Skipper! Skipper!" came a shout behind the two men.

Without turning, Brandon replied, "Lieutenant Strickland, what brings you to the conning tower?" He turned as the young communications officer forced himself through the scuttle and onto the conning tower.

"Sir," Strickland said as he pulled himself upright. He waved a message in his hand.

On the pier, Lieutenant Harwell ran around to the right side of the car and opened the rear door. Rear Admiral Clifton stepped out, solid gold epaulets across the shoulders of his calf-length wool conning tower coat, with two embroidered silver stars and anchors on top of the gold.

"Catch your breath, Mr. Strickland," Elliot said with a hint of irritation.

Brandon and he had their backs to the car.

"No heart attacks on the conning tower are the rule, COMMO," Brandon added.

The officer of the deck in port saw the admiral and hit the bells. The first two bells drew Brandon and Elliot back to the pier. Admiral Clifton glared up at the two men.

"Captain Brandon!" Clifton shouted from the pier.

Brandon raised his hand and saluted. He leaned down. "Officer of the Deck! Clear the brow for the admiral."

"Sir, this is for you," Strickland said, jamming the message into Brandon's hand. Then Strickland disappeared down the scuttle.

The second set of bells rang out across the pier.

"Working party!" Emano shouted. "Put your boxes down!"

All along the line, boxes were set at the feet of the sailors.

"Not you! Not you!" Emano shouted at the sailors on the brow. "Take your boxes on board the boat with you."

"Attack by the airdale and his aide," Elliot added softly. "Sounds like a good name for a horror movie."

"If you can get me on board the *Manta Ray*, Captain Brandon, I would like to have some important words with you."

"Yes, sir, Admiral." He leaned over to Elliot. "Something's wrong. He sounds almost sociable."

"He's an airdale. Probably forgot who you are by now."

Brandon grunted. "From this morning, I think he has my name tattooed on his palm."

Elliot laughed. "Then he's going to do more than use it as a memory tool."

"Remind me to add that last comment to your fitrep."

The last sailor left the brow. Admiral Clifton and Lieutenant Harwell were on their heels. The third set of bells rang out, and when the admiral stepped on the deck of the *Manta Ray*, a long bell announced his presence. Across the topside speaker system, the 1MC, the officer of the deck announced, "Naval Forces Keflavik arriving!"

"Hope he knows how to climb," Elliot said softly.

"I know how to climb."

"Sorry, sir, I didn't mean . . . "

"Cut the shit, XO. You must be the XO. Only an XO would try to be flippant at a time like this."

Brandon reached out to help the admiral.

"Do I look handicapped, Skipper?"

"No, sir."

Clifton pulled himself into the narrow space of the conning tower.

Behind him on the pier, Chief Emano was reconstituting the working party.

"Let's go below—somewhere we can talk."

The message in Brandon's hand fell to the deck at Clifton's feet. The top part of the message had "SECRET" stamped in big red letters across it. Brandon hurried to pick it up, but not before Clifton had seen the stamp.

"A classified discussion is what we need, if you know how to protect it, Commander."

A few minutes later they were seated in the wardroom. "Admiral, this is my classified briefing area."

"Reminds me of the classified briefing areas in the back of the EP-3E Orions or the Super Constellations of VQ-2."

VQ-2 was the reconnaissance squadron based out of Rota, Spain.

Brandon poured a cup of coffee each for the admiral and Harwell. A moment later they were all seated around the table across from the coffeepot. A steward quickly brought some fresh pastries. Elliot asked the sailor to close the pantry and give them some privacy.

When Brandon sat down, he felt the message he had jammed in his pocket and pulled it out.

"Any other time than now, Skipper, I would have my cryptographic custodians down here doing an audit of your books. Get your handling of classified material squared away. That's the last thing I'm going to say about it."

Brandon nodded and made a mental note to tie Strickland to the stern and drag him across the Atlantic.

"Un-wad your message, Skipper. I think it will tell you what I am about to elaborate on."

He read it quickly, then gave it to the XO.

"I just got an update from my intelligence officer, Captain Zewowski, before I came down here. Normally, I would have assembled everyone to discuss the situation, but orders are on their way to you."

Brandon took the message back from Elliot and folded it. Strickland stepped into the wardroom, saw the group, and did an about-face.

"COMMO! Secure this," Brandon said, handing the message to Strickland.

"As you can tell, Egypt and Syria attacked Israel about

thirty minutes ago. It was a surprise attack, with Syrian forces overrunning the Golan Heights, forcing the Israelis back. Egyptian forces are crossing the Suez Canal and have already established a foothold in the Sinai. On every front, the Israelis are retreating."

Brandon and Elliot exchanged looks.

"The first thirty minutes do not look good for the Israelis, but the Israeli Air Force has already started actions and may give their army time to get their forces together and react."

"Is that why we are heading toward the Mediterranean?" Brandon asked.

Clifton took a sip of coffee and broke off a bit of the cinnamon bun. "Originally, it was because the Soviets had increased the number of submarines in the Eastern Mediterranean and we wanted to equalize the number as much as possible. That is still the same reason, but the surprise attack less than an hour ago tells us why they have done it."

"I can get under way in the hour, sir."

"I know you can. I also know you know that I would not have come down here just to brief you on what is happening in the Middle East."

Brandon was surprised. It seemed normal that an admiral should come down and tell him about the Middle East. After all, he was the best known submarine skipper in the Navy.

"No, sir. I thought . . . " He stopped.

Clifton tossed the bit of bun into his mouth. "Don't flatter yourself, Commander." He swallowed. "Give me the paper," Clifton said to Harwell, snapping his finger.

Harwell opened the security pouch and pulled out a folder with the classification "TOP SECRET" stamped across it. "This is how we protect classified material," Clifton added as he took the folder. He slid it across to Brandon.

"Before you open it, let me tell you what I know."

For the next ten minutes, Clifton went over the report, from the half message German Naval Headquarters received from the *Silesia,* reporting the sighting of two submarines on the surface less than one hundred miles southeast of Keflavik. Then the merchant vessel went quiet.

They had been unable to raise it. At the request of the German Navy, Keflavik had dispatched a P-3C ocean surveillance aircraft to check on the merchant vessel. At daybreak this morning, the aircraft spotted wreckage at the last known location of the *Silesia*. A British destroyer was en route to ascertain what the wreckage, if it is wreckage, is. Meanwhile an expanding search of the area and low passes against merchant ships around there failed to turn up the *Silesia*.

Brandon sighed. "I suspect they want us to find and track the Soviet submarines that did this?"

Clifton shrugged. "First, we don't know for sure this is wreckage. The aircrew believes it is. They even think they saw a body or two among it. Won't know until we process the film and see what imagery shows."

"The orders you are going to receive," Clifton leaned close and whispered, "are to find and sink the Soviet submarines." Clifton leaned back.

"Are you sure, Admiral?" Brandon asked in disbelief.

"Well, I haven't seen the message yet, Skipper, but I know if you don't get one that says that today, sometime in the coming days you will. This isn't the Soviet Navy of the fifties and sixties. This is a Soviet Navy that has been waiting for the opportunity to show the world that it is a major Navy power. I think they are going to use this Middle East war to flex their muscles and recover their pride from having to back down during the Cuban Missile Crisis of 1962."

"They haven't done that much," Elliot said.

"Then you haven't been reading and keeping up with their Navy, XO," Clifton said. "They backed down because they had no aircraft carriers and no nuclear submarines. They had no air power reach to protect their fleet. The Mediterranean is a whole different kettle of fish. Their submarine force is for the most part nuclear, like ours. The Mediterranean the Soviets have always considered part of the Black Sea and part of their area of influence. And their air forces can reach the Mediterranean from their airfields." Clifton raised his finger. "Make no mistake about it. They want to confront us. They need to confront us." He lowered his finger. "Whether it comes to bullets and blood will be the key to how much they want to wear the mantle of the 'number one' superpower Navy of the world."

No one spoke. This was what Brandon had been living for. He'd always known they were going to fight the Soviets, and maybe Clifton was right. Maybe Brandon was going to be given his chance. Maybe even make captain out of it, though he had long ago given up that idea. His eyebrows furrowed and he looked at the admiral. "There has to be a why to this, sir."

"There is. But let's focus on what we know about the Soviet submarines in our own backyard. There are at least five Charlie-class submarines missing from the Soviet Northern Fleet inventory." He held up his hand, the fingers spread. "Five of them, and we suspected they were heading toward the East Coast as part of the Soviets' routine patrols, but initial reassessment is that those five attack submarines may turn and try to block the entrance to the Mediterranean. If they get in position where they can knock out a carrier battle group going into the Med, then we are stuck with our normal two-carrier battle group inside to fight off a massive Soviet Navy buildup."

"Are we going to send another carrier battle group, sir?" Elliot asked.

Clifton shrugged. "Too early to tell, but America is not going to let Israel lose." He looked at each of the officers. "And the U.S. Navy is not going to let the Soviet Navy keep it from entering the Mediterranean."

"And the Soviets cannot afford to let their allies lose," Brandon added.

"You are right," Clifton said. "I would be surprised if orders have not already been issued to both Commander in Chief Atlantic Fleet and Commander in Chief Pacific Fleet to prepare battle groups. Along with those orders will be orders to the Marine Corps to start emergency preparations for deploying to the Middle East." Clifton spread both hands on the table. "This may be it, gentlemen."

"It?" Harwell asked, drawing the looks of all three men. "Sorry."

"It is what we have known was coming for years. It is the confrontation between our Navy and their "wanna-be" superpower Navy. It always starts at sea, and if the Soviets are sinking merchant vessels, then the gloves are off."

"I have a full load-out of torpedoes and Harpoons, sir."

"I would put a couple of Harpoons at the ready, but I think you're going to be fighting an undersea battle in the coming next few days."

"Do we have any indication where the Charlies are now?" Brandon asked.

"The same P-3C reported visual recognition of an Ugra-class Soviet submarine tender. Side numbers identify her as the *Volga*. The *Volga* is heading west—going around Ireland is our best guess."

"Sounds like the same pattern they use when they are deploying to our coast for their patrols," Brandon offered.

Clifton nodded. "You are right. We could be wrong and the submarines are just going to take up a scattered north-south patrol along the East Coast. Then there is the idea that the *Volga* will continue west as a deception while the submarines turn south toward the Strait of Gibraltar."

"Or the submarine tender could turn south, drawing our forces with it while the submarines continue west," Brandon said.

Clifton sighed. "Lots of variables, but our doctrine says to expect the worse and you won't be disappointed." He pointed at Brandon. "Commander, you have two reputations. The one ashore is not pretty—Mickey? One day you'll have to enlighten me as to how you got that handle, or call sign as we flyers call it." Clifton slid to the left. "Find those Soviet submarines and blow them out of the water."

Clifton turned to Harwell. "Well, Lieutenant, you going to keep sitting there blocking me in or you going to move your ass so I can get off this boat before another airdale sees me and my reputation is ruined."

Harwell was standing at the doorway by the time Clifton finished his words.

* * *

CLIFTON buttoned his conning tower coat against the wind as the three stood near the car door held open by Harwell. "There is one thing I have learned about orders, Commander Brandon."

"Sir?"

"And that is that regardless of what happens, the United States Navy will never admit to those orders if it will embarrass our Navy. Everything attesting to them will disappear and everyone involved will have memory lapses, if it goes bad." He turned and slid into the car.

Harwell shut the door and rushed to the other side as the admiral's window came down. "Commander, if you have time, see my intelligence officer, Captain Zewowski. He may have more data since we last spoke, and most likely he can provide you some technical material that intel-types don't think we war fighters can understand."

IT was after eleven when Brandon returned. He was alone in the car during the short journey back and was pleased to see no sailors on the pier loading supplies. He bent down to look out the right rear window. Lieutenant Plummer, the boat's CRA, chemical and radiation control officer, was standing the officer of the deck in port. He leaned back as he heard Plummer strike the four bells announcing the skipper's presence and imminent return.

Navy protocol was something he could live without when it was for him, but that didn't stop him from recognizing a failure to render it. It wasn't that it was a sign of disrespect; usually it was a case of ignorance—not enough time in the Navy to know better—or a sign of being unready. Not knowing how to render honors was something he and other senior officers lived with and corrected quickly when needed. Being unready to render honors was a chink in the armor of overall readiness, and that was seldom tolerated mildly.

He thanked the driver and hurried across the brow, stopping just before he stepped on the boat to salute the ensign on the flagstaff at the stern of the boat.

"Report my return, Officer of the Deck," he said, stepping onto the deck of the boat. He looked up to his right at the conning tower. The XO waved from his vantage point.

A single bell rang simultaneously when his foot touched the deck, punctuating his return on board. At that moment, full responsibility for command once again settled on his shoulders. It had never left, but while he was gone, Elliot had been his voice and presence on the boat. The junior officer of the deck made the appropriate log entrance to report his presence back aboard.

"Welcome back, Skipper," Plummer said with a salute.

Brandon returned the salute. "Make ready for sea, Mr. Plummer."

"Sir, the *Manta Ray* is always ready for sea."

"Anything happen while I was gone?"

Plummer shook his head. "Postman came by and dropped off mail for us. The Special Services people exchanged our movies, so we should have several days out to sea before we start rewatching them."

"Good news all around, Lieutenant."

"Lieutenant Label said to pass along to you that he left your mail on your bunk."

"Thanks," Brandon replied as he worked his way to the scuttle on the conning tower.

Brandon had a way of reading people. Good leaders through history had this innate ability. He knew his wardroom would fight for him. He'd never quite figured out that officers' respect for him was built upon his respect for them. Like the time he demanded to be put in the brig with his officers if the Shore Patrol lieutenant commander in Rota, Spain, was not going to let them out. Fifteen minutes later, one telephone call with Commander Naval Forces Spain, and he and his officers were on their way back to the boat. Or the time when an officer returned from deployment to find his house stripped bare, his wife gone, and the children with her. It was Brandon who spent the evening getting the officer drunk and taking him to a tittie bar, using his own dollar bills, and convincing the about-to-be divorced officer of all the new joys of life coming his way.

Similar joy, from losing his first wife, came his way six months later.

Then there was the Congo Palace incident in Athens, Greece. The Congo Palace was the U.S. Air Force officers club. Air Force and Navy officers tended not to get along. The fight started with a joke that began with *There were three Air Force zoomies in a row boat* . . . When the combatant energy of both the Air Force and the Navy finally dissipated, which luckily was before the Air Police arrived, Brandon and the senior Air Force officer, who was commissioned Air Force out of the Naval Academy—*Lord, why in the hell did you go Air Force? Are your parents still speaking to you?*— decided that only a chugging contest of mythical proportion could settle the insults and slanders to each of their services.

The Navy easily won, but what in the hell was that thing called ouzo? It took two days for the *Manta Ray* to sail a straight course, but the good thing about being in a submarine is that no one can see the boat tacking under the surface.

Nope. There was no finer officer in the entire United States Navy, if you listened to his officers, to serve under. The man was a champion of the downtrodden, defender of his people, and a fighter for his Navy. If cut, he would bleed blue and gold.

And, of course, when Brandon heard someone telling him a sea story about his exploits, he laughed and wondered aloud where in the hell these things came from, because none of them were true. He was adamant that none of the stories he ever heard about himself were true. He once got on an elevator at the Bureau of Naval Personnel located on the hill near Arlington Cemetery, overlooking the Pentagon. The thing had barely started up before an officer in it confided that "Brandon" was in the building. Then the officer went on to tell how close he and Brandon were, before stepping off the elevator on the floor before his. To this day, he still did not know who in the hell that officer was, though the man had been wearing dolphins.

Nope, there was no finer officer to go to sea with or hit a port with than Brandon. His superiors preferred the going-to-sea part of his legend to the hitting-the-port part.

"How are we doing, XO?" Brandon asked as he pulled himself up to the conning tower.

"Have done everything you asked, Skipper."

"Load out?"

Elliot tucked his hand inside his foul-weather jacket and withdrew a folded sheet of paper from his shirt pocket. He handed it to Brandon. "Fully loaded out, Skipper: four Harpoons, five SUBROCs, and sixteen Mark-48 torpedoes."

Brandon unfolded the paper and scanned the weapons load-out report.

"Of course, we could always reduce our SUBROCs and replace them with more torpedoes or Harpoons. Not sure I agree with the admiral on the Harpoons. I think we need a couple in our tubes."

Brandon sighed and handed the folded sheet back to Elliot. "I know how you feel, XO. But we are definitely hunting submarines, so it will be torpedoes for the tubes. Keep a couple of Harpoons handy, but if we get to where we have to use them, then we will be in the Med. We are going to be looking for some Soviet submarines south of us."

Elliot looked surprised. "Anything more about the Israelis? Naval Intelligence have anything new?"

"We talked about it. Seems the Soviets must have known this was going to happen for some time. They have over twenty submarines in the Eastern Mediterranean. We have our normal two-carrier battle groups, which are now heading to the East Med." He shook his head. "You know, Dev, how we always talked about the 'someday' when the American and Soviet Navies would have it out? Would decide who is the baddest, meanest, sonofabitch in and on the ocean?"

"You mean kind of like the Congo Palace?"

"No, I don't mean like the Congo Palace. First, no one died, and second, the story is fabricated," Brandon replied, even as he knew Elliot had been with him in Athens.

"I mean all this bullshit we kept telling ourselves about how we were 'someday' going to kick Ivan's butt all the way back to Moscow?" Without waiting for an answer, he continued, "Well, that day may be here." He let out a deep sigh and smiled. "Kind of brings a warm spot to your heart, don't you think?"

"You recall the story of Admiral Nelson . . . "

"The British admiral at the Battle of Trafalgar; of course, I do."

"No, I mean the one seldom told about what he wore into battle."

Brandon gave him a puzzled look.

"He was on deck of the HMS *Victory* one day when the lookout reported three French ships of the line coming over the horizon. Nelson ordered his XO to bring him his red coat. The XO—"

"I don't think they called them XOs back then."

"Sir, do you mind? This is my story. Anyway, the XO told Nelson not to wear the red coat because it made him stand out and made him a target for the upcoming battle. Nelson put his arm around his magnificent XO—all XOs are magnificent by the way—and told him the red coat was because in the event he—Nelson—got wounded, he did not want the crew to see the blood and lose hope." Elliot paused.

"And the moral of this story?"

"There's more. The British met the three French ships and won a great victory and Nelson was not wounded. Three days later, the HMS *Victory* was sailing alone and over the horizon came ten French men-of-war. The XO looked at him and said, 'Should I bring your red coat, sir?' And Nelson replied, 'No, XO, bring me my brown pants.'" Elliot laughed. "So the question, sir, is will you be wearing red or brown when we go on this hunt?"

Brandon laughed. "Keep both ready because there are at least two Soviet Charlie-class submarines out there. Naval Intelligence thinks the five missing from inventory are all together. They also think the submarine tender is not going to try any operational deception to decoy us away. They think the Charlie-class boats have so many engineering problems down to and including being able to make potable water that the submarine tender will be heading in the same direction. Kind of a safety line for them."

"So it is a definite the submarines are heading for the Strait of Gibraltar?"

"Naval Intelligence is positively, completely convinced; energetically enthused to produce an analytical product that indicates there is a possible-probable chance they are going to do that."

"Sounds pretty positive to me."

"One of the Charlie-class boats is believed to be the Soviet test platform for weapons and class modifications—the K-321."

"Sounds like our boat."

"It did when I talked with Captain Zewowski. The K-321 has both forward and aft torpedo rooms and capabilities like us, unlike the other members of its class."

"The Soviets probably stole it from us. They stole our plans for building nuclear submarines."

"And they invented television, if you listen to their press releases. Anything else going on, XO?"

Elliot nodded. "The message came in from Chief of Naval Operations."

"And?"

"Pretty much says what the admiral told us. Steers clear of the words 'sink 'em' but does say we are not to allow them to take position to block the choke-point entry to the Mediterranean and we are authorized to use whatever means available to us to stop them."

"I would think they would send us some help," Brandon said, crossing his fingers and hoping the Navy didn't.

"No submarines available for the next ten days. It will take ten days for a Norfolk emergency deployment of five more submarines to reach us. Until then, we are on our own."

"We ready for sea?"

"Sir, the *Manta Ray* is always ready for sea."

"Déjà-vu, XO."

"Sir?"

"And we are to find them and trail them, right?"

"When do we sail?"

"As soon as possible. Once under way, have Lieutenant Strickland make sure everyone's page two is updated." "Page two" was that part of a service record where a sailor identified his next of kin. "We'll off-load the originals as soon as opportunity presents itself, but I want a message to BUPERS updating everyone's page two. And, XO, do it quietly. Do it like something we do routinely. It's a red coat type of thing."

"Supply says we still have a scheduled load-out at noon."

"Find out what it is, and if we can live without it, then we'll cancel it."

The supplies were mainly administrative stuff, with some food and emergency rations. By the time Brandon was informed, the trucks were on the pier, so the load-out commenced.

It took thirty minutes to finish loading this last-minute arrival of more supplies. Two of the movies Special Services had given them were two they had just off-loaded, but the admin officer, Lieutenant Label, managed to trade them with a nearby destroyer for a horror movie he had been hearing about, and something called *American Graffiti*. Brandon had doubts about both, but movies were important for crew morale. And he had not seen either.

BRANDON stood on the conning tower feeling the cold Arctic wind whip his face as the *Manta Ray* departed the port. He raised his binoculars and glanced back at Keflavik, Iceland. Another port to avoid for a couple of years, or until Clifton transferred. He listened to Quartermaster First Class Corley, who was sharing the small platform above the conning tower, pass bearings to the navigator, who was in the control room below.

Brandon lowered his glasses and looked to the left, at the shoreline that paralleled the departure of the boat. He wanted that jut of land off his stern before he turned west. He could have done this submerged, but with the overcast and the unscheduled departure of the *Manta Ray*, he doubted any Soviet TU-95 Bear reconnaissance planes would pick them up. Besides, Captain Zewowski said there were no Soviet recce missions scheduled for today. He wondered how the intelligence officer knew such things.

"Navigator, conning tower. Lighthouse bears two-six-zero," Corley passed.

Corley had been one of his sailors of the quarter earlier in the year. Brandon had already marked him as a future chief. He had ranked the man number two of sixteen first class petty officers on board the boat and number one quartermaster that he had ever served with. Words were powerful weapons, and selection boards read between the lines when they read evaluations. He had little doubt that with his name and Corley's rankings and prior performance, the man would be a chief selectee off this board.

Petty Officer Corley raised his head from the sight and pressed the sound-powered headset against his ears. "Aye, sir," the sailor said to the voice on the other end. Then he turned to Brandon. "Skipper, Mr. Label says we are smack-dab in the center of the channel, sir. Spot on." Petty Officer Corley smiled.

"Good work." Brandon turned forward, watching the boat maneuver straight. Iceland was a fishing economy. Fishing was ingrained in every Icelander, and everyone on this sparsely populated island owned some sort of fishing boat, from small rowboats he wouldn't take fifty feet from shore to huge trawlers capable of circling the globe. And each believed the sea was theirs and the rules of the road for navigation only applied to others.

Another reason for staying on the surface until he was well away from Icelandic waters. This way, he could avoid the nets and accidentally pulling an Icelandic fishing boat down. Submarines made terrible anchors.

AN hour later the *Manta Ray* was nearing the edge of the twelve-mile limit of Iceland's sovereign coastal waters. Brandon decided it was time to do what submarines do best: submerge.

He pulled the stopwatch from his pocket. Behind him, he heard the movement of the topside watches, and even Petty Officer Corley, preparing for what they knew was coming.

Brandon flipped open the brass covering of the sound tube. "Control room, this is the skipper: dive, dive!"

The *ah-hooh-gah* sound of the diving gong echoed across topside. He pushed himself against the railing as the watches slid down from the mainmast. Brandon looked over his shoulder as the sailors slid through the scuttle and down the ladder, propelling themselves through the access tunnel to the control room. He waited until Corley had left the conning tower; then he glanced forward as water started to flow across the bow, and then aft to make sure no one was above deck and that both the aft and forward escape scuttles were closed.

Satisfied, Brandon secured the brass sound tube and followed the sailors down, stopping just inside on the ladder to secure the topside escape scuttle to the conning tower. Then he was down the ladder, landing on bended knees in the control room. Behind him a sailor scurried back up the ladder to double-check his securing of the scuttle. There were no second chances on board a nuclear submarine. Rickover's dictum.

"Flood negative, flood safety!" Lieutenant Commander Fitzgerald commanded.

Brandon listened as his operations officer took the boat down.

Near the aft door, Lieutenant Commander Elliot stood near the Christmas Tree, looking over the shoulder of the sailor monitoring it. Even from where Brandon stood, he saw a couple of red lights. That was not good.

The "Christmas Tree" was a console that monitored the submarine's openings and valves that led to the water outside. The key to submarine survival was to keep the ocean outside of the boat. Most else was secondary. A series of green and red lights showed the condition of those openings and valves.

Brandon worked his way through the crowded control room toward the Christmas Tree just as the last two lights glowed green.

"I have a green Christmas Tree!" the sailor announced.

"This is a drill. Set battle stations!" Brandon announced.

Over the 1MC, he heard the gongs of general quarters along with the words "This is a drill, this is a drill. Set battle stations, set battle stations!"

"Three-degree down bubble," Fitzgerald ordered.

"Make your speed ten knots," Brandon added.

"Making my speed ten knots, aye!"

The echoes of orders rolled through the control room as the boat tilted forward and continued downward. At the weapons control station, Elliot received the reports from the *Manta Ray* departments, reporting "battle stations set."

Near the Christmas Tree, another set of lights told everyone the internal status of the boat as it went from peacetime sailing to wartime condition. This was no surprise to the crew. Every submerging was conducted as if it was an emergency submerging followed by immediate combat. Brandon doubted they would ever have to do it during his career, but he wanted to make sure that the "how to" was never lost as others followed in his footsteps.

"Battle stations set, sir!" Elliot announced.

"Very well." Brandon turned toward Fitzgerald. "Make your depth two hundred feet."

"Making my depth two-hundred feet, aye."

The *Manta Ray* shook for a moment, much like a car going over a speed bump.

"Easy on the bow planes!" Master Chief Torpedoman Hugh Tay snapped at the planesman.

Tay was the chief of the boat, the senior enlisted man on board the *Manta Ray*. Funny-looking guy when you first met him, with a broad chest mounted on such a small waist that it made you think if a strong wind came up, it would blow the top half of the COB away. The COB had arms that moved constantly, reminding Brandon of the rods that moved the wheels on old steam locomotives.

Regardless of the first impression, the COB was not a man to be trifled with, but then most master chiefs were not to be trifled with. They had reached as far as they would go in promotions in the Navy. They were the top one percent of the enlisted personnel of the Navy. And most grew up with the admirals that were in charge of the Navy today, and were not averse to calling them if they felt the need.

"Passing one hundred feet, three-degree bubble!" Tay announced.

"Passing one hundred feet, three-degree bubble!" Fitzgerald relayed.

And so it went as they continued a slow descent to two hundred feet. The helmsman reporting his course and speed. The planesman reporting the depth. The observers repeating each report and the officer of the deck acknowledging the report. And outside the chain of command was the quartermaster making log entries of each change. Even during combat, the log entries were a continuum of notations, so that when calm returned, the backseat drivers of the Pentagon could critique your success or failure. "Lessons learned," they called it.

"Approaching two hundred feet."

"Ease your planes," Fitzgerald commanded.

The angle of the *Manta Ray* began to level off and like a fine machine Fitzgerald reported exactly two hundred feet.

"Final trim. My depth is two hundred feet." "Final trim" was the nautical submarine term that told everyone the boat was level in the water at the designated depth; it was no longer on an angle.

Brandon hit the stopwatch. It showed five minutes. It had taken them less than forty-five seconds to submerge, which was not too shabby in his books. Two hundred feet was a good depth to give him the option of escaping and evading a superior force topside and at the same time to provide the latitude to reposition for attack.

"Good job, everyone. Took less than a minute—forty-five seconds—to submerge and just under five minutes to reach fighting depth. Secure from battle stations."

Over the boat's intercom the command to secure from battle stations echoed throughout *Manta Ray*. Brandon was not one to keep everyone bottled up just to show he could do it.

"XO, I'll be in my stateroom," he announced as he walked toward the aft hatch. "Check my orders for the watch and let me know if there are any questions." He did not notice the look of concern on Elliot's face as he left the control room.

Seconds later he was in his stateroom. Lying on his rack was the mail delivered earlier. He saw a couple of letters from Louise and smiled. The other letters included one that looked very official, from some company called Harrison-Johnson that had its Norfolk address embossed on the return envelope. He shook his head. He had seen these types of letters before, about overdue payments by his sailors or some sort of other legal problems.

He looked at the stamped dates on Louise's letters and put the older one on top of the more recent one. The smile on his face left as he read her first letter. By the time he opened the second one, a feeling of gloom had settled over him. When he finished the second one, he knew the letter from Harrison-Johnson was for him.

FIVE

October 6, 1973—Saturday

BY late afternoon on October 6, 1973, the surprise attack by Egyptian and Syrian forces had driven the Israelis back. Egyptian tanks were rumbling through the breach in the defensive Bar-Lev Line Israeli forces had built along the Suez Canal. The Egyptian Army was pushing into the Sinai, and the Arab world cheered as the "mighty" Israeli Army fled in front of it. The world was stunned.

The Egyptian Third Army poured across the Suez Canal behind its armor, quickly occupying this beachhead while the majority of its soldiers raced into the occupied Egyptian territory of the Sinai Peninsula.

The Sinai Peninsula had been lost by Gamal Abdel Nasser in the 1967 war. It was national pride which Anwar Sadat used to instill confidence in the army for this day. It was territory all Egyptians were intent on wresting from Israel.

The success of the Egyptian Army was a surprise to Sadat's government. It was also a surprise to the Egyptian Army, and it shocked the world.

The Egyptian forces were better trained than in 1967. Within hours, Israel had reconstituted a defensive front in the Sinai and its tanks counterattacked, slowing the Egyptian advance even as more Egyptian armor poured across the Suez Canal. Egyptian antitank forces, Soviet-trained, raced forward in the middle of the tank battle, stood their ground, and destroyed the majority of the Israeli tanks. But the Israeli counterattack had done its job. It had bought time for the encircled Jewish state to mobilize. It had caused the Egyptians to slow their advance. All along the Bar-Lev, Egyptian forces were digging in, turning the Israeli defensive line into their own.

Israeli Prime Minister Golda Meir addressed the nation, telling people how Israel had inflicted huge losses on the Egyptian and Syrian armies even as Israel was retreating. The opposite was true. Israel was suffering huge losses. Syrian forces had overrun Mount Hebron. Syria was attacking against the heavy Israeli defenses on the Golan Heights, and they were surprising themselves as they moved forward.

Israeli losses mounted in this first afternoon of the fighting, as the small nation, with the Mediterranean to its back, suffered loss after loss fighting against overwhelming odds. In the back of the minds of the Israeli leaders was the mantra of Nasser, who boasted that the Arab nations would push the Jews into the Mediterranean. When you looked at the map of Israel, you could see that there was no other place to retreat. For Israel, every war was a battle for survival.

The Israeli Air Force started a series of attacks; wave after wave of the elite air power pounded the attacking armies, but achieved little—a shocking failure for an Air Force seen as one of the best in the world, not only by the Israeli population, but by other Air Forces of larger nations. Without the Israeli Army engaged on the ground, the Israeli Air Force could not stop the slow advance of Egypt and Syria. Arab victories continued to pile up.

The Golan Heights became the focus by the afternoon. The Israeli Army fought pitched battles and held the strategic area thereby denying Syrian artillery and rocket forces an advantage from which all of Israel would have been threatened. The Syrian onslaught began to slow to a halt.

In the Sinai, the loss of the tank battle by Israel had left the door open to its western borders, but the Egyptians stopped. They started to dig in. The Israeli generals scratched their heads, wondering why the Egyptian Army had stopped at the Bar-Lev Line. There was nothing between it and the original 1947 Israeli border except a minuscule, disorganized Israeli Army scattered along a five-hundred-mile front.

No one in Israel could fail to know that the onslaught had only one purpose, which was to destroy Israel—wipe it from the face of the earth.

October 6, 1973, belonged to the Egyptians and Syrians. The Arab successes shocked and sent waves of fear through the Israeli population. The superpowers of the United States and the Soviet Union watched and started their own mobilization, for neither was in a position to allow their clients to lose.

Ironically, both were embarrassed by the actions. Kissinger had urged the Israelis earlier in the year not to take military action. Sadat and the Soviets were having political problems in that the Egyptians were beginning to believe the Soviets had too much say in Egypt. The nationalization begun by Nasser was ingrained in the Egyptian sense of independence and freedom. In the Arab world, where Egypt led the others followed. Israel had wanted to take preemptive action nearly a year before the attack, but Kissinger had convinced them to hold. Now both were experiencing the error of that decision.

Modern nations have contingency plans. The Israeli military jerked such a plan from the shelves. Within an hour Israel was mobilizing. Young men and women rushed from synagogues and families, some still buttoning uniforms as they raced with their weapons to assigned units. Even with such a detailed and ready response plan, and the experience gained through exercises, it takes time to reach the front, regardless of how many men and women are mobilized or how fast the mobilization occurs. Israel was already in extremis as they rushed to engage the approaching onslaught of the Arab armies. Without the supplies and logistic tail to support the fighting, no matter how patriotic your soldiers, no matter how well trained, no matter if God is on your side or not—your cause is lost.

By nightfall, Israel had asked the United States for a massive resupply or they would face the prospect of the destruction of the Israeli state. The fight was fully engaged by then, with other Arab states—themselves surprised and proud of the Arab victories—rushing to participate. Jordan and Iraq were the first to start their own Army units toward the front.

"MAKE your depth sixteen meters," Bagirli ordered. He was still fuming from having stood at attention in front of the other commanding officers for five minutes while Admiral Ramishvili both praised and chastised him. Praised him for sinking the merchant vessel that could have exposed their presence; then gave him an ass-chewing he would recall numerous times during the upcoming mission.

If he had not put the K-321 and K-301 on the surface when he did, then he—Admiral Ramishvili—would not have had to order the destruction of a NATO merchant vessel.

Bagirli took it. What else could he do?

"Making my depth sixteen meters."

The soft sound of water being expelled from ballast tanks came from every side of the compartment as the K-321 rose.

"Three-degree up bubble!" Lieutenant Vasily Kiselyov, the torpedo officer, announced. Kiselyov was the officer of the deck.

Bagirli nodded toward Demirchan.

"Very well!" Demirchan acknowledged.

"Up periscope," Bagirli ordered. He sighed. His career was dead.

The sound of hydraulics raising the scope from storage caused him to look down at the deck where the silver tube began to emerge. Almost perfunctorily he squatted, unfolded the handles as they came up, and put his eyes against the eyepiece. He watched the water cascade off the lens. The K-321 was alone. He had been relieved by Admiral Ramishvili.

His Navy was going to shit. A Uzbek on board his boat and a Georgian for an admiral!

He spun the periscope around, checking the water forward and aft for any signs of bubbles that might indicate a leak. He spun it around the horizon, searching the dark for contacts, though Sonar had reported six merchant vessels over the horizon, all of them traveling on straight-line courses and none of the headings to take any of them near the K-321. But then, it had been Sonar who told him the German merchant vessel was the Soviet submarine tender *Volga*.

"No contact. Down scope!"

Seconds later the periscope was stored.

"Tell Communications they can reel out the antenna."

"Aye, sir," Kiselyov acknowledged.

Bagirli scratched his chin. He squinted for a moment as he recalled that the last time he'd shaved was before the *Volga,* for the meeting with Admiral Ramishvili and the other Project 670 submarine skippers.

A different hum from the hydraulics of the periscope joined the other sounds of electronics within the control room. One of the starshinas lit a cigarette. Chief of the Boat Zimyatov walked over to the sailor, leaned down, and whispered something to the young man. A second later the cigarette was out.

"Communications reports they are reeling out the antenna, sir."

"Very well." He looked at the assistant weapons officer. Maybe this junior officer Kiselyov might be the one to relieve the sonar officer. He took a deep breath. The odor of sweat, oil, and stale air filled his lungs. Odors in submarines were less so today than when he first joined the Soviet submarine force with its diesels and less efficient battery power. But submariners became used to it over time as it slowly built up, and it was only when fresh air was pumped through the boat that they realized what they were missing topside.

The aft door opened and the operations officer, Lieutenant Commander Lepechin, entered. Bagirli said nothing as the operations officer spoke quietly with Kiselyov.

"Captain, this is Lieutenant Commander Lepechin. I am ready to relieve Lieutenant Kiselyov as officer of the deck."

"Very well," Bagirli replied.

Lepechin turned to the shorter Kiselyov. "I am ready to relieve you."

"I am ready to be relieved," Kiselyov replied.

"I relieve you."

"I stand relieved."

Lepechin turned back to Bagirli. "Sir, I have the deck and the conn."

"Very well." Bagirli looked at Kiselyov. "Lieutenant Kiselyov, you may return to your duties."

When he was at periscope depth, just as when he ordered the boat to battle stations, Bagirli wanted the operations officer as the officer of the deck. Demirchan stood near the weapons control station. Since the sinking of the German, the XO had seemed more distant. Most of the officers had, Bagirli surmised.

"Sir, we are steering one-nine-zero degrees true at a depth of sixteen meters. Engines one and two are both on line. My speed is eight knots. Radio reports antenna deployed for long-range communications."

Bagirli nodded. Someone had to pay for this mistake, and it was Sonar who had given him the wrong information. Trade the two in their jobs. Put Iltchenko as the torpedo officer and move Kiselyov to Sonar. His weapons officer, Nehoda, would complain, but it would be good for the boat. It would definitely improve his ego to punish Iltchenko. He would discuss it with Demirchan. He wiped his forehead. He hoped the crew recognized it as punishment, and he intended to make sure the sonar officer's personnel record reflected it as such.

Bagirli looked at the clock. Ten minutes until eight o'clock—or nineteen fifty hours for real people like submariners. He would remain at this depth for twenty minutes so Radio could receive any messages for the K-321. He wanted to read the GRU intelligence message on the fighting in the Middle East, for how the war was going there would affect his mission.

Demirchan walked up to the periscope platform and stood alongside Bagirli. Neither man spoke.

A starshina, wearing an apron, emerged through the aft door to the control room. On a tray the pot bellied sailor carried two cups of steaming tea along with several cookies. He smiled as he approached Bagirli.

At least some of the men on this boat knew how to show respect to the captain.

Demirchan reached out and lifted a cup from the tray before the starshina set it down on the nearby shelf between Bagirli and him.

Anger flew over Bagirli. His face turned red, but he said nothing. Demirchan's eyes widened.

"My apologies, Captain. I was afraid the man was about to spill one of the cups." He held the cup toward Bagirli.

Bagirli motioned him away, but said nothing. His anger calmed even as he knew Demirchan was lying. Was there no one on this boat who knew how to treat a senior officer?

"Thank you, starshina," he said curtly to the sailor, who smiled and nodded as he backed away. There was someone who knew how to show respect. Bagirli wondered for a moment what the man's name was and even thought of asking, but by the time he had decided to ask, the sailor was already opening the aft watertight door. He promised himself to ask next time and within seconds promptly forgot the promise.

Bagirli poured a few drops of cream into the tea, with a spoonful of sugar, and stirred it. "XO, has the logistics officer provided you with the updated status of our supplies?"

"I talked with him soon after we departed the *Volga*, sir. I presume—"

"No presumptions, please, Captain Third Rank Demirchan. Have Lieutenant Petrov come see us while we wait for the communicators to finish their messaging."

Five minutes later, Lieutenant Ziven Petrov emerged through the aft watertight door, ducking to avoid hitting the top of it as he came into the control room. Lepechin rolled his eyes as the supply officer sashayed toward the periscope.

"Captain, I am reporting as you ordered, sir," the slim officer said, a broad smile guarding his face.

"Yes, did. I shouldn't have had to, Lieutenant. What is the status of our supplies?"

The man's mouth opened for a moment before the smile returned—it reminded Bagirli of a young lady's. The man's long eyelashes only accented the image. Boats did not need men such as him on board.

"Sir, I am proud to say that we received everything we asked for. The pantry is topped off. My men are still storing some of the boxes. We may have to move some to the wardroom for storage—"

"You also received three torpedoes?"

Petrov's eyebrows furrowed. "Sir?"

"Torpedoes? You said we got everything we asked for, so I presume you asked for three torpedoes to replace the ones we fired."

The lieutenant's eyes cut toward Demirchan.

"I think what Lieutenant Petrov means, sir, is that everything we could get from the *Volga* we did. The torpedoes have been reordered, right, Lieutenant?"

The smile had disappeared. Petrov swallowed. "I have the message waiting to go, sir," he stuttered, his eyes going from the XO to the captain and then back to the XO for a moment.

"Then don't tell me we got everything we asked for if we are still shy three torpedoes, Lieutenant."

"Yes, sir. It will not happen again."

"And I presume the message will go out with this schedule?"

"Lieutenant," Demirchan added, "lay forward to your office and make sure your chief starshina has taken the message to the communicators. We would not want such a logistics gap to remain unknown at Naval Headquarters. They will not start replenishment of weapons without a request or an explanation."

"Yes, sir." Petrov looked at Bagirli. "With your permission, Captain."

"Permission granted. Let me know when the message is sent. I also want to know how long our resupply will last, until we have to rendezvous with the *Volga* again."

"Sir, we have enough food for sixty days."

Bagirli nodded curtly. "That is good. Sixty days. Report back to me when you have released the weapons resupply message."

He sipped his tea as the junior officer departed the control room. The tea was nice.

The *Volga* had a limited number of torpedoes on board, though it was primarily a submarine tender, capable of doing repair work and replenishing supplies. He still needed torpedo replacements, but to resupply them at sea—at night—during an Arctic October was something best delayed until later. Maybe once they reached the Mediterranean.

He could have mentioned it to Admiral Ramishvili, but to have asked for three torpedoes would have meant another round of chastisement. This time it would have been on why a Soviet submarine needed three torpedoes to sink an unarmed merchant vessel—Soviet submarine doctrine notwithstanding that tactics called for three well-placed torpedoes.

"What is our weapons load-out, XO?"

"We have six anticarrier cruise missiles, sir, and thirteen torpedoes."

"We do not have enough torpedoes or enough missiles to do either of the two primary missions, of sinking American aircraft carriers and sinking American submarines." Bagirli sighed.

Demirchan nodded with a grunt. "The newer Project 670 class will have better weapons systems thanks to what our prototype version has learned."

Bagirli started to say something negative about the boat, but to do so would violate the golden rule of skippers throughout the world: never, ever speak ill of your vessel. Bad luck. Bad juju. Their boat was their boat, and anything negative about it was his responsibility.

"We are with four other boats, Skipper. Between all of us operating together, we can slow the Americans from reaching the Mediterranean."

Bagirli sipped his tea for a moment before shaking his head. "Not any longer, XO. If we were part of the wolf pack, we would be formidable, but we are behind the others by at least a hundred kilometers." He paused before adding caustically, "We are the rear guard."

"Eventually we will reconstitute. Right?"

"I don't see how. The *Volga* will continue toward its area of operations, which is somewhere in the middle of the Atlantic Ocean. We are to head toward the Strait of Gibraltar and take position a couple of hundred kilometers west of the entrance. K-301 is already sprinting toward the American Norfolk Naval Base to watch for the Americans to deploy another aircraft carrier battle group to the Mediterranean."

"Do you think the Americans will do that?"

Bagirli smiled. "The Americans will do that," he said emphatically. "The Americans always send aircraft carriers to where they may fight. We, on the other hand, we send submarines." He looked at Demirchan. "Do you know why?"

Demirchan shook his head.

"Because we don't have aircraft carriers is of course the obvious answer, but the real answer is that we are still working toward being the superpower Navy we should be. As other Navies have in history. Submarines are the most formidable offense and defense available to stop surface might."

"I knew the answer about lacking aircraft carriers."

"The Soviet Navy will have its aircraft carriers one day. We will have more than the Americans, and we will outnumber them on the high seas. Thanks to our Arab allies, who never listen to us, that day may be pushed back."

"Communications reports that we have established contact with Naval Headquarters, sir!" Lepechin announced.

"Very well!" Bagirli acknowledged.

"We knew the Egyptians and Syrians were going to attack," Demirchan said. When Bagirli did not immediately answer, Demirchan asked, "Didn't we?"

"Yeah, we knew," Bagirli said, not sure if they did or not, but unwilling to admit he did not know the answer. Then he added, "We tried to stop them, but Sadat is not the ally we expected, and the Syrians are always lackeys for any opportunity to show they can whip the Jewish asses that keep whipping theirs. They are like the skinny bully on the playground who every so often decides to take on the biggest boy out there, only to get his ass whipped. Getting their ass whipped is something the Syrians are very good at."

"This is détente."

"Détente is nothing more than a pause between hostilities."

"So we will fight the Americans?"

Bagirli did not answer. He did not know. No one knew. Everyone believed they would one day determine who had the better ships, better sailors, better weapons. Right now he needed better sailors.

Demirchan sipped his tea and then, clearing his throat, asked again, "Do you think this time we will fight the Americans? Do you think the Americans knew the attacks were coming?

"All our warships in port in Syria and Egypt sailed from their berths yesterday before the war started. I think the Americans could have figured it out from just that message."

"The Americans should have suspected something with us doing that."

Bagirli shrugged. "I would have expected the xenophobic and paranoid Jews to have figured it out first." He sighed and sipped his tea again. "Ironic, isn't it?"

"What's that?"

"For the Arabs to actually surprise them! For them to ignore the warning our deployment from port gave them!" He shook his head. "It would not have been lost on us. We would have recognized it for what it was: a classic prelude to war. Ships don't sortie en masse unless something is about to happen or has happened."

"I did not think of that."

Bagirli forced a smile. "When you think of it, it means our enemies are not as smart or astute as we think they are. They are capable of mistakes. Their intelligence is capable of ignoring or missing classic indicators of war."

"MAKE your depth fifty feet, Officer of the Deck," Brandon ordered. "Up periscope."

He squatted as the low hydraulic hum raised the scope from its storage position. Brandon flipped the arms out as they cleared the tube. When the eyepiece came to eye level he leaned against it and pushed himself up as the scope rose. He felt the tightening of the muscles in his legs.

With the exception of the periscope and the few push-ups alongside his rack in the mornings, most of his exercising on board the *Manta Ray* was via his philosophy of "leadership through walking." He walked several times a day from one end of the boat to the other, pausing to talk to the sailors on watch and the officers, who he was sure forewarned one another as he traversed between the knee-knockers.

He blinked as the periscope broke water. Brandon did a three-sixty with the scope. "No contacts!" he reported. He leaned away from the periscope. "Sonar status?"

"Sonar reports no contacts, sir."

Brandon looked at the clock on the aft bulkhead. Twenty hundred hours. The movie on the mess decks would be starting soon. Serendipitously, the aft watertight door opened and Chief Rafael Emano entered the control room.

The supply chief walked right up to Brandon. "Sir, the movie is ready in the mess," Emano stated stiffly with his heavy Filipino accent.

"You may begin the movie, Chief. I think I am going to be here for a while."

Emano made a curt nod. "Aye, aye, sir." He turned sharply and was quickly gone.

Brandon sighed. Skippers had great powers at sea—under the sea, he corrected himself. They controlled everything from firing weapons to even determining when the evening movies started. Nowhere else in the United States military—or any other nation's military—did officers wield the historic powers that a United States Navy skipper under the sea did.

"No contacts immediate area, sir. They have a couple of merchants northeast of us. Looks as if they may be heading through the Iceland-UK gap. Navigation reports us a hundred miles north of Ireland. Time to turn is forty-five minutes, sir."

"Very well. Tell radio they can reel out the wire. Also, run up the electronic warfare sensor along with our mast antenna. Let's see if we have anything flying around us."

Nearly a minute passed before the EW operator started reporting radar from American P-3C antisubmarine warfare aircraft. At least four aircraft were flying at varying distances from the *Manta Ray*, but none were on a constant bearing, which would have meant the aircraft could be approaching them. Only the signal strength was being used to estimate ranges, and those ranges were more guesses than accurate.

"Am picking up some channel sixteen traffic," the quartermaster reported to Lieutenant Commander Fitzgerald, the officer of the deck.

"What you got, Petty Officer Jobs?"

"One of our aircraft is talking with a British fishing boat. Looks as if the boat rescued someone earlier this morning from a merchant ship that exploded last night."

"The man's lucky," Master Chief Tay said. "If he's been in the water this long and is still alive."

"What's the bearing to the fishing boat?" Fitzgerald asked.

"I have him bearing one-zero-six, sir."

"EW, you have anything out that way?"

"No, sir, Mr. Fitzgerald. Not a thing."

Brandon spun the periscope in that direction, but in the darkness he saw no lights. A wave washed over the periscope. He leaned away for a moment, feeling the boat beneath his feet. There was a slight rock to it. "We got weather topside," he said aloud.

"Yes, sir," Fitzgerald acknowledged. "Master Chief Tay and the planesmen are fighting the motion."

Brandon looked at the clock. Ten minutes at fifty feet. About another ten to fifteen minutes before Radio finished collecting their messages from the Navy broadcast. He would reel in the antenna as they went deeper.

The forward door opened and Lieutenant Tony Grant, the sonar officer, entered, ducking in a battle to avoid hitting the overhead as he stepped inside the control room. He lost, as the top part of the door clipped the brim of his ball cap, knocking it off.

"Damn," Grant said, picking up the cap and squaring it away on his head.

Grant drew everyone's attention for a second, before they all returned their full attention to the watch stations in front of them. Red light filled the control room. Grant moved toward Brandon, stopping at Fitzgerald to pass along a few words. After Fitzgerald nodded, Grant quickly reached Brandon.

"What's going on, Mr. Grant?" Brandon asked as the sonar officer reached him.

Grant adjusted the bill of his cap. "Sir, I would have had Sonar report this, but it was so nebulous that I wanted to explain it."

Brandon draped both arms over the handles of the periscope and leaned around it to face the sonar officer. "Okay. So explain."

"It may be nothing, but for a fraction of a second, our sonar technician thought he might have a Soviet submarine."

"When was this?"

"Less than a minute ago, sir."

"Un-uh," Brandon replied. "A minute can be a long time, Lieutenant. And what was the bearing of this possible submarine?"

"Sir, not sure it was a submarine."

"Then why did your sonar technician think it was a Soviet submarine, if he wasn't sure?"

"It was bearing one-nine-nine true, sir."

Brandon dropped his arms and walked around the periscope. One-nine-nine was southwest of *Manta Ray*. It was in the direction where Naval Intelligence figured the Soviet submarine pack would be heading. "I don't suppose your sonar technician identified it as a Charlie-class, did he?"

Grant shook his head. "No, sir. He didn't have time to do signals analysis on the contact before we lost it. I think we lost it because the signal was a convergence one. You know, oscillating up and down between the surface and the layer—"

"Thank you, Mr. Grant. I think I know what a convergence signal is," Brandon said with a smile. He looked over at Fitzgerald. "Officer of the Deck, make your course two-zero-zero and make it a slow turn. We still have the antenna out."

"Aye, sir. Making my course two-zero-zero, five-degree rudder."

Brandon turned back to the sonar officer, and in a low voice so only Grant could hear, he said, "Mr. Grant, I appreciate your concern about wanting to explain what Sonar had. In the future, report your contacts first, then come explain." Brandon smiled. "It gives everyone in the control room an opportunity to react in the event you are right."

Grant nodded. "Thank you, sir. I just wanted to make sure you understood we couldn't be sure."

"Passive signals are a bitch, aren't they, Tony?"

"Yes, sir," Grant answered.

The junior officer saluted and hurried away toward the forward watertight door. The door opened about the same time as Grant reached it, and the communications officer, Lieutenant Rolf Strickland, bumped into him. The two officers passed each other.

The familiar metal clipboard of the radio shack was in the communications officer's left hand. A moment later he was handing Brandon the message they had just received. Brandon read it. Clifton had been right. Wasn't a damn thing here he could hang his hat on if the shit hit the fan.

"Steady on course two-zero-zero, sir."

"Very well." The one-degree difference would put him slightly north of the possible contact.

Brandon handed the message board back to Strickland. "Have Mr. Fitzgerald read the operations order. Then find the XO and ensure he is aware of the orders. By the way, Mr. Strickland, I want a copy of the OP order given to Mr. Fitzgerald for the pass-down."

"Sir, it's top secret."

"And our entire submarine is filled with those cleared for top secret."

"But it says it is for your eyes only."

Brandon sighed. "Okay, don't put it on the pass-down log, but let Mr. Fitzgerald and the XO read it before you put it away."

"Yes, sir."

"Oh, and, Lieutenant. Belay my last. Don't put it away. Mount it so I can read it later. I want to scrutinize it closely so I make sure I fully understand it."

Strickland acknowledged Brandon's order and stepped down to where the operations officer stood. When Fitzgerald finished reading the message, the communications officer departed through the forward door, heading back to the radio shack.

You are ordered to use all means at your disposal to ensure access to the Mediterranean is assured for U.S. Navy vessels. This message is not meant to imply that offensive actions are authorized except in defense of your boat. Now, how in the hell does a submarine "peacefully ensure" any damn thing without surfacing, inviting the sonofabitch to have a beer, and arm wrestling him to see who does what? It seemed to Brandon that his only excuse for sinking a Soviet submarine, if it came to that, was to defend *Manta Ray*. Which meant he had to let the Soviet submarine know where he was and hope the Soviet captain was stupid enough to do something Brandon could call threatening. He smiled. Maybe this wasn't as bad as he thought. He nodded thoughtfully. This could be fun. Scary as hell, but fun.

Twenty-five minutes later the *Manta Ray* was at two hundred feet and the wire was reeled in. The boat was hunting now. He had the speed a few revolutions below twelve knots. He wanted to close the Soviet submarine, if it was one, as fast as possible, but he did not want to go so fast that the speed of the *Manta Ray* rendered passive sonar useless. If the quick hit sonar heard was accurate, he would find the Charlie.

"Sir, fifteen minutes until turn."

Brandon looked down. Should he turn to a new course or continue on this one? "Let's continue on two-zero-zero for another thirty minutes. Then we'll turn to our base course toward the operational area off the Iberian Peninsula."

It was nine-thirty when Brandon broke off the search and turned the *Manta Ray* toward the OPAREA. He waited until Fitzgerald was relieved as the officer of the deck before he signed the night orders and departed through the aft water-tight door, heading toward his small stateroom. He had put it off long enough. Time to open the large envelope. He might be lucky and it might be for someone else in the crew, but he knew it was for him. He recalled the last time.

"IT is an American submarine," Lieutenant Iltchenko said.

"Are you sure?" Bagirli asked, sipping his tea. "After all, you did think the merchant ship we sank was the *Volga*."

Iltchenko blushed.

Bagirli motioned to the sailor across the wardroom and pointed at his cup.

"Sir, it is definitely an American submarine. We had it for nearly a minute before we lost it."

"And it was bearing two-zero-zero, you tell me?"

"Yes, sir."

"Then it is behind us, but not in our baffles. For that we should be thankful." He reached over and lifted the handset from the internal communications device above the bench on which he sat. He pressed the button for the control room and asked for the officer of the deck.

When the OOD came on the line, Bagirli said, "Make your speed ten knots, Lieutenant, and I want you to clear the baffles every thirty minutes through the night." Clearing the baffles meant the submarine would maneuver right and left to make sure no adversary was attempting to use the one blind spot for a submarine to sneak up on them.

Bagirli sipped his tea, staying near the handset in the wardroom until it rang. He did not ask Iltchenko to sit down. The report was that no contacts were directly behind them, where the noise of the K-321 screws would mask their presence. He knew it. There was no submarine out there.

Bagirli hung up. "That should also give you and your team ample opportunity to regain contact on the American."

"Thank you, sir."

"If it is an American."

Iltchenko straightened. "Sir, it was definitely American."

"We will see, Lieutenant." He looked at the clock on the

forward bulkhead. "It is late. I am going to turn in before midnight. If you have further contact, then commence a target motion analysis on it so we can determine its course and speed."

"Yes, sir."

"Otherwise, I do not want to be woken until morning. You are dismissed, Lieutenant. Return to your sonar and make sure your sailors are awake." He watched with disgust as the man responsible for his disgrace parted the curtains and left.

"Incompetent," Bagirli muttered.

The sailor picked up the pot of tea and started toward him. Bagirli waved him away. "No," he said sharply.

SIX

October 7, 1973—Sunday

IT had been twenty-four hours since the surprise attack by Egyptian and Syrian armies drove the Israelis back from their defensive lines captured during the 1967 war. Syria had breached the Bar-Lev Line designed to hold back such an attack and had captured most of the southern portion of the Golan Heights. Israel was mobilizing as rapidly as possible, depending on its Air Force and small Army units facing the Egyptians and Syrians to slow the offensive until the bulk of the Israeli citizen Army could arrive. If the Golan Heights fell, Tel Aviv and all of northern Israel could follow.

Soviet Navy units in Syria and Egypt had sortied from their ports on October 5. America and its allies now interpreted this move as an indication that the Soviet Navy was going to protect their Middle East allies in this adventure.

At the Kremlin, lights burned through the night, working to stop the ill-advised Arab attack against Israel, but make it appear as a victory; for them and for their Arab allies. Soviet Premier Brezhnev had ordered the fleet out of Egypt and Syria to show their noninvolvement in this military action. This movement was misinterpreted by the West as the Soviet

Union being aware of the attacks and their Navy deploying to protect the seaward flank of their Arab allies.

President Nixon ordered the Sixth Fleet to sea.

The United States Sixth Fleet had been enjoying liberty in various ports throughout the Mediterranean when the Yom Kippur War started. The crew of the USS *Independence*, in port Naples, was ordered back aboard, and within hours of this second day of liberty, the mighty aircraft carrier was out to sea and heading east toward the war zone.

The Arab victories sent a chill through the Kremlin. If the Arab armies continued their successful offensive, Brezhnev was concerned that America might have little choice but to intervene militarily.

Nixon was advised that with the Arab victories so far, there was little reason for the Soviets to do anything other than gloat. But both Cold War leaders saw the two-day-old war as a catastrophic event pulling the two superpowers toward a confrontation that could engulf the entire world.

Nixon was angry, stomping about the Oval Office and demanding to know why intelligence did not foresee this attack. Why the emergent departure of the Soviet fleet from pierside Egypt and Syria was not seen as an indication of imminent war? He opined that the surprise attack was a Soviet move to control the Middle East and destroy the slow growth of American influence in the Arab world. Neither leader would allow his nation to be perceived as backing off from any superpower confrontation that may occur. Nixon pounded his desk and ordered the Chairman of the Joint Chiefs of Staff to provide him with a range of options.

As nervous as the string of victories was making the Kremlin, Brezhnev believed the Soviet Union had backed away from too many American face-offs since World War II. The Cuban Missile Crisis eleven years ago was foremost in his mind. He vowed not to allow it to happen again.

Brezhnev called Admiral Gorshkov, the head of the Soviet Navy, to his office and gave him his orders. The Soviet Union would not provoke a confrontation, but neither would they run from it. This time, this place, this "against his best advice" adventure by the Arabs had catapulted the Soviet Union into a position where serendipitously they had the stronger hand. They would not—"by Lenin"—back down. In the back of the premier's mind was the worry that the Arab successes would endanger the survival of Israel. He knew what would happen if that occurred. He was concerned that events might dictate his options.

It was strong talk inside the Kremlin for a politician who had led in the principle of détente with Nixon, but it was welcomed fodder for Gorshkov, the father of the Soviet Navy. A father who wanted to see how well his son played in the big sandbox of Navy might.

Nixon was more pragmatic, but he knew there was a line in that proverbial sandbox where America would not stand idly by and see a threat to the survival of Israel; even if it meant American troops on the ground fighting alongside the Israeli Army. It was a prospect he did not like or desire.

Israel would not lose, even if the intervention of American forces was required. By this second day of the war, the elite United States Army forces of the 82nd Airborne and the 101st Airborne were beginning to gear for immediate deployment. Even if Nixon was against the move, he had the mightiest military force in the world beginning to gear up for intervention. At this time, he told his staff and the Chairman of the Joint Chiefs of Staff that he did not intend to intervene in the war. What he didn't tell them was that events might give him few options.

By this second day, Israel had appealed to America. Its war supplies were being depleted quicker than what had been expected in their war plans. Israel could turn the tide, but they had insufficient war-fighting resources to do more than hold ground.

Israel neglected to point out they had never envisioned the Arabs ever winning against the superior training and competence of the Israeli Army. Overconfidence has lost more wars than any other intrinsic quality.

An immediate resupply effort was required. Nixon pushed back. If he started a resupply effort this early, the Soviet Union would have to do something—just what he wasn't sure. Kissinger and the brilliant staff he had surrounded himself with, proposed several scenarios.

The genesis for Operation Nickel Grass was laid. The United States Air Force started revving its engines, deploying its transports, and preparing for a modern-day Berlin Airlift operation, only this time it was for Israel. Nixon would not allow Israel to evaporate from existence, but he knew politically it was not the time for America to start such a large-scale resupply effort. American Naval forces were starting to appear in the Eastern Mediterranean.

Soviet Navy units were moving into surveillance position awaiting the arrival of the USS *Independence* battle group. Eyes in Naples told them the *Independence* was coming long before the aircraft carrier shifted colors and sailed.

Gorshkov told the commander of the Soviet Fifth Eskandra, Admiral Volobuyev, not to engage in risky behavior that might cause an incident. The orders were restricted to the Navy in the eastern Mediterranean. Meanwhile Admiral Yegorov, commander of the Northern Fleet, moved his wolf pack of Project 670 submarines into positions across the Atlantic so he could react if he was told to slow any American attempt to reenforce the United States Sixth Fleet.

THE Soviet Navy captain first rank finished his briefing on the current status of the war, showing where the Egyptian Third Army had crossed the Sinai and dug in.

"Why have they dug in? Why aren't they moving forward?" Admiral Georgye, one of the youngest three-star admirals in the Soviet Navy, asked.

"I do not know, sir," the briefer responded, his eyes cutting to the Chief Intelligence Directorate officer sitting in one of the observer seats arranged along the wall. The GRU officer quickly looked elsewhere.

"I will answer that," Gorshkov said from the head of the table. "It is because our Army has taught them Soviet tactics, when for this adventure the German blitzkrieg model would have achieved them greater success. The Egyptian and Syrian Armies would be knocking at Israel's 1947 borders if they had pushed forward instead of burrowing in like some mole afraid it is going to be discovered."

No one said anything. Gorschkov had the prestige, power, and known loyalty to the Soviet Union to state such a thing, but others around the table did not.

Gorshkov turned to the briefer. "Captain, good brief." His eyes turned to the GRU captain against the wall. "This afternoon, please tell your bosses that I want to know what the American Navy is doing and I want to know what NATO is planning."

Both captains snapped to attention and were soon out of the room, followed by several other lower-ranking officers.

When the room was cleared except for the Soviet admirals, Gorshkov continued, "As the captain briefed, even with the Egyptians dug in rather than pushing forward, the Israelis are retreating."

"That is good news," Admiral Georgye said, picking up a pencil and twisting it up and down in his hand, alternately tapping the point then the eraser on the table.

Gorshkov nodded. How had this man ever made admiral? he asked himself. He knew he had to have approved it, which meant since he did not know the man personally, someone in the Kremlin was his patron. He would know by this afternoon. "It is good news, but good news in war changes by the minute." He pulled the pad of paper to him and scribbled something on it, motioned his aide to him, and gave the slip to him. A moment later the man was out the door. "Plus, as good Navy officers, we know that politics are the ultimate determiner for what we do. I want to ensure that our Navy is ready for anything." He paused. "Including an actual armed confrontation with the Americans."

A chorus of agreement greeted his words.

"Let's go around the table. I want to hear from you what you are doing, what other orders you may have received, and the status of your forces in support of our 'Arab allies.'" Arabs were no one's allies. The next time he and Admiral Zumwalt talked, he wondered if he could offer a trade of allies? They would take the Israelis and the Americans could have the arrogant Egyptians and fawning Syrians.

For the next forty-five minutes, Gorshkov listened as fellow Soviet admirals briefed him on their war-fighting status, what they had been ordered to do—by him or others—and the status of achieving those orders.

The Soviets had no aircraft carriers, but history had shown Gorshkov that submarines could offset the power of aircraft carriers in the early stages of war, when forces were at sea. But for strategic advantage and control of the seas, aircraft carriers were the other matching bookend.

His submarines offset what he knew would be an ever-growing presence of the American Navy in the Eastern Mediterranean. He was sixty-three years old and had been the head of the Soviet Navy since 1956. No other fleet in the world had had a single person leading it as he had, and during this time he had taken the Soviet Navy to where it was today: a major power on the seas. He viewed the Cuban Missile Crisis of 1962 as a tactical setback early in his leadership. He had turned it into a strategic victory for the Soviet Navy.

Cuba still nearly cost him his job, but Gorshkov pointed out that diesel submarines caused them to turn away from the at-sea confrontation. If the Soviet Union was going to be a world-class power, then it needed warships capable of operating independently, away from Soviet shores. In 1956, when he took charge, the Americans had one nuclear submarine and they had none. He glanced at Zegouniov sitting near the end of the table to his right—Brezhnev's ear. But the Bear also owed allegiance to Gorshkov, for without Gorshkov, Anton would never have had the glory of being the first Soviet captain of a nuclear submarine.

As he sat at the table, the drone of the voices fading into the background of his thoughts, he reminded himself that the Soviet Union had nearly twenty-five percent more submarines than Germany did during the Great Patriotic War. He needed aircraft carriers, but because of the Cuban Missile Crisis of 1962 he had a fleet of nuclear submarines and his Navy knew how to use them. He had been unsuccessful in convincing the Kremlin to build an aircraft carrier. Maybe the first Soviet Navy aircraft carrier would fall to his successor.

He glanced around this table. These were the players given him to win this tournament. This Middle East adventure of their allies would be his legacy. It was time to show the Americans that there was a new kid on the block.

Gorshkov looked at the clock on the wall and raised his hand. "Enough."

Immediately, the discussion stopped and everyone turned toward the head of the table.

He pointed at the flag officers. "Your orders—" Then he patted his chest. "My orders are to make sure the Americans do not intervene in this war."

"But, sir, we warned the Egyptians of the consequence—"

"And you were stationed there, Alex. Did they listen to you as the senior admiral of our forces, Admiral Sergeyev? Did they have any respect for our support?"

"My apologies, Admiral. I am—"

Gorshkov smiled. "Don't be." He patted the top of his receding hairline. "I have this from trying to walk the same paths you did with our Arab allies." A quiet smattering of laughter came from the table.

He sighed. "The issue, my fellow admirals, has little to do with our allies and all to do with the Soviet Union. This is not 1962. This is not Cuba. This is the Mediterranean, an adjunct to the Black Sea. And it is the Eastern Mediterranean, where we have a historic right of presence from as far back as the Russo-Turk war in 1787. The Mediterranean is as much a part of our Naval history as the Black and Baltic seas." He clasped his hands together and rested his chin on them for a moment.

"Here is what we have." He grunted. "Some lessons from the Americans. When you go to war, you go less prepared than you want to be. If Armies and Navies waited until they were fully prepared to go to war, there would be no wars, for like engineers who have never met a project they could not improve, we never reach full preparedness. There is always something else you want in your war chest."

He chuckled, which was unusual for Gorshkov, and he immediately turned it into a cough.

"We have over eighty ships in the Mediterranean, most in

the eastern part where we need them. The Americans have less than ten, with one of them anchored off the eastern end of Crete watching our anchorage there. Of our eighty warships, forty-seven of them—a mix of surface and submarines—are capable of launching surface-to-surface missiles. Right now, we are the superior force in the Mediterranean."

Several smiled. Georgye drummed his pencil on the table. He was going to have to go—Gorshkov made a mental note. *It is a wonder someone has not taken that pencil and shoved it . . .*

"Do you think we will have an incident with the Americans, Admiral Gorshkov?" Admiral Zegouniov asked.

"We do not want a confrontation with the Americans, but we must prepare for one." He listened to the acknowledgments, aware that a few of them around the table had been on the same short list as him for accusations during the fallout from the Cuban Missile Crisis.

"Two days ago, when the war began, I, like all of you, believed the Israelis would quickly rout our friends and we would be called upon to help extract their Arab butts from this fiasco. The status quo would return and life would go on as normal. Right?"

They agreed, for no one disagreed with Gorshkov.

"It didn't happen. Instead, our 'allies' have Israel's back to the wall. The Main Intelligence Directorate tells me that the little Israeli madam, Golda Meir, is already appealing to America for more supplies." He paused. He enjoyed weighing the body language of his audience, especially his subordinates. It dawned on him that someone at this table could be his replacement someday. He knew it would not be the pencil drummer.

He had not been the commander of the Soviet Navy for this number of years by failing to be political astute.

"Two days ago I instructed Admiral Yegorov, commander of the Northern Fleet, to take actions to give us the options of restricting American access to the Mediterranean. Admiral Chernavin has assumed command of this strategic and tactical execution." He paused again, to let the message sink into their minds. He wanted them supportive and confident that the Soviet Navy was ready to take its place at the table of maritime dominance.

"He had five Project 670 submarines conducting group training in the Arctic. Chernavin has ordered them to the Atlantic." Gorshkov turned to an aide and nodded. "The screen," he said.

The aide pulled down a projection screen at the end of the table as Gorshkov stood.

"While we prepare for possibly confronting the American Navy in the Eastern Mediterranean, we cannot discount the fact that the Americans will sortie additional aircraft carrier battle groups to the Mediterranean. If I was Zumwalt, I would be preparing my amphibious ships to bring United States Marines to the fight."

Gorshkov frowned.

"At this time, they have yet to start preparing for such a move, but when they eventually decide to execute it, they will move with their usual haste. We can expect the first aircraft carriers and their escorts to deploy within the next forty-eight to seventy-two hours. I would be disappointed if the Americans failed to do so."

The slide projector showed a map of the Atlantic on the screen. Five red lines projected out from near Iceland.

"The red lines are our forces. The black line, running from Norfolk, Charleston, and Jacksonville to converge here about one-third of the way across the Atlantic—that is the projected path of the American battle groups that will come to the Mediterranean."

Gorshkov paused to give the audience a moment to take in the chart of the Atlantic. To the left was the American East Coast. To the right on the chart were the Iberian Peninsula, the far western coast of Europe, and the Strait of Gibraltar, where the black line ended.

"American battle groups seldom travel alone if they can combine their forces. It gives them greater kill power. Look at the red arrows," he said, motioning toward the screen.

Two arrows ended near the United States East Coast, with one ending directly opposite Norfolk and the second one midway between Charleston, South Carolina, and Jacksonville,

Florida. A third ended one-third of the way between the Strait of Gibraltar and the eastern United States coast, and a fourth complemented it along the projected path of the American Navy buildup. A fifth arrow ended at the choke point of the Mediterranean: the Strait of Gibraltar.

"Sir, if I may, I understand we have already had an incident with the Americans?"

Gorshkov turned, his eyes wide. It was the drummer. "Are you talking about the sinking of the merchant?"

"Yes, sir."

"It was unfortunate, but one of our submarine commanders allowed himself and a sister submarine to be spotted on the surface." He crossed his arms. "Gentlemen, this is an important— No! It's more than important. This is a critical moment for the Soviet Navy. Either we are a world-class superpower or we will always be living in the shadow of America."

A chorus of agreement echoed from those around the table.

"These five Project 670 submarines will tell us when the Americans are coming, what firepower they are bringing with them, and they will provide us with the capability of ensuring the Americans do not arrive in the Mediterranean, if we decide it is to our tactical and strategic advantage to take them out." His voice rose as he accented each of the last few words.

Silence greeted his statement.

He grunted and pressed the button on the table in front of him. The door opened and an aide entered. "Bring me some more tea." The man scurried out the door.

"Listen to me and understand this," he said when the door closed. "We are not going to have another Cuba! Do you understand?"

A chorus of "yes, sirs" filled the air.

"Do we all support this?" he asked, his voice demanding.

A second chorus of "yes, sirs" filled the air, but his gaze fell on Admiral Georgye, the pencil drummer, who met his eye contact.

"Good. I am briefing you on the Atlantic provisions. Supporting our submarines will be round-the-clock, twenty-four-hour reconnaissance flights by the Air Force Tupelov-95s."

"Sir, if we decide to take on the Americans . . . " Georgye started. The man had stopped drumming his pencil and was now flipping it between two fingers like a baton.

"There is not a decision to be made, Admiral. The decision has already been made," Gorshkov said irritably. He uncrossed his arms. "You do support this decision, don't you?"

Gorshkov was gratified to see the man's face turn white.

"Of course, Comrade Admiral. I am very supportive. I only want to ensure that everything we do results in success."

"Then I suggest you start by agreeing with our decision."

"Sir, I am in full agreement."

"Good," Gorshkov said curtly. The door opened and the aide brought tea over to the admiral of the fleet. He motioned to the aide. "Go take that damn pencil from Admiral Georgye before I break it myself."

Georgye dropped the pencil, letting it roll across the table. Zegouniov picked it up, winked at the unfortunate man, and handed the pencil to the aide.

SEVEN

"GOOD morning, Lieutenant Strickland. Do we still have contact?" Brandon asked, ducking as he stepped into the control room.

"Sporadic, sir. But Sonar still holds the contact on a steady course."

"Which is?" he asked with a yawn.

"Two-one-zero degrees. Slight left bearing drift."

"How old is that information?"

Strickland glanced at the clock. "About twenty-five minutes, sir."

Brandon nodded as he moved toward the chart spread out on the nearby plotting table. "Get an update, if you would."

The two sailors standing at the plotting table stepped aside to give the skipper room.

Brandon ran his finger down the line of bearings. "Looks to me as if Mad Ivan might be making a slow turn south."

"It has been a slow one-degree-by-one-degree left-bearing creep, sir."

"Creep?"

"Drift, sir."

Brandon smiled and shook his head. "I think 'creep' is an apt expression. He's probably past the Irish landmass and turning down the western side of it." He glanced back at Strickland. "What's your status?"

Stickland straightened and turned toward the bank of controls along the starboard bulkhead. "We are still on course two-zero-zero degrees, sir, at two hundred fifty feet, speed ten knots."

"When was the last time we cleared our baffles?" He looked at the clock. It was zero seven ten Greenwich Mean Time, which considering where they were—north of Ireland—was also the local time.

"Thirty minutes ago, sir, per your standing orders."

His standing orders called for a sharp port or starboard turn at least once an hour at random intervals to check their aft quadrant. He did not want Mad Ivan "creeping" up his ass. Of course, having contact on one Mad Ivan bearing two-two-zero did not mean it was the only Soviet submarine out here looking for a quick hero status back home by bagging an American submarine.

Brandon took another sip of the fresh coffee. "Any messages?" he asked as he turned from the plotting table and walked across the control room, glancing at the gauges and trying to be nonchalant about it. He was following Rickover's leadership principles: Know your job; know your subordinate's job; check work; be consistent; and, don't be afraid of taking *fucking* risks. Of course, the "f" word was Brandon's contribution to leadership.

Strickland lifted the clipboard off the hook and handed it to Brandon, who climbed up and sat down in his chair. For the next fifteen minutes he read the messages, scribbling instructions on the top of certain ones, writing questions on others, and asking certain officers to get back to him after they read the message. Most were routine messages that had arrived earlier in the watch, when he had authorized a periscope depth maneuver to give Radio an opportunity to receive them.

The messages were divided into three categories on the board. On top were the messages directly addressed to the *Manta Ray*. There he found a message from Commander U.S. Second Fleet ordering him to chop the *Manta Ray* to U.S. Sixth Fleet once he reached the vicinity of the Strait of Gibraltar. Routine message, but because the Navy split the area of responsibility between the Second Fleet and the Sixth Fleet at the entrance to the Strait of Gibraltar, Second Fleet wanted to ensure Brandon knew that if he was on the west side of the strait, he was going to be working for Sixth Fleet.

Another had to do with his supply officer failing to sign for some supplies loaded in Keflavik, and another was a follow-up message from the irate four-striper at Holy Loch about Chief Norman wanting to know the disposition of his case. The Navy captain also wanted his three hundred dollars in damages to the club sent immediately or he was going to turn it over to Legal.

He smiled. Reading between the lines, he could see that if Norman paid the three hundred dollars, then the captain would drop the issue and go on with normal base life. If the *Manta Ray* failed to come up with the money, then the four-striper was going to forget the money and come after the chief and the boat. Alongside the body of the message, he wrote "Let's talk" in a note to the XO.

"Looks to me, Chief Norman, as if you're about to be out three hundred dollars," Brandon muttered to himself.

The second category contained what he called informational messages—messages that were sent to everyone in the Navy or that informed the *Manta Ray* of certain logistical, personnel, or administrative changes. Those messages he usually scan-read to see if there was anything requiring an immediate reply or implementation. Sometimes action messages got mixed up with them.

The third category was the one he was most interested in. It held the intelligence reports and the news reports from Navy Public Affairs. He reached the Naval Intelligence messages on the war in the Middle East and nodded when he'd finished. He knew it wouldn't take the Israelis long to regain their footing and push back.

The forward watertight door opened, and Tony Grant, the

sonar officer, entered. He saw Brandon and made a beeline for him. "Sir, we have a problem."

Brandon closed the message board, figuring to come back to it later and finish the intelligence news section.

"We have lost the contact."

"How long ago?"

"About forty-five minutes now, sir."

"It was twenty-five minutes earlier," Brandon said, his head still in the message board. Brandon glanced up at Strickland. "Mr. Strickland, you told me we still had contact."

"Not his fault, sir. It's mine," Grant said. "We thought we had regained contact twenty-five minutes ago, but after analyzing it, we decided it must be a bounce back from the original contact or a different one. Then it disappeared."

Brandon held up a hand. "Wait a minute. Did you say you had another contact? Another submarine out there? Another Mad Ivan runnning around . . . What was the bearing to it?"

Grant glanced at Strickland, then back to Brandon. "It was two-eight-zero. But it did not stay up long enough for us to qualify it as a possible submarine. It could have been environmentals."

"Could the Soviets have detected us and maneuvered north of our position?"

"We thought of that, Captain, but the signature data was different from the one southwest of us."

"So we do have two contacts out there?"

Grant grimaced. "I think we do, sir, but we failed to hold the second contact long enough to determine if it was truly a possible submarine."

"Possible-probable-definite—the problem is we have two contacts. Contacts that are most likely submarines." He bit his lower lip. "The Soviets think this part of the Atlantic belongs to them just because it's closer to their homeland than ours." He laughed. "Go figure. The problem, Mr. Grant, is that there is a chance we have two submarines out there. And if they bear along the lines you indicate, then they have bracketed the *Manta Ray*." He turned to Strickland. "Ask the XO and the OPSO to join me in the control room."

* * *

DEMIRCHAN stuck his head into Bagirli's stateroom. The skipper lifted his arm from across his eyes. "What is it, XO?"

"We've lost the American submarine."

Bagirli reached over and sat up. He flipped on the desk lamp and then bent over, putting on his shoes. "When did we lose it and what was the bearing when lost?"

"We lost it about thirty minutes ago—"

"Why wasn't I informed then?" he asked as he tied his shoes.

"The passive signal had been coming and going. We'd have it for long periods of time—"

"What is a long period of time?"

"A few minutes to several minutes, then it would fade away for a few minutes before returning."

Bagirli stood up. He nodded toward Demirchan, who blocked the doorway. "Sounds like a convergence zone."

Demirchan stepped back into the passageway as Bagirli walked past, heading forward toward the control room. Demirchan fell in behind the captain.

"When did Sonar decide they were not going to regain the contact?"

"They called me after ten minutes. I cleared our baffles to make sure the signal was not lost in the cavitations of our propellers." When Bagirli failed to respond, Demirchan continued. "By the time I finished the maneuvers, it had been over twenty-five minutes. It was then I came to notify you."

Bagirli stopped, nearly causing Demirchan to run into him. Turning, he faced his XO. "Wish you had come sooner," he said gruffly, knowing even as he said it that Sonar would not have been any more successful whether he was in the control room or not.

He turned and opened the watertight door to the control room, entering quickly. "Status!"

Behind him, Demirchan spun the wheel sealing the watertight door.

"Sir," Lieutenant Commander Lepechin answered. "We are at two hundred meters depth. My course is two-four-zero at ten knots, sir."

"What is the layer depth?" Bagirli asked the navigator as he walked along the bank of gauges, reading the information off each.

"Two layers, Comrade Captain," Lieutenant Victor Zaharovich, the number two navigator, answered from his plotting table near the forward bulkhead. "One layer is at the three-hundred-meter depth—one hundred meters below us—and the second layer is around the one-hundred-twenty or twenty-five-meter depth—above us."

Bagirli turned to his operations officer, his feet spread, and hands clasped behind his back. With a deliberately calm voice, he asked, "What time did you lose the contact?"

"Zero six forty-five, sir."

He looked at the clock on the aft bulkhead. It showed seven-thirty. "I understood it was thirty minutes, earlier, Commander. It's nearer forty-five than thirty."

"Yes, Comrade Captain," Lepechin replied.

"What was our depth when we lost it?"

Lepechin exchanged looks with Chief Ship Starshina Zimyatov, who looked away. Lepechin walked briskly over to the starshina responsible for recording the orders within the control room. His finger went down the entries quickly before he jabbed his finger at a specific spot. "Sir, we were in the process of returning to base course after checking our baffles. We were descending in the maneuver from one hundred fifty meters to two hundred meters depth."

"Make your depth one hundred twenty meters," Bagirli ordered.

Lepechin turned to the helmsman and the planesman. "Three-degree bubble; making my depth one hundred twenty meters, sir!"

Bagirli was surrounded by youth and inexperience. He had a great desire to say incompetence, but that would have been a reflection on him. Incompetence was something a good skipper rid the boat of either through good training and counseling, or by firing the officer who was untrainable. An untrainable officer was guilty of crimes against the state because obviously he was deliberately not applying his full attention to the personal improvement program devised by the *zampolit*.

The boat tilted slightly as the K-321 started its ascent. Later Bagirli would want the XO to explain why they had gone so deep, but first he needed to check his standing night orders to ensure there could have been no misunderstanding.

BRANDON looked at the clock. It was seven-thirty. The division officers would be holding their quarters in thirty minutes to commence daily work. Thirty minutes after quarters were held, he would do his morning walk-through of the boat. He'd ask the chief of the boat, Master Chief Hugh Tay, to accompany him, a moment for the COB to give him a dump on crew morale, concerns, et cetera. It was also the time for him to find out any problems on the home front.

When he thought of the home front, he thought of the letter from Louise and the other letter from her lawyer. It was good that the Service Members Civil Relief Act protected him until he returned. He knew of officers and sailors who had returned from six-month deployments to discover an empty house staring back at them. Most times military neighbors within the close-knit Navy community would be the ones to spill the story of a wife unable to cope on her own with the kids, unable to relate to the other wives, and then the neighboring wives would tell how one day while standing in the playground across the street they watched moving vans arrive to ship her and the kids back to their hometown.

Hometowns were the bane and the satisfaction of Navy families. Bane when the wife decided parents and old friends were more important than being loved by a guy who was never home. Satisfaction when you knew there was one special place that no matter how long you were away, always welcomed you back. Families were those people who had little choice but to take you back.

Not him though. No brothers, no sisters, both parents dead. The Navy was his home and his family. Brandon never understood the attraction of the single place others called home. Home was the boat.

"Sir, Sonar still reports no joy on regaining contact."

"Status?" he asked, already knowing the answer.

"My course is two-two-zero, ten knots, at two-five-zero feet, sir," Strickland answered.

"Let's take her up one hundred feet, slowly." He raised his hand when he saw Strickland open his mouth to execute the orders. "Before you do, tell Lieutenant Grant what we are doing. Tell him we are going to do it at one-degree bubble. It's going to be a long, slow process, but he is to tell you immediately if he should get any signs of contact. Got that?"

"Yes, sir."

"Good. The moment he reports contact, trim the boat at that depth. Got it?"

"Yes, sir."

"Good. Make your course two-four-zero, the course we last had the Charlie on. Maintain ten knots."

"What are you doing?" Elliot asked.

"We could be below or above the layer where the Charlie might be hiding. I don't want to go any lower, so let's go up and see if the change in depth improves Sonar's hearing."

Brandon stood and walked toward the forward watertight door as behind him he heard the familiar orders relayed in proper sequence to maneuver the boat upward and onto a different course. At the plotting table he leaned down to the quartermaster. "Check our location and make sure we don't intrude into Irish waters or start heading toward shallow waters."

The first-class petty officer nodded and replied, "We're far enough on track, sir, that at this distance and speed the closest we'll come to Ireland's territorial waters is about fifty nautical miles."

"Good. Let's keep it that way." Fifty was still too close for his comfort.

Everything had to be done perfectly on a nuclear submarine. While everyone thought this applied to engineering, the fact was it applied everywhere.

He opened the door and turned down the passageway toward the sonar spaces a few feet away. He wanted to see the sonarmen at work and watch the passive rainfall ride down the green screen. Not that his eyesight was better than theirs, but having the skipper looking over their shoulders made sure everyone understood how important the "old man" thought what they were doing was. Management through walking worked.

He felt the slight forward rise of the boat as the *Manta Ray* started her ascent. When he opened the door to Sonar, Grant was hanging up the handset on the internal communications set.

"You heard?"

"Captain!" Grant said, startled. "Yes, sir, Lieutenant Strickland relayed your orders to me." Without waiting for Brandon to reply, Grant relayed the news to the sonar technicians.

Brandon stepped inside the small compartment and slid along the interior bulkhead until he stood behind the technician who was watching the sonar console for signs of a passive signal. The green screen had a constant wave of electronic lines running slowly down it, hence the term "rainfall." This was the passive rainfall of noise in the ocean, as picked up by the hydrophones along the bow of the *Manta Ray*. When an extra noise was picked up, the lines would split or change color or come together in such a fashion that the person watching would get a visual display of the sound emanating through the ocean.

"How you doing, Petty Officer Bullet?" Brandon quietly asked the sonar technician manning the console. He patted the sailor lightly on the shoulder. *Wonder if your wife will be waiting for you when you return.*

"Pretty good, Skipper."

"Got anything?"

"Did have, sir; but as you probably know, it disappeared."

Grant moved closer to Brandon.

The door opened, momentarily blocking the two officers. The voice of the Sonar Division chief, Chief Bob Davis, filled the compartment. "All right, you assholes, the captain is out somewhere doing his walk-through. At least look busy," he said, his voice trailing off when he saw Brandon. "Sorry, Captain. Didn't see you there."

"More management by standing right now, Chief."

"Sorry, sir . . . "

Brandon smiled. "Quite all right, Chief. Been there, done that. Your men were hard at work when I walked in a few seconds ago."

Davis handed a cup of coffee to Grant. "Sorry, sir. I came through—"

"Chief, there is a saying in the Navy: when you find yourself in a hole—quit digging." Brandon grinned as he said it.

Brandon glanced at the Fathometer above the consoles. It showed the *Manta Ray* inching above the two-hundred-foot mark. He glanced at the screen, but the steady unbroken rainfall trail continued to flow down the screen. Bullet slipped on his headset, pressing one side against his ear as he twirled the hydrophone settings, changing them slightly in the hopes of improving reception.

"What's the layer?" Brandon asked.

"We have a layer beneath us, sir—about a hundred feet—but nothing above us in this cold water," Chief Davis replied.

Brandon stood and watched for a couple more minutes before excusing himself and heading farther down the passageway toward the radio shack. Never hurts to surprise the radiomen in the morning. Besides, they always had the better coffee, though he'd never let Chief Emano know.

A few minutes later he was sitting on a stool inside Radio sipping fresh coffee in a ready cup they kept for him. He flipped through copies of the messages he had read earlier.

"Nothing new here, Petty Officer Cornell," Brandon said about halfway through the heavier and thicker board.

"Haven't had another comms period, Skipper. But on the good side, being deep means not having to bother you with a lot of routine message traffic."

Brandon nodded and leaned back against the bulkhead. Somewhere out there—*cross your fingers and hope to die*—and in front of them was a Soviet submarine that was being credited with sinking a German freighter. He wondered if the captain was aware that the *Manta Ray* was hunting for him. He took a deep breath and let it out. He would love to finish out a Navy career with a Soviet submarine painted on the conning tower. He just didn't want to finish it wearing prison gray before the paint dried.

It was nearly eight-thirty when he started back toward the control room. He had listened to the negative reports over the internal communications systems speaker.

BAGIRLI sat at the wardroom table while Lieutenant Iltchenko and Captain Demirchan stood in front of him.

"Do you have anything else to say, Lieutenant?"

"No, Comrade Captain," Iltchenko replied, his voice loud and steady.

"I appreciate your leadership in accepting the responsibility for falsely identifying an enemy merchant vessel as a Soviet warship. But I cannot fathom how such a mistake could have been made by someone who has been trained by the best our Navy has to offer. Because of your professional incompetence, we were forced to sink the ship or endanger the mission of the Project 670 submarines."

"I understand, Comrade Captain!"

"I am going to transfer you out from your job as assistant underwater weapons officer. I am moving you to Engineering, where you will have an opportunity to regain my confidence."

"Aye, Comrade Captain!"

"And if you should regain that confidence, then I will write it so in your record."

"Thank you, Comrade Captain."

"You are dismissed. Turn over your duties to Lieutenant Kiselyov this morning. When finished, report to the XO, and when he is satisfied, you both are to report to me. Do you understand?"

"Yes, Comrade Captain."

"You are dismissed."

Iltchenko did a forty-five-degree turn on his heels and marched out of the wardroom. Demirchan continued to stand. Bagirli motioned the XO to sit down.

"What do you think?" Bagirli asked.

"I believe he understands the error of his ways."

"Get with Volkov and make sure he understands what we have done, why we did it, and the corrective actions we have put into place." It was important to Bagirli that the *zampolit* knew his side, so that the unseen logs and papers submitted through Volkov's channels complemented what he did.

"I will brief Volkov personally, Captain."

The two men sat in silence for a few more minutes, Bagirli sipping his lukewarm tea and Demirchan waiting to see if the skipper had anything else to add. Eventually Demirchan excused himself and disappeared through the doorway.

The sailor who had been ordered away during the event with Iltchenko returned and without being asked refilled Bagirli's cup. He set a small plate, with three sugar cookies on it, in front of the captain. Bagirli nibbled at them as he weighed the responsibilities on his shoulders, of commanding a boat filled with the worst dregs of the Soviet Navy.

Iltchenko was only one of the problems he had on the K-321. Problems the admiral expected him to resolve, but it was hard when he was surrounded by so many incompetents. Destroying the German merchant had not solved his problems. He knew it. He had to do something spectacular. He needed the recognition a Hero of the Soviet Union medal would bring. The officers and crew of the K-321 would fight against him as he tried to regain favor, but then on his last boat, when he was the XO, he'd had many in the wardroom who worked to make him look bad in the eyes of the skipper. He smiled. In the long run, it had been them who had been shipped off the boat.

Lieutenant Commander Nehoda walked into the wardroom. "Captain, you asked to see me?"

Bagirli nodded curtly and spent five minutes informing the weapons officer why he had relieved Iltchenko as his assistant. Bagirli wanted to make sure Nehoda understood that by relieving Iltchenko, he had also noted Nehoda's failure to properly train his officer. Lieutenant Kiselyov, the torpedo officer, was now being moved to replace Iltchenko, and if Sonar had another failure in leadership, Nehoda could expect himself to be looking for another home.

When the shaken weapons officer left after the one-sided conversation, Bagirli was enthused over the reaction. It helped to keep officers and crew on their toes. They needed to know he was watching and capable of taking action when necessary or . . . Or what? The XO? He shook his head. Demirchan was loyal? He wasn't sure, but he knew the officer would do whatever he was told and execute it flawlessly. He would use Demirchan as long as he could to help whip this crew into shape. But he knew from his last experience that the XO wanted his job and would do whatever it took to become the captain.

BRANDON wiped his lips and laid the napkin on the table as he slid out of the booth. Breakfast-lunch-dinner and an ever-ready stable of croissants, breads, and cakes kept the wardroom and the crew's mess a steady traffic area.

"Nice lunch, Chief," he said to the head steward as he left the wardroom. It was a few minutes after one.

A few minutes later he was in the control room. Most of his days and evenings were spent in this compartment. Either with his arms draped over the periscope handles when they were at scope depth, or sitting in his chair listening to the soft patter of checks and balances echoing softly as the officer of the deck kept the boat at final trim.

"Captain on the bridge," the quartermaster announced as he stepped through the aft watertight door.

"Carry on," Brandon replied as he worked his way to his seat. "Status?"

"Sir, my course is two-four-zero; depth is one hundred fifty feet, and speed is ten knots," Lieutenant Junior Grade Schaefer, the *Manta Ray* torpedo officer and on-duty officer of the deck answered.

"Any success?" Brandon asked.

Lieutenant Junior Grade Schaefer shook his head. "No, sir. Still no contact."

It had been over five hours since they had lost contact with the Soviet Charlie-class submarine. He had hoped the slow crawl upward earlier would have allowed the *Manta Ray* to pass through a convergence zone where they might have regained the contact.

"Tell Radio we are preparing to go up to periscope depth. They can plan on doing their communications stuff."

Schaefer acknowledged, and Brandon waited until Radio reported ready. "Bring me the message board with a blank message slip. Ask the XO and the OPSO to join me."

While he waited for Elliot and Fitzgerald, he drafted the message to Submarine Forces Atlantic, notifying them of the lost contact. Moments later, when the two men arrived, he handed them the message. They both read it and agreed with it.

"Very well." Brandon turned to Schaefer. "Make your depth fifty feet."

"Aye, sir; making my depth fifty feet." The young officer turned away from the other three. "Up three-degree bubble. Make my depth fifty feet. Maintain course two-four-zero, speed ten knots."

The *Manta Ray* tilted upward as the submarine started its change of depth. Five minutes later, the periscope was up. Brandon scanned the horizon. A rain squall was passing close by. Radio had the wire out. At least he would have new messages to read later, after Radio had printed and collated them onto the board. Immediate and urgent messages would be brought to him without waiting for posting to the board.

"Scope down," he said, stepping back from the mechanism as it slid into the storage position. Above the surface he kept the electronic warfare antenna out. Sonar was watching for any sounds of surface ships, but the EW system was the only warning he had of—

"Sir, the WLR-1 is showing faint contact of a TU-95. I have its maritime surveillance radar on scope, sir!"

"What variant is it?"

There was a slight pause before the electronic warfare operator answered, "Not sure yet, sir."

"Let me know as soon as you are."

"Aye, Skipper."

The TU-95, NATO code name Bear, was the Soviet's premier reconnaissance aircraft. Capable of flying from the mainland of the Soviet Union, conducting a mission along the eastern or western seaboard of America, and returning.

There was little chance of it spotting the small EW antenna above the surface, but like every submariner, Brandon wanted to take no chances.

"Bearing?"

"Bearing zero-one-zero, sir," the EW operator reported.

"Officer of the Deck, ask Radio if they have finished with their message trafficking."

Less than half a minute elapsed before Schaefer reported. "Still receiving message traffic, sir, and they still have your message to send."

"Tell Radio to send my message now and report!" He looked toward the electronic warfare suite for a moment and then left the periscope area to walk hurriedly toward it.

Brandon glanced at the gauges as he passed them. "Make your speed five knots!"

At ten knots he could be leaving a wake on the surface. All an aircraft had to do was see the wake and follow it to the submarine. The ocean was big though, so the chance of the aircraft spotting—

"I have a rapid-bearing drift!" the EW operator shouted, interrupting his thought. "Right to the left—off our starboard side! Signal strength increasing."

Brandon did a quick turn and ran to the periscope. "Up scope!" He knew when he ordered it that he should be ordering the *Manta Ray* down. But a Soviet Bear shouldn't be able to detect him even at periscope depth—unless it was ASW-equipped.

He rode the scope up, flipping open the handles and pressing his eyes against the eyepiece. When the scope broke the surface, he turned it to the right and swept the horizon from the bow to the stern. Nothing. He saw nothing.

"I have a constant bearing! The radar is searching, sir. Contact bears zero-one-four degrees true."

That would put the aircraft off the *Manta Ray*'s port aft quarter, Brandon translated, envisioning the left rear side of the submarine.

"Short Horn?"

"No, sir. It has switched to fire control radar, Skipper, the Clam Pipe."

"Sweeping or lock-on?"

"Sweeping, sir; no lock-on at this time," Lieutenant Junior Grade Schaefer replied.

The Soviets and Americans had agreed that locking their fire control radar on each other opened the opportunity for a mistake to occur. Fire control radars had a narrow beam, and while sweeping, they were searching. That caused a lot of angst, but only if the operator of the fire control radar focused a constant fire control radar beam on the target it was said to have locked on. To lock on an adversary was considered an act of war.

The compass direction was off the *Manta Ray*'s starboard aft quarter. Brandon turned the periscope, aligning it through the reflected compass inside the lens. Nothing. But he kept it aligned, and just as he was about to take the periscope down, a burst of reflected sunlight drew him.

"Clam Pipe?" he asked aloud, hoping the Soviet aircraft had shifted back to his surveillance radar.

"Still active, sir, and still in search mode!"

There it was. Nose-on toward the *Manta Ray* and flying at a low level. The four double-turbo props blurred, an eerie silent rotation from beneath the ocean, knowing that if you were topside on the bridge, the noise would have been heard long before anyone could have seen the aircraft. The TU-95 had spotted them and was heading directly toward them. And the bomb bay doors were open.

"Down periscope! Make your depth three hundred fifty feet! Flood negative; flood safety!"

"We have the wire out, sir!" Schaefer reminded Brandon.

"Take her down! Use five-degree bubble; flood negative and safety! Tell Radio to wind that wire in ASAP. Maintain current course." What he wanted to do was get some water over him and then change course to avoid the Soviet reconnaissance aircraft, but a quick maneuver could sheer off the long-wire antenna and without the long-wire, the *Manta Ray* would have no long-range communications.

"Five-degree down bubble; making my depth two hundred feet; speed five knots."

"Increase bubble to ten-degree!"

"Increasing my bubble to ten-degree, sir!"

The *Manta Ray* tilted forward precipitously, causing everyone standing to grab hold of something. The boat was heading down and heading fast.

Brandon stood aside as the periscope slid into storage. His right hand held onto the overhead pipe as he leaned aft.

"Make your speed ten knots!" They had been spotted. It could hardly be serendipitous detection. It was the notorious Clam Pipe fire control radar. Clam Pipe was the NATO code name for the TU-95 fire control radar. If the TU-95 was painting *Manta Ray* with its fire control radar and it had opened its bomb bay doors, then Brandon had to assume it was developing a firing solution.

In the era of the Cold War, the potential for hot situations had arisen more times than he wanted to recall.

"Making my speed ten knots, sir!"

"Very well," Brandon acknowledged.

"Passing one hundred feet!" Schaefer announced.

"Ease your bubble to three degrees!"

"Aye, sir, I am easing my bubble to three degrees."

It took a few seconds before the bow of the *Manta Ray* began to creep upward from a ten-degree downward angle to a more reasonable three-degree.

"Radio is whirling in the wire, sir!" Schaefer reported.

"Battle stations submerged, Officer of the Deck," Brandon said. He didn't believe the Soviet TU-95 would attack them, but its ASW variant, the TU-142, had the capability, and there was always the chance they might find a torpedo or two dropped over them. And the only differences between the two Soviet maritime reconnaissance aircraft was their weapons capability.

The beeps of battle stations echoed throughout the *Manta Ray*.

"General quarters! General quarters! All hands man your battle stations; this is not a drill!" came the announcement alongside the beeps to general quarters.

"Ready decoys!" Brandon ordered. Chill bumps raced up his spine. Even in drills the call to battle stations created a similar rush of adrenaline. He knew this was just one more instance of cat and mouse, and so Brandon chalked one up for the Soviets. They had caught an American submarine on the surface. Never mind that he was fifty feet below the surface—the fact was he had been detected. This would give Admiral Clifton a cataclysmic orgasm of delight when he read the SITREP.

"Decoys ready! Christmas Tree green!" Schaefer reported.

Throughout *Manta Ray*, sailors who had been on off time and napping flew out of their racks, scrambling into dungarees and shoes, buttoning shirts as they bumped into one another on their way to their battle stations. Others left what they were doing and ran toward to their battle stations, shutting the watertight doors and hatches behind them.

Once the watertight doors of the *Manta Ray* clanged shut, they would remain shut, for neglect of that on a submarine could send it to the bottom.

The control room aft watertight door opened and Elliot entered, followed quickly by the operations officer. Fitzgerald went to Schaefer and began the turnover of the OOD functions to the operations officer. Schaefer's battle station was the forward torpedo room.

Elliot hurried to Brandon.

"What's going on?"

"We've been spotted."

"EW antenna stored!" the EW operator reported.

"TU-95 Bear. EW picked up a Soviet reconnaissance radar off the long-range maritime reconnaissance aircraft."

"Fire control?"

"It is now. Clam Pipe radar," Brandon said.

"Fire control," Elliot stated matter-of-factly. "If it's spotted us, it could be a TU-142."

"Only one aircraft. EW identified it as a Bear, but was unable to identify the variant, so we don't know if it is the antisubmarine variant or not."

"Did you get a visual on it, sir?"

"I flipped the periscope in the direction he reported. Flash of sunlight and there it was bearing down on us at low altitude."

Elliot glanced at the gauges.

"This is Lieutenant Commander Fitzgerald. I have the conn and the deck! I have three-degree bubble, passing two hundred feet. Making my depth three hundred fifty feet. My course is two-four-zero and my speed is ten knots."

"We ought to change course," Elliot offered.

"Can't. Radio has the wire out. If I change too quickly, we break the wire. If I turn too sharp or go down too fast, we run the risk of wrapping the wire about the shaft. Already took a chance with a ten-degree bubble."

"We can cut the wire."

Brandon nodded. "We can, but then we still lose our long-range communications. Would leave us with only line-of-sight comms. Won't be able to send—"

"Or receive." Elliot bit his lower lip.

"Engineering reports battle stations; forward and aft torpedo rooms report manned and ready," Fitzgerald reported from the Christmas tree, where the row of green lights confirmed the verbal reports.

The forward hatch opened as several sailors dashed into the control room and Schaefer headed out of it.

Brandon sighed. "Of course, without the wire, I would not have to send the SITREP," he said with a weak smile.

"I'll write it," Elliot offered.

"Let me see it before it goes."

"I don't think the Soviets are going to do anything."

"Neither did that German merchant."

Brandon looked at Fitzgerald. "Mr. Fitzgerald, I want a sonar report. Tell me what we have in our area."

"What are you thinking?"

"Don't know, but do know I want to know what the surface looks like. I want to know what type of clutter that Soviet airdale is seeing."

Another minute passed before the *Manta Ray* reported battle stations achieved and all watertight doors secured.

"Passing two hundred eighty-five feet. Maintain planes at three-degree bubble," Fitzgerald ordered from near the helmsman.

"XO, take your position near the firing console," Brandon said. "And give me weapons status."

"Sir, I don't see what we can fire against."

A moment of anger flashed across Brandon over Elliot's push-back, but his voice was calm and low. "We cannot allow the aircraft to distract us from the fact that we have at least two Soviet Charlie-class submarines out here somewhere. We don't know if they are working in conjunction with—"

"Sir. Sonar reports two merchant-type vessels northeast of us; we have multiple small contacts nearer the Irish coast, and several more ahead of us crossing our bow with right bearing drift."

"Very well," Brandon replied. He looked back at his XO. "Anyone of those ahead of us could have a Charlie hiding under it."

Elliot nodded. He had crossed a line he was unaware existed.

"Yes, sir; I will man my position."

Brandon sighed and rubbed his face. "Dev, I need your advice, but I also need your calm demeanor with the only weapons we have. I think we will be out of this shortly, but if it goes the other way, then I want to make sure we are not overeager in any response we make."

"I understand, Skipper," Elliot replied as he eased his way across the control room to the position behind the weapons control panel. The Christmas Tree glowed green, showing everything ready for anything that might be thrown at them.

The interior communications speaker squeaked, causing everyone in the control room to cringe from the sharp sound. A frantic voice came across it. "Control room, this is Sonar. We have splashes ahead and to starboard of us. Multiple splashes. I have multiple splashes!"

"Make your depth five hundred feet," Brandon said sharply. "Increase bubble to ten degrees. Officer of the Deck, left full rudder; set new course one-eight-five, speed ten knots."

"Making my depth five hundred feet, left full rudder; making my course one-eight-five! Increasing bubble to ten degrees," Fitzgerald echoed.

Unbeknownst to Brandon, Radio had managed to rewind some of the long-wire, but as the *Manta Ray* spun downward, making a sharp turn on its way, the hundred feet of wire still protruding whipped close to the churning propellers, missing them by inches. The maneuver caused the long-wire antenna to kink, shredding some of its copper cabling through the insulation and snarling itself at the point where the antenna exited the boat. As Radio continued to pull in the antenna at maximum speed, the copper wiring started to shred further. Kinks appeared along the vital antenna as it entered the boat and the storage reel.

BRANDON moved from the periscope deck to his chair and fought against the angle and tilt of the *Manta Ray* as he pulled himself into it and strapped in. He heard the familiar click of other seat belts following. To his left Elliot held firmly to an overhead pipe. Master Chief Hugh Tay, his feet spread and knees bent, maintained his equilibrium with both hands spread apart along the bulkhead near the gauges of the planesmen.

"Control, this is Sonar. I have no fast rotations. I have no blade rotations," the voice announced, a lot more calmly than the earlier one seconds ago.

"Sonobuoys," Elliot offered.

"Sonobuoys," Fitzgerald seconded.

Brandon acknowledged the analysis. Splashes could mean anything from the worst case of torpedoes being dropped on them, to sonobuoys.

Sonobuoys were small cylindrical sensors about a yard long, dropped to detect submarines. They could be preset to different depths to compensate for underwater layers, and once they reached their depth, flotation devices were released to deploy a short-range antenna above the water. Then the aircraft operators flew around and listened.

"Make your speed five knots," Brandon ordered. If they were sonobuoys, the increased cavitation caused by the propellers would be quickly picked up.

He listened as Fitzgerald repeated the order. He took a deep breath. The new course was completely away from their original course of two-two-zero—more importantly, the new course was away from the sonobuoy field the Soviet Bear was laying.

"Has Sonar plotted the splashes?" Brandon asked. They should, he knew, but it would be a minute or so before the outline of the field would show.

BAGIRLI smiled. The K-321 hovered at sixteen meters. The antenna protruding above the ocean surface was receiving the data information from the ASW reconnaissance aircraft. He was too far away to receive the sonobuoy data directly, but he smiled knowing the tactical advantage between him and the American submarine had changed.

"We have the enemy plotted," Lepechin said.

Bagirli glanced toward the plotting table where his operations officer stood. "And?"

"The American submarine was caught with its pants down, Comrade Captain. It was on the surface. There will be egg on the skipper's face today at the Pentagon."

Bagirli's smile departed. Was Lepechin making an oblique comment about Bagirli's leadership? It had been less than three days since he, too, had been caught on the surface.

He caught a quick glance from Lepechin. If the officer apologized, he would cashier him on the spot. "Very well, Operations Officer. And what is the course and speed of our adversary?"

"Sir, the Tupolev reports the course as two-one-nine—"

"Bullshit!" Bagirli snapped. "No commander goes on a course of two-one-nine! Like us, they round them off to a five or a zero unless they are entering or leaving port." He motioned at Lepechin. "Mark him as going two-two-zero—and his speed?"

"Ten knots, sir," Lepechin replied.

"That makes sense. At least the Air Force knows how to estimate speed. And the pattern?"

"The communicators are relaying the information from the aircraft, sir. The sonobuoys had contact for nearly a minute before they lost it."

"Do we have radio contact with the Tupolev?"

"No, sir; just receive. They are out of range of our bridge communications suite."

"What is our range to the American?"

"One hundred sixty-six . . . one hundred sixty-five kilometers, sir."

"We are ahead of them. How long until they reach our vicinity?"

"At ten knots, it will take the American about sixteen to seventeen hours, sir."

Bagirli nodded. It would take longer because the American was no fool. Bagirli was not a fool, and he did not want a fool for an adversary. The American was maneuvering. His sonar . . . Bagirli grimaced. The American sonar team would be much better than the novices they had assigned to his boat. The American sonar would have detected the splashes. The American skipper would have taken evasive action, thinking they could be torpedoes.

Why was the American at periscope depth during the daylight? Bagirli thought about it a few seconds before he realized the only reason for a submarine to be at that depth during daylight was for communications. If the American submarine was doing its communications, then it, too—like the K-321—would have its long-wire out. This would restrict the man's maneuverability.

Bagirli weighed this thought and then started considering what he would have done in a similar situation. The reconnaissance aircraft data showed that the American had gone deeper, so the American knew the aircraft was there. The American sonar team would have detected the sonobuoys splashing into the waters around them. Then what?

He took a deep breath and envisioned the scene in his adversary's control room. When the man's sonar failed to pick up any high-speed rotation, he would have taken his submarine deeper, slowed the speed to decrease sonobuoy detection, and he would have changed course. To which direction would Bagirli have taken the K-321 in such a situation? He grunted as he thought.

"The aircraft reports it has lost contact, sir."

Bagirli shook his head. "They've only just started monitoring their field. Are they planning to abandon an active sonobuoy field and go home? What is wrong? Did the Air Force run out of hot food or is their toilet full?"

Lepechin shrugged. "I do not know, sir."

Bagirli clinched his lips. He needed the aircraft to stay on station for at least another thirty minutes to an hour. The American had to return to his base course, if, as Bagirli suspected, the American was chasing him. He would wait here for his American adversary. The game of cat and mouse continued. If the American passed near the K-321 and he could find it, track it, and do whatever he had to do, then it would show Admiral Ramishvili that the K-321 was his best boat. It would redeem Bagirli in the eyes of his peers and the Northern Submarine Fleet.

BRANDON sat passively in his chair, occasionally glancing at the gauges as the boat made its way along course one-eight-five. The XO walked up from his left.

"Sir, it's been three hours," Elliot said. "May I recommend securing from battle stations to give the men a chance to hit the heads and grab a bite to eat?"

Brandon looked over Elliot's shoulder at the clock on the bulkhead. It showed a little after noon.

Without replying, Brandon turned back to Fitzgerald, who was watching. "Officer of the Deck, make your course two-two-zero, speed ten knots, and make your depth two hundred feet."

"Aye, sir," Fitzgerald replied. "Making my depth two-hundred feet, returning to base course two-two-zero, and increasing speed to ten knots."

"Very well. Once you've steadied up, Mr. Fitzgerald, secure from battle stations."

He turned to Elliot and in a low voice said, "Dev, I apologize for being sharp with you earlier."

Elliot shook his head. "You were right, sir. My battle station position is at the weapons console. That is where I should have gone first."

Brandon nodded. His thoughts for most of the past two

hours had been on his family situation. Was he going to be one of those sailors who returned home from a six-month deployment to an empty house? Was he going to be one of those sailors whose entire pension went to the wife who ran away with someone else? He grimaced. Louise would never have an affair. If she was leaving him, then it was because of his career. She would never cheat on him, as he had never cheated on her. He ran his hands through the two rows of hair growing alongside the slick spot across the top of his head. Guess he would have more letters—official type—once they reached Rota.

"Officer of the Deck, have Sonar keep searching for that Soviet Charlie-class." He looked at Elliot. "We've lost him for sure now."

"Secure from battle stations; secure from battle stations; all hands, secure from battle stations," came the announcement over the internal communications system.

Brandon unbuckled his belt and stepped down from his chair. "Let me know if we regain contact."

The forward watertight door opened, and Radioman First Class Cornell stepped through it with the gray metal-covered clipboard in his hand. He came directly to Brandon.

"Sir, your message to Commander Second Fleet made it out before we had to cut communications. We were able to copy the broadcast and I have a couple of action messages for you."

Brandon took the board, read the messages, and handed the board to Elliot. "Looks as if our trip to Rota may be delayed."

"SIR," Demirchan said. "It's been three hours since they lost contact."

Bagirli nodded. "I know. Can you believe they monitored their field for less than an hour and then turned tail toward home? A sailor would never do that. We would have laid more fields, used our sonar, even going active if we had to, but we wouldn't throw out a field of sonobuoys, wait a few minutes, and declare we have nothing. Then wave our hands in the air in mock disgust so everyone will believe we did our job as we put full bore to the engines so we can get home in time for dinner and sex."

Demirchan grinned. "Air Force, sir; what do you expect?"

Bagirli sighed. "I know." He leaned back in his chair.

After a couple of minutes Demirchan cleared his throat. "Sir, we can turn to our base course if you want and continue toward our assigned area of operations."

"No, XO, we're going to wait here."

"Wait here?"

Bagirli nodded, but said nothing for a few seconds, drawing on Demirchan's angst. Then he spoke. "The American was following us. Probably assigned to find and sink us, XO. Even if the Air Force went home sooner than we both would have liked, they at least did detect him on the surface. We can assume his base course was two-two-zero."

"Yes, sir."

"Eventually, the American is going to go back to his base course. That base course from where he was detected will take him near us."

Demirchan grinned. "You're going to wait for him."

"That is right. We are going to wait for him to come. But you and I know we can't wait forever, so we will give him twenty-four hours. If he doesn't show, then I am wrong and he was not following us."

"SIR . . . sir." Bagirli heard the voice calling him. He shifted in his seat for a moment and then came awake.

"Yes?" he asked as he blinked his eyes.

"Sonar has picked up the American," Demirchan said.

"Submarine?"

Demirchan nodded and glanced toward Lieutenant Commander Lepechin. "He is northwest of us."

"Northwest?" Bagirli smiled. Sonofabitch. The American must have turned left when he was detected. The left turn had brought the American closer to him when the enemy submarine turned back to base course.

"His drift will take him behind us soon. Recommend we come right to course one-nine-zero."

Bagirli straightened. He was fully awake now. "Status?"

"Sir, my depth is sixteen meters on course one-zero-zero, making way at four knots."

"Quietly, Commander Lepechin, bring up around in a starboard turn to course one-eight-zero. Keep our speed at four knots." He held up his hand as Lepechin turned to start the chain of commands to execute Bagirli's orders. "Wait until I finish."

He leaned forward. "When Sonar loses contact with our enemy, cut all engines and let the momentum take us onto course or until Sonar regains contact." Bagirli looked at Demirchan. "I don't want them to detect us during that time when they are in our baffles and our propellers are pointed at them. The long circle turn at four knots should give us the momentum to take us on course and for Sonar to regain contact." They never would have thought of that, which was why he was the skipper and they never would be. Clever, he told himself.

TWENTY minutes later the K-321 Project 670-class Soviet missile submarine was steady on one-eight-zero at periscope depth with four knots of speed as Sonar continued to report growing signal strength of the American submarine as it approached. Two hours later the bearing drift of the American was right-to-left, and it was rapid, indicating that the enemy was close off the K-321 starboard side.

"We should ease behind it," Demirchan suggested.

"We wait," Bagirli said. He wanted to get in his adversary's baffles so they would hide the noise of the K-321 from the American sonar.

Adrenaline rushed through him over his self-congratulations. He was brilliant, and when he sank this enemy, Moscow and the rest of the Navy would recognize Bagirli for the warrior he was. Two ships sunk in one deployment, and he would be the one to have done it.

No other Soviet submarine skipper had sunk two in one

deployment. Forget about the *Scorpion*—that was a story hidden in so many layers of classifications and security no one would ever know the truth or know that somewhere near the remnants of the found American submarine was a Soviet submarine.

Underwater surveillance was like reading a book. Everything was envisioned and painted on the brain, for nothing was visual. This time it was the K-321 out of sight and the American in danger. He smiled.

Demirchan and Lepechin saw the faraway look in Bagirli's eyes, and the enigmatic smile. They exchanged unsmiling glances before returning to their positions.

An hour later Bagirli maneuvered the K-321 directly behind the American submarine, quietly taking the boat down to one hundred meters. He did not know how much distance separated them, but he figured it had to be at least five nautical miles. It was near midnight when he finally left the control room for bed.

EIGHT

ADMIRAL Zumwalt waited until the door to the tank closed before turning to the other flag officers sitting around the conference table. His bushy eyebrows rose as he let out a deep sigh. "Well, gentlemen, we just heard Rex tell us what Naval Intelligence is seeing on the front."

The door to the tank opened and a well-dressed civilian entered. "My apologies for my tardiness, Admiral, but I was at the White House." Without waiting for an answer or acknowledgment, the civilian walked quickly to the end of the conference table and took the seat that the Director of Naval Intelligence had just vacated.

Zumwalt looked at the three-star Marine general to his left. "General?"

The Marine flag officer pushed his chair back and stood. "Admiral, the commandant sends his regrets; he is down with his Marines at Camp Lejuene. Down there giving the men encouragement and focus for the days to come."

Camp Lejuene, North Carolina, was the main East Coast base where the Marine Corps kept its amphibious forces ready for deployment.

The general reached forward and laid a flimsy on the flat face of the projector that was directly in front of the Chief of Naval Operations. On the front screen a row of dates appeared with numbers alongside them.

"This is our timeline for outfitting the amphibious task force being readied for deployment, Admiral. By the end of the week we will have started our movement to Morehead City, North Carolina, for pickup." He nodded to the flag officer at the end of the table. "We are working closely with Commander Amphibious Group Two, as his ships prepare for shifting colors out of Little Creek and Norfolk, Virginia, en route to Morehead. By the time the ships arrive, our Marine logistic team will have everything arranged."

Amphibious operations required meticulous arrangements for loading and off-loading. Off-loading properly with the right combination of men and material made all the difference in whether an amphibious landing was successful or not.

The general knew this, as did every admiral sitting around the table. Though no one said anything, everyone assumed the Army flag officer sent over by the Army Chief of Staff understood amphibious operations, and as things were unfolding so rapidly in the Middle East, if the Air Force general didn't understand, someone would explain later.

"Looks good, General," Zumwalt said. He looked around the table, then at his watch. "We've been here a long time, gentlemen. I know we have other things to do, and with the afternoon waning, most of us will be here through the night." Zumwalt stood. "Good night, gentlemen." He sighed. "I am sure all of us will be seeing more of each other in the days to come."

Chairs scraped along the carpet as the attendees stood.

At the door of the tank, Zumwalt turned. "George, come see me when you are finished here."

Admiral George Ellison, one of the sixteen four-star admirals in the Navy, acknowledged the request and waited with the others until the Chief of Naval Operations had gone. After the Chief of Naval Operations departed, they began to pick up the notebooks and papers in front of them.

Admiral George Ellison held up his hand and smiled. "I apologize, everyone, but unfortunately, I need to keep you a few more minutes." Ellison was the head of Naval Expeditionary Operations. He shared the job with his deputy, a three-star Marine general—Octavius McNamara—who had little time for anything having to do with a meeting that had the potential of lasting more than thirty minutes. Unless it was a meeting on the battleground.

Everyone sat down.

"General McNamara is with the Commandant at Lejuene and sends his regrets. As you know from what Rex told us and what most of us know from our various staffs, the Israelis have asked President Nixon for additional war supplies. War supplies they say are critical for Israel's survival." Ellison took a sip of water.

"I spent this morning with the CNO, the Commandant, and Admiral Moorer, the Chairman of the Joint Chiefs of Staff. The Chairman spent a large part of yesterday and early this morning at the White House. The Israeli counterattack the press has been reporting, the one yesterday by General Sharon, apparently was unauthorized by the Israelis." He smiled. "The attack is succeeding, but he launched it without prior approval. And his success in pushing the Egyptian Third Army back has also opened up the Israeli flanks. As General McNamara opined, Sharon has made the whole Israeli front f-ing vulnerable."

The Marine general laughed. "Knowing Octavius, I doubt he used the word f-ing without the 'u-c-k' in there somewhere."

Everyone laughed.

"You know him well, General." But then who didn't in the Marine Corps? General McNamara was a Korean and Vietnam veteran with so many combat ribbons and Purple Stars his uniform shirts only lasted a month at most before the weight of the ribbons tore the fabric.

Ellison continued. "The Israelis are hastening to fill in the holes that Sharon's success has opened."

"Good for him," the Army general said.

"Oohrah!" the Marine general agreed.

"Unfortunately for us, gentlemen—and the Israelis—the Soviets are using this Israeli Army offensive as an excuse to start preparation to airlift war supplies to both Egypt and Syria. They informed President Nixon early this morning. We can expect it to hit the press probably tomorrow. Meanwhile, the White House has decided to honor a request by Prime Minister Golda Meir."

Ellison paused and ran his hand across his receding hairline and through his sparse hair before he looked around the table. "Tomorrow, El Al will start flying round-robin efforts to resupply Israeli forces. The staging area will be Dover Air Force Base in Delaware."

"El Al—the Israeli commercial airline?" the Air Force general asked.

Ellison nodded. "Yes, sir, the same. And you would be right if you didn't think they will be able to meet the fighting requirements of the Israeli Army."

"That is right. It's a commercial airliner for the most part, and to do anything approaching commercial airlift they need to be able to load fast, take off rapidly, and unload fast." The Air Force general shook his head. "They're primarily a passenger carrier with the exception of a few aircraft designed for mail and commercial goods. That means that, with the exception of those few aircraft, everything loaded on El Al aircraft will have to come and go through doors designed for passengers."

Everyone agreed.

"The Chairman agrees with your analysis, General. He also does not think El Al is sufficient. The four Joint Chiefs agree with him, including the Air Force Chief of Staff. The Joint Chiefs are in agreement that in the near future— possibly as early as the next two to three days—we are going to be asked to step into the breach. Therefore, the Chairman has ordered preparations to begin for a massive airlift of war-fighting materials, if necessary."

Several flag officers nodded, including the two-star supply officer drumming his pencil at the end of the table. No supplies went anywhere without the proper paperwork, and it was the Navy supply corps who would locate, ship, and track each piece of Navy material sent.

"General," Ellison said, raising his bushy eyebrows and nodding at the Air Force two-star. "You probably have more information on this than I do."

The general stood and cleared his throat. The wings of a fighter pilot shined on his left breast. Two stars shined on each shoulder of his neatly buttoned Air Force dress blue uniform. "Thank you, Admiral. The Chief of Staff of the Air Force has already ordered the dispersal of our key transport aircraft. While El Al will do its damned best, in the final analysis, it is still just a commercial carrier. As we discussed briefly a few seconds ago, there is no way it can deliver the war-fighting supplies that Israel needs, regardless of how many hours they fly or how heroic the pilots and crew may be."

"Here, here," the Army general said.

"Therefore, our C-141 Starlifter and C-5 Galaxy transport aircraft will be ready for a massive resupply of Israel. The name of the operation will be Nickel Grass—the aerial re-supply of Israel."

Ellison was impressed at the dramatic pause by the Air Force major general. He smiled. The Air Force really knew how to do a briefing and capture the attention of the audience. And they knew how to do aerial operations on a global scale, which was much more important even than the future arguments the Air Force would use against the Navy aircraft carriers.

"By tomorrow, the C-141 transports at Travis Air Force Base in California and Dover Air Force Base in Delaware will begin dispersing to the various arsenals scattered throughout America. The C-5 aircraft will follow shortly afterwards."

"Do you have a list of those arsenal locations and the airfields that the Air Force will be using?" Ellison asked.

"Yes, sir."

"Please see that I, along with General McNamara, get a copy of those locations. It will be vital for our operational planning."

"Yes, sir. I understand that the operations plan for Nickel

Grass is being prepared for the Chairman's release. I can check and make sure that you are on distribution for it."

"I would appreciate it, General."

"Nickel Grass. Who comes up with those names?" one of the admirals asked, but no one responded.

The Air Force general continued. "Nickel Grass will overshadow what we did in the Berlin airlift of 1948 to 1949 in terms of flight miles and number of flights. We don't think it is going to last the eleven months the Berlin airlift lasted." He nodded to Ellison and held up a flimsy. "If I may, sir?"

Ellison nodded and motioned to the overhead projector.

A moment later a full-color graphic appeared on the screen, encompassing the world between the East Coast of the United States on the left side of the graphic and the Middle East on the right side. Red lines ran from Charleston, South Carolina; Norfolk, Virginia; and Fort Bragg, North Carolina converging off the East Coast, with arrows pointing west.

The general picked up a pointer and went to the front of the room. "The Air Force Military Airlift Command will be in overall tactical charge of Nickel Grass when the President orders us to implement it. While we are dispersing our air fleet to the various arsenals across our great nation, we are going to have to land them along the East Coast before they start the huge transit from here to Israel."

"When?" the Marine Corps general asked.

The Air Force general nodded. "When?"

"You just said 'when the President orders'."

"Yes. When is the key. There is no way unless a miracle happens that Israel can hold out against the Arab forces arrayed against it if the Soviets start pouring war materials into Egypt and Syria without direct U.S. intervention."

"I don't think we are going to intervene militarily," Ellison said.

"No, sir. If I gave that impression with the use of the word, I apologize. What I mean is that there is no way the Israelis can hold out without the United States taking up the slack in the resupply effort. That is the intervention I am referring to."

"I understand."

"In the face of a Soviet resupply of its allies we will have to respond in kind. This war is going to be one of who has the best arsenal rather than who has the best fighters," the Air Force general added.

Turning back to the projection on the screen, the general continued, "While we will have in-flight refueling capability, we expect to use Lajes in the Azores, and if necessary we will ask the Spanish for permission to use Rota, Torrejon, and Moron. The Italian and Portuguese governments have given us tentative permission to use Lajes and Sigonella. We are waiting for Spanish approval. Both Rota and Sigonella are Naval air stations."

The general glanced at the screen. "Earlier today, forward command elements of the Air Force deployed to both Rota and Sigonella to act as liaison with the Navy during the operations."

"How long do you expect this operation to last?" the Navy supply rear admiral asked.

"We can sustain the flying part of it indefinitely. We see two critical elements that can interrupt the loop." He motioned the pointer between the East Coast and Israel. "The most critical one is in Israel. We are going to be using Lod Airport in Tel Aviv as the arrival point. We already have an Air Force forward command post set up there. They arrived this morning and have already made arrangements with the Israeli Army to take charge of the supplies as they arrive."

"That's impressive, General," Ellison said.

"We have been working with General Willis, your head of air operations."

General Willis was the Air Force lieutenant general who headed up the air power section of Ellison's Joint Expeditionary Operations group.

The general directed his comments to Admiral Ellison. "Admiral, we will have to discharge our cargo, refuel, and take off within forty-five minutes of landing. If we don't, Lod will become a bottleneck with aircraft beginning to stack up and eventually bringing the operation to a halt."

"Forty-five minutes? That's cutting it close, isn't it?" Ellison asked.

The Air Force general nodded. "Yes, sir, but we have no choice but to keep a constant, steady stream of resupply aircraft flying a constant loop. This plan takes into consideration everything from in-flight refueling, to loading and unloading, to crew rest for our people."

"Quick planning," Ellison commented.

"Prior planning, sir. The Air Force always knew that sometime in the future we might have to do a contingency operation just like this. It was a matter of blowing off the dust on the operations plan and tweaking it for this."

"And the other critical element?" the two-star representing Commander Second Fleet asked.

"The amount of war-fighting supplies we have in our own arsenals."

The Navy supply admiral straightened in his seat and quit drumming his pencil.

"How's that?" Ellison asked.

"The war-fighting material we are going to have to ship to the Israelis is going to come from our own reserves, our own arsenals, Admiral. We have been told by the Joint Staff that with the exception of the Marine Corps, we will be using the reserve materials from all the services, to include the Air Force air-to-air missile inventories. As you can guess, none of us have that much depth."

"How are you going to manage the other services' inventories?" the supply officer asked.

"The Air Force Chief of Staff will be formally asking all of the military services, including the Marine Corps, to put a liaison officer on the Military Airlift Command staff."

A moment of silence filled the room until the gentleman in civilian clothes sitting across from the supply officer cleared his throat. "You realize this is a slippery slope of one-upmanship,"

"How's that?" Ellison asked.

"Well . . . the Soviets do a resupply effort; we do one. The Soviets disperse a massive number of warships to the Eastern

Mediterranean; we disperse a massive number of warships to the Eastern Mediterranean." The civilian sighed. "Eventually, the Soviets will have to threaten military intervention, and I don't mean the intervention of logistics that our Air Force flag is preparing to execute. I mean actual boots on the ground." He leaned forward to look at the Army general. "If I were you, General, I'd start getting the 82nd and 101st Airborne ready."

The Army general smiled. "They are always ready."

"Desert gear or gear for fighting the Soviets on the German plains?" Without waiting for a reply, the civilian continued. "I apologize to those who may not know who I am. I'm Gerry Spyra from the Department of State, and I am considered one of our Middle East experts. I was asked here today by the Chairman. Admiral Zumwalt was gracious enough to invite me to the tank for this briefing, and Admiral Ellison was kind enough to allow me to stay. I apologize for my presumptuousness, but if you follow where we are now—nearly five days after the war started—the Soviets are determining what we do. We are racing to get ships into the Eastern Mediterranean; they aren't. We are racing to start an airlift; they're not.

"This is a typical escalation ladder, common to other crises we have had with the Soviets, except for one thing." He held up one finger. "They are leading and we are with the others playing catch-up. Most times we have led, with the exception of small brushfire wars. This is not a brushfire war and they are leading. We are chasing."

"I think we're doing a good job," Ellison said.

Spyra nodded. "Yes, sir. We are and you are. But the fact is we are the ones racing to catch up regardless of how fast we are sprinting."

There were several exhalations of disagreement before Spyra raised his hand while shaking his head. "I'm not taking issue with what you are doing," he protested. "I don't think most of us at the Department of State or the Department of Defense recognize where this crisis can take us. But it can take us to the brink of war—and pray to God no further."

There was silence around the table.

"I don't think that will happen," the Air Force briefer said. "We both have too much to lose."

"You may be right, General. I hope you are, but Brezhnev is a new type of premier. He came to power when the Soviets had to back down when we pushed our might at them. We have to recognize that here—here in 1973—the Soviets believe they are at a point in their history where backing down is no longer an option."

"CHIEF Norman, you're in a whirl of shit," Elliot said.

The recalcitrant chief petty officer stood in front of him, legs spread and arms positioned behind his back. Alongside Norman was the chief of the boat, Master Chief Hugh Tay, and Chief Norman's department head, Lieutenant Commander Daniel Washington.

"Yes, sir; I know, sir."

"Stand at ease, Chief." Elliot looked down at the papers in front of him as Norman relaxed, letting his arms fall along his sides. "Do you know specifically why you are here, Chief?" He shook the papers in front of the man.

"Because of my altercation in Holy Loch, sir?"

"You're asking me? You're asking me! Why? What other instances could I be referring to, Chief?"

Norman glanced at Tay, who glared at him. "Answer the XO."

Norman swallowed. "Sir, it wasn't my fault."

"Funny thing, Chief. Everyone at the club, the shore patrol, even the four-striper commanding officer of Holy Loch seems to think it was your fault." Elliot held up a sheet of paper. "According to this, you started a fight with three other sailors off the USS *Greenling* . . . SSN-614 . . . a sister boat to the *Manta Ray*," Elliot said, his voice rising as he spoke.

Norman grinned slightly, dipping his head as he did.

"This isn't funny, Chief. Two of those men had to be taken to the hospital for stitches, and one of them has a fractured arm; not broken, but close to it."

"But, sir . . . "

Elliot held up his hand. "Just stand there and keep your mouth shut unless I ask you something."

"Yes, sir."

"I said keep your mouth shut!"

Tay elbowed him. "Shut up."

"Additionally, you caused over three hundred dollars of damage to the club during the fight. And, if that wasn't enough, after the fight you decided the shore patrol had no right to 'take a chief into custody because the Secretary of the Navy promoted you to chief,' and then you demanded a phone call to the SECNAV!" Elliot looked at Norman and let out a huge sigh. "Chief, do you think maybe you had had a little too much to drink that night?"

Norman's eyes widened. "You know, sir, I think those sailors may have sneaked something into my drink."

Elliot leaned forward. "The only thing that was in your drink that night was your lips, Chief, and they were in too many drinks." Elliot lifted Norman's service record. "Chief, it amazes me that you are a chief petty officer. This record reads like a Huckleberry Finn of World Wide Wrestling. This isn't your first XO mast, nor will it be your last mast, if I decide to send it forward to the old man."

Norman opened his mouth to reply. Tay elbowed him again, grimacing at Norman when the man looked at him.

"Here is what you are going to do, Chief, and you're going to do it on your own volition. Do you understand?"

"Yes, sir."

Tay elbowed him.

"He asked me a question, Master Chief."

"Here is what you're going to do. You are going to write the club a check for four hundred dollars."

Norman's eyes widened. "But, sir, it was only three hundred in damages."

"That's why you are going to be one stand-up guy and send them four hundred. And you're going to write them a letter of apology, and the master chief is going to read it to make sure it sounds contrite enough. Do you understand?"

"Yes, sir, then I can mail it."

"Good try, Chief. The master chief will mail it after your department head, Lieutenant Commander Washington, has reviewed it. He may want to endorse it."

"Aye, sir."

"And you are going to confine yourself to the *Manta Ray* for the next two port visits."

Norman took a deep breath. "But, sir . . . "

"The other choice is captain's mast, and believe me, you do not want to go before Captain Brandon. He will have your nuts for a garter and your khakis for grease rags. People will be calling you 'Petty Officer' if not *'Seaman'* before tomorrow afternoon."

"Yes, sir. I understand."

"Are we in agreement about what you are going to do?"

"Yes, sir."

"Then by taps tonight, I want a letter and a check in the master chief's hands."

"Sir, I don't have a bank account. I don't have a check."

"Then, you better hope you can get to the post office and find a postal clerk who will sell you a money order, because at taps tonight, I have to tell the skipper what my recommendation is on you, and right now, it's to toss you overboard without us surfacing."

"HOW did it go, Steve?" Chief Electrician's Mate Leroy Nash, known as Bubba, asked.

"It did not go well," Norman said in the passageway leading to the engineering control room.

Nash handed him a cup of coffee. "He didn't ask about me, did he?"

"Oh, fuck off, Bubba. I didn't rat you out, and I didn't say anything about you being with me that night in Holy Loch."

Nash let out a deep breath. "I'm sorry . . . "

"About what? Running off and leaving me to get my ass beat up by a bunch of fellow bubbleheads?" He made quotation marks with his fingers. "'A sister ship to the *Manta Ray,*' the XO said."

"You didn't exactly get your ass kicked, Steve, and I didn't exactly run off. You sent three of them to the hospital."

"I went to the hospital, too, shithead."

"Yeah, bruised knuckles."

"And you did run off."

"Look, shipmate, word is getting around to avoid you on liberty. Every chief petty officer in the goat locker worked hard for those khakis. We aren't going to endanger our careers and our families so you can get shitfaced and try to fight everybody around you." Nash shook his head. "Hell, man, you tried to fight me a couple of times in the club."

"You should have stayed. One of them kicked me in the balls."

They stepped inside the engine room.

"Shit, man," Nash said in a whisper. "If I had been them, I'd've kicked you in the balls, too. It was the only way to stop you, you know. I didn't run. I didn't leave until I heard the Shore Patrol sirens. I tried to stop you, but I doubt you remember that. You punched me when I tried to pull you away from the fight."

Norman sighed. A deep one that filled the compartment. He rubbed his head. "I don't know what comes over me when I have a little too much."

"It's the 'smart' syndrome."

"Smart syndrome?"

"Yeah, the more you drink the smarter you think you are, the smarter your jokes become, and the smarter you think the women think you are."

"And that's wrong?" Norman asked with a laugh.

"No, it ain't wrong, but you want to whip everyone's ass as well as being smart. When you're sober . . . "

"I don't need an electrician's mate telling me what's wrong with me; I got an XO, the chief of the boat, and by tomorrow my division officer telling me how fucked up I am." He looked over at the broad-shouldered Nash and for a fleeting moment wondered if in a fight he could take the muscle-bound oaf. "You know I gotta give Tay a check for three hundred dollars by taps tonight."

"What for?"

"Damages to the chiefs club."

"You didn't do that much damage. I think one chair . . . maybe a table was destroyed in the fight, but nothing else."

"You and I know that, but the XO said the base commander sent a message saying three hundred dollars' worth of damage." He didn't mention the extra hundred dollars the XO ordered him to pay. He didn't have three hundred, much less four, and he had no idea yet where he was going to beg, borrow, or steal the money.

"They must have had other stuff they been waiting to buy and along comes you and those others to pay it."

"They don't have to pay."

"I wouldn't bet your bottom dollar on that, shipmate. I bet the *Greenling* got the same message, only their four or five sailors were assessed three hundred dollars *each*. You know how nice that club is going to look when we get back to Holy Loch? And it is all thanks to you and the others." Nash laughed.

"Don't laugh at me."

Nash's laughter stopped and his face grew red. He put both hands on his hips and leaned forward into Norman's face. "Man, I ain't laughing at you. I'm laughing with you. They might even name the club after you. What you going to do, Steve? Fight every fucker on the boat and everyone you meet from now to eternity? You got to get your drinking under control before you kill yourself or—worse yet—someone else."

Norman ignored the words, and when Nash leaned away, he said, "We'll check when we get back."

"Check what?"

"How much damage I did and how much improvement they did. I'm going to be one pissed muther if we show up there and it looks like—"

"Yeah, we will," Nash interrupted softly. "Well, I gotta get back up to the office. Radio has a kink in its wire, so I have a couple of my sailors working on the thing now. If we can't get it straightened out, Radio says we may be without comms for a while."

"Well, we are the silent service."

A few minutes later, Norman left the engine room and worked his way aft to a storage closet, then looked both ways before stepping inside. He shut the door before he turned on the small light. Norman licked his lips as he shoved aside the cans of cleaner and pulled out a box of liquid shoe polish. Nearby he pulled out a loaf of bread he had taken from the mess this morning and arranged the loaf over a bucket. Then, he started straining the shoe polish through the bread, smelling the grain alcohol as it emerged from the other end.

"TAKEN care of?" Brandon asked as Elliot approached.

Before Elliot could answer, Lieutenant Tony Grant said in a loud voice, "Sir, I make my course two-two-zero, depth two hundred feet, speed ten knots. Sonar reports no possible submarine contacts and is tracking ten surface vessels probable commercial."

"Very well, Tony. Keep me apprised of any changes to the status in our condition or any contacts that might be of interest. Meanwhile, keep steady on course, depth, and speed unless otherwise told differently or for the safety of the boat you have to make some change."

"Aye, sir."

Brandon turned to Elliot. "And our little problem?"

"I think it's taken care of."

"Good. Let's go to Radio and see how they are coming on that casualty to the wire. It's got to be either a kink in it or something wrong with the reeling mechanism. We missed the evening communications check. They are going to start getting worried at Submarine Forces Atlantic if we miss the second one."

Brandon glanced at the clock as they headed toward the forward watertight door. It was twenty hundred hours; eight PM for civilians, he thought. Maybe if he retired, his married life would come back together. Maybe he could pump gas somewhere in Norfolk.

"So we didn't know about this until they tried to reel it out?"

Brandon opened the door. "Nope. They streamed out about a hundred feet and it locked up."

Elliot pulled the door shut behind him and swung down the latch to secure it. "So it's still out there?"

"So far. We still have a hundred feet of wire streaming behind us. That's why I reminded the officer of the deck not to change our course, speed, or depth. I don't want to wrap the wire around one of our shafts."

Brandon punched in the code to the cipher lock on the radio shack, waited for the click, and opened the door. Inside was a maelstrom of activity and noise, with tools clanging, sailors cursing, and a too crowded compartment greeting the two men. And everything and everyone was focused on the box at the bottom of the end rack, where Chief Nash and two of the electronic technicians were bent over the opened electronic equipment.

Lieutenant Strickland stood off to one side with his arms crossed. Turning and seeing the skipper and XO standing at the hatchway, he shouted, "Attention on deck!"

The maelstrom came to a complete halt.

"Carry on," Brandon said. Everyone went back to what they were doing, but the activity was more muted as whispers instead of loud voices filled the compartment.

"Lieutenant, what is our status?"

"No change, sir. The electronic technicians are trying to see if it's something electronic. Engineering is checking the hydraulics and the motor. Everything seems perfect except the wire won't wind in or wind out now."

"When was the last time the maintenance check was done on it?" Elliot asked.

Strickland shook his head. "Done on time, XO," he replied calmly. "All our 3M is done on time or ahead of time, but never late."

Neither Brandon nor Elliot commented, because both knew it was true. Strickland ran a tight division.

Chief Nash stood and wiped his hands. He looked at Brandon and nodded as he walked over to the three officers.

"It doesn't look as if there is anything wrong with the electronics, Mr. Strickland. It has to be in the motors and hydraulics. I'm going to go down to Engineering and check on their progress."

"Chief, do you have any idea how long all of this is going to take?" Brandon asked.

Nash shook his head. "No, sir, I don't. I know we have done all we can here until Engineering completes their checks on the motor and the hydraulic system. Once that is done, I can conduct some additional tests to see if the internal electronic relays are working."

"And if everything is working?" Strickland asked.

"It's like this, Lieutenant. If everything is working internally—motor, electronics, and hydraulics—then we got a kink in the wire, and that kink is most likely located either right inside where the wire leaves the boat . . . " Nash paused.

"Or both?" Elliot asked.

"I don't think so, sir. If it was outside, then we could roll the wire out. I think it has to be inside if the wire itself is the casualty."

"When you say kink, Chief, do you mean a big wad of wire?" Elliot asked, his hand cupped as if holding an imaginary softball.

"It could be, XO, but most likely it means the wire has split. When the antenna wire splits, all those individual copper strands making it up shoot out of the skin holding it together and they go every which way. If we have a kink, we have a problem."

There was a moment of quiet among the four before Brandon added, "It means we are stuck with the wire protruding one hundred feet behind us until we get to Rota, where we will have to pull in and have their immediate maintenance folks repair it."

"We could jettison it," Strickland said.

Nash pursed his lips. "Can't jettison it, sir. If we could jettison it, we could wind it out or wind it in."

Brandon held up his hand. "But the problem isn't that we can't get rid of that hundred feet of wire. The problem is that getting rid of it could cause some flooding to the boat, because most likely it will leave a hole that the wire is currently plugging."

"We aren't taking on water," Strickland added. "I checked

with Lieutenant Grant and with Engineering when the wire failed to move."

"I know," Brandon added. "If we were flooding, I would know." He looked at Strickland. "Do we have any message receive or send capability with a hundred feet of wire behind us?"

Strickland nodded. "Not much, sir, if any. We were unable to make a good synch with the available communications frequencies earlier, and we couldn't send anything. We can keep trying. Lots of times it's atmospherics that cause the problem. Maybe in the early morning hours before dawn we can try again."

"Then we'll try then."

"I just don't know how well yet, or even if it will work, but we will try, Skipper."

The three officers looked at Nash, who raised his hands. "Sir, all I can tell you is the system is working for winding out or in the antenna wire."

Strickland looked at the leading petty officer, who had been eavesdropping on the four from near his workbench.

"Yes, sir?"

"Will we be able to send or receive messages if we are unable to fully unwind the wire?"

The petty officer nodded. "Oh, yes, sir, but it won't be as effective and we might miss something. We can easily determine if we miss something, but we might not know if something we sent got received."

"Well, that's some good news," Brandon said.

"Sir, I'll have to recalculate the frequencies we can use, because they will have to be frequencies that can operate on the length of antenna we are streaming."

"Then, make it so, Petty Officer Cornell," Brandon said.

"WHAT next?" Elliot asked as they stood in the passageway outside of Radio.

"Well, we will have to issue a CASREP, and when you write it, XO, ask Rota to stand by with its local force and see if they can provide some immediate maintenance availability when we arrive."

"I thought our Rota visit was canceled."

Brandon nodded. "Our mission is to ensure the Strait of Gibraltar stays open to U.S. forces. The Soviet submarine force is scattered throughout the Atlantic and the Mediterranean. Most likely they are going to put some boats at the Strait. Shutting down the Strait of Gibraltar is easy. Lay a few mines, and the only way into the Med is the Suez Canal. Our mission is to see that that doesn't happen."

"Someone else may have to take our place."

Brandon grunted. "Unfortunately, there is no one else. *Greenling* is tracking west toward the center of the Atlantic. Naval Intelligence thinks the Soviets have deployed some of their attack submarines there. The boats from Norfolk are deploying today and tomorrow to clear the lanes for the carrier and amphibious battle groups." He shook his head. "Seems like everything is moving forward for a classic 'oh shit' confrontation."

The two men turned aft toward the control room. "Wonder what happened to the Soviet Charlie we were tailing."

Brandon shrugged. "As long as he isn't tailing us, I'm happy." He swung the watertight handle up, but held the door closed for a moment.

"What you thinking?"

Brandon took a deep breath and sighed. "I was thinking of clearing our baffles, but we cleared them earlier before the antenna went broke-dick on us. Don't want to maneuver too much if we can avoid it, until we have finished everything possible to get that wire back in."

He opened the door and entered the control room, glancing at the quartermaster who quickly noted his presence at the announcement of the officer of the deck. It was something learned from years of boring holes in the depths of the ocean. Consistency was the key to survival. Consistency was the key to responding quickly to an emergency situation. And consistency was something submariners practiced and lived on a daily basis. For without it, this boat that intentionally sinks itself might never rise again, so even the smallest thing done on board a submarine had to be meticulous in its execution. Consistency was also one of the biggest vulnerabilities of a submarine.

VOLKOV hugged the navigator to his body, laughing. "You have given me such pleasure over how well my Party-political work with you has taken, Victor Zaharovich." The *zampolit* released the number two navigator and flopped down on his rack. "You see, too many of our officers fail to understand their responsibility to the Party, to report such incidents." He pointed at Zaharovich. "You on the other hand have an immaculate record. A record that one day will see you command a boat such as the K-321."

"Thank you, sir."

"Don't call me sir. Call me Mikhail. Mikhail is my given name, my friend." Volkov reached over and pulled out his notebook. "I need to write down what you have told me, Victor. And I may need to ask you some questions, so if you do not mind waiting while I write it down, I would appreciate it."

Zaharovich acknowledged the Party-Political officer, looking around the small stateroom.

Volkov grinned. "I am sorry, but I have no chair." He patted the space beside him on the bed. "Sit here beside me."

"So when did you witness this confrontation between the XO and our skipper?" he asked.

Zaharovich started his story once again, relaying the nuances as he understood them and the growing awareness within the wardroom as to how much the captain had changed since the sinking of the *Silesia*. The failure of the captain to acknowledge a directive from the admiral of the wolf pack and telling the communicator, Lieutenant Karimov, that he— Bagirli—would write the response and get it back to him. To date, to the best of Zaharovich's knowledge, no such reply had occurred, and the captain had ordered Radio into silence. He told everyone that it was because they were tailing an American submarine, but Zaharovich and a few other officers were concerned that the captain might be thinking of doing something irate. Something designed to regain his prestige and honor with the Navy.

"Who are the other officers?" Volkov asked, pausing as he took notes.

"Do I have to tell you?"

Volkov put his hand on the nervous navigator's thigh and squeezed. "Yes, you have to tell me." He did not remove the hand and Zaharovich did not object. The hand began to move up the young navigator's thigh. Ten minutes later the notebook lay on the deck of the stateroom.

NINE

"WHAT is going on?" Bagirli asked as he entered the control room.

"We are not sure, sir," Lieutenant Commander Lepechin answered.

"We have not lost contact on the American submarine, have we?" he asked, afraid for a moment that his chance to impress the Soviet Northern Fleet command had vanished. "Has he cleared his baffles yet?"

"Depends, sir, on how you want to define it. No quick turns, nothing that indicates a tactical maneuver to see if anyone is behind him. Just what I would identify as normal turns—slow to hide any possibility of cavitations," Lepechin answered, shaking his head. "Either he is very confident that the Soviet Navy is incapable of detecting and tracking his *superior* American submarine, or something is stopping him from making sharp turns. No, sir; it has been over two days since we have seen the normal American tactic."

"This is an enigma. Are you sure he has not tried to check his stern area? Americans are predictable."

"Sir, up until two days ago, this captain has been consistently clearing his baffles once every hour to one and a half hours. He would do a sharp turn, steady for a minute, and then finish off with a second parallel sharp turn. The last time we had the enemy in a sharp turn was sixteen hundred hours Tuesday, sir—two days ago. Then he did a starboard ninety degrees followed two minutes later with a one-eighty to port. Since then, no sharp turns. We have had several small turns—not many, but no sharp turns."

"Maybe he is overconfident?" Bagirli asked.

"He could be, sir."

"Or maybe he has had an equipment casualty that restricts his maneuverability. Maybe a rudder casualty," Bagirli said, the right tip of his lip curling upward in a half smile. He chuckled. "Would not that be something?"

"That could be it, sir, but he has not surfaced since then."

"I am sure he has changed his depth. They are like us when it comes to communications—they have to come up to periscope depth. What is their technical data, Lieutenant Commander Lepechin?"

Bagirli waited a few seconds then explained, "His course?"

"We have a very good passive profile of the American, Captain Bagirli. Our target motion analysis shows they turned earlier in the morning to a base course of one-six-five. We do not have a depth or range to the contact, but considering that we are at two hundred meters, they are also above the three-hundred-meter layer."

Bagirli grunted. The bottom layer had moved up one hundred meters since yesterday. Normally, he would question why the change, but his interest was focused on his American submarine.

"Most submarines never venture that low," Bagirli said. "Even at two hundred meters that is the same as over six hundred feet. We tend to stay at lower depths than the Americans. The Americans want to be able to swim to the surface if they have to, so going low would be an anomaly."

"If I may recommend, Captain, since we are discussing depth, may we change our depth to one hundred meters?"

"Why? Are you afraid of the depth?"

Lepechin blanched for a moment before his face turned red.

Bagirli watched the color change and fought the urge to smile at the discomfort. "Well? You are the operations officer. If you want me to authorize a change of depth, then you must have a reason?" Bagirli made no attempt to lower his voice. From the corner of his eye he saw the chief of the boat, Chief Ship's Starshina Totya Zimyatov, slap the back of the head of one of the planesmen and point toward the gauges. The crew must always know who the skipper of the boat is.

"My thoughts, sir, were to refine our targeting information on the American. To see if working with our Sonar we could refine the depth and the range to the contact."

"Our Sonar?" Bagirli thought. *They couldn't find their way to the outhouse without some imbecile showing them the path.* "They have had contact with the American submarine for over two days, haven't they?"

"Yes, sir."

"And during that time we have come to periscope depth at least twice," Bagirli continued, holding up two fingers. "And they still had the Americans then, right?"

"Yes, sir, but the signal faded in and out. Maybe for a couple of times they even thought they lost it."

Bagirli waved the comment away. "Comrade Operations Officer, of course they probably lost it. They lose everything. They just never tell us until we demand it. My question, though, isn't whether they lost it, but if they maintained contact, then why didn't Sonar calculate the Americans' depth then? Why must the K-321 go through a series of maneuvers that may alert the Americans to our presence? Why do we do it now, my operations officer?"

"Sir, if I may," Lepechin said, his voice low. "When we are coming up to periscope depth, we are rolling out the wire and making lots of noise."

"The K-321 does not make noise."

"My apologies, Comrade Captain, I did not mean intentional noise. When we are coming shallow, the crew of the K-321 is focused on trailing the wire, raising the periscope, and concentrating on the shipping in the area that may detect our presence."

There! I knew it! Lepechin was deliberately rubbing the incident of the German merchant in his face. An incident that was the result of faulty sonar. He looked around the control room. It seemed that every eye was on him; sailors glancing from the corners of their eyes. Officers staring indiscriminately. Chiefs smiling at him.

Bagirli shut his eyes for a moment, and when he opened them, routine had returned to the control room, everyone attentive to his console.

Now Lepechin wants to let Sonar try to show it was capable of performance!

"And if Sonar should lose the American and not regain him? What then, Lieutenant Commander Lepechin? Do we send a message to Northern Fleet Command and tell them that we not only lost contact, but we lost contact because we were maneuvering to better refine our solution on them? Some solution we developed, wouldn't you say?"

There was a moment of silence in the control room, broken by the sound of the aft watertight door opening. Captain Third Rank Demirchan entered, trailed by the chief engineer, Lieutenant Commander Semyon Mashchenko. Spotting Bagirli, the two men headed toward the center of the control room. Demirchan's eyes flickered between Bagirli and Lepechin.

"Comrade Captain," Demirchan said in greeting as the two men reached Bagirli and Lepechin.

"Comrade XO, our esteemed operations officer wants to conduct a series of maneuvers to see if we can refine the position of the American submarine. He wants to take a chance on us losing the valuable contact we have had for over two days."

Demirchan turned to Lepechin. "Comrade, do you have anything further to discuss with the skipper on this insane idea?" he asked calmly.

Lepechin shook his head. "No, sir, XO." He nodded at Bagirli. "With the skipper's permission, I must conduct my hourly check of the condition of the boat." He turned and walked to the forward part of the room to start his inspection. Lepechin leaned over the navigator's shoulder.

Bagirli turned back to Demirchan and nodded sharply. *There! That should put Lepechin in his place. Sonar has screwed me enough on this trip and once the K-321 returns to Severomorsk, I am going to have the Soviet Northern Submarine Fleet relieve the entire sonar team off of the K-321. There is too much incompetence on the K-321. Maybe Demirchan does understand this. Thank Lenin.*

"I will speak with Lieutenant Commander Lepechin later, Captain," Demirchan said quietly.

"Do that, XO. I can't afford to lose this contact. A lot of maneuvering would no doubt alert the Americans to our presence."

"I understand, Captain."

"The Northern Submarine Fleet headquarters has already commended the K-321 on maintaining contact this long. Tonight, when we transmit our situation reports, it will mean three days of nearly constant contact." Bagirli thought of the secret list of names he had compiled in his stateroom. Names of those he suspected of being disloyal and incompetent. Demirchan's name was on the list, and for a moment he considered removing it.

"That is well on its way to beating the length of time the Soviet Pacific Fleet submarine held contact on the American last year."

Bagirli guffawed, but fought the urge to smile. This was serious business. "But they did it when there was no crisis. When there was no opportunity for a direct confrontation. We are doing it while ramping up to confront the Americans in what they have always considered their European lake—the Mediterranean."

"That is very true, Captain. What you are doing will also break new ground on how to do antisubmarine warfare in a time of crisis."

"That is true, Yerik. I am leading the finest submarine . . ." He stumbled when he realized what he had just said, then after a couple of openmouthed attempts, Bagirli continued, ". . . in the Soviet Northern Fleet, tracking an American who seems to be heading toward the same area of operations as us—and doing it surreptitiously." *If only I had a strong crew, a complete crew who knew their jobs.*

"That is true. Tonight when we pass our situation report to Severomorsk, we will be able to tell them the same information we have told them for two days: the course of the American contact."

"Course? Yes, we will be able to tell them the course. And we will be able to say with certainty that we are still trailing their wake, hidden in their baffles." He laughed, but it sounded more like a giggle gone bad before he abruptly stopped.

It washed over Bagirli like an unexpected wave on a cold Arctic night. Demirchan had identified something he should have thought of. The Northern Submarine Fleet would want to know more; Admiral Yegorov would want to know the range to the American. The commander of the Northern Fleet would demand to know at which depth the American was operating. And, something so simple to calculate, he would want to know the base speed of the American submarine. All of these things meant the K-321 would have to maneuver.

Demirchan nodded at Mashchenko as he changed the subject. "Skipper, Lieutenant Commander Mashchenko and I have completed our periodic inspection of the engineering spaces."

"And?" Bagirli asked sharply. Why didn't the two of them just step away for a few minutes? Let him concentrate on how to derive this additional data on the American without having his stupid sonar team lose the contact.

"Nothing critical to report, sir. The slight malfunction in the number one motor and reduction gear lubricating oil sump has been repaired. Commander Mashchenko's black gang was able to take the spare on board for the number one main engine sump pump and jerry-rig a couple of parts. The lubricating oil sump now works to specifications."

Bagirli's eyebrows furrowed, the thoughts of the American submarine shoved into a recess of his mind to be jerked forward later when he finished with this. "What happens if the main engine sump pump suffers a casualty, Comrade Chief Engineer? Will we have sufficient spares to resolve that casualty immediately?" *Why did everyone on his boat think they could do anything they wanted without his permission?*

"Sir?"

"You know what I am saying, Lieutenant Commander Mashchenko! We can make do with the motor and reduction gear oil sump having a slight problem, but if the main engine sump pump breaks, we could find ourselves having to route around it. Or we might even have to shut the engine down until we fix it. If we have to do that, then it means we could lose the American we are tracking." Bagirli shook his head back and forth several times. He raised his finger toward the two men, took a deep breath, and then after a couple of seconds let the breath out slowly. Finally he uttered softly, "Did you think of that?"

Bagirli rubbed his hand across his face. He was tired. The most sleep he had had in two days was four hours in a row. Even then he had woken with a fit of anxiety over what his incompetent crew might have done while he slept. This was just another example of why he needed to be everywhere on his boat.

Demirchan's and Mashchenko's eyes widened.

"No, sir, not immediately . . . "

"How many spare parts do we have for the main engine sump pump?"

"Captain, that was our only spare part. The pump was making too much noise, sir. You said—"

"You would endanger an auxiliary piece of critical equipment that protects our ability to make way, to resolve a slow fuel transfer problem? Seems to me that while the initiative is very well understood, Commander, you should have asked me before starting it."

Demirchan cleared his throat. "That is my fault, Comrade Captain. Commander Maschenko approached me with the recommendation. You were very tied up with the more important challenge of leading the boat tracking—"

"I am never tied up so much that any element within my command lacks my personal attention. Especially, any change that affects the ability of the K-321 to fight must never escape my notice or interest."

"Aye, sir. I will have the crew remove the spare part and return it to storage."

Bagirli motioned him away. "No, you have done it." He nodded sharply a couple of times. "Most likely we will not need the spare part, and maybe your effort will be rewarded by us not needing it." He noticed Demirchan nodding in agreement. "XO, you have a question?"

"Oh, no, sir, I do not. I realize now I have let you down and you have my apologies." He turned to Mashchenko. "Chief Engineer, if the skipper is finished, you may return to Engineering."

"I have nothing else."

Bagirli waited until Mashchenko had departed the control room and the wheel on the watertight door had spun closed. "I am sorry for the slight outburst, XO. I am concerned we have too many officers with great ideas for resolving problems and refining data who may make unintentional mistakes that rush us into making decisions we will not only have to live with, but have to explain to our bosses."

"I understand, sir. They are only trying to please you. When you tell them to make the boat as quiet as possible, they go searching for things causing noise, such as the lubricating oil sump pump. Sometimes we try too hard, and then you must focus our attention as you have done."

"You are right, XO. I am glad one person on this boat understands the challenges I have with command."

"Yes, sir."

"What would you recommend on developing new data on the American we are tracking?"

"It would mean doing some slight maneuvering in terms of course changes and depth changes, but nothing quick. Do it very slowly to come to a right-angle course for a few minutes so our target-motion-analysis team can develop the speed of the American. It would mean several right-angle course changes against our baseline course of one-six-zero. Once we have calculated the target's speed, we will know the distance."

"We should also use the layer to calculate the depth of the American."

"That will mean changing our depth."

Bagirli scrunched up his face for a moment before relaxing. "I do not want to go too shallow." He recalled Lepechin a few minutes ago revealing that Sonar had sometimes lost the signal when they were at periscope depth.

Demirchan nodded. "The Americans like the shallow depths, but like us they know the importance of remaining below the topmost layer. Since we are below the top layer and a hundred meters above the next lower level, we already know the American cannot be higher than seventy-five meters or lower than four hundred meters. I would submit we already have some feel for the depth of the American."

"My thoughts exactly, XO, so I don't think we have to do too many depth changes where the sound of water going in and out of our tanks will resonate."

"No, sir. When we change depth, we should do it very slowly so as to minimize any noise in the water. Your crew is very capable, sir."

"If I authorize this maneuvering, then I want the port-starboard turns done independently of depth changes. We are either turning or we are changing depth, but not both together. It only increases the opportunity to lose the American if we try to be too cute in our target-motion-analysis effort. It also increases the noise in the water."

"I will ensure it, Comrade Captain."

"And you will be here while it is going on?"

"Of course, sir; if that is what you want."

"That is what I want. And I want to be notified prior to any course change or depth change regardless of where I am."

"Yes, sir."

"I am going to the wardroom and have some tea. Call me if anything happens."

A few seconds later, as Bagirli departed the control room, Demirchan walked up to Lepechin. "Go ahead, Operations Officer."

"Sir?"

"Put into action your plan you discussed with the skipper. He has decided that you were right."

Lepechin's eyes widened for a moment before he grinned. "Thanks, XO."

Demirchan nodded, but said nothing as he walked toward

the periscope platform. He could sit in the captain's chair, but the urge to do so had evaporated over the course of this deployment. He lifted the handset to the internal communications system and buzzed the wardroom.

"CAPTAIN Demirchan, forget that last order," Bagirli said into the handset. "Only notify me if we are going to leave the layer." He held the handset to his ear with his shoulder while trying to butter his croissant. For the past four hours, every few minutes someone had been chasing him down to get permission for course changes and depth changes. Most of the course changes were one to four degrees off base course, then they were chasing him down in the wardroom. He hung the handset up. "Must I do everything on this boat?"

"My apologies, Comrade Captain. I did not understand."

Bagirli looked up at the steward. "I said I would like another cup of tea." Slow turns to develop better localization data on the American. His eyes widened and he stared at the bulkhead across from him. The photograph with Lenin looking to the left filled his sight. This was what the Americans had been doing for the past two days: slow turns and then back on course.

Bagirli's eyes widened. "My God!"

"Sir?"

He slid his chair back suddenly, bumping the arm of the steward behind him, sending tea and china flying everywhere. He did not apologize as he dashed out of the wardroom, heading toward the control room. Why did his sonar and his operations officers not realize what the Americans were doing? Why was everything left to him to figure out?

GORSHKOV walked slowly along the massive hallway of the Kremlin. Age was beginning to slow down his body, but his mind was still as intent and active today as it was in 1956. While others saw danger in confronting the Americans, Gorshkov saw an opportunity to catapult his Navy ahead of the West.

His young executive aide trailed a few inches behind on his left. Left was the position of subservience, where juniors positioned themselves, a legacy learned from the British centuries ago and now a Soviet tradition.

Gorshkov swerved suddenly and stopped at one of the nearby windows. Windows along the interior of the Kremlin reached from near the floor to near the top of the high ceilings of the building. They were more than two of his shoulders' width from side to side. He stared across the internal grounds of the seat of government. A second later the reason for him stopping appeared.

General Pavlovskii strolled up and stood silently beside the admiral. Army General Ivan G. Pavlovskii was the Deputy Minister of Defense for the Soviet Army Ground Forces.

"You have my respects, General," Gorshkov said without looking at the taller Army officer. "Yours is a task that is much more complicated than mine."

"And you have my respects, Admiral, as you always have."

"It is a challenging position our Arab allies have placed us in, isn't it?" Gorshkov asked satirically.

"I am certain the Americans feel the same." Pavlovskii sighed. "It is one we both knew would come someday."

"You mean you and me, or us and the Americans?"

"Both."

"Unfortunately, Ivan, I doubt the Americans believe we had little to no influence on these events unrolling in the Middle East." Gorshkov snorted. "As superpowers, we and the Americans should be deciding when and where we confront each other, not having desert Bedouins pushing both of us down this slippery slope of confrontation. I always thought we would start it on the high seas." He turned to Pavlovskii. "You know most wars are fought when nations are incapable or lack the will to commit their people, land, and fortune to an adventure."

"I agree, Admiral." Pavlovskii sighed.

In the hierarchy of the Soviet military, Gorshkov was a legend. One of the few remaining veterans of the Great Patriotic War still wearing a uniform. He was recognized even now as the father of the modern Soviet Navy. Only the premier called the great man by his first name—Sergey. To everyone else, he was "the Admiral."

Pavlovskii continued, "The Soviet Army has always focused on a European war. A war of tanks and infantry slugging across the Polish border to push back the Americans and their NATO allies." The husky army general shoved both hands out, pulled them back slightly, and then shoved them out again. "Surging forward, conquering land, pausing for more forces to come forward, and then completing the victory." He grunted as he dropped his hands. "Maybe throwing in a few tactical nuclear bombs to help speed their retreat. Alas, we now must turn our attention south."

"Your men will do you proud, Ivan. It is unfortunate that the Israelis were able to reconstitute their army so fast. The attacks today along the Golan Heights and the pell-mell retreat of the Syrian Army have exposed Damascus to the Israelis. It would serve them right if the Israelis did a victory dance through their streets."

"As Premier Brezhnev just pointed out, we cannot afford to be seen as deserting our allies, even when they do stupid things."

"The Americans are not going to be happy. They will feel they have to respond in kind."

"They already have their airborne forces at Fort Bragg on alert. All we are doing is matching their stage."

"With one exception," Gorshkov said, raising a finger. "We are telling the Americans that if the Israelis cross a certain point or threaten Damascus, we will deploy your airborne forces to Syria." He laughed. "That's a little stronger statement than just doing the one-rung-at-a-time climb to the top."

"Their ally isn't losing now."

"Their ally is lacking supplies. The Americans are going to have to do something."

Pavlovskii nodded. "But the Israelis have already started a resupply effort."

"The American Air Force has always wanted to show the world a demonstration of another Berlin-type airlift," Gorshkov said, ignoring Pavlovskii's comment. "I don't think the Israelis are going to be able to mount the logistic chain they will need to airlift war-fighting supplies from the American mainland to Israel."

"It's the Israeli commercial carrier El Al," Pavlovskii protested. "They might be able to hold out."

"For the time being." Gorshkov shook his head. "You have read the same intelligence reports I have; the American Air Force has already deployed its heavy transports to key American airfields."

"I interpret that to be a dispersal, kind of a preventive maneuver against one of our supposedly surprise nuclear attacks," Pavlovskii said, referring to the Soviet belief that paranoia drove most of America's military actions.

Gorshkov nodded. "You could be right, but why would they disperse their heavy transports to locations near the war-fighting arsenals of their military?" He motioned General Pavlovskii quiet as he continued. "No, the Americans may not have made the formal decision yet, but they will eventually start a massive resupply of Israel."

"We are resupplying Syria and Egypt."

Gorshkov nodded. "That we are, my good Comrade General, but not on the scale the American Air Force can put into the air." He leaned down and with a smile added, "Let's not tell Chief Aviation Marshal Kutakhov that I said that."

Pavlovskii smiled. "He does not take kindly to criticism of his Air Force."

"I have met his counterpart on the American side. He doesn't either." Gorshkov pointed up. "Must be the low air pressure at high altitudes that create . . . " He grasped for the right word for a moment before adding, "Oh, you know what I want to say."

"I think the Americans will wait to see what we will do."

Gorshkov turned away from the window and started down the hallway, and General Pavlovskii fell into step to the admiral's left. Gorshkov and Pavlovskii's aides walked several feet behind the two flag officers.

"What the premier did not say in the short conference, Ivan, is that our ambassador in Washington, Comrade Dobrynin, has already told Kissinger that we would send your troops to defend Damascus if the Israelis threaten the Syrian capital."

"Yes, I know."

"Do you know what Kissinger said would happen if we do? He said America would deploy its troops to integrate and fight alongside Israeli forces."

Pavlovskii nodded. "I heard something similar, but America is still reeling from Vietnam. Its people would not support such a move."

Gorshkov glanced at the Army general. "The key here is the threat to integrate the American Army into the Israeli Army." Gorshkov grunted. "That is something we have already ruled out. We are not going to integrate our military into the Arab military."

"It would be a disaster. We would not know how long they would stay in the fight before they cut and run," Pavlovskii answered.

"If Nixon decides to do the airlift, and he will," Gorshkov continued, "he will tell the American people afterwards and context it with the survival of Israel. No, General Pavlovskii, we are on the slippery slope toward confrontation, and neither we nor the Americans seem able to stop it." He glanced at the taller officer. "It is up to our allies to decide to stop fighting and our politicians to find a face-saving solution that ends this. It is one thing for me to take them on at sea, but once your and their airborne forces exchange the first shot, then it becomes a matter of prestige and nothing will stop it from exploding around the world."

"You don't seem enthused over the prospect."

"Anyone who fought in the Great Patriotic War and suffered the pains of war can never be called mentally competent if they long to do it again. This time, there would be no civilization to resurrect our world, if total war ever occurred on the scale of the one with Germany." He stopped and took a deep breath. "Enough of this evening gossip, Ivan. Your men will do you, the Party, and the Soviet people proud. Nothing will stop them if they go into battle. That includes a combined American-Israeli force."

"I have always wanted to know how we would stand in a face-to-face battle with the Americans. I am confident we would prevail."

Gorshkov nodded. "I understand how you feel, Ivan. I, too, have confidence that in a war-at-sea battle, we would win, but both our Navies would be bloodied. It would not be a pretty victory." He smiled at Pavlovskii. "I do not think any general or admiral anywhere in any country fails to wonder how his forces will stack up in a fight with whoever is his rival." He sighed. "But while we wonder, let's hope we go to our retirement homes feeling confident we would win, but without having to find out."

"I agree," Pavlovskii said and then added, "You know the one thing that could hurt us if we airlift our troops to Syria and Egypt?"

"They become Moslems?" Gorshkov asked with a slight chuckle.

"I could order them away from that, but what I cannot do is change a hundred thousand uniforms from wool to cotton overnight. I am more concerned with heat exhaustion than I am with any tactical challenge the Israelis or Americans can throw at them."

"It is the air picture that will hurt you most." Gorshkov uncrossed his arms. "The Americans and Israelis will own the air unless Chief Marshal of Aviation Kutakhov can figure out a way to forward deploy his fighters to Syria."

Pavlovskii grunted. "It would be nice to have our own fighters overhead when we engage the Israelis and the Americans."

"We might not even engage them, General. You might get your troops down there and find they spend their time more as a political ploy than in a military adventure."

"I hope not," Pavlovskii snapped. "If we deploy a hundred thousand airborne troops, they are going to get their opportunity to learn the Americans and the Israelis are not supersoldiers, but mere flesh and blood like everyone else on earth."

Gorshkov grimaced as the two officers approached the elevator. "I will do what I can to reduce the American threat from the sea, but there is little to naught that my Navy can do to stop the air threat. That will be your most dangerous enemy . . . after the heat."

"It would be good if we could show the American military we mean business."

"That will occur Sunday, Comrade General."

Pavlovskii turned, and when Gorshkov said nothing further, he asked, "How?"

"We have a declaration with Turkey . . . "

"An American lackey."

Gorshkov laughed. "Don't tell the Turks that. They think they march very well to their own music."

"The Ottoman Empire is dead."

"But we continue to give them hope that we would like to see it rise again."

"So, how, my good Comrade Admiral, will you let the Americans know we mean business?"

"I am sending two amphibious ships through the Dardanelles into the Mediterranean—the *Voronezhskii Komsomolets* and the *Krymskii Komsomolets*." He shrugged. "They are smaller ones than I would like, but I need to continue to grow the size of the Fifth Eskandra. The Americans must understand that we mean business."

"Sometimes, even when we tell them we mean business, they ignore us."

"Sometimes we talk too much. Maybe this time, we will *show* them we mean business."

Gorshkov's aide ran forward and pressed the down button.

The admiral and general shook hands, wished each other the best, and when the door opened to the elevator, Gorshkov and his aide stepped inside. When Gorshkov turned around and the doors started to close, General Pavlovskii had disappeared. Most likely heading down the hallway to talk with the air marshal, which would be good politics and good military. Gorshkov looked down. His Navy was ready for the tasks to come, but instead of it being Navy against Navy, the true success of the Soviet Union in standing up to the Americans would rest in all three military services working together.

He had read the American treatises on fighting as a joint warfare unit, but right now he was more concerned about the American Navy's battle group defense strategy. It was a strategy designed to defeat his tactics of massive cruise missiles from the sea working in a combined attack with the air marshal's long-range cruise missile aircraft. But with the events in the Middle East drawing the attention of the Politburo, he doubted that any fight in the ocean would be strictly his Navy against the Americans.

It might not be a bad idea to provoke a slight confrontation. Something where the Americans had to use their carrier air power. He might be able to use the consequences of such a confrontation to push for his Navy to build an aircraft carrier. This was 1973. Britain had an aircraft carrier. France had one. Even Italy and Spain had one, but not the Soviet Union! They were a superpower without an aircraft carrier. If his Navy had at least one aircraft carrier, he would have a true triangle of at-sea war-fighting might.

"Did you say something, Comrade Admiral?" the aide asked.

Gorshkov shook his head. "No, Comrade. I was probably talking aloud to myself." He looked at the young officer. "As you get older, thoughts sometimes echo out the mouth before they finish their trip around the brain."

The doors opened. Might be time to see what his American spy in Norfolk had to offer.

IVAN still behind us?" Brandon asked, leaning over the shoulder of Tucker Bullet.

Chief Bob Davis, known as "the dome" because of his shaved bald head, straightened and pushed himself off his seat.

Petty Officer Bullet smiled and slid his left earpiece to one side. "He's still there, Captain. He's definitely trailing us." The slender sailor reached up and tapped the green screen with his finger.

Brandon smiled and squinted as his eyes followed the sailor's finger. His keen non-sonar-technician eyes could not tell the difference in the green waterfall coming down the screen.

"Chief, Petty Officer Bullet, I hate to tell you, but I don't see a thing."

The two men chuckled.

"It is hard, Captain," Chief Davis said, "until you correlate the passive noise with the right steady line on the console. Then it's a matter of making sure the visual line and aural noise are always together. Us being at the bottom of the top layer helps." Davis leaned forward and with a pencil touched the center green line. "It's a faint signal and has been since Bullet detected it a couple of days ago."

"Good work."

"Every now and again it fades to almost going away, and then it comes back." Davis tucked the pencil back in his khaki shirt. "Thing is we could lose it anytime, but based on it remaining almost constant, I would say 'old Ivan' is between the layers—top and bottom—going about the same speed as us—ten knots—and going in the same direction."

Brandon smiled. "Good analysis, Chief. Looks to me as if you both are right and he's tracking us. The speed thing is something I had not considered, but it makes sense."

"Same signal strength, same direction—makes it seem to be same speed, Skipper," Bullet added.

Brandon had already ordered anti-submarine torpedoes loaded in the aft tubes, keeping a couple of Harpoon cruise missiles in the forward torpedo tubes—just in case, he had told himself.

Bullet jumped in. "Crazy Ivan hasn't even done his normal one-eighty either, sir. He's confident he's got us and he's confident no one is trailing him: otherwise he'd be clearing his baffles."

"Well, he'd be right, Petty Officer Bullet. There is only us out here. No other American boat within five hundred miles."

"He's developing a targeting solution on us, Captain," Chief Sonar Technician Davis said.

"Why do you say that, Chief?"

"We've watched him do some slow turns. Not the turns associated with clearing his baffles, but turns that would give his passive tracking team different lines of bearing on us, different angles. Similar to what we would do if we wanted to refine our range and bearing to a target."

"You think he is refining his targeting profile on us?" Brandon asked aloud, leaning down to look at the green screen again.

"Sir, that's a definite," Bullet said. "He's trying to develop a better target-motion-analysis picture on us."

Brandon scratched the stubble on his chin and glanced at the bulkhead clock. Navy clocks were ubiquitous on ships. With the exception of passageways, every compartment usually had one.

"He might be getting his training hours in," Davis offered.

"Or he might be preparing for—"

"Don't say it, Bullet," Davis said.

Brandon smiled. Tracking each other was a God-given maritime right. Even targeting each other, as long as you did not turn on your active sonar, was expected. But right now American and Soviet forces were beginning to square off in the Eastern Mediterranean.

The 1MC piped up with a boatswain whistle followed by the announcement "Taps, taps. All hands maintain quiet throughout the ship. Now, taps." Twenty-two hundred hours.

"How long ago, Chief, did they start doing their slow turns?"

Davis's lower lip pushed up against his upper and his eyes narrowed for a moment before he reached out and touched Bullet, who had replaced his earpiece. "When did we notice the first slow turn?"

Bullet slid the earpiece off to the side. "About four hours ago, Chief."

"We had not seen them do any turns prior to then?"

"Only when they were changing course to stay behind us, sir," Bullet answered. He turned back to the console and then excitedly added, "There he goes now, sir."

This time Brandon could detect the motion on the screen, as a light green line near the center of the console began bending to the right. The three men stared as the noise line disrupted the pattern, causing a spoke to separate the steady green like a stick being dragged through the water.

"Right-hand turn," Davis said. "Always first a right-hand turn, followed by a left. Has yet to do it the other way—asshole commie. No innovation, always the same direction."

"We might have the better of him," Brandon said. He touched Bullet on the shoulder. "Good job, Petty Officer Bullet. Chief, I'm going aft to the control room. I think we can keep our tattletale behind us from refining his targeting solution."

He stepped to the watertight door and was opening it when Chief Davis added, "Sir, good luck."

"Let's hope I don't screw up our own targeting data on our new friend behind us or cause you to lose him."

Several frames, one watertight door, and a couple of sailors later, Brandon was inside the control room, standing over the Gold Team who was doing the target motion analysis on the Soviet Charlie-class submarine.

It had been a serendipitous event two days ago, after the casualty with the wire antenna, when Bullet had detected the Charlie. The *Manta Ray* had been heading to periscope depth in an attempt to transmit their casualty report to Commander Second Fleet, when Sonar reported a brief contact. The officer of the deck at the time, Lieutenant Strickland, had been quick on his feet and noted the depth as just below the two-hundred-feet mark.

After Radio was unsuccessful in transmitting the casualty report, Brandon had taken the *Manta Ray* back down. Fifty feet—*exactly*—below the depth noted by Strickland, Sonar regained steady contact. For the past two days *Manta Ray* had remained near the two-hundred-feet mark, watching the Soviet submarine—convincing the Soviet submarine that it had sneaked up on the *Manta Ray*.

Bullet had eventually identified the noise as some sort of engineering pump on a Soviet Charlie-class submarine. While the petty officer had been able to identify the noise as emanating from a faulty pump, neither he nor the other sonar technicians had been able to discern which part of Engineering the pump supported.

Then, earlier today, the noise of the pump had disappeared, but Sonar knew what other sounds the Charlie-class submarines made. So when the pump disappeared, they had other sounds radiating along the same line of bearing. The new noises were fainter, but thanks to the faulty pump giving Sonar a line of bearing, they had been able to exploit the other signals in the water. Otherwise, there would have been a good chance they would have lost the noises amid the noisy underwater life of the ocean.

"WHAT you got?" Brandon asked Lieutenant Grant who was running the Gold Team.

"We are still tracking the contact, sir. Sonar says he is in a turn, and while we are tracking his turn, we are ignoring it for our calculations. These turns can screw—"

"I know, Lieutenant, and I think I am going to do some maneuvers to mess up their calculations."

"Their calculations?"

Brandon smiled. "They're doing slow turns, aren't they?"

"Yes, sir. They have been doing them for about four hours—maybe longer."

"Why have we been doing slow turns, Mr. Grant?"

"To refine our TMA . . . " His voice trailed off.

"Exactly. Ivan has decided it's time to refine his targeting picture. He doesn't know how much distance separates us. If he did, he wouldn't start doing targeting maneuvers, something he should have been doing when he first detected us. He'd be speeding up to close the distance—get within torpedo range—but he hasn't. At ten nautical miles—*twenty thousand yards*—it would have to be a long-range torpedo shot, a Hail Mary."

"What are you planning, Captain?"

"Some maneuvering of our own. Make them work to determine how far apart we are."

"He's had four hours."

"But he doesn't have our sonar team or our professionals calculating speed, range, and course based on noise spokes." Brandon smiled. "But when I start making turns while Ivan is making turns, then we are going to run the risk of having to start our targeting solution all over again. Can you handle it?"

Grant smiled. The three sailors around the plotting table smiled. "Captain, there is nothing the Gold Team can't do with a few lines of bearing. After all, sir, we already know his bearing, speed, and course. What more does a good math team need?"

"Good. We're going to pit American geometry against Soviet geometry," Brandon acknowledged and quickly moved to his chair. He hoped the Soviets' geometry was not as good as their chess skills. "Lieutenant Strickland, give me a status report," he ordered, looking at the officer of the deck.

"Sir, I make my course one-six-zero; my depth is two hundred feet, and my speed is ten knots."

Brandon mentally crossed his fingers. Sonar had been able to keep the Charlie on its rainfall, but the noise was faint. He ran the risk of losing contact, but then in ASW you always ran the risk of something—including being sunk. Right now he had the upper hand. Ivan might be tracking him, but in his heart he knew his Soviet counterpart did not know how little distance separated them. Ten miles was just a healthy sprint.

He smiled and let out a deep breath. When you're going to fight with someone your own size, it's best to take the uphill position. And he was uphill.

"Very well, Mr. Strickland. Ask the XO, OPSO, and the chief engineer to join me, if you would."

"Aye, sir," Strickland said, nodding to the quartermaster, who immediately lifted the handset and started dialing.

The aft watertight door opened and Elliot entered, followed closely by Fitzgerald.

"I love it when XOs read your mind. I just asked the OOD to send for you two," Brandon said.

Elliot tapped his head. "That is why XOs are psychic, sir."

Brandon turned again to Strickland. "Let's do a left-hand turn." He hummed for a moment as he thought and then added, "Say about forty degrees off base course."

"Aye, sir. I am making my course one-two-zero degrees, maintaining ten knots and a depth of two hundred feet."

"What's going on?" Elliot asked.

"Ivan is targeting us. I thought we'd just throw him off with a little maneuvering of our own."

"Good idea, Skipper," Fitzgerald said. "Is there any chance we might lose our contact with him?"

Brandon smiled. "A good question, OPSO. There is that chance, but we both know what our base course is. He's not going to give up a chance to track an American submarine." He chuckled. "It's not like the Soviets have had great success in tracking us, and I don't want him to lose us—yet."

BAGIRLI rushed into the control room. "They're tracking us!" he shouted. He saw that the Uzbek was the officer of the deck and his angst grew.

All conversation stopped, with the exception of the ASW team, where one of the starshinas announced, "The target is in a left-hand turn."

"Sir?" Lieutenant Karimov asked.

"Quiet, Lieutenant! Did you hear what ASW just said?" he asked. His eyes bored into the young officer while his hand pointed to the plotting table. "They are in a turn! They are in a turn and we are in a turn! He's targeting us!" Bagirli shouted.

Bagirli turned and rushed toward the periscope platform near the starboard side of the control room. "Sound battle stations. He's preparing to fire at us. Increase speed to fifteen knots, hard left-hand turn. Put a knuckle in the water! Make your depth three hundred meters!" He needed Lepechin as his OOD. The operations officer would know how to fight the boat. *Wait! Lepechin was on his list! But that mattered little right now. The operations officer was his best, even if the man was untrustworthy!*

He'd never thought he would be put in this predicament. Bagirli touched his chest. His heart was pounding. A bead of sweat burned his eye. Bagirli blinked it away.

The sound of battle stations echoed through the boat as the K-321 tilted into a left angle, as the officer of the deck shifted his rudder to hard left and increased the angle of his planes. The K-321 was heading deeper.

"Am making my depth three hundred meters, increasing speed to fifteen knots, and coming to course one-eight-zero!"

The aft watertight door burst open. Sailors and chiefs rushed into the control room. A few raced across to the forward watertight door and dashed through it.

Bagirli shouted after them. "Do not use the control room . . . !" But they were gone before he could finish. No one was to use the control room as a passageway! They were to use the deck below.

The boat tilted forward as it started a sharp dive.

"Five-degree bubble," Karimov announced.

Bagirli grabbed a handhold above him, just as Demirchan came stumbling through the aft hatch and started working his way to the weapons control panel.

Good, Bagirli told himself. *At least, one loyal officer is here to witness this event.*

The boat continued in its hard left turn.

Karimov looked toward Bagirli, waiting for the next order.

Demirchan saw the hard left rudder. "Officer of the Deck, what course are you coming to?"

"I do not have a course yet, Comrade Captain."

Bagirli heard the exchange. "Rudder amidships!" he ordered.

"Rudder amidships!" Karimov commanded.

The K-321 continued downward as the boat righted itself.

"Passing two hundred fifty meters, sir; I am easing my planes to three-degree bubble."

Bagirli said nothing at Karimov's announcement.

"Is the American still turning?" Bagirli asked the ASW team.

"We don't know, sir. We have changed course and speed. We will have to start—"

"Are you incompetent?" he shouted. "Has Sonar lost contact?"

"Yes, sir— I mean no, sir."

"What do you mean?"

Demirchan reached the weapons control panel, looked over at Bagirli, and nodded.

"Planes eased to three-degree bubble," Karimov said.

"Three degrees! What is your depth?"

"Captain, we are passing two hundred fifty meters. Am approaching final trim."

Before Bagirli could say anything, the K-321 started to level off. He wanted to scream at the Uzbek, order him off the control room floor. But, at that moment, Lepechin rushed through the forward hatch. Bagirli touched his chest. He was breathing too fast. He forced his breathing slower. The American was preparing to fire on him. This had gone all wrong. He should be the one firing, and now he was going to be the one to have to run—

"Check with Sonar and see if they still have contact," Demirchan said to the ASW team.

Bagirli straightened. He was not going to run. The Soviet submarine force had run enough, and this was his chance to regain his loss of face with the Northern Fleet submarine force. No one would stop him from replacing those disloyal to him when he won this battle with the American. He knew what he had to do.

"Bring us back slowly to base course one-six-five!"

"Making my course one-six-five," Karimov answered.

"Reduce speed to eight knots." Fifteen knots put too much noise in the water. The sharp turn, the burst of speed, and now the lower speed should reduce the noise in the water the Project 670-class was known to generate.

The K-321 coasted into a right-hand turn as its speed started to come down.

"I have the deck and the conn," announced Lepechin.

"Lieutenant Commander Lepechin has the conn!" Karimov echoed as he quickly moved toward the forward bulkhead, his square body nudging aside Chief Ship's Starshina Zimyatov, who was standing spread-legged above the planesmen. Karimov was heading toward his own battle station in Communications. A second later the Uzbek communicator was out of combat and the forward hatch secured.

Bagirli breathed a sigh of relief. He would discuss relieving Karimov with Demirchan after this was over.

"Steady on one-six-five, final trim depth three hundred meters."

"Very well," Bagirli acknowledged. "Open forward torpedo tubes one, two, three, and four."

"Sir?" Demirchan asked.

"I said, open the forward torpedo tubes and make ready to fire."

Bagirli failed to see the glance between Demirchan and Lepechin.

TEN

ELLISON gently placed the telephone back in its cradle and leaned back. Clasping his hands together, he rested his chin upon them for a few seconds before he looked across the desk at Gerry Spyra.

A few seconds passed before the man from the State Department asked, "So, is there anything you can share with me about the other end of that conversation with Admiral Moorer? I heard enough to know that something has happened . . . something that will involve the State Department."

Admiral Moorer was the Chairman of the Joint Chiefs of Staff, one of the few World War II veterans still on active duty, and destined to retire in the coming year.

Ellison lifted his chin and glanced at the clock on the wall behind Spyra. "Do you know that across the Atlantic, it's ten o'clock—twenty-two hundred hours—taps, as we say. Sailors, soldiers, airmen, Marines are all listening to the playing of the bugle, the firing of the evening cannon, or the sound of a boatswain whistle." He smiled at the confused look on Spyra's face, and then chuckled. "Sorry,

Gerry, just thinking of where our forces are and what they might be doing that is a symbol of stability and peace. That symbol right now is taps. Five hours away in Rota, Spain, and London, England, Navy personnel are crawling into their racks as taps sound. Add another hour, and taps has passed gracefully through Naples and Sigonella; another hour—seven hours from where we sit—it's midnight and a war rages that threatens to pull America and the Soviet Union into a confrontation."

Spyra nodded as if he understood, drawing another smile from Ellison. Spyra cleared his throat.

"Let me see, Gerry. I probably should have asked you to step out when the telephone call came through, but I wasn't aware the admiral was calling about official business. I thought it had to do with an official function Admiral Zumwalt and I were to attend tomorrow."

"If you feel the conversation is something that should be kept between you two, Admiral, I would not want to put you in an awkward position."

"And you wouldn't, Gerry." He sighed. "Admiral Moorer was trying to reach Admiral Zumwalt, who is on the other side of town at the Defense Intelligence Agency."

Ellison leaned back in his chair. "Thing is, if you were back on your home turf of the State Department, you would already know what the Chairman just shared. Seems Soviet Ambassador Dobrynin has paid a courtesy call on your boss. He has informed Secretary Kissinger that if the Israeli offensive threatens Damascus, the Soviets will be compelled to deploy their airborne troops to protect the Syrian capital."

"Wow," Spyra said softly.

"And, in true Kissinger style, your esteemed boss informed the Soviets that if their troops enter the Middle East fray, the United States would be compelled to do likewise."

"That doesn't sound good."

Ellison stood, walked to where an aide had put a decanter of water earlier in the afternoon, and poured himself a glass. "I doubt either they or we are going to deploy troops into the theater."

Spyra stood and joined Ellison at the decanter, and poured

himself a glass of water. "I don't know if I agree, sir. The Soviets have been looking for an opportunity to confront us since 1962. They have never really forgiven us for making them back down in the face of our overwhelming Navy superiority."

Ellison laughed. "You're just saying that to make me feel good."

Spyra smiled. "You could be right. After all, I am a diplomat. But the truth is the Soviets have put a lot of the national economy into their military since then."

"They have been doing that for decades, Gerry. I tend to focus on their Navy, and regardless of your thoughts on Admiral Gorshkov, he has turned the Soviet Navy from a coastal Navy into one that is capable of going anywhere in any ocean."

"True, but it's only been since 1962 that their Army and Air Force strength has been focused."

Ellison took his glass and walked toward the four soft leather guest chairs arranged in front of his hardwood desk. Spyra followed.

"Yes, you are right. That's because Navies and Air Forces do not win wars. Boots on the ground win them. You win because you take the other guy's land." He took a drink. "But their focus has been on winning a European war, not a fight in the Middle East," Ellison added as he sat down, enjoying the softness of the armchair after an hour of his butt pressed against the seat of the hard desk chair, which was shoved back from the desk in front of him, touching the green felt curtains that framed the windows.

Spyra sat down. The late afternoon sun came through the thin panels of the blinds, casting alternating patterns of shade and light throughout the office and across both men's faces. Ellison thought about getting up and closing the blinds, but the sun was something he was getting little of except in his office, and even then it was on his neck. What a fiasco in the Middle East! Fiasco? Now, why would he call it that?

"And our focus?"

Ellison brought his thoughts back to the topic of their conversation. "Focus," he said aloud, then turned to Spyra.

"Our focus has been on countering the European strategy of the Soviets, not fighting in the Middle East," he answered.

"But we and NATO have not built up our armies to conquer Russia."

Ellison nodded in agreement. "History has shown that it's nigh impossible to conquer Russia—*the Soviet Union*—by invading it. The boots on the ground would get mired in the depth of the country. Napoleon tried it. Hitler tried it. You can even go further back, to Genghis Khan, who tried it. You might cut a swath through it, but it would be something that would cause a conventional war to fail. An invasion of Europe by the Soviets would either end quickly with a negotiated peace or escalate rapidly into nuclear war." He shrugged. "Both sides know that, but we plan on a European war because the planning keeps the Mutually Assured Destruction Doctrine— MADD—in place and functioning. You stop planning for a conventional war, then what happens?"

"Everything stops."

"Could. But more likely one side or the other would believe they had stopped the buildup with more toys on their side than the other. Then the conventional war would stop anyway."

"But we have had confrontations. We have fought them."

Ellison said nothing. "I can neither confirm nor deny what you say. But think of it this way: fighting in the middle of the ocean, away from the watchful eyes of the press and civilians, gives the event an almost 'never happened' quality."

"So you think they won't deploy," Spyra said, changing the subject.

Ellison shook his head. "I think both we and the Soviets see the Middle East events catapulting us toward a confrontation that neither they nor we want, but which neither of us can back away from." He set his glass on the small side table separating the two chairs. "Whether it comes to that most likely rests in the hands of your department."

"But it could be the military that causes—"

"We have rules of engagement and operational plans that drive our responses. I would be very surprised if Soviet intelligence isn't smart enough to extrapolate what those ROEs are and figure out where we are in our operational plans." He shook his head, looked at Spyra, and gave him that famous one-lip-curled-upward grin. "Do you know where the most likely place of confrontation would be, if the Soviets really wanted to prove they had moved past the Cuban Missile Crisis of 1962?"

Spyra shook his head. "Along the European front?"

Ellison shook his head. "Just like we touched upon—at sea. Most wars start at sea. They then migrate to land when the adversaries have had their at-sea tiff. The Soviet Union is a seagoing power. We recognize that. But I'm not so sure they have yet." Pointing his finger at Spyra several times for emphasis, he continued. "If you think the Soviets are going to deploy their Army airborne forces to Syria, then all you have to do is watch what they do at sea."

"How's that?"

"They are going to have to close the Mediterranean because their spies will have already told them of our preparations to deploy. They cannot afford to have us build up our strength in the Mediterranean. We will have to fight our way into the Mediterranean, and if I was Gorshkov, I would start that fight in the Atlantic."

Spyra made a face. "You really believe that?"

"My job is to prepare the Navy for the worst case scenario. Right now—and this is top secret, Gerry, so don't share it with your *Washington Post* friends down at that drinking hole near State—"

"Admiral, I would never do that," Spyra protested, his eyes widening. "I never share anything from our meetings except with my superiors."

"Calm down, Gerry. The classification is real; the comment about the *Washington Post* is half-real. We have a testing gauge here for what we do. It's called the '*Washington Post*' test. Whenever we are doing something and wonder about its appropriateness to the situation, we ask ourselves is this something we would want to wake up in the morning and read as a headline in the *Washington Post*?"

"Oh."

"But what I was going to add was that the Soviets have already deployed submarine forces to meet a surge in American Navy forces. You already know about the twenty-plus submarines in the Mediterranean. Most of them are cruise-missile-capable. If just one missile or torpedo is fired between surface combatants, then we are going to be forced to react with massive retaliation to take the Soviets out. We have to for our own safety. In the Atlantic, my counterpart, Admiral Gorshkov, has deployed submarines along the East Coast."

"He would never!"

"Gerry, sometimes I think the State Department is filled with some of the brightest, most naïve stars we have from our country."

"Sir . . . "

"We always have his submarines off both our coasts. Everyone in America knows about the boomers the Soviets keep within firing range of our nation. Few know about the anticarrier-capable submarines that also patrol."

"Guess he would want to take the aircraft carriers out before they reach the Mediterranean."

"He would, but most likely he won't."

"Why?"

"There has to be a catalyst. Some event that forces either him or us to fight. I think he wants to see us have some sort of exchange . . . some sort of confrontation . . . and I don't mean accidental brushings between our ships. An actual exchange of weapons fire."

"That would be disastrous, sir, but it counters your argument that the Soviets would not deploy their forces to Syria."

"Not really, Gerry." Ellison leaned toward the State Department envoy. "A war-at-sea between two Navy powers doesn't carry the weight of putting armies against each other ashore. We could have a battle that would last thirty minutes or thirty hours, and when it was over, both our bloodied Navies would disengage, and while the sabers might rattle on both sides, nothing would happen."

"We would win. Right?"

Ellison nodded. "The Soviets aren't on par with us yet. But given the right circumstances, they could inflict pain before we cleared the seas of them."

Spyra smiled as if satisfied with the answer.

Ellison leaned back. He wondered if given the right surprise circumstances, the Soviets could actually win a war-at-sea. The answer was always yes. Soviet tactics involved a massive armada of warships, submarines, and aircraft filling the skies with wave after wave of cruise missiles. That was their basic tactic of destroying a carrier battle group: cruise missiles.

"The destruction of an aircraft carrier battle group would be too massive of a sea battle to stop at sea. It would be met with American retaliation. So what is Gorshkov planning and why?" At that moment, Ellison realized that the Office of Naval Intelligence assessment briefed to Admiral Zumwalt over two years ago was right. Gorshkov had his sea going Navy, but no way to project power ashore as long as he had no aircraft carriers. Ellison thought about sharing this epiphany with Spyra, but when he opened his mouth, he decided against it. This was something for Zumwalt.

The sun drifted downward between two of the blinds. The bright rays caused Ellison to squint. He tilted his head slightly to avoid it. "Of course, even though we would win a war at sea, Gorshkov would have gotten what he wants."

"What's that?"

"A surge in morale within his Navy because they can fight the Americans and survive. Of course, my job is to see that they are bloodied so bad that he achieves just the opposite."

"So he would do this just for morale?"

"No. He wants something else. Something he doesn't have." *He just hasn't convinced the Politburo to fund them.* The briefing Ellison had reluctantly sat through two years ago was now more poignant than ever. Gorshkov was going to use this war to force the hand of the Soviet Politburo.

"I would think he would want to support his forces ashore," Spyra said, setting his drink on the side table.

"Of course, he does. I do, too. But, from the U.S. Navy perspective, as long as he doesn't, I can whup their butts in any sea at any time."

"What if they get aircraft carriers?"

Ellison shrugged, surprised that the man from the State

Department grasped the one element that ensured the U.S. Navy superiority. "If they started building them today, it'd be five years before the first one sailed down the ramp and another three to five years before they developed some expertise in using them. By the time they have enough aircraft carriers to challenge the West, Gorshkov will be dead and I will be rocking on that proverbial front porch playing with the grandchildren."

"So how does he create a confrontation big enough to convince the Politburo of the need for carriers and yet keep it small enough so it doesn't cause both our nations to go eyeball-to-eyeball?"

Is Spyra reading my mind? Ellison thought.

"If he is bloodied, which is my job, he can argue that if he had had aircraft carriers, this loss at sea would never have happened."

"But they could relieve him also. Tell him he screwed up, pack his bags, and he can go home to play with the grandchildren—couldn't they?"

"Possibly, but Gorshkov has friends in very high places, and I wouldn't be surprised if the old goat had photographs to help ensure his survival as head of their Navy."

The sun hit Ellison's eyes again, and in that instant he knew how he could bloody Gorshkov and yet still deny the man the political argument needed to get his carriers. It was his second epiphany of the moment, because he also knew that if he thought it, Gorshkov had figured it out much earlier.

"Gerry, you are going to have to excuse me. I need to talk with Admiral Zumwalt and relay to him what the Chairman has told me."

"He's back from the DIA?"

Ellison glanced at the clock. "Not yet, but I have to get some notes together for him. The boss likes to have a one-pager—we call them blue-blazers—so he can have a quick reminder if he needs to refer back to them."

A few minutes later Spyra was out the door. Ellison's aide entered. "Captain, get me Admiral Cousins on the phone." The aide did an about-face and was nearly at the door when Ellison added, "And get me the current status of the *Manta*

Ray. I want to know if they are still tracking that Soviet Charlie-class."

"Yes, sir," the aide acknowledged, and was nearly through the door when Ellison spoke again.

"And ask Admiral Rectanus to join me with Admiral Zumwalt when the CNO returns."

The clock above behind him showed five-thirty. Rex Rectanus, who was the Director of Naval Intelligence, and Zumwalt had been together through other tours of duty. The CNO depended on the DNI's advice for understanding how the Soviets would react to what the United States Navy was going to do or had to do. The senior intelligence officer in the Navy was the key when Ellison voiced his suspicions to Zumwalt. If Rectanus agreed, then Zumwalt would agree.

"SONAR reports loss of contact on the Charlie, sir," Fitzgerald replied.

"Probably because we're in a turn. Probably got him in our baffles," Brandon replied, hoping his guesses were right. "Tell Sonar to keep searching, and let's wait until we are out of our turn to see if they regain contact."

"Passing two-four-zero in a starboard turn," the petty officer on the helm reported.

Brandon glanced at the gauges above the helmsman. They were still at two hundred feet, with a speed of ten knots. This would really throw off the Soviet captain's analysis. Brandon thought he should have realized turning might cause his Soviet counterpart to slow the speed of the Charlie. A slower speed meant better targeting refinement by reducing the noise signature of the boat.

"Passing two-four-five."

Only fifteen more degrees to go. He glanced at the internal communications system, expecting any moment for Sonar to report they had regained contact.

A minute later the helmsman began to ease off the turn as he neared the ordered heading of two-six-zero.

"Ask Sonar if they have regained contact."

Fitzgerald grabbed the handset.

"Put it on the speaker, Commander Fitzgerald, and leave it on."

The speaker squeaked for a moment and then the voice of Chief Davis emerged. "OOD, this is Sonar."

"Any contact, Sonar?"

"Nothing, sir. We lost it when we went into our turn. We are still searching, but everything seems to have gone down— disappeared. We are—"

Suddenly frantic shouts inside Sonar garbled Davis's voice. Brandon didn't understand a single thing being said. "What are they doing?"

The ICS went quiet for a moment before Davis came back on line. "Control, Sonar. We have high-speed rotations— probably torpedoes—bearing three-four-five!"

"Sound battle stations!" Brandon ordered. "Make your depth four hundred feet. Prepare to deploy decoys! Right full rudder, steady on course three-four-five." Get his bow dead-on to the torpedoes. Reduce the profile of the Manta Ray.

"Tell Engineering to cut the wire." He couldn't have the antenna trailing if he needed to do some high-speed maneuvering. He'd have to worry about communications later.

Davis came back on line. "Rotation noise is faint, sir. I repeat, rotation noise is faint, but definitely torpedoes. We are seeing a slight left bearing drift on the noise spoke, sir."

"Make your speed five knots!" Brandon said.

Fitzgerald looked back at Brandon, his face questioning. "Sir, slow down?"

"Slow down, Lieutenant."

"Sir, I recommend increase speed."

"Increased speed only increases his ability to track us. Slowing us down decreases it."

"But, sir, we have torpedoes inbound."

Brandon grinned. "Not from ten miles out we don't. Execute my orders." Slowing the Manta Ray down would decrease the opportunity for those torpedoes—how many?—to home in, by reducing the amount of noise the submarine was generating into the water.

Noise in the ocean rides the currents and bores through the water, searching for the easiest way to travel. Temperature, pressure, current, and even the salinity of the water determine how far and how fast sound will travel underwater. Just because Chief Davis said the noise was faint meant little if the wrong combinations were occurring. The two submarines could be much closer, even if the geometric calculations of the target-motion-analysis team showed the Soviet Charlie about twenty thousand yards from them. TMA was not an exact science.

"Ease your bubble to three degrees, Officer of the Deck," Brandon said.

"Three-degree bubble?" Fitzgerald asked.

"Take her down slowly." The boat continued in its hard right rudder, with the deck tilting slightly to the right as the boat continued its course change to meet the torpedoes head-on.

"Passing three-zero-zero degrees," the helmsman reported.

"Very well," Brandon said. He smiled, for he knew his counterpart on the Soviet Charlie submarine had no idea how far *Manta Ray* was from him, while he, on the other hand, knew the Charlie was around ten nautical miles away. Too far for Soviet torpedoes. His forehead wrinkled. At least according to Naval Intelligence, the Soviet had no torpedoes capable of that range.

"We don't want those torpedoes to get into our baffles. Even if the Soviet captain fired from twenty-thousand-yard range, there is always a chance they might lock on our propellers." *Besides,* he told himself, *if the torpedoes get behind the Manta Ray, Sonar won't be much use.*

"I am making my depth four hundred feet, three-degree bubble, coming to course three-four-five."

Brandon smiled. Time to show the Soviet captain that tracking the *Manta Ray* was one thing. Trying to sink her was another.

"Engineering reports wire cut, flooding controlled."

There went his communications with Momma Navy.

"Passing two hundred fifty feet."

"Make ready forward tubes one, two, three, and four," Brandon ordered. He was glad now he had ordered the Harpoon missiles in two of the forward tubes replaced with Mark-48 torpedoes.

"Making ready forward tubes one, two, three, and four, aye, sir!" Elliot repeated from the weapons control panel. On the panel in front of the XO, Elliot passed the information to the forward torpedo room.

At the bow of the *Manta Ray,* a deck below the main deck, the men manning the forward torpedo room hurried in their efforts as they thoroughly went through the checklist for battle stations. The checklist covered many of the requirements for firing torpedoes, but the chill bumps and rush of adrenaline with the order to prepare to fire them was unexpected. The American submarine Navy of 1973 was not filled with a lot of underwater warfare experience, though it was thoroughly trained in how it was supposed to be done. But then, the same was true for the Soviet submarine force. The World War II veterans that had led both nations' submarine forces to their current level of readiness and strength had long since retired, with only a few senior officers still at the helm of their services. Gorshkov was one. Zumwalt was not a veteran of World War II; he was the new breed, of Vietnam and the Cold War.

THE tube captain of the *Manta Ray*'s forward torpedo room did a quick sound-powered telephone check with the control room. Satisfied, Petty Officer Carpenter steadied himself at his position between the two banks of torpedoes, his eyes glued to the gauge board. He checked the gauges visually to see if the circuits were functioning. Firing the torpedoes was done by the XO at the weapons control panel in the control room. His job was to fire them manually if the solenoid firing mechanism failed electrically. Like the other five sailors in the compartment, he had the training; he'd had his personnel qualification standards approved, and he had his dolphins. Carpenter knew the *Manta Ray*. Blindfolded he could trace any line, pipe, or valve throughout the boat. With every light out on the boat, Carpenter could walk the boat from one end to the other, locate every critical valve and find every emergency lantern, but even knowing all he knew, like the others on *Manta Ray* he had never fired a torpedo in anger. And in this case, if he had to fire the torpedo it would not be in anger; it would be in fear.

Fear is a hard creature to conquer. It rises from the bowels of men and can be contagious. And Carpenter's fear of revealing that to his fellow shipmates was greater than his fear wondering if he could fire the torpedo if so ordered.

A hand touched his shoulder, causing him to jump slightly. "You'll do fine, Petty Officer Carpenter," Chief Torpedoman Tommy Martin said.

Carpenter nodded. His throat constricted for a few seconds before calm settled over him. "Sure thing, Chief."

"The rest of you listen up," Martin continued. "This is just like training. Step by step, be sure everything is done according to the book, and when the torpedoes are out of the tubes, I'll tell you when we start reloading." He wrinkled his nose. "Remember one thing, my fellow sailors: once those torps are off and running, our job is over. All we have to do is rig the next set like we usually do." The chief paused. "Only a little quicker than usual."

Fear is a contagious force. What keeps fear contained is confidence in what you are doing and knowing the men surrounding you are as competent as you are. Carpenter felt better. The chief could be a pain in the ass, but right now Carpenter would panic if the older man wasn't there. Carpenter had read enough books about the Navy and the military to know the literary concept of men who allowed fear to cause them to run, leaving comrades to die in battle. Men fought because their shipmates fought, and that bond among warriors was stronger than any fear. Carpenter took a deep breath and let it out.

Chief Torpedoman Tommy Martin turned to Carpenter. "Got comms?"

"Yes, Chief."

Martin was the senior enlisted man in the small torpedo room. His job at battle stations was to manually work the manifold of valves and levers if the torpedo tube doors failed to respond to the electrical command to open or close. Carpenter could only fire his torpedoes manually if those tube doors were opened. Tube doors had to be opened from the torpedo room—either electrically or manually. On board the Permit-class submarines, the control room could fire the torpedoes, but the torpedo circuitry would not allow them to be fired if the torpedo tube doors were shut.

Behind the two men, two more sailors stood ready to reload the tubes. The aft hatch opened, and Lieutenant Junior Grade Peter Schaefer entered, quickly latching the watertight door behind him.

"Where are we?" he asked.

Martin quickly brought him up-to-date. Schaefer made sure Control knew they had achieved battle stations.

"FORWARD torpedo room ready in all respects, sir!" Lieutenant Commander Fitzgerald reported from his position near the helm.

"I concur!" Elliot seconded, monitoring the Christmas Tree from the weapons station.

"Very well," Brandon acknowledged. The boat was doing well. Battle station reports had slowed to a trickle, but the critical areas were manned and ready. He glanced at the clock on the bulkhead. He didn't know how long it had taken for them to achieve battle ready status, but the logbook would have the time. He made a mental note to check the time when this was over.

"Passing three hundred feet."

"Easing my rudder," the helmsman reported. "Coming to course three-four-five."

"We had contact!" came a shout through the speaker.

Had? That meant they'd lost it again.

"Control room, this is Sonar. For a fraction of a second we had a noise spike."

"Make your depth three hundred feet," Brandon ordered.

"Making my depth three hundred feet!"

The planesmen, under the watchful eye of the COB, quickly eased the planes of the *Manta Ray* from a downward angle toward a more level one.

"Take her up at three-degree bubble."

Fitzgerald grabbed the nearby sound-powered telephone

talker and instructed the sailor to inform Sonar of what they were doing. The officer-of-the-deck had his hands full driving the boat.

"Steadying up on three-four-five," Fitzgerald reported.

"Very well," Brandon replied.

On the weapons control panel, four green lights glowed, showing the four torpedo tubes were ready, their outer doors still closed, and if Brandon needed, he could launch all four within seconds of his orders. The lights would change to red once the outer doors were opened.

"Steady on three-four-five!" the helmsman shouted.

"Steady on course three-four-five," Fitzgerald relayed.

"Very well," Brandon acknowledged.

"Final trim," came the cry from Master Chief Tay as the planesmen leveled their planes. The boat was at three-hundred-feet depth, level deck beneath everyone's feet, and heading forward at five knots.

The *Manta Ray* was now in position, and Brandon had four loaded torpedoes ready for launch.

"Prepare to fire torpedoes on my command." Brandon's voice sounded more confident than he felt. He was probably the only one on board to have ever fired a torpedo at an enemy vessel, if you could call a North Vietnamese sampan a vessel. What the crew did not need to know was that the torpedo spread, accurately executed and expertly fired, had sailed harmlessly beneath the high-riding North Vietnamese vessel to explode on the beach behind it.

"Control room, Sonar. Torpedoes now bear three-two-zero; signal strength remains constant."

"What do you think, Skipper?" Elliot asked from his position against the aft bulkhead.

"They're searching. Torpedoes are on a left bearing drift. There is not much difference except for accuracy between their torpedoes and ours. They'll run out so far, and if they don't detect a contact, then they'll go into a circular pattern until they either find one or run out of fuel."

Brandon shook his head and shrugged. "Make your course three-two-five, Commander. Let's try to keep us bow-on to the torpedoes. It'll help mask our propellers and keep them out of our baffles. I want to know where they are, so modify your course accordingly, but keep your speed constant for the time being."

The rote of rolling down orders from the skipper echoed through the compartment.

"Twenty thousand yards, you'd think he had us dead to rights," Elliot said.

"I don't know why he fired. Maybe he didn't mean to fire?"

Both men knew better. The Soviets controlled every aspect of life ashore and afloat. No one executed anything without some direct order from above. To do so, they risked Siberia, according to Naval Intelligence. Naval officers studied their adversaries. Knowing weapon performance, tactics, and strategies was important to win a war at sea.

What Brandon failed to appreciate was that the Navy skimmed over the leadership and organizational training of the Soviet Navy. While Brandon knew the weaponry and tactics of the boat he faced, he had little knowledge of the officers and men who manned it. How were they trained? What was the internal organization of the boat? The only thing most U.S. Navy officers knew about the Soviet Navy organization was the presence of *zampolits* on each vessel.

Fitzgerald turned to Brandon and reported, "Final trim; my depth is three hundred feet, sir, speed five knots."

Brandon looked at the clock. The Soviet torpedoes had been running nearly five minutes. Five minutes at a normal speed, and those torpedoes should have covered half the distance to the *Manta Ray*. Every second brought those torpedoes closer to his boat. He glanced at the ASW plotting table and was able to see the chart between the bodies surrounding it. Target motion analysis was more a science than an art and if the team had their distance wrong . . . They didn't. His teams were too good to screw it up, and they had had days to determine the distance.

"Is aft torpedo room prepared with the decoys?"

"Aye, sir," Elliot answered. "We have two ready for dispersal."

"Very well." Brandon looked around the room, and then raised his voice. "Listen up, everyone. Those torpedoes were fired from far out, but they are still coming this way, even if they have a slight left-bearing drift. We have time in our favor, so here is what we are going to do if we have to take evasive action. First and foremost, each of you has to focus on your job. You know what you have to do. You've been trained to do it." He laughed. "Ivan has really screwed the pooch on this one, gents."

A few forced laughs echoed in the compartment.

Several in the control room wished they had run by the head on the way to battle stations.

Brandon started talking, telling the crew what they were going to do; how they would deploy the decoys if needed and how he intended to maneuver the boat to further reduce the ability of those torpedoes to acquire the *Manta Ray*. He told them of his intentions if they decided to return some of their own torpedoes to the Soviet Charlie who had fired first. Then he told them he reserved the right to change everything he had told them and do something different, so they had to be on their toes and ready to execute with perfection, which he had no doubt each of them was capable of doing. Silently, he hoped he did.

Brandon had intrinsic leadership talents; talents others studied through books and classrooms, never quite achieving a level where those talents came naturally. Even if Brandon had been asked why he had said what he'd said when he said it, he doubted he could have told them. But, deep down inside, he knew his words had relaxed the tension a little in the control room.

"Request permission to open torpedo tube doors," Elliot said.

Brandon took a deep breath. It would take several seconds to open the doors. Opening torpedo tube doors created noise in the water. But, then again, they had not heard the Soviet doors open, so maybe the Soviets would not hear theirs.

"Open torpedo tube doors on number one, two and three."

Several seconds passed before Elliot reported the three torpedo doors opened.

Brandon cringed, expecting to hear Sonar announce that the torpedoes had changed direction, that they had detected the torpedo doors opening; but after nearly a half minute with no such word, Brandon pushed one more concern from his list.

The *Manta Ray* was ready. Would he fire if the Soviet torpedoes ran out of fuel and disappeared?

"We have contact again!" the voice of Petty Office Bullet came loud and clear over the speaker.

A second later, Chief Davis came on the speaker. Brandon smiled. He imaged the scene in Sonar, with Davis taking the intercom from Bullet.

"Control room, Sonar. We have regained contact with the Charlie. She bears three-four-zero."

With his arms crossed Lieutenant Strickland watched silently from his position at the TMA plotting table. The sound of trace paper being pulled off the table joined the other background noise in the control room, the battle station team starting their plots again. As more lines of bearing arrived, their solution would become more accurate.

CHIEF Norman opened his eyes. The gauges in front at the throttleman position seemed to waver in and out of clarity. He reached down and rubbed his right side. The last few days he had been having a lot of pain about right there where he pushed his fingers into his side. He had run out of shoe polish the other day and had stolen a bottle of rubbing alcohol from the corpsman. Even mixed with bug juice, it was terrible stuff. He shut his eyes for a moment. The signal would alert him if the captain wanted to change speed again.

"Chief, you okay?" Petty Officer Miller asked.

Norman opened his eyes and looked at the nearby sound-powered phone talker. "If I'm not okay, I'll tell you. Okay?"

"Okay, Chief. I just thought . . . "

"Sailors aren't paid to think," he replied, scrunching up his face as a shot of pain wracked his body. Must be the flimsy two-inch mattresses he was forced to sleep on.

"Sorry."

"Yeah, I bet you are."

Miller slipped the earpiece back on his ear and thought

Screw you, Chief, as he turned his attention away from Norman. *Damn drunk.* The chief's eyes were always red, and while no one smelled the alcohol on him, all the sailors in Engineering knew he had some somewhere. Miller would love to find it, might have a drink himself, but if he found the chief's stash, he was going to piss in it. Might even invite his other friends who'd had to endure the man's wrath and arrogance.

"SIR, you have fired on the Americans!" Lieutenant Commander Lepechin said, his eyes wide.

"They were about to fire on us."

"But they haven't, sir."

"Then it worked, Commander." Bagirli leaned forward, his eyes narrowing. "Are you questioning me?"

Demirchan spoke up, drawing Bagirli's attention to the weapons console. "Sir, the torpedoes are running true. No wires attached."

"Who ordered the wires broken?"

"Sir, the distance was too far away for wire guidance. I recognized from your orders that you would want the best opportunity for a hit. Without wires, the torpedoes will travel faster and go farther, if the American submarine is farther away than we think."

Bagirli started to say something, but didn't. Demirchan was right. No one knew how far away the American was, but a long-range hit would be prestigious. It would earn him the notoriety he so richly deserved.

"Torpedoes are on course one-six-five. Torpedoes one and two are set for one hundred meters. Torpedoes three and four are traveling at two hundred meters. We have a two-degree separation between the four torpedoes, so the farther they travel the wider their search area."

"That is good," Bagirli replied.

"They should bracket the Americans, and if they make sonar contact, then their own fire control will take over and take them into the enemy's boat."

"Good thinking, XO," Bagirli acknowledged. No one understood him or his tactics as well as Demirchan. With the crew turning against him and now Lepechin openly questioning his orders, he needed the loyalty of officers. He wondered again if he should remove the XO from his list.

"Has Sonar regained contact?"

Lepechin passed the question to Sonar. A moment later, he turned to Bagirli and said, "No, sir. They are requesting that we ascend slowly so they can see if the noise quality is better at different levels."

"It would cloud our depth to the Americans," Demirchan added.

"What is our status now?"

"Captain, I make my depth three hundred meters, course one-six-five, speed eight knots."

"Make your depth one hundred fifty meters; maintain current course and speed."

"I am making my depth one hundred fifty meters, speed eight knots, course one-six-five." Lepechin turned to the planesmen. "Three-degree bubble. Slow rise to depth one hundred fifty meters." He turned toward Demirchan at the weapons console. Their eyes met for a moment before Lepechin turned back to driving the boat.

Three minutes passed before Bagirli asked, "Has Sonar regained contact?"

"Sir, they are reporting no joy on contact. They are also reporting no torpedoes."

"And our torpedoes?"

Demirchan answered, "They are still traveling straight and true, sir."

"Range traveled?"

"Approximately five kilometers now, sir." When Bagirli did not reply, Demirchan added, "They have fuel for another ten kilometers, Captain, but they are programmed to go into a search mode in another five minutes."

"Very well."

Search mode would send the four torpedoes in a circular pattern, the fire control sonar in their nose searching for something to attack. Submariners knew that something could even be them if they came within detection range. Bagirli would change the course of the K-321 when the torpedoes began to search.

The quietness of the control room was different. There was always a low level of murmur that rode just below the comprehension range, but there was nothing now. He could have whispered and his crew could have heard him. He liked it.

"Sonar reports no contact," Lepechin reported.

Bagirli nodded, but did not reply. He was enjoying the quietness. It calmed his thoughts. He had fired the torpedoes in a great spread. The American was dead, even if the American was thinking of firing at him, which he was, of course. It was only Bagirli's quick thinking and action that would keep the K-321 from being sunk. He was amazed that only the XO understood why he'd had to fire. The torpedoes would find the American submarine. They had to. And once they did, he would show his crew, the Soviet Northern Submarine Fleet, and his peers which one of them was ready and willing to fight.

"Torpedoes one and four have begun circular search pattern, sir," Lepechin reported.

The torpedoes should not be going into search mode this early, Bagirli told himself. *They should still be going forward until they found the American.*

The internal communications system beeped again. A moment later Lepechin reported the other two torpedoes in search mode.

Search mode meant they would run out of fuel in three minutes or less. His shots had been for naught.

"The Americans may have picked up the torpedoes," Demirchan said.

Bagirli looked at him but said nothing.

"Recommend we reduce speed, Captain, and wait here until the torpedoes detect the American."

Sweat dripped into his eyes, causing Bagirli to wipe his brow. His XO was right. To keep going forward risked endangering the K-321 with its own torpedoes.

"Make your speed three knots; continue to one hundred fifty meters," he muttered, but in the quiet of the control room his voice carried easily. Maybe he should go to periscope depth? But if he did, the *zampolit* would want to transmit his messages, and what would he achieve by that?

"Making my speed three knots, maintaining course one-six-five, passing two hundred meters, three-degree bubble."

Bagirli glanced toward the helmsman and the planesman positions. Chief of the Boat Zimyatov expressionlessly met his gaze for a moment, before turning back to the gauges above the planesmen.

"TORPEDOES are in search mode, Captain," Fitzgerald reported.

"Direction?"

"They bear two-eight-zero, sir."

"Very well. Maintain speed and depth, but keep the torpedoes at a relative bearing off our forward port quarter. I don't want to give them a better noise opportunity by exposing our props to them."

"Aye, sir." Fitzgerald turned to the helmsman, pulled the sound-powered phone talker closer to him, and began translating the bearings from Sonar into course changes for the *Manta Ray*.

Brandon walked over to the weapons console, where Elliot stood.

"Your thoughts?"

Elliot shrugged. "Not sure. The Soviet skipper has to know his torps failed, or are about to fail."

"He should have fired another salvo by now. You know what I think?"

Elliot nodded, and a slight upward tug on the left side of his lip returned a half smile. "He doesn't know where we are."

Brandon's grin spread over his entire face and his eyes lit up. "He doesn't know where we are. How dumb is that?"

"What should we do?"

"We have the advantage. Right now, I think he is slowing down waiting for his torpedoes to stop their circular search mode. Be a hell of a thing to explain to Moscow how you managed to sink your own boat."

"We might be able to get behind him."

Brandon turned. "Commander Fitzgerald. Contact status, if you please."

A second later, the officer of the deck replied, "Sonar holds the contact bearing three-four-zero."

"He's maintaining his course. No zigging or zagging," Elliot said. "We could wait for him."

"We could. I would like to have a little bearing drift so we don't wait for him to come down our throat. A ramming at sea is bad, but one beneath the surface is worse."

Elliot forced a grin. "Of course, we could move away, vacate the area, and report the incident to Second Fleet."

"You could be right. Most likely we should. But, you know something, XO, what if we do and our adversary detects us? Going shallow really creates noise in the water that spreads in all directions."

Elliot nodded, knowing Brandon was exaggerating.

"Okay, XO." Brandon sighed. "We'll go up for morning communications, though with the wire cut, I doubt we'll be able to establish any communications."

"Aye, sir."

"But before we do, I want to get behind this asshole that tried to sink us. That way, when we do go to periscope depth, we'll be in his baffles. That should help mask our noise."

"We could come to an all stop. Keep just enough forward motion to hold us steady."

Brandon thought for a moment. He had always been a commander who believed in quick maneuvers to get in position, but in this instance the target was coming to him. "Good idea, XO. If there is any sinking to be done, then we are going to be the ones to do it." He turned to Fitzgerald and gave the orders. *Manta Ray* was going silent—deadly silent.

ELEVEN

THE first arms shipment via El Al began to arrive at Lod Airport in Tel Aviv. The amount was insufficient to replace the munitions Israel was expending against the combined armies of Syria and Egypt. The Israeli Army had now reached full strength through the rapid mobilization of its reserves.

The armor needed to reinforce the front lines was moving out—heading north toward Syria and west toward Egypt—engaging and defeating the Arab armies. But even with the Israeli victories, the Israeli government knew that without the necessary materials to wage a sustained battlefront, Israel had little choice but to hope for a quick victory against the onslaught.

A major loss now would find them once again fighting a retreat. A retreat with nowhere to go but into the sea, where the former Egyptian tyrant Gamal Abdel Nasser had many times threatened to push them.

The United States Air Force preparations for a gigantic Berlin-like airlift from the United States, taking United States war-fighting reserve munitions and weapons to the

Israelis, was making the admirals and generals nervous. Those reserves were earmarked for the eventual battle with the Soviet Union.

Air Force C-141, C-5, and the already vintage C-130 transports were idling on the airfields near the strategic arsenals that held the missiles, weapons, and munitions capable of sustaining a major war for thirty days. Thirty days is such little time when you are fighting a foe the size of the Soviet Union. In thirty days, Soviet armies could reach the English Channel. In thirty days America could run out of the reserves it needed to carry the battle to the Soviet homeland.

"CHIEF, you okay?" Miller asked, glancing at the clock on the bulkhead behind them. "We've been at battle stations for over three hours."

Norman raised his head off his chest. His head hurt, screaming at him, begging him to shut his eyes again. "I'm okay, I've told you. You're not listening?"

"I thought you were asleep."

"Chiefs don't fall asleep," he slurred slightly.

Miller opened his mouth to say something, but then shrugged and went back to being bored. Four more months and he was history. He wouldn't have to put up with asshole chief petty officers like Norman anymore.

Miller took a deep breath and stepped away from the gauges and Norman. He pulled a pack of chewing gum from his pocket and slipped a stick into his mouth. Gum was illegal on most submarines. Sailors chewed it and then would stick it most anywhere, though the underside of the tables in the crew's mess was the usual receptacle for the discarded gum. The taller members of the crew learned the hard way about how hard gum was to get out of dungarees when their knees brushed against the fresh stuff beneath the tables.

Norman blinked his eyes several times. Here lately he had been having these bright spots springing up in his vision. The doc told him yesterday he might be having migraines. It had been while the corpsman was in the next compartment counting out aspirin for him that he had slipped a bottle of rubbing alcohol into his jacket. This morning he had taken some bug juice and mixed a shot of the stuff with it. "Horrid" was the word that came to mind. Norman forced a grin across his pallid lips—but the drink had packed a hell of a kick. He pulled his handkerchief from his pocket and wiped his eyes. He failed to see the dark smears across the white cloth as he wadded it up and jammed it weakly into his back pocket. But in the red light of the compartment, blood would have been a dark black.

Norman sighed. He checked the gauges. Two knots speed. Just enough to keep the boat level and hovering in the water—talk about a final trim. Like some giant sperm whale— he laughed. *Now that's apropos,* he wanted to say, but for some reason he couldn't make the words come forth.

"You say something, Chief?"

"I said, that's what the *Manta Ray* is," he garbled.

"What? I didn't understand a word you said, Chief."

Norman growled.

Miller's forehead wrinkled. If he ever decided to make the Navy a career—and it would be a cold day in hell before he did—he would never understand chief humor. "That's really funny, Chief."

Norman turned.

Miller's eyes widened.

"What's a matter?" Norman asked with a smile.

"Nothing," he said, trying to keep his voice calm. It was the red light, he told himself. The man's eyes had disappeared into his sockets like black pits with no bottom.

Miller shivered at the slender dark trickles that lined the sides of Norman's face. Just what he needed. To be stuck in the engine room with a zombie. He had seen *Messiah of Evil* before they departed Norfolk, with its living dead people. Norman reminded him of the movie. Miller glanced toward the watertight door and edged closer to it. It would be double-bad if Norman was one of the living dead, because he was a chief also.

Norman's headache crashed outward like shards of glass, causing him to clinch his eyes tight. More blood vessels erupted around his eyes and in his eyeballs. They itched and burned. The tinge of his skin had turned a sallow color during the evening, and the red light hid that well also. He took a deep breath and leaned back in the chair.

Miller moved closer to the watertight door. If Norman stood up, he was out of there. This might be his duty station, but he'd be damned if he was going to die at the hands of a madman, a chief who was a dead man. Wow! Wait until he told the other sailors.

Norman never knew what hit him. During the day the rubbing alcohol had reached a saturated liver with such impact that the cirrhosis already killing the vital organ soared forward. Impurities that the organ would normally have kicked out of the body had been building up. Between cigarettes, alcohol, and lack of exercise—you name it, Norman had or hadn't done it.

The detection of the Soviet Charlie-class had shoved everyone's thoughts in a different direction, so for the past couple of days, Master Chief Tay had not bothered him about the money. But eventually the man would want to know where it was. That was his last thought as his heart picked up beats, racing forward for several seconds before fluttering a few times and then stopping. He lived for a few seconds more, unable to call for help or move a muscle.

Norman absorbed impassively the loss of feeling through his body. His thoughts began to twinkle out. There was no white light at the end of the tunnel; there were no family members waiting. One moment he was a living, breathing human, and the next he was just a hunk of meat beginning to decay.

Behind Norman, Miller saw the chief jump slightly before the man's head tilted forward a little. No way was he going to bother the man. If the control room called and he had no choice, he would. He glanced at the gauges. He didn't understand them fully, even though he was working on his dolphins. Though he didn't understand why he was working on them, since he was going to finish these last few months and hit the beach.

Back to Chatham County, Georgia, back to Stephanie—if she still remembered him, as she hadn't written for the two years he had been in. Last time in Savannah, she had had a hair appointment and so was unable to go out with him. He was going to get himself a job down at the piers. His time in the Navy ought to count for something. Maybe he'd even use the GI Bill and go off to college. Of course, he'd have to finish high school first. Miller basked in his daydreams, leaning against the bulkhead as the boat hovered at one hundred fifty feet. Like most junior sailors, he had no idea what the officers were doing. Basically he didn't care, but as long as the chief stayed asleep and no one bothered him, he was satisfied, if not happy.

"STATUS?" Brandon asked, stepping back into the control room after a quick trip to the head. When he entered, a mess cook stood near the watertight hatch and handed him a fresh cup of coffee. "Thanks," he said.

"My course is three-four-zero, speed two knots making way, and depth is one hundred fifty feet, sir."

"Very well. And our contact?"

"Still bears three-four-five, sir. Constant bearing."

"Okay, lets put a five-degree left rudder on, Mr. Fitzgerald, and start getting a right-hand bearing drift on Ivan. I want to ease behind the Charlie, not have him crash into us."

"Aye, sir. Right five-degree rudder!"

"Five-degree rudder, aye," the helmsman acknowledged.

Brandon, Fitzgerald, Elliot over at the weapons console, and Master Chief Tay, hovering continuously over the planesman, watched the small shift of the wheel as the petty officer turned the *Manta Ray*.

"Make your course three-three-five."

"Aye, sir. Making my course three-three-five," Fitzgerald echoed before directing his orders to the helmsman. "Steady up on course three-three-five."

At the TMA plotting table, the sailors cleared the trace paper off and laid a fresh sheet. As soon as the *Manta Ray* steadied on its new course, the target-motion-analysis team would start a new geometric pattern. The old data from the prior sheet was quickly written in pencil in the corner of the paper. With luck and data, the team might be able to fathom the exact location of the enemy submarine. Of course, depth was a different issue all together.

The helmsman started to ease his rudder. Brandon sipped his coffee from a position slightly behind Fitzgerald, while the operations officer watched the compass steady onto course three-three-five.

"Steady on three-three-five," the helmsman announced.

Fitzgerald repeated the petty officer's announcement, and Brandon acknowledged the report. At the navigation station, the quartermaster notated the course change.

"Check with Sonar and make sure they still have contact," Brandon said.

He moved toward his chair and set his cup in the holder. He thought about letting the crew take a head break. He glanced at the Christmas Tree and saw a light blink quickly from green to red. The sailors were already making up their own minds about the head break.

"XO, Commander Fitzgerald, if you please," Brandon said, motioning the men to him.

"Here are my thoughts about the next phase of this plan of ours," he said when they reached him. "The Charlie isn't going to come right. If he has us, I think we'll see him start maneuvering the closer he gets. At this range, I don't think he'll fire again. He's probably more nervous about his torpedoes than we are. We're going to continue on this course. The torpedoes he fired are long dead now. When the bearings from Sonar show us the Charlie is passing our bow, we will make slight left-hand turns. Left-hand turns to put us behind it, on its stern, and keep our stern away from his hydrophones."

"How long do you think that will take, sir?" Fitzgerald asked.

"That depends on how far away it is. It was about ten miles when he fired those torpedoes."

"Why did he do that?" Elliot asked, his face betraying bemusement.

"Why does anyone do anything precipitously? Because one," Brandon said, holding up his index finger, "he had bad targeting data, or two," the second finger went up, "he got nervous."

"Scared?"

"Don't know, XO. But he fired, and he shouldn't have. Bad decision at the very least."

"Maybe his torpedo room fired without his orders?"

Brandon shook his head. "You could be right, Mike," he said to Fitzgerald. "But if the firing was accidental, then why is he continuing on a closing course? If he was scared, then he'd be running. No, this captain isn't scared. It wasn't accidental. He fired on purpose. If it had been one torpedo, then maybe I could see it being an accidental firing. But then he should be turning away, getting out of the area, going to periscope depth to report the incident while he can." Brandon shrugged. "At least that is what I would have done."

"Then he is leaving us little choice," Elliot added.

Brandon grinned and shook his head. "He has left us with all the choices. We know where he is. He has a broad concept of where we are. He does not have our range," Brandon held up crossed fingers, "and I would bet you that right now he doesn't have us on his passive sonar."

"WHERE is the American?" Bagirli demanded, his voice filling the control room. "Get me Lieutenant Kiselyov back here now!"

"Sir, he is at battle stations," Demirchan cautioned.

For a moment Bagirli glared at his XO, but then he seemed to relax. "I know, XO, but he is so new to Sonar that Chief Starshina Luzhkov is really running it. I want to ensure he knows the importance of maintaining a tight rein . . . " He looked back at Lepechin. "What did I say? Get Lieutenant Kiselyov back here now," Bagirli repeated, emphasizing each word.

Lepechin quickly repeated the order into the ship intercom system.

Bagirli turned back to Demirchan. "XO, you are the only officer on board who understands that we are at war with the Americans. We must not let the enemy get away, and the only way we can find and destroy him is if our stupid Sonar can maintain some semblance of professionalism and track the bastard."

The forward watertight door opened and Lieutenant Kiselyov entered, securing the door behind him. "Captain, you sent for me, sir?"

"Yes, I did, Lieutenant. How long have you been the sonar officer?"

"Since Monday, sir, when I relieved Lieutenant Iltchenko."

"And are you comfortable with the position, Lieutenant?"

"Sir, there is a lot to learn."

"And you are learning it."

"Sir, if I may, right now I would feel more comfortable in the torpedo room—the forward torpedo room, sir."

"That is where Lieutenant Iltchenko—"

"Sir, we moved him to Engineering," Demirchan said.

"Then who is in the forward torpedo room?"

"We have Chief Starshina Ortoff."

"The Finn?"

Demirchan started to reply.

"We have an enlisted person in the forward torpedo room? Who is the officer that is supposed to be there?"

"Sir, I could go there," Lieutenant Kiselyov volunteered.

Bagirli looked at the taller officer. *What to do?* he asked himself. *I am trying to sink the American and I have no forward torpedo room officer? Everyone is against me.*

"Sir, if I may suggest, we should send Lieutenant Kiselyov to the forward torpedo room now."

"And Sonar? Who will run Sonar?"

"Sir, we are at battle stations. When your decision to relieve Iltchenko was made, we did not expect to have to fight an underwater battle. We are now in one. If I may suggest, regardless of his problems in leadership, he has the most experience in Sonar."

Bagirli nodded. "That makes sense, XO. Tell Engineering to send Lieutenant Iltchenko to Sonar." He turned to Kiselyov. "And what are you waiting for, Lieutenant? Get to the forward torpedo room and help me sink our enemy."

Kiselyov grinned, and his shoulders lifted as if a massive

weight had been taken from them. "Yes, sir, I will, and you will not be disappointed."

The watertight door clanged shut behind the junior officer as Kiselyov hurried forward toward familiar territory. The man's enthusiasm grated on Bagirli, but the safety and success of K-321 might depend on that very quality. The fact that the torpedoes had missed was more the fault of the team doing the passive noise analysis than his. He would never have fired if they had known the true range, but it was a firing in self-defense. Obvious to him and it should be to the others. If he had not fired those torpedoes, the Americans would have fired. The fact that no American torpedoes were fired proved that his tactic worked.

A moment later Iltchenko walked through the aft watertight door to be met by the XO. Bagirli moved away so he would not have to watch this officer who was most responsible for the problems he was facing now. "Don't think you are getting away with it," he mumbled aloud.

The aft watertight door opened again, and a steward from the officers mess entered carrying a tray filled with hot tea. At least someone on this boat knew what he was doing. Bagirli took the first tea, thanked the starshina, and while he sipped, his eyes trailed Iltchenko as the disgraced sonar officer returned to Sonar.

His eyes and Demirchan's locked for a moment when the forward watertight door shut. Demirchan nodded and returned to the weapons control station. Bagirli wondered what was going on in his XO's mind. He wondered for a moment if the XO was truly concerned for Bagirli's vision for the K-321 or even understood how his future was directly tied to Bagirli.

"Contact status?"

Lepechin flipped on the intercom system and requested an update.

Bagirli took a deep breath. The compartment smelled heavily of human sweat, riding the soft breeze created from the background hum of the circulating system. It was an odor not uncommon among submariners. Only when the boat surfaced and brought fresh air from the outside did most notice the change.

Demirchan walked up to the raised periscope deck, where Bagirli sipped his coffee. "They were the new torpedoes, Comrade Captain."

Bagirli nodded. "The torpedoes are the new fifty-three sixty-fives, XO. We fired them for fast speed, for defense against the imminent attack by the Americans."

"Yes, sir, but we had no range on the enemy."

Bagirli glared at Demirchan for a moment. "And for that we have our expert sonar team to thank," he replied sharply but in a whisper. "At fast speed they would have been traveling over sixty-five knots."

"This limits their range to ten kilometers. The American is more than that from us. We know that now."

"If we had fired at the slow speed . . ."

"The American might have had time to fire his own spread," Demirchan offered. "You made the right decision."

Bagirli needed to hear that. He needed to know that someone on this ill-crewed boat understood tactics as well as he did. "Do you have a suggestion, XO?"

"Sir, we have to assume the enemy heard the torpedoes. We have to assume he used decoys, though we did not hear them . . ."

If we had a good sonar team we would have heard them, Bagirli told himself. He had not thought of them missing something as noisy as a decoy until Demirchan mentioned it. *And now I have Iltchenko back in there with the rest of the misfits.*

" . . . and he is attempting to do one of two things."

"One or two? Why not more?"

"Captain, it may be more, but when torpedoes are coming toward you, you can take evasive maneuvers and leave the area, or you can evade the torpedoes and start maneuvering your boat for your own best firing position."

"They don't know where we are."

"They may have a better sonar team."

"Any team is a better sonar team," Bagirli said, his voice slightly louder.

Several heads turned inside the control room, including Lepechin and Zimyatov's. They glanced at the two men briefly before returning to their gauges. Zimyatov slapped the back of the heads of the planesmen and pointed at the gauges.

"I would submit, Comrade Captain, that the Americans are not known for evading and leaving."

"Good. When we get within range, we will fire again. Have the tubes been reloaded?"

"Yes, sir. They are reloaded, with number one tube being the only one not loaded."

"Why is that?"

"A slight problem with the hydraulic pressure to close the outer door. The torpedo room expects to have the problem fixed shortly."

"Good. Let me know when it is fixed, and find out why I was not told when it occurred."

"Sir, as for the Americans, we are not zigging, zagging, or changing our depth. If I may make the suggestion, we should start our own defensive maneuvers."

"It will further complicate sonar passive analysis of their signals."

"We do not have any contact right now, sir. If we maneuver, we might be able to gain an advantage against them, move into position where their noises appear to Sonar."

Bagirli thought for a couple of seconds and realized the XO was right. "I would want to orient any changes in course to our base course. We still have our primary mission of denying access to the Mediterranean to any American forces deploying there."

"I agree, sir."

Several seconds passed.

"Sir, would you like me to give the tactical commands?"

Bagirli's lower lip pressed upward for a few seconds as he pondered the reason why the XO would want to take those powers, but then he visibly relaxed. He would be listening and able to stop any unconventional or dangerous orders his number two officer might give.

"Very well, XO, but remember my caution."

"Yes, sir."

* * *

"THANKS, Rex. I value your advice."

The Director of Naval Intelligence shook Ellison's hand and left quickly through the door. There was much to do based on what the Chief of the Naval Operations wanted. Ellison's aide watched until Admiral Rectanus was outside the office, before responding to the boss's motion to him.

"You called, sir?" Captain Mulligan said. There was an ease of familiarity between the two Naval officers that had been earned through several tours together.

"Harvey, contact CINCLANT Fleet. We are moving forward with our plan. Bring me the latest data on the *Manta Ray* and her communications ability."

"She still has contact?"

Ellison glanced at the clock. "According to Admiral Rectanus, she still had contact nearly twenty-four hours ago."

"That's a long time in ASW action, Admiral."

Ellison nodded. "Submariners are notoriously bad communicators. If they had their way, the only way they would talk with us is by letter."

Mulligan nodded in acknowledgment. "The only problem we know, sir, is the casualty to their wire antenna. It's still trailing out about a hundred feet behind her."

"I know and they know and I'd be surprised if the Russians don't know, but sometime tonight someone is going to want to talk with Commander Brandon."

Mulligan nodded. "We still have the ELF communications prototype up in Michigan. I hear that with the right power and frequency it can talk with anyone anywhere."

"And the farmers up there say it's stopping their cows from giving milk."

"It's nearly the weekend. The farmers should be off."

Ellison's busy eyebrows bunched. "Harvey, we have got to get you outside the office a little more."

"KEEP her on a steady trim," Brandon said.

"Sonar reports a slow right bearing drift on the contact, sir."

"Rudder?"

"Still two-degree starboard, Captain," Fitzgerald acknowledged. "We're keeping our bow toward the target."

Elliot walked over to Fitzgerald and whispered something. The operations officer nodded.

Elliot raised his head and announced, "I have the conn."

Fitzgerald announced, "Commander Elliot has the conn. My course is three-two-zero, speed four knots, right two-degree rudder, depth one hundred fifty feet."

"Very well," Elliot said, then he turned to Brandon. "Sir, I have the conn."

"Very well. Maintain your current course, speed, and depth."

A moment later, Fitzgerald was through the aft watertight door. Brandon had been allowing the men a few at a time to take a ten minute comfort break, but no flushing of the toilets, which meant the assortment of human odors that filled a fighting submarine was going to take on new meaning for the next few hours. Flushing a toilet in a submarine required that the sailor know the right process and execute it in the right order. It also meant not being seated on the john when they cleared the tanks.

The Soviet Charlie-class had been slowly approaching the *Manta Ray* for over two hours. It was nearly one o'clock in the morning. The crew was hungry. They were tired. Sitting, standing—it didn't matter; the inability of moving around and other things was fatiguing to the crew. But Brandon needed to have the Charlie off his nose and know that the *Manta Ray* was in the submarine's baffles before he started securing the crew. He was taking a chance giving them this ten-minute break, but better the smells emanating from the heads than from every battle station on the *Manta Ray*.

DOWN in the throttle room, Miller was dancing from one leg to the other. Norman was asleep. That was easy to tell. The man was a drunk, and wherever he was getting his booze, he was having one hell of a sleep-off. He'd tell someone, but all that would do is get him put in the firing hairs of the chiefs.

Getting the goat locker on your ass was not a career-enhancing thing. It also tended to impact getting your liberty chit. He shut his eyes for a moment, thinking of that Moroccan honey in Rota, Spain. Last year—*ten dollars*—a pussy that could milk you dry without you having to do a thing but moan. He had saved several ten-dollar bills for the Rota visit, and with Radio having its antenna problems, *Manta Ray* might be there for several days. Sleep he could get once the submarine got under way again.

"Chief, they're letting everyone go to the heads. I'm going to go, or do you want to go first?"

No answer.

Well, he had done his duty. He had asked. Miller told the control room of his intentions, took off his sound-powered headset, and left the throttle compartment.

Eleven minutes later he returned, checked in with the control room, and was chewed out for being a minute late and not having anyone answer. He started to tell the petty officer on the other end about Norman, but then decided to hell with him. Why should he say anything to the asshole first class? The man had just chewed him out for being a minute late. There'd been a line and the head stank to high heaven.

He pulled out a stool and sat down. He had even lain down for a moment on the hard deck, but when Norman said nothing and Miller woke suddenly to discover he had dozed off for nearly five minutes, he stood up. Norman might get away with napping, but newly minted third class petty officers became seamen again and found themselves doing shitty jobs, and after his quick visit to the head, he knew what the job would be.

There were certain things about the Navy a sailor learned in his first four years. One of those was that being a third class petty officer was the best pay grade in the Navy. You were high enough they didn't give you any shitty details and low enough they didn't give you any responsibilities.

"SHE'S easing past our starboard quarter, sir. Rapid bearing drift."

"Range to contact?" Brandon asked, looking at the TMA team.

"We hold her less than four nautical miles, sir."

"Mr. Fitzgerald, increase your rudder four degrees."

Brandon listened as the officer of the deck executed his order. What he needed was to be in a position where the Soviet Charlie was dead-on to the bow of the *Manta Ray* with no bearing drift. This would mean they were in the Charlie's baffles.

The clock on the bulkhead showed zero two hundred hours. They had been at battle stations since yesterday afternoon. Another hour and he should be able to secure from battle stations.

"Sir, Sonar reports the bearing drift is picking up speed and the lines of bearings have less separation."

"Shit!" Brandon said. The Soviet skipper had changed course or speed or both. He would be in *Manta Ray*'s baffles in a few minutes unless Brandon did something.

"Increase speed to eight knots, but do it slowly."

"He may have picked us up," Elliot offered.

He should not have been so quick to let the crew have a comfort break, but alternatives are too late once the die is cast.

Fitzgerald went through the chain of repeating the order. The command went from the control room to the engineering room to the throttle compartment.

MILLER saw the command echo up on the gauges.

Ah, shit, he thought. *I'm going to have to wake Norman. Why not just leave it at two knots?*

"NO response," Fitzgerald said. He grabbed the handset and buzzed Engineering, then talked rapidly into the mouthpiece for a few seconds before hanging up. "Sir, no response from the throttle compartment."

"MILLER, what the hell is going on down there?" the voice screamed into his ear.

He wasn't going to the brig or to clean those heads for Norman. "The chief's asleep."

"Well, wake him."

Miller reluctantly stepped forward and touched Norman on the shoulder. Nothing. He touched him again. Still no response. He reached forward a third time and shook the shoulder roughly while trying to ignore the screaming in his ears. "Chief, wake up! Wake up!"

Norman rolled to the side and fell onto the deck.

"Shit, man, muther fuck!" Miller screamed, using the common Navy expletive several times as he backed up.

"What's going on?"

"He's dead or something!"

"Who's dead?"

"Chief Norman!"

By the time two of the engineers from a compartment away arrived, all they found was Norman's body on the deck and a discarded sound-powered telephone outfit nearby. Chief West, the daytime engineering officer of the watch slid into Norman's seat, but only for a second before jumping up.

Dead people void their body fluids, and it took several seconds of cursing before Chief West reached forward and increased the speed to eight knots.

"What you want to do with the body, Chief?" the first class asked.

"Roll it over to the other side and take over the sound-powered position. Tell Mr. Fitzgerald we have remanned the throttle compartment with one casualty: Chief Norman."

The first class was still fiddling with the sound-powered telephone outfit as the ship began to pick up speed.

"HE'S behind us, sir," Fitzgerald reported.

"Belay my order. No increase in speed. Make your speed two knots. I want just enough way to keep us at a hover."

Before the order could be executed, Brandon felt the slight increase of power as the *Manta Ray* picked up speed, heading toward eight knots. Behind the submarine, the noise of the propellers was amplified as the disturbed ocean water ricocheted away from the props.

A submarine moving at a constant speed maintained a constant disturbance behind it, but when speed increased that disturbance increased, as if the ship were climbing a big hill, until the new speed settled itself.

"Make your course zero-niner-zero, maintain eight knots," Brandon countered his order again. He had no choice. He must stick with eight knots, and he had to muffle the noise the *Manta Ray* had just jolted into the water. If Ivan didn't hear this one, then he must have a team of deaf men for his Sonar.

TWELVE

"CAPTAIN!" Lepechin shouted. "Sonar has regained contact! Enemy bears two-two-five with rapid right bearing drift and is in a turn. Noise signature is weak."

Bagirli jumped, hot tea spilling on his hand. He had not expected Sonar to regain contact. "Very well," he said, his mind racing. The American was near. *How near?* Near enough that his bearing drift was quick, shifting right, which meant the American was trying to get behind them. Bagirli glanced at the weapons control panel. He had to fire torpedoes again, but he needed to know how close the American was.

"Weapons status?" he shouted.

"Forward torpedo door one is still open. It is the only tube unloaded. The other five doors are closed," Demirchan reported. "Aft tubes have torpedoes in tubes one, two, and three. Tubes four, five, and six have decoys."

"Commander Lepechin, bring K-321 right, three-degree rudder. Maintain your current depth and speed." Bagirli was surprised how calm his voice sounded, but he was the captain, and a captain must stay calm even as his heart raced.

"Aye, Comrade Captain."

The aft watertight door opened and the *zampolit* entered, whistling. "Good morning, everyone," Volkov said jovially as he worked his bulk past a couple of sailors at the plotting table.

"Lieutenant," Demirchan said, "please hold your voice down. We are in close contact with the American."

Volkov brought a pudgy finger to his lips and nodded in acknowledgment. "Aye, XO."

The K-321 tilted slightly to the right as the boat responded to the small rudder change.

"Tell me if Sonar is able to increase its signal strength on the enemy," Bagirli ordered.

Lepechin leaped to the task. Tension rose in the control room as the Soviet Project 670–class submarine started a maneuver to close the enemy.

"Sir, do you want to increase speed?" Demirchan asked.

"No!" Bagirli snapped. *Stay calm.* He took a deep breath. "We don't know how close we are to the contact." With this crew, the K-321 might sink the American by ramming it.

"Sonar says signal strength constant, Comrade Captain."

"Very well, Commander Lepechin. Tell Sonar we are going to increase our rate of turn. They are to tell us when the signal strength increases and then starts to fade. They are to keep a running report on the bearing to the contact."

Lepechin nodded and once again jerked up the handset. A moment later he jammed the handset back into its seat and reported Sonar's acknowledgment.

The tension in the compartment was strong. No one spoke. Everyone focused on his console and gauges. The strong, potent odors from humans forced together for days beneath the sea had long ago ceased to be noticed. Unlike on the *Manta Ray*, Bagirli had not shut down the toilets, and it was at this time that an unknown starshina decided to flush.

"IVAN is in a turn, sir," Fitzgerald announced. "Right-hand turn; we have a rapid right bearing drift. Looks as if he is trying to get in our baffles . . . "

"As we are trying to get in his," Brandon finished. It was a good plan, but the failure of Engineering to put the speed on when he'd needed it had cost the *Manta Ray* the element of surprise. What now? If he turned left, he would expose his stern to the enemy and lose sonar contact, and Ivan had already shown he would attack.

"Rapid right bearing drift, sir."

He took a deep breath. "Right full-degree rudder, Mr. Fitzgerald. Increase speed to fifteen knots."

"Fifteen knots?"

Brandon glared at his officer of the deck. "Now is not the time to question my orders unless they endanger the boat. I want a full-right rudder and simultaneous speed increase to fifteen knots! And make your depth one hundred feet." If Ivan wanted to play circle the wagons, then he'd give him a stampede to deal with.

The *Manta Ray* picked up speed almost instantly. The nuclear reactor never changed a gauge in its ability to provide power when required. It just needed to be told.

"Sonar reports loss of contact," Fitzgerald said. "Wait! Wait! They have something."

Brandon nodded. He knew they would, but he needed to get the *Manta Ray* in a better position. Right now, Ivan had the better tactical position though neither was in position to fire. *What's your depth, you bastard?*

Behind the *Manta Ray* a slight knuckle emerged. Water churned for a few seconds, sending tendrils of noise emanating from it.

"Sonar picked up a toilet flushing on board the contact! That toilet bears one-six-five true!"

Lieutenant Strickland and his TMA team bent over the plotting table.

The fact that the boat was increasing its speed would not be lost on the Soviets. He might even get them to fire their torpedoes prematurely again, but this time, he knew exactly where they were.

A few seconds later, Strickland raised his head. "Gold Team holds the contact bearing one-six-five range two thousand yards at eight knots."

"Two thousand yards?" Brandon asked. "Sonar said they had them increasing speed."

"The faster the speed, Skipper, the closer the contact."

Brandon knew that. And the slower the speed, the farther out it could be, but the rapid bearing drift indicated the two submarines were close to each other.

"Prepare to fire. Weapons status?"

Elliot turned to the weapons console. "Six forward tubes armed and ready; tubes one, two, and three opened and ready for firing. Back tubes still closed, with tubes three and four holding decoys. Recommend opening aft tubes one through four."

"Very well, open aft tubes one through four," Brandon said. He reached up and grabbed hold of one of the pipes running through the compartment. His hand grasped and relaxed as the tension grew. Increasing speed was a risky maneuver. If Ivan didn't have him located now, he needed to fire his sonar team.

"Aft tubes one through four open!" Elliot shouted.

At the navigation table, the battle station quartermaster was rapidly making log entries of the commands bouncing around the compartment. In neat but quick flourishes, the pencil flew across the page, marking the time when the aft torpedo tubes were reported open. A bead of sweat dropped on the page, bringing a quiet "damn" from the sailor.

"Make your speed five knots, come to course one-eight-zero." Time to figure out how astute his adversary was. How good was Ivan's Sonar? "Prepare to launch decoy."

"Decoy ready for launch."

There should be a good-size knuckle in the water after that fifteen-knot turn.

"THE American has increased his rate of turn, sir!" Lepechin announced, his voice steady, loud, and firm. "Means he has—"

"Increased his speed or we are closer than we think," Bagirli finished. A rush of adrenaline filled his body. This was what he was meant to do. His life was meant for this moment.

"Give me full-right rudder, decrease speed to four knots, and make your depth one hundred meters." If the American thought he could panic the K-321, he did not know Bagirli.

Several crewmembers licked their lips and exchanged glances. Demirchan and Lepechin looked at each other, their eyes meeting for a moment. Volkov's whistle seemed a little shakier. The *zampolit* worked his way as innocuously as he could toward the navigator position near the forward bulkhead. The apologies he whispered as he bumped into sailor after sailor joined the other background noise in the compartment.

"Sonar reports contact bearing three-five-five. The American is in a right turn, sir."

"Making my depth one hundred meters, three-degree up bubble, full-right rudder, sir!" Lepechin announced.

"He's trying to get behind us," Demirchan added.

"I know," Bagirli agreed. He reached up and grabbed an overhead pipe. His hand gripped and relaxed, repeating the gesture over and over. What to do? He was in no position to fire. But he had to do something. Every action required some sort of response. "Decoy status?"

"Decoys loaded in aft tubes one and two, sir," Demirchan reported.

"Open outer doors on aft tubes."

"Sir?"

Bagirli glared at Demirchan. "I said: open outer doors on aft tubes."

"Opening outer doors," Demirchan reported.

Bagirli knew the risk he was taking. The American might detect the torpedo doors opening. The American would not know there were only decoys behind them and might think the K-321 was preparing to fire again.

He amended his order. "Open all aft torpedo doors,"

"Opening all aft torpedo doors," Demirchan answered.

If the American fired when he heard the doors opening, then Bagirli wanted the ability to defend the boat. He grinned. The American was not going to fire. They were both going in a right-hand circle, trying to get into the baffles of each other. Like a never-ending merry-go-round, waiting for the other to dismount first. He wondered for a moment what his counterpart on the American submarine was thinking.

"SIR, Sonar reports loss of contact."

"Make your speed three knots," Brandon ordered, and before waiting for a reply, he turned to Elliot. "XO, launch a decoy."

"Aye, sir." Elliot turned to the weapons control console and hit the aft torpedo tube number three red button.

In the aft torpedo room, the canister shot out of the torpedo tube, the compressed air sending it about fifty feet before the water slowed the instrument. Then the decoy began generating the noises of submarine propellers as the *Manta Ray* moved away from the decoy that was generating imitation noises as if it were a submarine.

"Passing six knots, making my speed three knots, sir."

Strickland crossed his arms again, reached out, and shook his head when the first class petty officer started to rip the trace paper away from the plotting table. Instead, the senior petty officer leaned down and began to erase the lines of bearing they had, leaving the last plotted location of the contact along with course and speed on the paper.

"If we are right, the very first line of bearing will cut through the contact course. If we aren't," Strickland said softly, "then we will know its speed."

"SONAR reports the contact has further increased its speed and we now have a constant bearing on it, sir!" Lepechin said, his voice filling the control room.

"Increase your rudder to full," Bagirli ordered. He had to know. Was the American running? Seemed to be. If the American was pointed right at him, his Sonar would never have heard the propellers. His Sonar could not find a bag of shit in an outhouse, much less track his American enemy.

"Passing one hundred fifty meters, on my way to one hundred meters depth, sir," Lepechin announced.

"Very well," Bagirli acknowledged.

"Recommend current depth, Captain," Demirchan said.

Bagirli's forehead wrinkled.

"Sonar has contact and we don't know what the American is doing. The ballast tanks are putting noise into the water."

Bagirli nodded. "Final trim, Officer of the Deck, at this depth."

"Aye, sir; making my depth one hundred seventy meters."

"One hundred seventy meters," Bagirli acknowledged. The American would have to have a sonar team as stupid as his if they failed to hear the sound of compressed air pushing or water rushing into the ballast tanks. He should have thought of that, but during the time Bagirli was changing depth, Brandon had the *Manta Ray* at fifteen knots, going too fast for Sonar to have heard the ballast tanks.

"**WE** still have no contact with the target, sir," Fitzgerald said.

"Damn!" Brandon said, slapping his hand against the overhead pipe. He had little choice but to break off. He thought about changing depth, but the noise of water going in or out of the ballast tanks could distract from the decoy.

"Make your course one-one-zero," Brandon said.

"Aye, sir; making my course one-one-zero."

"Maintain three knots speed."

Somewhere off his starboard quarter was a Soviet Charlie-class, but the Soviet skipper must be one smart sonofabitch. He had countered Brandon's attempt to get behind him. Of course, he could have exchanged a frontal attack with Ivan; kind of a shoot-out at the OK Corral. But he wanted to take the submarine out without risking the *Manta Ray*. What is the use of winning an undersea battle if you can't rub it in the faces of your fellow skippers at the club?

"We're going to break off," he announced. "Too many unknowns. Let's stay this course for the time being, Officer of the Deck. Once we are clear of the area, we'll come back to one-six-five in a couple of hours and continue on to Rota."

Behind them, the decoy finished its job and went silent as it drifted toward the bottom of the dark Atlantic.

"**WE** have lost him, sir," Lepechin reported.

"Of course, we have lost him." If he had a half-decent sonar team, he could have gotten behind the American. Now he had no way to know if the American was sneaking up his ass or not.

"What is your course?"

"We are passing three-five-five, sir. Rudders at ten degrees."

"Shift your rudders and come to course one-six-five."

"Aye, sir; making my course one-six-five."

The K-321 broke from its right-hand turn and began a slow turn to port as the submarine started a one-eighty-degree turn.

If the American was behind him, he'd know in a moment.

"Prepare to fire forward torpedo tubes two through four," he ordered.

Demirchan acknowledged the order and flipped up the protective covers over the red firing buttons.

"Passing course two-seven-zero," Lepechin announced.

Five minutes later the K-321 was steady on course one-six-five. Sonar had no contact. And unknown to both Bagirli and Brandon was the fact that the two submarines were separating from the area of confrontation.

The K-321 returned to its base course, while the *Manta Ray* continued eastward for a while before returning to a similar course, both submarines heading for the same strategic entrance to the Mediterranean.

IN the Sinai Peninsula, Israeli tanks surged forward in a classic pincher maneuver. Egyptian armored units were warned of the approaching Israeli armor and prepared to engage. Both sides were preparing for the largest tank battles since World War II.

Jordon and Iraqi forces started to arrive in Syria, to the ongoing slugfest battle for the Golan Heights.

"Stop the Israelis!" was the cry being heard throughout the Arab world, as people ignored the reality that it was the surrounding Arab nations that had initiated the conflict. Unknown to Egypt and Syria was the rapidly diminishing Israeli war-fighting supplies. Israel was down to less than forty-eight hours before it would have to ration its munitions and weapons and take a defensive stand.

For the past twenty-four hours the Israeli military had been enjoying victory after victory. Every engagement had the Arab armies retreating. In some places the retreats were routs, but the Israelis were surprised to discover that the Arab armies were better trained and led than the ones they had faced in 1967.

Fierce fighting was using up the dwindling war-fighting supplies Israel needed to keep the offensive moving.

In the States, American sailors, Marines, soldiers, and airmen had thrown open the doors of the American arsenals. The silence within the locked bunkers, waiting for the call to war, was now broken by the noise of forklifts, trucks, and men shouting to one another as they hurriedly moved the supplies to waiting trucks.

Large trucks rolled out of the arsenals and headed to multiple airfields scattered throughout America, where United States Air Force transport aircraft were quickly loaded and took off.

The arsenal of democracy was on the move.

By this Saturday morning some of those aircraft had already passed the East Coast of the United States and were over the Atlantic. The largest resupply effort since the Berlin airlift was under way, with the knowledge that if it failed, Israel would lose.

The only backup plan was the intervention of American and other Western forces. Intervention, everyone knew, would start a cavalcade of events, with the Soviet Union deploying its airborne forces, which were on alert, armed, and ready to deploy to Syria.

Israel had to hold out without the Arab nations learning of

its supply problem. Israeli logistic forces were waiting at Lod Airport in Tel Aviv. When the American aircraft landed, the arriving munitions and weapons would be off-loaded directly to trucks that would whisk away the supplies directly to the airfields and battlefields where they were needed. There was no middle stop between the resupply and the fighting. All Israel had to do was to hold out until the resupply rhythm between the two forces was established, working well, and rearming the country.

In the weeks to come, throughout the continental United States, America's arsenal for defense would work its way toward depletion, as its own reserve munitions, kept in readiness for fighting the Soviets, were sent overseas to fight a war that could catapult the world into another global conflict—global conflict with weapons of such mass destruction it would take centuries for the world to recover.

"HAVE a good nap, Skipper?" Elliot asked, sipping his coffee. He slid over to let Brandon sit down.

"Anything left from lunch?" he asked, his voice groggy from lack of sleep. "Two hours is enough for any submariner. I think it doubles my sleep time for the past two days."

"Sandwiches. The cooks did well for breakfast, considering we were at battle stations until six."

"They did. I managed a bite of breakfast before spending the rest of the morning in Engineering. How about you, XO? You've been up as long if not longer than me."

"I am considering studying the back of my eyelids later." Elliot glanced at the clock. "It's fourteen hundred—two P.M. for civilians. We have to go up for our communications checks in a couple of hours."

"They take care of Chief Norman's body?"

"Doc put it in plastic. It's in the supply refrigerator until we arrive in Rota."

"He knows what killed him?"

"He suspects too much drinking. Won't know until we turn it over to the morgue in Rota. Doc says they'll either do an autopsy there or ship it back stateside and it'll be done there. Either way, the man is dead."

"I'll write the letter to his next of kin. Would you pull his service record for me and have Admin drop it off on my desk in my stateroom?"

"Already have pulled it. His page two lists a mother in Florida. No wife, though the master chief told me he had some kids in Charleston. His page two doesn't reflect any. He left his insurance to his mother in Jacksonville."

Brandon nodded. He wondered for a moment what the story was on Norman. Everyone had a story. If the chief had kids, why leave his insurance to his mother?

"Master Chief Tay said the man never received any mail, so it appears Norman may have been one of those loners who see the Navy as their family."

Brandon let out a deep breath. "We'll take care of the paperwork and let his relatives work out the details. I'll write the letter to his mother."

"Aye, sir."

"Has Sonar been able to regain contact?" Brandon sipped the coffee, tasting the touch of the tannic acid of old coffee around the edges of the tongue. By seven tonight, the acidity would turn the tongue with its depth.

Elliot shook his head. "Nope. Seems Ivan has disappeared. Probably slinking off home with his tail between his legs."

Brandon smiled. He shut his eyes for a moment, to discover he didn't want to open them. Sailors grew used to fatigue, as something to live with on board a boat. Watches four hours long followed by four hours off, with no hope of a quick nap before the cycle started again.

"I don't think this Soviet skipper has snaked off home, Dev. I have the feeling this Soviet skipper is looking for us as much as we are looking for him."

"We are still on base course of one-six-five at eight knots, at two hundred fifty feet depth. I double-checked with the officer of the deck to ensure he understood to clear our baffles several times during his watch, but at no set time. No sign of Ivan."

Brandon sipped his coffee. "He's out there. He wants to sink us as much as I want to send him to Davy Jones's locker. Let him breathe the fresh salt water down there," he said, finding that while he spoke the words he did not feel them emotionally. In his younger days in the Navy he would have said the same thing with vigor and belief. *Maybe it's age,* he thought to himself.

"Did you say something, Skipper?"

Brandon put both hands around the hot cup. "I was just thinking about what I said, Dev. Fifteen years ago I would have truly believed that was what I wanted to do—send a commie pinko down to the bottom of the ocean. But after all these years under the sea, sending fellow submariners to the bottom lacks the appeal it once did."

"I know."

"You know."

"We do what we are ordered to do. Sometimes that means sinking boats, ships, or even surfacing within sight of land and landing SEAL teams ashore. The latter is something that I really hate to do."

Brandon nodded. "You're right. We just never think of the human casualties involved in executing those orders."

"Maybe the Soviet skipper feels the same way."

"Not sure I want to put a human face to my enemy. Don't want to wonder about his family or the men who serve under him. Don't want to know how many fatherless orphans will result because of anything we do. And I am sure he isn't putting a human face to us."

Elliot nodded. "It's a cruel profession we chose."

"I don't think I was ever meant for another one. I don't think I could have worked a nine-to-five job, going home to the same house night after night." His thoughts slid to Louise. He wondered if she was still at their base house at Norfolk Naval Base or if she had already shipped home the household goods, thrown the keys at the housing officer, and was back in Savannah with her folks.

"I think my wife would have left me if I spent that much time at home," Elliot said.

"I think my second wife just left me because I didn't."

"Louise? Yes, I know."

"You know?"

"Linda wrote me. Got the letter in Keflavik. Didn't want to say anything."

"I got my letter before we departed Keflavik. And got the divorce papers from her lawyer. Seems she has had enough of single parenting and wants to return to Georgia."

"She sent you divorce papers? While you were deployed?" Elliot asked incredulously. He and his wife, Linda, had been married for seven years. "I got the impression from Linda that Louise wanted a divorce, but Linda thought you two would work it out."

Brandon shrugged. "Been through it once before."

"I'm sure you can patch things up once we return."

Brandon nodded. He knew better. Things had been heading south when he left. Too many late nights out with the shipmates, too many late nights at the job . . . just too many late nights. He sighed. Maybe men such as sailors were not meant to be married. Maybe they were meant to be one-night stands, spewing their sperm with every woman they could, and leaving an untraceable trail of offspring wherever they went.

The wardroom door opened and Lieutenant Strickland stepped inside. He was breathing heavily. "Sorry, Skipper, XO. Hate to interrupt you, but we got a message from Commander Second Fleet to come up for a special communications."

"ELF?"

"Yes, sir," Strickland said, handing the one-line message to Brandon.

ELF stood for extremely low frequencies. Naval Research Laboratory was experimenting with this capability to communicate with submerged submarines. So far, the capability was proving successful, but the ability to send long messages had yet to be achieved.

"ELF will never prove valuable for submarine comms," Elliot said.

Brandon shrugged. "It's still in its infancy. Give it a few years." He reached up and took the single sheet of message traffic and quickly read the one-line message. "It's got some coordinates here," he said, handing the message to Elliot.

Elliot was already sliding out from his side of the table as he grabbed the message. He read it as he stood. "Looks as if I need to get to the control room." He looked at Strickland. "Has the officer of the deck seen this?"

Strickland shook his head. "Said 'eyes only' on it, sir."

"Eyes only" meant for the skipper alone.

Elliot shook his head and let out a deep sigh. "Why would they send a one-liner with "eyes only" on it?" he asked, not expecting an answer. "Waste of firepower for such a slow mode of communications."

Brandon pushed himself out of his seat. "We ought to go see how far away we are from this position." He looked at Strickland. "Are we going to be able to communicate even if we go to periscope depth?"

"I don't know, sir. We still have the VHF/UHF communications, but with the wire gone, we have no HF comms."

"Can we pick up messages?"

"The chief seems to think we can't. Says the wire antenna both transmits and receives, and right now we have neither."

"What you want to do, Skipper?" Elliot asked.

He glanced at the clock again. "We got two hours to get to this position. Let's do what the message says; after all, it is from Second Fleet."

"Maybe it's a change to our mission."

"Could be, but unless this rendezvous changes our mission, we are going to continue toward the Strait of Gibraltar and then take up our duties of ensuring access to the Mediterranean for our fleet."

"That will be after we do port call at Rota, Spain, to get the communications capability repaired?" Elliot asked.

"That will be after we do our intermediate maintenance availability at the port. Should not take them long. After all, we already sent them the logistic request with the parts needed to repair it."

"Let's hope the supply system works."

Brandon nodded. "If not, we might be doing this mission without any communications except what we have on the conning tower."

VOLKOV sat in his underwear on the edge of his rack, smoking a cigarette. The smoke whiffed upward toward the small ventilation shaft. In the armless chair near the door leading into the stateroom, Zaharovich sat in his underwear. Sweat spread slowly beneath his armpits, further staining the yellowish T-shirt.

"So what happened then, Victor?" Volkov asked, smoke encircling each word of the *zampolit*'s.

Zaharovich shrugged. "It was the strangest thing. Before anyone could say anything, the skipper fired four torpedoes at the American." A nervous laugh escaped. "We were scared at first, then like the others in the control room, I felt a surge of pride over firing at the Americans."

"Did it last?"

"What last?"

"This feeling of pride."

Zaharovich shook his head. "When the torpedoes kept running and running and failed to find the Americans, I think everyone of us became apprehensive. I thought we would hear a report from Sonar that the Americans had fired on us." Another nervous laugh came from the number two navigator. "But then the torpedoes went into a circular search mode. We never heard the Americans again, until early this morning, when it looked as if we were both trying to get into position to sink each other."

"I remember," Volkov said with a chuckle. He reached over and stroked Zaharovich's leg. "I came over and stood near you. But back to the firing of the torpedoes." He removed his hand. "I was not in the control room for this incident. Did anyone recommend to the captain to fire at the Americans, or was it his idea alone?"

Zaharovich shook his head slightly, then stared directly at

Volkov. "I don't know. I was the navigator on duty. One moment I was reporting our location and time to turn, then the next we had four torpedoes in the water. We should have sunk the American."

"Didn't the skipper have the wire guides on the torpedoes?" Volkov raised a hand above the bed and twisted it. "Couldn't we have guided the torpedoes?"

Zaharovich shrugged. "I'm not sure, but I know the wire broke soon after the torpedoes were fired, because I heard the officer of the deck report it."

Volkov grunted. "Did we do a fancy maneuver or change depth quickly or did the captain order the wire to be cut?"

"I think we did a quick turn away and changed our depth." Zaharovich looked down at the floor. "I am not sure, my dear friend . . .

Volkov forced himself upright and in a sharp voice said, "You need to get dressed and leave me alone for a while. I have reports to write."

"But, I thought . . . "

Volkov laughed. "Navigators don't get paid to think. They get paid to chart the right direction."

"But . . . "

Volkov held up his hand. "Let's not spoil our special relationship by believing it is anything more than two sailors helping each other out while at sea."

Zaharovich's expression dropped.

Volkov reached over and ran his hand along the man's face. "Victor, you are such a young officer with such a great future ahead of you. I have already written praise of your support to the Party and the importance of making sure you are placed in positions of greater responsibility. Positions where you may grow in rank . . . rank, prestige, and power."

"Thank you, *Zampolit*."

Volkov dropped his hand, stood, and slipped his pants on. "And such smooth skin. Now, get your pants on and get out of here. We would not want anyone to start talking about how closely you are following your Party-political studies with the *zampolit*, now would we?"

Zaharovich nodded. He thought about telling Volkov that his boss, Lieutenant Commander Obukhov, had already cautioned him about the time being spent in the *zampolit*'s stateroom.

"It is two o'clock, comrade. Time for me to get dressed and make my rounds."

Zaharovich stood and said, "Good-bye, comrade." Commander Obukhov was more concerned that Zaharovich's actions might cause him—the number one navigator—to be forced to come to Party-political meetings. That would be catastrophic for the world of Soviet navigators, who had no other duties but that of navigating. But behind that cautioning, Zaharovich had detected that Obukhov suspected that more than party work was occurring. When he had left Obukhov earlier this morning, Zaharovich was blushing from his own interpretation of what Obukhov suspected.

Volkov did not see the redness of Zaharovich's face as the navigator glanced once more at the *zampolit* before pulling the door shut behind him.

LEPECHIN stood quietly in Demirchan's stateroom. "What if he comes in?"

"Then I am chewing you out for arguing with the skipper while we are fighting the Americans."

"He is dangerous. He is very paranoid."

"That is mutinous talk, Commander," Demirchan cautioned.

Demirchan turned, letting his pencil drop onto the top of the desk. The slight clicking sound stopped as the pencil rolled from the edge, coming to rest against the back of the desk. "He is the skipper. We must be very careful about what we say."

"XO, we both saw what we saw."

Demirchan pinched his nose and took a deep breath. He and Lepechin had discussed the changes in Bagirli since the sinking of the German merchant ship.

The meaning of Bagirli's public reprimand by Admiral

Ramishvili, in front of his fellow Project 670 skippers, was not lost on Demirchan and the other officers of the wardroom.

Bagirli would be relieved once this crisis was over. And Demirchan would be very surprised if he did not join Bagirli in whatever the Navy decided. Guilt by association was a Soviet tradition generated by the great Stalin.

"He is trying to recover his position," Lepechin offered.

"I would watch what you say, Lieutenant Commander Lepechin. Even if what you say is true," Demirchan said quietly, though he knew Lepechin was right. "He is still the skipper, and because of that only the *zampolit* or medical officer can relieve him. For you and I to discuss such a thing is mutiny. Mutiny is the same regardless of whose Navy you are in—ours, the Americans, the British, even the Polish and Italian."

"I am concerned he might get all of us killed . . . "

"His orders are to keep the American Navy from entering the Mediterranean. If he believes the American submarine is here to prevent him from carrying out his orders, then he must sink it."

Lepechin guffawed. "We cannot do that by ourselves."

"Sink the American? Of course we can."

"I didn't mean that, XO. I meant we—one submarine— cannot stop an American fleet from entering the Mediterranean. We need many more to be effective."

"You are right, Pyotr. We are not alone in this mission, though it seems we are by ourselves. The other four Project 670 boats are taking positions along the most likely path of the American fleet when it leaves its East Coast ports. Our orders are to take position near the mouth of the Mediterranean, near the Strait of Gibraltar, off the coast of Rota, Spain."

"The Spanish Fleet is in Rota."

Demirchan wrinkled his nose. "It is hard to call a small carrier such as the *Dedalo* and its handful of destroyers a fleet."

"It is still an aircraft carrier."

"It is an American castoff. An ancient American aircraft carrier with the capability of carrying six to eight Harriers."

"They could join the Americans to protect entrance to the Mediterranean."

"And they could attack the Soviet Fleet, if they were foolish enough to do it. But we know they will not."

"Because our fleet is in the Eastern Mediterranean," Lepechin said with a grin.

Demirchan grinned. "Touché, my operations officer. Because we are in the Eastern Mediterranean, but also because we are submarines and the Spanish Navy is for self-defense. If we don't attack the Spanish, they will leave us alone."

"But if we attack the Americans while they are in Spanish waters . . ."

"We won't."

"Are we sure? Captain Bagirli may have different ideas."

"I will talk with him."

"He has ordered a zigzag course to the area of operations. He is still searching for the Americans."

"He is right to do so." Demirchan looked at his watch. "I have reports to write, including an update to the situation report we sent earlier. The Soviet Northern Fleet will want to know if we have reestablished contact with the American submarine."

Lepechin acknowledged the dismissal and quickly left the stateroom. Only three staterooms on the Project 670–class had doors: the captain's, the XO's, and the *zampolit*'s. Curtains covered the entrance to the small, tightly confined two-man staterooms for the rest of the officers.

When Demirchan next looked up, thirty minutes had passed. The two-page situation update was finished in double-space rough so Bagirli could make any changes he wanted. Then Demirchan would read it once more and suggest any additional corrections to Bagirli before delivering it to Communications.

The next communications period, when the K-321 was at periscope depth, would be when this situation report would go—even if the situation changed four hours from now.

Demirchan stood, picked up the report, folded it so it would fit into his pocket, and left the stateroom. Down the passageway he saw Zaharovich leave the *zampolit*'s stateroom. The navigator was spending too much time with Volkov, Demirchan thought. He patted the report in his pocket and took two steps toward the wardroom, where Bagirli was waiting, before he stopped. He bit his lip a couple of times before he turned around and reluctantly headed toward Volkov's stateroom.

THIRTEEN

October 14, 1973—Sunday

THE Israeli and Arab armies engaged in the largest tank battle since World War II. Egypt lost over two hundred tanks. Syria had captured part of the Golan Heights and was prepared to move forward, unaware of what was waiting for them. Jordanian and Iraqi army units began to arrive in Syria, to the shouts and cheers of the Arab population.

General Sharon had exploited a gap between the Egyptian Second and Third armies, racing his armor units between the two main Egyptian armies and rapidly encircling the larger Egyptian Third Army.

The Egyptian Third Army was now isolated, surrounded by the Israelis. The Egyptian Second Army began fighting an organized withdrawal.

Loose elements of the Egyptian Army, cut off from the main bodies, had fled before the fierce fighting. Those catching up with the Second Army turned and joined the fight.

With the Third Army encircled and the Second Army fighting a magnificent battle in retreat, Israel discovered there was nothing between the Israeli Army and the Suez Canal.

Expecting the Third Army to surrender, Israel was surprised to discover a hard-core element of fighting spirit within the Egyptians. They fought the Israelis and held them off, while calling for reinforcements and relief.

In Cairo, Anwar Al Sadat berated his Army generals and demanded they turn the Second Army around and send it to rescue the Third, but the defensive withdrawal was too far along and the Israeli pounding was too near for the Egyptians to turn their retreat into an attack.

The Egyptian Third Army was left alone. The Egyptian Air Force was unable to help either. Israel owned the skies.

In the north, Israeli armor and infantry attacked, pushing the Syrians off the Golan Heights. Even with the Israeli forces vastly outnumbered at the beginning of the surprise attack, the best the Syrian Army was capable of doing along its front was to overrun the Israeli fortification at Mount Heron. The Israelis recaptured the fortification, bloodily pushed the Syrian Army back, and engaged an approaching Iraqi Army reserve force coming to the Syrian rescue.

The Iraqis were quickly neutralized. When the smoke cleared on Sunday, October 14, 1973, the Syrians had little organized capability on the ground. Their army was in full rout. There was nothing between the Israeli forces and Damascus but a few Syrian fighting units.

The Soviet Union began earnest preparations to deploy its airborne forces. Israel was about to cross an unidentified red line in the sand drawn by the Kremlin.

Soviet transport aircraft had already been pre-staged at several military airfields, and troops were drawing weapons, munitions, and gear for defending Damascus.

Ambassador Dobrynin hurried to the United States State Department and warned Kissinger that the Soviets would defend Damascus even to the point of engaging the Israeli military forces directly if they continued to advance.

It was a nose-to-nose confrontation in Washington as Kissinger warned the Soviets that should such a deployment occur, American troops of the 81st and 101st Airborne would immediately join the Israeli forces. Even as the two men exchanged "frank" diplomatic discussions, a Soviet command and control unit arrived in Damascus and within hours the Soviet military had set up the necessary command structure to take charge of Soviet forces once they began to arrive. For the Soviet military, the decision to deploy and fight had already been made.

When the Yom Kippur War started, there had been the normal tension between the Mediterranean fleets of the Soviet Union and the United States. Neither side was in a position to confront the other. By October 14, the Soviets had over eighty ships in the Eastern Mediterranean. America had fifty-two, led by the aircraft carriers *Teddy Roosevelt* and *Independence*. The Soviets had over fifteen submarines in the area to the American four. The American Sixth Fleet had canceled all shore liberty at the beginning of the war and now began moving into the Eastern Mediterranean. The air powers of the two carriers were told to prepare to commence combined operations with the Israeli Air Force and to expect a long-range air attack by the Soviet Air Force.

Tensions had skyrocketed daily as the ebb and flow of the war ricocheted between the interests of the two superpowers.

The Kremlin had had a night of shouts and arguments as Party leaders fought to determine how best to show their support for their irate allies, without finding themselves in an escalating war of nerves with Washington that could turn into the Third World War. There was no easy answer, as similar discussions raged late into the night at the White House and the Pentagon.

If the Soviets were going to deploy their airborne forces into the Middle East conflict, the Soviet Army demanded they have Soviet fighter and attack aircraft supporting them. The Arab Air Forces were incapable of providing the ground support needed for the Soviet airborne troops being committed. By evening on this eighth day of the war, the Kremlin agreed.

Chief Aviation Marshal Pavel S. Kutakhov was given the go-ahead for the Air Force to deploy its tactical fighters to Syria. Iraq gave permission for the aircraft to overfly its territory.

Turkey quickly warned Washington of the new request by

the Soviet Union to overfly its territory, but when the Turkish General Staff realized that the aircraft were fighters and bombers, they denied permission. Turkish air defense and its Air Force began to increase readiness and quietly warned the Soviet Union that any fighter or bomber aircraft approaching Turkey would be considered hostile. Turkish fighters began defensive combat patrols along the country's northern and western borders. Other NATO nations were being notified by America of the Soviet intentions. Lights began to burn late into the night in every NATO capital in Europe.

The rush to a superpower confrontation that neither side wanted was rolling rapidly down a slippery slope the end of which neither knew.

"WHAT do we do now, Boss?" Elliot asked, pouring a cup of coffee.

Brandon sat at the end of the table. Strickland and Fitzgerald flanked him. "Guess we do what the ELF message says." He drummed his fingers on the table. "Submarines are great instruments of power, you know."

Elliot nodded with a grin.

"The one thing that probably hurts our ability to function effectively with battle groups is our communications ability."

"Or lack of it. Most of the time we are too deep for them to contact us except by this ELF experiment Naval Research Labs is doing, and even then a one-line message could take fifteen minutes to receive, not to mention we can't even acknowledge we received it.

"We went to periscope depth last night, but received no messages, nor did we have any communications," Brandon continued. He looked at Strickland. "We have a problem if the only comms we have is ELF."

"They are saying come up again on VHF, sir."

The clanging sound of metal trays disturbed the discussion for a few seconds, followed by the rattling of silverware as the stewards began washing the luncheon utensils.

The air recirculation system kept the air scrubbed and clean, but the smell of fresh air was really needed. Brandon wondered for a moment about surfacing and spending several minutes topside tonight to flush out the air system. It wasn't as if the air was bad. It was pure, but there was something about knowing fresh air from outside was being percolated through the boat that made you feel as if you were topside.

The *Manta Ray* was five hundred miles off the coast of northwestern Spain. Not much chance of a Soviet overflight.

"It's thirteen hundred now," Brandon said. "They want us to surface at fourteen hundred." Surfacing during daylight was anathema to a submariner. It was like making love with the lights on and curtains open; you never knew when her husband was going to show up. He laughed.

"Something funny?"

"No, just thinking how ridiculous it would be to come up for these unscheduled communications and get discovered."

"When I came from the control room a few minutes ago, I double-checked the course, speed against the coordinates. We will be within ten miles of the destination at fourteen hundred, Skipper."

"Let's hope we are able to do something. If they want us on VHF comms, then we can suspect that there will be some platform nearby that can relay to us."

"Maybe it's an aircraft battle group," Fitzgerald offered.

"And maybe it's not," Elliot replied.

"Sonar has no surface contacts in the vicinity at this time," Fitzgerald offered.

"We have another hour to go. Keep searching for any contacts in the area. We're in the middle of a major sea-lane, so I'd be surprised if there aren't some merchants floating about. And it goes without saying to keep searching for Ivan."

"I think he may have beat feet after our dance of the underworld yesterday," Elliot said.

Brandon shook his head and took a deep breath. "No, he's still around. He's out there, and like us searching for him, he is searching for us." He sighed. "We're going to cross paths with him again."

"And if we do, sir?" Fitzgerald asked.

Brandon cocked his head to the side. "Then, unless things have changed, we are going to sink him."

No one spoke for several minutes.

"I do not understand why we are unable to find the American," Bagirli said. Standing before him were Demirchan and Iltchenko. "I have restored you to the position of underwater weapons officer, Lieutenant Iltchenko, and as soon as you reach your position, we lose the American. It is not lost on me that maybe you are not cut out to be an underwater weapons officer. Maybe you are better qualified to be a deck officer, someone in charge of chipping paint and taking care of the boat's hinges." It was, however, lost on Bagirli that Sonar had let the American slip away before Iltchenko was restored. It was the reason Demirchan had successfully argued for Iltchenko to be reinstated.

"Yes, Comrade Captain," Iltchenko replied.

When Bagirli did not reply immediately, Iltchenko continued. "Does the Captain want me to return to Engineering?"

"I think the Americans lost us also," Demirchan said, bringing Bagirli's eyes to him and off the hapless junior officer. "We need more time to find him."

Bagirli grunted. "Every minute means he is farther away." *Or closer,* he added silently.

Iltchenko cleared his throat. "Sir, does the Captain—"

Bagirli slammed his fist down on his desk. "Don't be more stupid than you already are, Lieutenant. When I want you to return to Engineering, I will tell you! Do you understand?" Bagirli's words came like bullets from a machine gun—fast, clipped, and drilling into Iltchenko.

"Lieutenant, please do not speak unless spoken to," Demirchan said softly, once again drawing Bagirli's attention back to him.

"Yes, sir," Iltchenko muttered, his eyes glistening.

"So what are we going to do, XO?"

"Sir, I believe you have done everything you can and are doing everything you can now. We still have our orders—"

"To stop the Americans from entering the Mediterranean."

Demirchan's eyebrows furrowed. "Sir?"

"I said our orders are to stop the Americans from entering the Mediterranean. Why? You interpret them differently?"

Demirchan shook his head. The orders said to deter, delay, but did not say "stop." Stop would mean engaging the Americans. Deter and delay meant just letting the Americans know that a Soviet submarine was in the vicinity, and that would be sufficient to delay them. It would mean playing cat and mouse with the American ASW forces, but the K-321 was more than capable of doing that. Even now, Demirchan had Lepechin and his department developing a tactical plan for such an operation, a plan he intended to present to Bagirli later this afternoon.

"You don't seem convinced, XO."

"I am sorry, sir. I read the order as saying we are to deter and delay the—"

"Yes, it did say that, Captain Third Rank Demirchan, and that is what we are going to do. And the only way I see for us to do that is to sink an American warship," his eyes shot back to Iltchenko, "or this submarine that our Sonar has lost." He hated this lieutenant. Everything that had gone wrong with this voyage was because of this piece-of-shit lieutenant. Bagirli had led this boat through the bulk of the American forces surrounding Iceland, American forces bent on sealing up Soviet access to the world's oceans, but he had avoided them, sneaked past. Until this piece of shit had misidentified an enemy freighter as the *Volga*.

"Lieutenant, get out of my sight," he said, his voice low but venomous. "When I want to see you, I will send for you."

Iltchenko saluted and without further urging was out the door.

Only Demirchan and Bagirli remained in the small administrative office that served as the captain's work space.

Neither spoke for a moment, before Demirchan said, "He is young."

"He is stupid. Stupidity does not discriminate as to what age a man is. In his case, he comes from a background of stupidity."

"He does?"

"He has to, doesn't he, Yerik? A man does not grow up being stupid unless his parents drilled it into him or he inherited it. He is lucky his ancestors survived Comrade Stalin during the Great Purge."

The Great Purge was a Soviet period in 1937 when Joseph Stalin had conducted an immense roundup of supposedly anti-Soviet personages throughout the Soviet Union—sending most to Siberia, uprooting and moving millions of families far away from Moscow, and executing hundreds of thousands. Millions died in the Great Purge, through starvation or execution.

"There was a man who knew how to wield the whip, a man who did so much for consolidating our great melting pot of nations into what the Soviet Union is today."

Demirchan tried to keep his face expressionless. Premier Khrushchev had denounced Stalin in 1956, and since then Joseph Stalin had come to epitomize everything wrong with the Soviet Union.

"Don't you agree?"

Demirchan cleared his throat. "Sir, I will talk with Iltchenko and develop a training plan to improve his performance," he said, trying to deflect the question.

Bagirli felt the blood rushing to his face. His eyes narrowed. "The man is stupid, XO."

"Yes, sir, but maybe under your leadership and my mentorship, we can transform him. Maybe we can use him as an example to the crew . . . "

"I would like to do that. But, if we execute him, where would we put the body?" Bagirli asked with a slight grin.

"Sir?" Demirchan asked with shock in his voice. "We cannot—"

Bagirli motioned him down. He sighed. "I know, XO. I know what you mean. I was thinking of how the great Stalin would have resolved this issue, and while things have changed in today's world, there is still sometimes a longing for how we used to clear up our problems in the past."

"Sir, as your XO, I must caution you not to say such stuff in front of the crew or the other officers."

"Yerik, you are my XO. If I cannot express myself to you, then who can I? To Volkov? Mr. Party-political himself? He barely knows what he is doing on the shitter, and less what is going on within the boat."

Demirchan nodded. "Sir, my apologies. I thought you were serious."

"About executing Iltchenko or about Stalin?"

"Stalin I understand, sir."

"Let's change the subject." Bagirli took his foot and shoved a chair over toward Demirchan. "Sit down and get comfortable."

After Demirchan sat, Bagirli continued. "You are obviously concerned about my interpretation of our orders."

"I am never concerned about your orders, Comrade Captain," Demirchan lied. "I just did not think they included the concept of sinking an American warship."

"What did you think we tried to do earlier, Comrade? Ask the American submarine commander aboard for a shot of vodka?

"There is a chance we won't sink an American warship, but already they know we can. That knowledge will do more to deter and delay an American battle group than letting them know Soviet submarines are in the vicinity. I think the days for playing antisubmarine war games with the Americans are a thing for the past. We are at war. You need to recognize it as I do."

Bagirli paused and took a sip of his tea. "I think when we sink the American submarine that is out here somewhere, it will send the right kind of deterrence. It will delay the Americans trying to send another fleet into the Mediterranean." He paused. "Why? Do you have a better idea?"

Demirchan bit his lower lip and then started telling Bagirli about the operational plan being developed by Lepechin, and which was nearly ready for delivery to Bagirli. Bagirli listened, but as the names of those involved in developing the concept rolled off Demirchan's lips, Bagirli realized that they were all working behind his back. Why did he not know of this and why had Demirchan ordered this done without consulting with him? So this recent belief that his XO supported him was in error. Back on the list went Demirchan's name.

"MAKE your depth fifty feet, Officer of the Deck," Brandon said to Fitzgerald. They were on their way to the surface. He glanced at the clock. Two o'clock on the nose and he was only a hundred feet from periscope depth.

"Making my depth fifty feet, sir!"

"Very well."

Brandon listened as Lieutenant Commander Fitzgerald relayed the orders to the bridge team, followed by the back-and-forth play as everyone repeated the commands, each making sure the reply accurately reflected the orders.

The Quartermaster at the navigation plotting table hurriedly made a log entry on each command and each reply. And so throughout the United States Navy, whether on surface ships or submarines, similar commands and logging of them continued. Along with those entries went everything of note, to include the location of the skipper as he moved about the boat. Brandon recalled a few years back when a new third class quartermaster had even logged his visits to the head, before the chief had slapped the third class upside the head and told him to line out each of those entries. Lining out drew eyes to the entry quicker than the entries themselves and invited questions as to why an entry was lined out, but it was against Navy regulations to erase anything once it had been entered in the ship's or boat's logbook. Entries that needed changes or that should not have been entered had a single line penciled through them, accompanied by no explanation. Brandon had joked that it was a good thing he had not identified whether he was doing "number one" or "number two" because the teenage quartermaster would have entered that also. Imagine how future history books would have remembered the skipper of the *Manta Ray*.

Air pressure started to clear the ballast tanks. The bow lifted slightly as the three-degree bubble took effect. The submarine was rising to the domain it hated: the surface.

"Tell Sonar to be alert," Brandon warned. The noise being put in the water as the boat changed its depth was more than the *Manta Ray* had generated in the past twenty-four hours. Somewhere out there was a Soviet Charlie-class, and Brandon doubted the XO's theory that they had chased it away. If the Soviet skipper had had the balls to fire at the *Manta Ray* earlier, then Brandon doubted he would suddenly lack a set and flee the area.

"Passing one hundred feet."

Brandon eased over to the periscope. He checked the gauges along the side of it and looked at the deck and overhead mountings as if he expected water to be easing through them. The clock showed five minutes after two. *Fourteen-oh-five for us military types*, he thought to himself.

When Fitzgerald announced passing sixty feet and started the orders easing the planes toward final trim, Brandon ordered the periscope up.

As the scope rose, he flipped down the handles and positioned his eyes against the eyepiece. The water cascaded away from the glass as the periscope broke surface. He turned the scope completely around in a three-hundred-sixty-degree move. He saw nothing, but he also knew the eye of the periscope was not that far above the water.

He leaned back and announced, "All clear visually. EW, you have anything?"

"Searching now, sir. I show no mainstream commercial radars in the area."

"Let me know—"

"Sir, I have an APS-134 dead ahead of us, bearing one-six-five true. No bearing drift."

"APS-134?" Brandon asked as he spun the periscope to align it along their heading. He tilted the glass up slightly, but saw nothing. Spotting an aircraft with a periscope was hard to do unless motion or a glint of the sun drew your eyes to it.

"EP-3E Aries aircraft, sir," the EW operator added.

"Probably VQ-2 out of Rota," Elliot added from his position near the weapons console.

"Raise the VHF antenna," Brandon said, still searching.

"Think they've detected us?" Fitzgerald asked.

"I would think so. The APS-134 is a maritime search radar. It's one of those with the sensitivity to pick up a periscope, and even if they don't have us on their radar, I'm sure our scope is making enough of a wake that they can see it."

The hydraulic sound of the antenna being raised rode the hums of the background noise. What was a VQ-2 reconnaissance aircraft doing out here in the Atlantic? According to the situation reports flying across the broadcast— before the *Manta Ray* lost its wire—the EP-3E and EC-121M reconnaissance aircraft were going to provide littoral patrols across all of North Africa for the heavy airlift the Air Force was expected to start. Maybe the airlift has already started?

THE banging on his door woke him. Bagirli's eyes flew open, and he was out of the rack before he was fully awake, stumbling into the small storage compartment installed alongside the bulkhead.

"Captain! Captain!" The pounding continued.

He glanced at the clock on his small deck. Two o'clock. He pushed the papers around and flipped a couple of them upside down. Last thing he wanted was for them to think he'd been sleeping. "Coming! One moment, I'm coming."

He opened the door. Lieutenant Commander Obukhov stood there with his fist poised to knock again.

"Sir, Captain Third Rank Demirchan asked that I come get you, sir."

"He could have called."

"I think they tried, but your internal communications system must be off the hook or—"

"Why did he send you, Commander?" Bagirli interrupted. He did not recall hearing the faint siren noise the ICS made when someone buzzed his office. "Who is doing the navigation?"

"Sonar has regained contact. The XO has eased the K-321 course for better reception. And Lieutenant Zaharovich is on the navigation—"

"The American?"

"Yes, sir, the American submarine. It is northwest of us. We are slowing—"

"I am coming, step back." Bagirli pushed the slim track star out of the way and hurried by him. Maybe Sonar had lucked out and really did have the American. He would not be surprised if they were tracking a whale. Behind him the footfalls of the number one navigator followed.

"BEARING?" Brandon asked.

"Hold the EP-3 directly off our stern now, Skipper," Petty Officer Early reported from the AN/WLR-1 electronic warfare position. "It's on a constant bearing, sir. Probably coming right up our ass."

"Early, that's enough," Master Chief Tay said from near the planesmen. "Just report the data; no colorful commentary, if you please."

"Aye, Master Chief."

Brandon smiled. Funny . . . he liked the colorful commentary. Colorful commentary was something he had been told to temper down a few times during his own career. *Early, you're flag material.*

"We got the VHF on the speaker yet?" he asked.

Fitzgerald reached to turn up the volume. "Would you like me to call him?"

Brandon nearly said yes, but instead blurted out no. He would let the airdales call him first. He had the periscope aligned with the bearing EW was reporting, but he had yet to spot the aircraft. Then suddenly it filled his vision, blocking out everything—and then it was gone. He discovered he had ducked involuntarily when the low-flying aircraft zoomed directly overhead the *Manta Ray*. The submarine vibrated slightly from the noise the aircraft generated in the water. If Brandon had had any doubt that the aircraft had spotted them, this had resolved it.

"What was that?" someone asked in the control room.

"That was a close-flying aircraft trying to submerge alongside us," Tay said.

"Well, it vibrated the boat . . . ," Early offered.

" . . . like a dog shaking water off its back," one of the planesmen added.

"Keep the noise down," Fitzgerald told everyone.

Tay slapped the back of the planesman's head. "You guys are making calluses on my palm. Now, pay attention and keep your lips shut."

"Charlie One, this is Charlie Two," came a voice through the static of the VHF radio. "Do you read me?"

"Who is Charlie One?" Fitzgerald asked.

"We are," Brandon answered. "When you don't have someone's call sign, you make one up." He lifted the microphone near the periscope and replied, "Charlie Two, this is Charlie One."

"Stand by for coded message, Charlie One."

Brandon looked over at the quartermaster. "Petty Officer Terrance, take it down." Who better qualified than the person responsible for the ship's log? Brandon also knew that the radiomen would be copying the message down from their speaker watch.

He put his eyes back to the periscope.

"He's circling us," Petty Officer Early said. "I have a quick circular bearing drift on the WLR-1." He pronounced "WLR-1" as "Whirly-One," giving it a nickname the way most sailors did, to hardware systems, each other, and certain women of the night known for their exotic skills.

"Commander Fitzgerald, has Radio finished enciphering our situation report?"

The forward watertight door opened and Lieutenant Strickland stepped inside with one of the radio shack metal clipboards.

For the next four minutes, the EP-3E radio operator or the communications officer on board the aircraft broadcast NATO phonetics. At the navigation position, Terrance wrote one letter after the other until the aircraft reported finished.

While this went on, Brandon checked the plaintext message. He and Strickland talked in a low voice. Elliot joined them at the periscope platform. Satisfied, Brandon gave the message to Elliot and told the XO once he gave the go-ahead, for him to broadcast the report to the VQ-2 aircraft.

From the overhead speaker, the voice from the aircraft started to repeat the message to ensure complete delivery.

When it was finished, Brandon took the microphone and told the aircraft to stand by for a situation report.

As he talked, he watched Strickland take the hand-scribed message from the quartermaster and disappear toward the radio shack, where he and his radiomen would compare it with theirs and then decode the message. Brandon wondered again what message could be so important for the Navy to have a submarine come to the surface—for a submariner periscope depth was nearly the same as surfacing—and to send a limited asset such as the EP-3 to deliver it.

The XO started relaying the top secret message—one NATO phonetic at a time. Within the situation report, *Manta Ray* told of the underwater action with the Soviet submarine firing at them and how now Brandon found himself without long-range HF communications. Five minutes later the aircraft reported receipt, and EW watched them head off southeast, back toward the Portuguese border and eventually Rota, Spain.

"Let's get out of this area. Make your depth two hundred feet, maintain eight knots speed."

"Aye, sir. Making my depth two hundred feet, speed eight knots."

"And let's clear our baffles. Don't want Ivan to have used this moment to sneak up on us."

BAGIRLI listened as Demirchan guided the K-321 onto a constant bearing course with the American submarine. Why would the American make such noise with its ballast tanks? Was the American going up or going down? What would cause the American to deliberately put noise into the water?

"My course is one-four-zero, speed ten knots."

"Sonar believes he is surfacing," Lepechin said. The operations officer stood near the plotting table, alongside Lieutenant Commander Nehoda.

"Make your speed five knots," Bagirli ordered. Ten knots put more noise in the water than five. The winner of this duel was going to be the submarine that could be quieter. But it would also be the submarine that got behind its contact first.

"Making my speed five knots," Demirchan repeated.

"Pass the word to the crew to maintain silence about the boat."

Bagirli had the senior officers of the boat in the control room. Only the engineering officer was absent, and that was only because Bagirli could not figure out what Lieutenant Commander Mashchenko could bring to the undersea battle.

"Sir, Sonar believes the American is changing his depth. He's either surfacing or going deeper."

Bagirli shook his head. "So they believe detecting baffle noise means changing depth?" he asked sarcastically. When no one answered, Bagirli continued. "No, he is going to periscope depth." Only a few reasons to go to periscope depth during the daylight hours: He could have an equipment casualty that endangered the boat. He could be rendezvousing with another American warship, but Sonar had not reported any surface contacts in the immediate area. Bagirli glanced at the clock on the wall and smiled. *Communications. How stupidly simple.*

"He's coming up to communicate," he said. He rubbed his chin as he smiled. "Either to receive or transmit or both."

Demirchan stared for a moment, then his face changed as he realized Bagirli was right. "Can we be sure?"

"We are never sure in the dark of the netherworld," Bagirli said, "but it is fourteen hundred hours." He pointed at the large clock mounted on the aft bulkhead. "It is right on the hour. It is daylight. And he is going up to periscope depth. If he surfaces, then he has an equipment casualty."

The officers nodded.

Chief Ship's Starshina Zimyatov's face glowed, and he slapped one of the two nearby planesmen on the head and whispered, "Did you see how the captain figured everything out, so fast, while we were wondering what the Americans were doing?" He did not wait for an answer, but slapped the other planesman on the back of the head. "Pay attention and learn." The chief of the boat rubbed his hand and wondered for a moment if his counterpart on the American submarine had similar discipline problems.

"Yes, Chief of the Boat," the starshinas answered.

Bagirli overheard the chief's comment and glowed for a moment in the admiration. The COB and the sailors were the only loyal ones he had at the moment. He looked at Demirchan and knew the loyalty he expected, and had thought he had, had disappeared. At least the sailors were still loyal to him.

"My speed is five knots, sir," Demirchan reported.

"Very well, XO. We are at one hundred fifty meters depth now. What are your thoughts?" *Let's see, my friend, if you are thinking like me.*

"Sir, with the American masking our noise with his own as he goes shallow, we could easily change our depth without them hearing us."

"I agree." *So we continue to have something in common.* "Let's bring us up to fifty meters, XO. Fifty meters sound reasonable to you?"

"I concur, sir. At fifty meters, we will be below the Americans and still have depth above and below us if we have to . . . maneuver," Demirchan finished.

Bagirli felt a rush of blood to his face. Demirchan was going to say *run.* "The K-321 will not run, everyone."

They all agreed with enthusiasm.

"Status of our weapons?" Bagirli asked.

Chief Starshina Grishuk, one of the torpedomen, was manning the weapons console. "Sir, forward tubes one through six are loaded with fifty-three/twenty-seven torpedoes. Tubes are closed. Aft compartment has two fifty-three/twenty-seven torpedoes in tubes one and two, with decoys in tubes three and four."

"Who gave the order to close the tubes?"

Demirchan and Lepechin looked at each other, then Demirchan turned to Bagirli, clearing his throat. "Sir, I did."

"Why may I ask did you do that?"

"Sonar told me we were putting noise into the water. You were not available, so to increase our opportunity for finding the Americans, I ordered them shut."

Bagirli bit his lower lip and took a deep breath. "Next time, let me know when the status of my boat changes, XO."

"My apologies, Comrade Captain."

"Open the forward tubes."

Demirchan started to object, concerned about the distinct noise created when torpedo tube doors opened.

"Aye, sir; opening forward tubes," Chief Starshina Grishuk repeated as he flipped open the protective coverings and hit the switches.

"Sonar reports increasing right-hand bearing drift on the American," Lepechin said.

"Does the plotting team have a range, course, or even a speed on our contact yet?" Bagirli asked. If other captains in the world's growing "soon-to-be most powerful Navy" had crews as incompetent as his, they would surface, line them up, and shoot the lot of them.

Nehoda, who was running the passive motion analysis, turned and faced Bagirli. "Sir, we know he is between ten to twenty kilometers from us. He is traveling a base course between one-five-five and one-seven-five. The range and base course are determined on his speed and as yet we have not calculated it."

"Did you not report the bearing drift was increasing?"

"Yes, sir. That is what Sonar reports."

"Let's say that this time Sonar is correct. If so, then not only do we want to record it for posterity, but it would mean the American is closer to us rather than farther away. Since Sonar is tracking the ballast tanks and cannot hear the submarine propeller, would you not say that we are facing more toward the American's bow area than his stern?"

"Sonar reports the ballast noise has ceased, but they have hydraulic noise from the American submarine and . . ."

"Raising its periscope and whatever else they have on their conning tower," Bagirli interrupted.

The four senior officers exchanged glances with one another for a moment before all four nodded in unison. "Yes, sir. You are probably correct," Demirchan said.

"Of course, I am correct. I am the captain. So what is the best course and speed for our contact now?"

"Two minutes, sir," Nehoda said, his words running together as he bent over the plotting table.

It is so simple to me, Bagirli thought. Why must he be the only one on the boat to figure these things out?

"Forward torpedo tubes one through six are open, sir."

"Say that to me again, Chief Grishuk, and say it correctly."

"Sir, forward torpedo room reports tubes one to six opened. Torpedoes are ready in all respects."

"That is better, but not entirely correct. Lieutenant Commander Nehoda!"

Nehoda's head shot up from the plotting table. "Yes, sir!"

"Schedule Chief Starshina Grishuk for instruction on proper command and control reporting in the control room."

Nehoda looked at Grishuk, who had assumed a position of attention. He looked back at Bagirli. "Aye, sir, I will do so."

"Good."

Nehoda looked at Demirchan for a moment before crouching back over the plotting table.

Words have power, and in the control room where the undersea battle is fought, everyone must report things in an orderly, correct way so that information is conveyed in such a manner that everyone grasps the significance simultaneously. If everyone used his own way of reporting, you would never get the right picture. Confusion would reign. Why was he the only one who saw all of this at once? Bagirli thought.

The boat tilted as it began its ride upward.

"Watch the ballasts, XO," Bagirli cautioned. If he was able to find the Americans through their own carelessness, then he did not want them to find him through his.

"Sir, we believe the American submarine is between

twelve to twenty kilometers from us on current bearing. His base course is between one-five-five and one-six-five," Nehoda said. "And he is traveling at five to eight knots," he added with a vocal flourish.

"Good!" Bagirli said sharply. He left his position near the periscope and went to the plotting table. "Now, show me."

"This is Commander Lepechin. I have the deck and the conn."

"Very well, Commander," Bagirli said. "XO, please take the weapons control panel position." He had had enough of incompetence today. How could he depend on a chief starshina to fire torpedoes if the man could not even give the replies in proper order?

"**EASE** the planes," Fitzgerald said as the depth gauge showed the *Manta Ray* approaching two hundred feet.

Brandon sipped his coffee. It had taken them nearly an hour to exchange the messages with the VQ-2 aircraft and then creep down to two hundred feet.

"Sir, Sonar reports a slight noise anomaly off our starboard quarter."

"Tell Sonar I hate the word 'anomaly.' Give me a name for it."

Elliot stepped over to the plotting table, where the Blue Team now manned the antisubmarine warfare target-motion-analysis effort. They were sitting around the chart waiting for a bearing from Sonar.

A few seconds later, Fitzgerald put the handset back in its cradle. "Sir, for a second they thought they might have regained contact on the Soviet."

"Bearing two-five-zero."

Over at the TMA table, the sailors rose and crowded around the plot. The sound-powered talker put his headset back on and began to make communications checks with Sonar. The junior officer leading the Blue Team was Lieutenant Junior Grade Peter Schaefer, Brandon's torpedo officer.

"That would put him off our aft starboard quarter," Brandon said, visualizing the contact bearing northwest from the back right side of the *Manta Ray*.

Brandon walked over to the plotting table and looked down at it. The team had marked the track of the *Manta Ray* on the trace paper laid over the chart of the area. The chart had the western coast of the Iberian Peninsula showing on the east side of it, while the vast expansion of the Atlantic Ocean filled the remainder. The previous tracking of the contact was still on the chart.

Brandon put his finger on the last estimated position of the contact. "Run me a line from where we lost Ivan. A line that shows us where Ivan would be if he had continued along the same course we estimated before we lost him."

"Aye, sir," Schaefer said, motioning to the first class petty officer across the table to him. "Leander, do it."

Brandon watched as the hefty petty officer took a set of clappers and quickly drew a line projecting out the Soviet submarine course. The course cut through the line of bearing from Sonar, but then any course would do that.

"And speed?" Brandon asked.

The operations specialist took a mathematic compass and opened the twin-legged drawing tool. He measured the estimated speed and walked the instrument out along the projected course of the Soviet submarine. When he crossed the line of bearing, he stopped.

"When would he have reached this line of bearing based on your calculations, Petty Officer?" Brandon asked.

"Fourteen forty-five, sir."

He looked at the clock. It was three-fifteen. "It's him." Brandon turned to Fitzgerald. "Sound battle stations."

As the quiet beep to battle stations sounded through the *Manta Ray*, Brandon turned to Elliot. "XO, weapons status."

"Sir, forward torpedo tubes fully loaded, armed, and ready for firing. Torpedo tube door number one has been reset."

"Aft?"

"Torpedo tubes one and two loaded with Mark-48 torpedoes, sir. Decoys in the remaining two."

The call to battle stations echoed softly through the boat as racing sailors hurried to their assigned war-fighting places. Everyone in the *Manta Ray* knew there were no more drills in this deployment.

FOURTEEN

GORSHKOV paced, hands behind his back. Three stone-faced Soviet admirals from his staff stood quietly behind the couch and the two soft leather chairs that faced his desk, which filled the middle of the large Kremlin room. All three men wore the submarine devices of command at sea. Gorshkov turned to the slender, balding admiral standing in the center of the three, Admiral Karl Papanin, the senior man within his submarine staff.

Gorshkov cleared his throat.

"Admiral Papanin, your submarine commander fired at the Americans and missed." He picked up a message from his desk and waved it in the air. "I'm amazed. He fired without authority."

Bagirli was not subordinate to Papanin, but from Gorshkov's perspective anything having to do with submarines was the responsibility of his staff, even if they had no authority over who manned what submarines, how the commanding officer was selected, or even what constituted the right level of professionalism.

"Yes, sir; I will see that . . . "

Gorshkov waved away Papanin. "*Nyet.* That's not what I meant, Karl. I meant, here is a Soviet captain of one of our most modern nuclear submarines taking on the Americans single-handedly, and he misses. He misses when we need him to succeed. Because he misses, we have lost an opportunity to steer the morale of our fleet. That is my problem with him firing." Gorshkov grunted. "I'm not angry that he attacked."

Papanin visually relaxed. "Yes, sir. He is brave."

"Brave, stupid, intelligent, courageous. Bullshit. I don't care why he did it, I'm just glad we have a captain who is able to think for himself without waiting for us to tell him when to take a shit. We need our captains able to think immediately when they need to—but he missed. Do you realize what that means?"

"No, sir, Comrade Admiral of the Fleet."

"Oh, stop your buttering up, Admiral Papanin. If it becomes knowledge that our first encounter with the Americans was a failure, it will cast doubt on other elements within our Navy. A doubt at this time with our 'allies'—and I use the word very loosely—may result in us having to do more, where we might have broadened the opportunity to show the Americans that we are a superpower Navy. Same as theirs." He laid the message back on the desk. "Tell me, what are you going to do to rectify this?" he asked, crossing his arms and leaning back against the desk.

"Rectify?"

"Yes, rectify. What are you going to do so this officer knows that he has to find and sink the American submarine he missed?"

"Sir, he reports he is on his way to the mouth of the Mediterranean."

Gorshkov nodded. "I know, and he has orders to delay the Americans from entering the Mediterranean as long as he can."

"We could tell him—"

Gorshkov interrupted. "But if he is a too loose-cannon, he might do something worse than sinking a German merchant vessel. Do we know if this Captain Bagirli intends to sink the

American battle groups when they come? Does he intend to—" Gorshkov stopped, feeling that increased pressure in his chest that seemed to come more often as he grew older. He touched his chest.

"No, sir. Captain Bagirli is well thought of within the submarine community," Papanin lied.

Gorshkov dropped his hand from his chest. "I want him to sink the American submarine. I do not want him to take on an entire American battle group."

The submarine admiral motioned to the seats. "Sit down and let me tell you why I want us to do something such as this."

Gorshkov pulled his chair out and sat down. A desk between him and his subordinates ensured no one forgot who was the admiral of the fleet of the Soviet Union. He was. Everyone knew it, but this was a critical moment in the history of the Soviet Navy and it had taken him since 1956 to reach it.

He pressed a button, and a Navy starshina entered, wearing a crisp, starched white uniform. "Tea, gentlemen?"

The steward served the three and Gorshkov as they made small talk waiting for the young starshina to depart.

Gorshkov knew the three admirals in front of him welcomed the brief respite of tea, for it gave them time to think about his question. He needed them to see the strategic picture for the Soviet Navy and understand how the tactical mission he needed now influenced it.

The three men sat in front of the father of the Soviet Navy, the admiral whose brilliance had brought the Navy from barely a fledgling with coastal capability to a force that was now on the precipice of confronting the American Navy. And the Soviet Navy was going to confront them in the Mediterranean, a sea the Soviet Union believed was an adjunct to historical Russia and by default theirs to control. It had always been an affront to them when the British controlled it, before the Americans ascended to the role.

When the young man departed, Gorshkov put his cup down. The *ting* of porcelain china as it touched the saucer barely echoed off the walls of the huge office. *For a commu-*

nist nation, Gorshkov thought, *we still love the feel of fine craftsmanship such as that of the artists who made this cup.*

"So, do any of you have the answer to my question?"

"Sir," Papanin offered. "We need to sink the American submarine to show that we are prepared to engage the enemy whenever and wherever we encounter hostile actions."

Gorshkov nodded. "That is true. But why do we need to do that now? Why not last year or the year before?"

The three men looked at one another, and after a brief moment, Papanin said, "Sir, we hesitate to answer that for fear of sounding stupid or offending you."

Gorshkov let out a deep sigh. "In 1960, we had to turn back from confronting the Americans because our diesel submarines were incapable of facing the might of America in its own backyard. It caused Premier Khrushchev to back down. Like dominoes, we suffered a wave of global public humiliation as we were forced to bring our defensive missiles back."

"I remember it," Admiral Papanin said with a tinge of sadness in his voice. "We were forced to bring our submarines back."

"But Premier Khrushchev achieved a secret pact with the Americans for them to move their missiles from their lackey Turkey," the submariner admiral to the left of Papanin added.

"And it took them three years to do what they forced us to do in six months," Gorshkov shot back. "Treaty! A consolation by the Americans so we would have something to show, something we could secretly share with our allies to show how our plan all along was to have those missiles moved."

No one spoke.

"Behind every thunderstorm—even 1960—there is opportunity for growth, and we took it. We used the humiliation to convince the Politburo to build the mighty Soviet nuclear submarine force we have today." Gorshkov waved his right hand at the three flag officers. "Your nuclear submarines." He looked at Papanin. "Admiral Papanin, how old were you when the Great Patriotic War ended?"

"Twenty-seven, sir."

"You remember the diesel submarines."

"We all do, Comrade Admiral. All three of us have served as captains of a diesel at one time or another during our careers."

"Then all three of you understand what I am saying. A nuclear submarine can go anywhere, execute any mission, and do so with the knowledge that our primary adversary, America, is well aware of our growing power."

The three nodded.

"I do admire Bagirli for attacking the American, for whatever reason he did. But you submariners are a most independent lot, and while I admire the man's gumption, I am somewhat concerned about his propensity for action. What Bagirli did near Iceland is haunting us and has earned me some sharp questions by the premier."

Gorshkov took a sip of tea. "The German Naval attaché has quietly filed a demarche through our Navy-to-Navy liaison office, asking for a full investigation and explanation."

"Do you intend to provide this?" asked Papanin.

Gorshkov shook his head. "We intend to feign innocence and blame the sinking on the Americans." He shrugged. "Eventually it will go away, and in the midst of this Middle East fiasco caused by our Arab friends, it has lost Western media interest within twenty-four hours of its happening."

"We could relieve him," Papanin offered, "but then, he does have some qualities that you believe may benefit us."

"Part of me says to do just that. But he is trying to sink the American submarine even if he has lost him. He may provide us the opportunity for what I believe will be the next 'great leap forward' for our Navy."

Gorshkov saw the puzzled look on the faces of the men across from him.

"We can warn him to be more careful. To use due caution."

"Karl Papanin, that may not be necessary. Right now he seems to be the only one standing up to the Americans, and he is doing it somewhere where if he is successful, only we and the Americans will know. It will be enough to shatter their belief that their Navy controls the seas. It will set the stage for what we may have to do in the Eastern Mediterranean."

"But he could also be sunk."

Gorshkov nodded. "That is true. In which case, we have an incident started by the Americans, with the intention of raising the level of confrontation. It will not change the war plans. It will only change the story for our Navy, which is sailing in harm's way down there."

"We should tell Captain Bagirli of your concerns, Comrade Admiral."

Gorshkov shook his head. "No, no," he said, quickly motioning the suggestion away. "Sometimes I like to think aloud about what is going on and how it may affect our Navy. This is one of those times. It does not mean that anyone has to rush out and relieve a captain because, though I like what he is doing, at the same time I am distrustful that he even knows what he is doing. He may have gone off the deep end and have this paranoid belief that every ship or boat on his sonar is out to sink him, so he has to sink them first."

"I don't think . . . " Papanin started to object.

"I don't think he does either, but we need to send him a message. A message that is carefully worded so that he knows we have both concerns and admiration." He looked at the admiral to the right. "Admiral Kagin, you wrote that book a few years ago—what was its name?"

"That was my treatise more than a book, Admiral Gorshkov . . . "

Gorshkov laughed. "I hate you young kids who have to be so exact with words."

Kagin blushed, causing Gorshkov to laugh again. "No, I admire your book, if you don't mind me calling it that. Words are very powerful, and to be able to write so much and have so many read it is something to be admired."

"Thank you, Comrade Admiral."

"You are very welcome. Now I want you to write a message for Admiral Papanin to release telling our good Soviet Captain Bagirli how much we admire him and how much we are scared that he is going to bungle something. I want him to know he should sink the American submarine, and at the same time I want to forbid him to do so."

The three submariners exchanged glances.

"It is obvious you three have not been in the Kremlin long."

"Sir, I can do that," Kagin said.

"I know you can. You know why we want Bagirli to sink the American?"

"Because they are our enemy, and you can use his victory to stir morale in the fleet," Papanin answered.

"I think I just said that. You are right, but for every tactical victory there must be a strategic reason." He saw the puzzled look on their faces.

"You win enough battles and you win the war. The war is a strategic target. You stop a battle group from reaching its objective, you change the balance of power on the fight ashore—everything tactical in a war has a place on the strategic stage." Gorshkov pushed the teacup to one side and leaned forward. "This war we did not want," he said, his index finger emphasizing each word by tapping the desk. He leaned back. "We tried to steer our allies away, and like all Arabs, they refused to listen. Therefore, we must use current events in the Middle East to help the Soviet Navy."

"How do we do that, sir?" Papanin asked.

"Bagirli is part of the strategy this war presents for us to build the future of our Navy."

"More submarines?"

"Admiral Papanin, don't you think you have enough submarines now?" Gorshkov chuckled. "No, I mean aircraft carriers. We have a great Navy with no tactical air cover for operations outside the reach of land-based aircraft. For the Soviet Union that means aircraft that are based on Soviet soil."

Where Gorshkov was taking this discussion seemed obvious now.

"No, we need aircraft carriers. I promise you this, comrades, when this misadventure is finished, we will have the Politburo screaming for aircraft carriers. From this face-to-face confrontation—even if neither we nor the Americans sink anything of each other's—the Soviet Navy will grow a carrier fleet."

"Sir, that is brilliant," Kagin said.

"We are in a no-lose situation," Gorshkov continued. "If we fight the Americans and win, the world will know. If we lose, then the Politburo will have little choice but to give more money to improve the Navy. If we only pose and posture and face off the Americans, then the world will also notice. Whatever happens, I will use this to build a better, bigger, stronger Navy. I will not be satisfied until the seas belong to the Soviet Union."

"How can we help, sir?" Papanin said quietly.

Gorshkov gave these thoughts some rein, imaging the sight of a Soviet carrier battle group sailing into the Caribbean, taking the Soviet Navy presence into the front yard of the Americans.

"Sir?"

Gorshkov's bushy eyebrows rose. "What?"

"I asked how may we help?"

"I heard you. Captain Bagirli is where you can help."

"We could direct him away from the Strait of Gibraltar and substitute one of the other Project 670–classes in the wolf pack."

Gorshkov took a deep breath. "No. It would take too much time. He is the only boat heading toward the Strait of Gibraltar. The other four are scattered along the East Coast of America or in the middle of the Atlantic, to help slow or delay the deployment of a battle group. I think we have to leave him to his mission."

"Once this is over with, Admiral—if I may suggest—we should relieve Bagirli and bring him home."

"For what, a medal or a court-martial?"

"We can decide once he is back."

Gorshkov nodded. "Sometimes, Admiral Papanin, I think you are as devious as all the other submariners I have met."

Papanin grinned, his skin wrinkling upward across his long forehead. "Sir, we are known for our humor more than for our devious nature."

Gorshkov grinned. "There is a right way, a wrong way, and the submariner way. I think your Captain Second Rank

Bagirli has combined all three." The grin faded. "Leave him be for the moment. Let's see what happens." He leaned forward. "Admiral Papanin, find out what the *zampolit* is saying about the K-321. Let's make sure we aren't fighting some party hack who has a differing opinion from us of the good captain or is about to relieve him. And, Admiral Kagin, I would like to see your message before Admiral Papanin releases it."

THE doors shut behind the three men. Gorshkov stood and moved to the window, looking out at the evening sunset as the shadows crept up the opposite side of the Kremlin from him. Shadows that reminded him that everyone was dispensable; time was the agent that determined when that moment arose. "Good luck, Captain Bagirli, and may your time not arrive until you have done your strategic duty."

THE faint hum of the ventilation system recycling the air filled the background in the warm radio shack, alongside the quieter noise of the electronics. Brandon always found the white noise of Radio comforting in comparison to the quietness of the nuclear generators in Engineering. The three radiomen on watch moved among their equipment doing their maintenance checks and making sure the communications gear would operate when needed.

Communications was the bane of submariners. Only when they came to periscope depth, where the antennas could penetrate the surface of the ocean, or they actually surfaced could the silent service rejoin the endless command, control, and communications of the Navy.

The rest of the time, the submarine disappeared from the Navy, while ashore, in such 24/7 command posts as Submarine Force Atlantic, watch station personnel pushed small blue magnetic submarine models across a wall-size chart—models that inaccurately tracked where everyone believed submarines were located. And eerily, small red models dotted the chart where Naval Intelligence believed Soviet submarines operated.

Brandon bit his lower lip. Of course, right now at SUBLANT, the watch-standers would be updating the location of *Manta Ray*, and near the *Manta Ray* model they would be slapping a red model. He had been stationed at SUBLANT for two years of what should have been a three-year tour, but shore duty disagreed with him. If you weren't under way playing hide-and-seek with the Soviets, all you were was a glorified shore-pounder—a landlubber doing things any civilian could do. For a moment he thought of Louise and the kids. The kids he would miss.

Brandon leaned back in the radio shack, nearly falling as the chair tilted quickly to hit the forward bulkhead.

"Hate to lose a captain to an irate chair," Elliot said.

"That chair is dangerous, Skipper," Lieutenant Strickland said as he handed the message to Brandon. "I've decoded it. Sorry it took so long, but we had to open up the two-man controlled keys for it."

"Keys" was the term associated with the cryptographic messaging system, or CMS, used by the Navy. The cryptographic cards were sealed tight in packaging that once opened could never be resealed. CMS was the key to secure communications, and as long as the Navy kept good security on the program, their communications were protected from the prying eyes of the enemy. Unfortunately, back in Norfolk, Virginia, a Navy warrant officer was fattening his bank account with Soviet money for delivering those keys to his handlers.

The internal communications squawk box broke the working noise of the sailors. "Skipper, Control room," came the call.

Elliot reached over and pushed the toggle switch down. "XO, here, Commander. Skipper is listening."

"Sir, final trim depth two hundred feet. *Manta Ray* is steady on course one-seven-zero, ten knots."

"Very well, Commander Fitzgerald. Set the normal underway watch and report to Radio when you are relieved."

"Aye, sir."

Brandon lifted the message and began to read. It was short.

One paragraph, and the impact of it sent his heart rate soaring. The chair slipped forward onto all four legs, and he looked up at the faces surrounding him.

"What is it, Skipper?" Elliot asked.

BAGIRLI stood on the periscope platform. He watched the control room, waiting for the next mistake by his crew. They'd do it. He had little doubt of it. Sonar had reported a noise signature of ballast tanks operating. This meant the American had either gone higher in depth or lower. Bagirli made a humming sound in his throat as he thought about what the American would do. Several seconds passed before he decided the American skipper was now going deeper. If the American had gone to periscope depth for communications, then the comms period was done, and now Bagirli's American counterpart was seeking the safety of the depths.

"Steady on course one-six-five. My depth is two hundred meters, and my speed is eight knots, sir," Lepechin said.

Bagirli wondered briefly what his American counterpart was like. Did the man have the same love of country that he felt for his own? Did he have a family with children such as he did back in Murmansk? Then, he thought of the American sailors on the enemy submarine and wondered if they all wore blue jeans even when they were on board a warship.

Bagirli felt an affinity with this American he was going to send to a watery grave. He crossed his arms. The boat was on a level trim. He glanced at the gauge above the head of the helmsman. Two hundred meters. Too deep? he wondered.

"Plotting table, where is the American?"

Nehoda looked up, cleared his throat, and answered, "Sir, the contact bears one-two-zero from us on a right bearing drift. We estimate his speed as five knots."

"Where does that put us in relationship to him?"

"Sir?" Nehoda asked with a puzzled expression.

"I am asking, where are we in relationship to our contact? Are we off his stern? Are we directly in front of his bow? Are we on his port or starboard side? Where are we in relationship to our contact?"

"Sir, based on his bearing drift and our course, I estimate we are aft of his starboard beam, nearer his stern than his amidships."

"It is called starboard aft quarter, Lieutenant Nehoda."

"Yes, sir, starboard aft quarter," Nehoda said, his voice shaken.

"Officer of the Deck, what is our status?" Bagirli asked, turning his attention away.

"Sir, we are at two hundred meters depth on a course of one-six-five, speed eight knots," Lepechin repeated with a quick glance toward Demirchan.

"Officer of the Deck, make your depth one hundred meters," Bagirli ordered, then listened to the roll of orders as they echoed their way to the helmsman, who was less than six meters from him. If Nehoda was correct, then he was already in a position to take advantage of the American sonar on the bow of the enemy's submarine—a sonar that was pointed forward with a maximum coverage of 120 degrees on either side.

He had paid astute attention to the GRU briefings on the abilities of the American submarine sonars, never realizing until now how valuable this intelligence was going to be.

The American was in the same arm of the Navy as he was. Bagirli knew the training of the Americans and knew from the GRU briefings the career path his counterpart had taken to reach the level where he had his own boat. It was not that dissimilar from his own. Most likely they were both the same rank, with the same number of years in the submarine service. His counterpart might even have had a little more experience at sea because of the years the Americans had controlled it.

The right side of Bagirli's mouth curved upward in a kind of half grin. *But, in minutes, my American counterpart, I am going to change the world opinion as to who owns the seas.*

"Three-degree bubble. Making my depth one hundred meters, sir."

His ears detected the slight hum of the air pressure pushing the water from the ballast tanks. Bagirli was confident that he was in the 120 degree area where the American sonar, pointed away from them, would be unable to detect most any normal operating noise made by the K-321. It would even be hard for *his* crew to screw this up.

BRANDON handed the message to Elliot as he walked over to the ICS and pushed the toggle switch down. "Control Room, this is the skipper."

"Skipper, Officer of the Deck here," came the familiar voice of Commander Fitzgerald.

"Commander, belay my last about setting the normal under-way watch within the control room. I would like for you to remain in charge for the time being."

"Aye, sir. May I ask why?"

"I'll show you when we get there." Brandon released the toggle switch, paused, and then pushed it again. "Mike, let's do a quick clearing of our baffles. I want to make sure we haven't picked up a tail. All this flooding and emptying the ballasts must have put a whale of a lot of noise in the water. Let's make sure Ivan hasn't made use of our distraction."

After Fitzgerald acknowledged the order, Brandon turned back to Elliot.

"Looks as if we are at war," Elliot said.

Brandon shook his head and took the message back. "Not yet. Did you read it closely?"

"Says we are to find and sink the submarine that attacked us."

Brandon nodded. "Not exactly, but I think your interpretation of the message intent is correct. What it says is that we are to engage any submarine that fires on us."

The question Brandon saw in the future, when they stood him in front of the green table to ask why he'd sunk this specific submarine, was, How did he know it was the submarine that fired on them? And there would be a dickhead on the board. All Navy boards had a dickhead on them and that dickhead would push the envelope on the question, wanting to know how Brandon knew it was not another Soviet submarine. How did Brandon know the submarine he sank was not just ole Ivan boring holes in the water, humming the Soviet national anthem, "The Internationale," and thinking erotic thoughts of his wife, who was coming home from a day spent at the mills welding missile heads to rockets, and lo and behold, here came a couple of American torpedoes to ruin his day?

"Should be an easy answer, Skipper."

"How's that, XO?"

"Whatever submarine we sink is the one that fired on us."

Silence greeted his words.

Brandon nodded. "There is only one submarine anywhere near us, and if we find it, we are going to sink it."

"Aye, sir."

The *Manta Ray* tilted to starboard as the boat went into a sharp turn.

A short, rolling vibration rocked the control room, causing Bagirli to reach up and grab one of the pipes running across the overhead. A metallic shriek followed for a few seconds, and then the boat returned to normal.

"What was that?" he asked.

Demirchan pushed the Bch-5 toggle on the internal communications systems squawk box. "Engine room, this is the control room. What is going on?"

"Sir, it was the number one motor and lubricating oil sump, sir. We have shut it down."

"What is the casualty?"

The voice of the chief engineer, Mashchenko, answered, "Sir, number two is on line and functioning properly. Whatever speed is needed, there is no—I repeat no—impact to the performance of the boat. I have a repair team on the sump pump now. We will break it down—"

"Sir! Sonar reports the American is in a sharp starboard turn!"

"They heard it," Nehoda said.

Couldn't have heard it, Bagirli said to himself. *We were in their null spot. I know we were in their null spot. GRU intelligence said we would be in their null spot.*

Demirchan finished his discussion with orders to

Mashchenko to keep him apprised of the situation. Turning to Bagirli, he offered, "Maybe the American is just clearing his baffles? Doing a check."

Bagirli shook his head. "Too coincidental. I don't believe in coincidence. They heard us."

"Stop your ascent!" Bagirli shouted. "Level her up now!"

"Aye, sir," Lepechin acknowledged.

The K-321 began immediately to level off.

"It is possible they did not hear us," Demirchan said.

"Then we will know soon enough, but the worst case is that the Americans heard the sump pump noise. If not, then we will return to our approach," Bagirli mumbled.

"Orders?" Lepechin asked.

The tilt of the boat began to come down.

"No change to orders. Maintain current speed and report your new depth, Officer of the Deck. Let's hope the Americans did not hear that noise. If they did, any further changes to our speed and depth will only focus their search effort," Bagirli finally said.

"Final trim, sir. We are at one hundred fifty meters on course one-six-five with eight knots way."

"RADIO, Control room! Sonar has a contact bearing three-zero-zero. Brief noise, but definitely man-made."

"I'm on my way," Brandon said.

FIFTEEN

BAGIRLI tightened his hand on the overhead pipe, then reflexively relaxed it for a moment, before gripping tightly again for a few seconds. The American was still on sonar. Other than the unexpected turn to the right, there was no sign to show the enemy had heard the K-321. But Bagirli's American counterpart was every bit as good a skipper as he when it came to the cat-and-mouse game of antisubmarine warfare. There were no coincidences in this drama, as there were none in life. Everything was cause and effect.

He squeezed the pipe again. Bagirli would have his engineering officer's nuts for this. Mashchenko was fully qualified to be the engineering officer. The officer had known the pump was suspect. Otherwise Mashchenko would never have cannibalized a more critical part to fix it. The chief engineer should have been ready and paying more attention to a piece of equipment that had been repaired with the wrong spare part.

"Depth one hundred fifty meters, course one-six-five, speed eight knots, sir," Lepechin said from near the helmsman.

Bagirli acknowledged the report. He had been right about them using the wrong spare part. He should have listened to his own advice and ordered them to remove the part meant to support the number one main engine sump pump.

"The American target—"

"He is the American enemy," Bagirli corrected Demirchan.

"My apologies, Comrade Captain. The enemy has steadied up on a westerly course. May I suggest we ease into a right-hand turn so as to keep our position off his starboard aft quarter?"

Was that a good suggestion or not? Bagirli thought for a few moments, weighing the XO's recommendation. He dropped his arm and with both hands grabbed the upper stanchion of the platform. In his mind he could visualize the two submarines on the same plane separated by only a few kilometers of water, both jockeying for position. He raised his head. "Officer of the Deck, right rudder three degrees; maintain eight knots."

"Aye, sir. I am making right three-degree rudder until further orders."

Motion by helmsman as he eased the rudder to the right caught Bagirli's attention.

"Very well," Bagirli acknowledged, his eyes fixed on the planesmen, wondering if the helmsman was qualified to be doing this.

"What is my weapons status?" he asked.

Lepechin and Demirchan exchanged glances. Bagirli saw it, but ignored the obvious indiscretion. He shut his eyes for a moment. He had only asked for the information a few minutes ago, but it was his boat and he could ask for it one time or a hundred times. It was his boat, not theirs.

"I have three-degree rudder on, sir," Lepechin announced, and received no acknowledgment.

"Sir, forward torpedo room tubes one, two, three, four, five, and six are loaded with class fifty-three/twenty-seven active torpedoes. Aft torpedo tubes one and two also have class fifty-three/twenty-seven active torpedoes in them with remaining tubes three and four loaded with rapid fire decoys," Demirchan reported.

"Very well, XO. And the torpedo tube doors?"

"Forward torpedo tube doors are opened per your instruction. Aft torpedo tube doors remain closed."

"Let's open aft torpedo tube doors."

This time, Bagirli missed the eye contact exchanged between his two most senior officers.

"Sir, if I may recommend," Demirchan said, his voice respectful. "We have the forward tube doors opened. Recommend we do not open the aft doors at this time."

"Why?"

Demirchan looked directly at Bagirli. "It would lessen the noise we are generating and putting into the water. Additionally, sir, if the American has detected us and is tracking us, if he detects the opening of the torpedo doors, it may precipitate an attack by him."

"Have we heard them open their torpedo doors, XO?"

"No, sir, but—"

"Then the submarine with its torpedo doors open first can fire first, putting the other submarine in the awkward position of targeting, evading, decoying, and trying to fire effectively. Besides, our aft torpedo tubes are pointed away from the enemy. They are pointed in the same direction as our propellers," he added sarcastically. "If we are going to sink the American, then all we need is to be one step ahead of him."

No one spoke. Bagirli knew he was right. He was going to sink the American. He had heard nothing from Moscow to tell him to stop trying. And he didn't want to be on the surface when such an order came through. This was his moment. It was a moment for the Soviet Union. It was a moment to redeem himself from the inept performance of a poor crew.

"I strongly recommend not opening the doors, or limiting them to two, sir."

Bagirli's face grew red with anger. So it was true. Demirchan was against him also. Like a virus, mutiny was spreading throughout the K-321. He would speak to the *zampolit* and recommend Party members be armed—trusted Party members. He realized that while he had a list of those disloyal to him, he did not have one of those he could trust. Bagirli took several breaths and then replied as calmly as he could, "Captain Third Rank Demirchan, don't you think the American knows we are out to sink him? After all, we have already fired a spread of torpedoes at him. If anything, he is trying to sneak away. We are in his baffles. The tactical opportunity does not get much better." Bagirli chuckled, the anger easing even as his suspicion grew.

"Yes, sir. You are right, Comrade Captain."

"The American is fleeing," Bagirli said again. Typical Americans believe everyone loves them. They are amazed that someone might want to kill them, surprised when they discover the world is more complicated than they'd suspected.

"Opening aft torpedo tube doors."

Bagirli listened for the familiar *whoosh* sound as the doors opened. The soft vibration whispered through the control room.

"Aft torpedo tube doors opening, sir; forward torpedo tube doors opened."

"Very well, Captain Third Rank Demirchan," Bagirli acknowledged. He turned to Lepechin. "Officer of the Deck, keep the boat trimmed so the American is constantly off our starboard bow. Keep us in his baffles."

"SIR, Sonar has regained contact with the target. Reports pressure noise possibly associated with opening of torpedo tube doors. Target bears zero-four-five degrees!" Fitzgerald shouted, his voice tight as emotion flowed through the operations officer.

"Sound battle stations!" Brandon ordered, stepping quickly down from the periscope platform and heading toward the plotting table.

The crew of the *Manta Ray* responded. The soft beeps calling the crew to battle stations echoed through the boat, sending sailors scrambling for where they were needed to fight the boat. Sailors jumped from their racks, quickly pulling on dungarees and shoes, buttoning their shirts as they ran through the narrow confines of the passageways. In the back of everyone's mind was the attack three days ago south of the British Isles.

"All weapons ready, sir."

"I need a firing solution," Brandon said to no one, but meant it for all.

The ASW team at the plotting table worked furiously, with clappers and pencils flying, trying to link together the sparse information into the best firing solution they could provide. They needed more from Sonar, more lines of bearings.

"Sonar reports additional torpedo tube doors opening sir; reports contact bearing zero-five-zero, sir!" Fitzgerald reported.

"He's opened both his forward and aft torpedo tubes," Brandon said, believing the sonar report applied to both torpedo tube locations on the Soviet Charlie-class.

"I concur," Elliot said, thinking the same thing as Brandon.

"He's made us," Brandon said.

"He's tracking us. Why else would he open his torpedo tube doors?" Elliot added.

"Weapons station, make preparation for firing," Brandon ordered, and then he turned to Fitzgerald. "Officer of the Deck, right full rudder, all ahead fifteen knots. Maintain two hundred feet depth."

The *Manta Ray* tilted to the right as its nuclear engines kicked up a wee bit more power. The propellers responded almost instantly, as they surged from ten to fifteen knots. Behind the *Manta Ray*, the waters of the Atlantic churned and roiled upon themselves, creating a huge knuckle of water and sending noise vibrating 360 degrees through the depths.

"Weapons, stand by, forward torpedo tubes."

At the weapons control station, Elliot placed his hand on the plastic coverings of the firing switches, ready to open them and press the switches when so ordered. The electrical switches would automatically fire the Mark-48 torpedoes. If something happened and the torpedoes failed to fire, the men in the forward torpedo room would fire them manually. Either way, the weapons were going to be put into the water and sent on their merry journey.

Brandon licked his lips. He thought he should feel some fear—maybe the dryness of the mouth was it. But he didn't feel it overtly. He knew he was going to win. It was like hitting a winning hand in poker, when you knew before you turned it over that the card you needed was there.

"Officer of the Deck, steady on course zero-one-zero."

"Aye, sir, making my course zero-one-zero," Fitzgerald acknowledged, quickly turning to the helmsman and repeating the orders. The quartermaster of the watch, still waiting for the navigation officer to man his battle station, made nervous entries into the boat's logbook, capturing each and every word said in the control room. Eventually, this logbook was going to be the main source of reconstructing the actions ongoing at this instant.

"Weapons, fire one decoy. Officer of the Deck, make your speed five knots, maintain current depth."

Elliot lifted the plastic covering of the aft torpedo tube three switch and pressed the large red firing pin.

A slight bump vibrated through the control room as the decoy fired from the rear of the boat.

"Prepare to fire forward torpedo tubes one and two, XO." Brandon turned to the ASW team. "Firing solution? What do you have?"

"Sir, based on his right bearing drift and his bearing, we estimate he is between six thousand to ten thousand yards from us, currently bearing zero-five-zero," Lieutenant Grant answered from his position at the plotting table.

"And his speed?"

"Between five and ten knots."

"Lots of unknowns there, Lieutenant Grant," Brandon replied. "Tell me why you think he's only three to five miles from us."

"Sir, if he was going faster than nine knots, Sonar would hear him even with his stern pointed away from us. Rapid bearing drift and slow speed means he's close, sir."

Brandon nodded. "Good."

"Sir, best we can do. Once you fire the torpedoes, I suspect we'll get a lot more information off the asshole."

Brandon grinned. "I hope you're not saying that to make me feel good, Lieutenant."

"Sir?" Lieutenant Grant asked.

"Officer of the Deck, turn the speaker on for Sonar so we can hear their reports."

Fitzgerald reached over and flipped the switch.

"Weapons, contact bears zero-six-zero," Brandon said, adding ten additional degrees to compensate for the rapidly changing bearings of the Soviet submarine. "Prepare forward tubes one and two. Target angle on the bow ten starboard; set range eight thousand yards."

"Forward torpedo tubes one and two set; angle on the bow ten degrees starboard; range set eight thousand yards."

The aft watertight door opened, and Lieutenant Label, the administrative and navigation officer, dashed inside, securing the door behind him.

"Fire forward torpedo tubes one and two, XO."

"Fire one!" Elliot announced as he flipped up the protective cover and pressed the first firing button. "Fire two!" quickly followed.

Every crewmember felt the stronger vibration of the two torpedoes as they shot out of the forward tubes. Those still racing to their battle stations quickened their pace.

A couple of seconds after the vibrations of the firings rolled through the control room, Elliot turned to Brandon and announced, "Forward torpedo room reports all torpedoes fired electrically. Torpedoes running true on zero-six-zero. Time to target three minutes."

"Very well." Brandon turned to Fitzgerald. "How are we doing on setting battle stations?" The sooner he had *Manta Ray* at full battle stations, with all the hatches locked down and secured, the safer the boat would be.

"Sonar reports torpedoes are running true," Lieutenant Davis said from the plotting table. "One moment, sir." Davis pressed the sound-powered headset down tighter across his ears. "Sir, they have steady noise signature from the Soviet contact, sir. It must have heard our torpedoes."

"Sir, easing rudder to steady on course zero-one-zero," Fitzgerald reported.

"Very well, Officer of the Deck."

From the ICS squawk box came the voice of Chief Davis. "Contact bears zero-five-five."

"Won't be long," Brandon said.

Elliot looked at him.

"His sonar team has to hear those torpedoes headed his way. XO, have the forward torpedo room prepare to launch tubes three and four."

Brandon turned his attention toward the plotting table. To the left he heard Elliot relaying his orders to the forward torpedo room.

"Sir, Engineering reports battle stations set. *Manta Ray* is at full battle stations."

"Roger, Commander Fitzgerald. Lieutenant Label, ensure proper log entries are entered to keep track of everything going on."

"Aye, sir," the young officer replied, before leaning down to double-check the quartermaster first class, who had a slight resentment that anyone could believe he had missed anything.

"Time to target two minutes, torpedoes running true zero-six-zero."

"Very well, XO."

What would he do now if he was the Soviet Captain? was the question racing through Brandon's mind. If he was on the receiving end of the inbound torpedoes, what would he do? Fire decoys, certainly. He lifted his head. Most submarines carried their decoys in their aft tubes. That meant when the Soviet captain fired his decoy or decoys, the man was going to try to do something similar to what Brandon had done. Put a knuckle in the water, come about? Would he turn to engage the *Manta Ray* or would he head for deep water and seek shelter beneath the layer? He did not believe his Soviet counterpart was someone who would run.

"What was the last line of bearing?" Brandon asked.

"Zero-five-five, sir."

"Control room, Sonar. Ivan has picked up speed. Bearing drift accelerating. Bearing zero-six-zero, and we show him in a right-hand turn."

He was right. His adversary was turning toward them through a right-hand bearing drift. Could be the Soviet submarine was just picking up speed, but you did not stay on course when torpedoes were heading your way. You took action, and part of that action involved evading, turning your propellers away from the inbound weapons—anything that reduced your profile to the seeker heads in the torpedoes. The Soviet submarine was turning toward the *Manta Ray*.

"Weapons, prepare forward tubes three and four for firing. Have aft torpedo room report when the decoy expended has been replaced."

Brandon took a deep breath. He visualized the positions of the *Manta Ray* and the Charlie-class submarine. Ivan was maneuvering to put his bow toward the *Manta Ray*. Give the Soviet captain credit for not running. The man was going to defend his boat against the inbound Mark-48s, while bringing his boat into position to fire at the *Manta Ray*.

"Left full rudder. Increase speed to fifteen knots!" Brandon said.

The nukes kicked in again, and the speed was felt instantly as the *Manta Ray* leaped forward into a left-hand turn, leaving another knuckle behind them. The active seekers in the nose of any torpedo coming could be fooled into driving through the artificially created dense water roiling upon itself.

Several seconds passed.

"Control room, Sonar. Contact is in a turn. Contact bears zero-five-nine and is easing out of his turn. We have a left bearing drift on this course, Control room."

Brandon was putting *Manta Ray* in a dangerous position with its starboard beam broadside to the Soviet submarine, but if the Soviet captain held off firing his torpedoes a few more seconds . . .

"Weapons, fire decoy number two!"

Elliot reached over, flipped up the cover, and pressed the firing mechanism. A soft vibration rippled through the control room.

"Decoy fired electrically."

"Very well. Officer of the Deck, rudder amidships, maintain speed." Brandon looked at the clock on the bulkhead. If he did this right, the enemy torpedoes would see a quarter-mile-long false image of the *Manta Ray*. If he did it wrong, then he would not have to worry about explaining his actions.

He wanted to get in the baffles of the Soviet submarine, get in a better position that gunfight at twelve o'clock. Submarine warfare was not the Old West seen on television. It was okay to shoot the enemy in the back in submarine warfare.

"Control room, Sonar. Decoy working. We show it directly astern of us. We show our torpedoes still on true course with left bearing drift due to our course change."

"Sir, decoy replaced in tube number three, sir, and ready for firing. Sonar in process of replacing decoy in number four."

"Good," Brandon whispered with a nod. It was coming together.

His eyes watched the clock on the bulkhead. Thirty seconds he needed. Thirty seconds for *Manta Ray*'s surge, from its last knuckle at fifteen knots, to churn the water. What he was doing was the equivalent of a surface ship laying a smoke screen. The first knuckle would last a few minutes, he thought, even as he knew the water had started to dissipate. The decoy was echoing effectively. Thirty seconds.

The second hand on the clock reached the thirty-second mark. It was time. He took a deep breath. If this worked, it was his crew who'd done it. If it failed, then he doubted anyone would know what had happened.

"Officer of the Deck, right full rudder!"

"Aye, sir, coming right full rudder. Speed fifteen knots, depth two hundred feet."

"Weapons!" Brandon shouted, pointing at Elliot. "Fire decoy tube number three now!"

The soft vibration went quickly through the boat. Throughout *Manta Ray*, the crewmembers felt each of the vibrations and knew four firings had occurred. It was only the veteran submariners who could tell the difference between a torpedo exiting the tube, with its rapid rotating propellers, and the decoys being fired, with the propulsion to take them several hundred yards before they started falling toward the bottom of the ocean.

"Officer of the Deck! Make your speed eight knots!"

"Aye, sir; making my speed eight knots."

"Steady up on course zero-one-zero again."

"Making my course zero-one-zero," Fitzgerald repeated.

"One minute to impact," Elliot said from his position at the weapons control panel

Beneath his feet, Brandon felt the *Manta Ray* decreasing its speed. The boat was coasting away from the false image he was leaving behind off his aft starboard quarter. At eight knots, he could put them some distance from the ghostly sonar image he'd created, and at this speed he wouldn't create a lot of noise in the water.

"Control room, Sonar. Contact bears zero-niner-zero now, with right bearing drift due to new course change."

The bearing would change drastically because of the *Manta Ray* maneuvers. "Come on, come on," Brandon said aloud.

"Sir?" Elliot asked.

"The Soviets are about to fire," Brandon said.

"Sir?"

"Control room, Sonar. We have high-speed rotations in the water. Two torpedoes inbound starboard bow, rapid right bearing drift."

"Officer of the Deck, reduce speed to five knots." The Soviet torpedoes had to pass down the starboard side of *Manta Ray,* and even if they were about a mile or two away—he hoped—he did not want to give them anything to change their headings. The watery and man-made decoy should be about a mile from *Manta Ray* now.

Two thousand yards was not a lot of distance when you were evading torpedoes. As long as the passive and active seekers on those Soviet torpedoes had their narrow range of detection focused toward the decoy-knuckle cloud off Brandon's starboard aft quarter, they should miss detecting the *Manta Ray*, even with her propellers starting to become unmasked.

"Making my speed five knots."

Torpedoes had both active and passive radar seekers in their noses. They were designed to use passive means first to detect a target, but when that failed, they went active. While the decoy put false noise into the water, the knuckle presented a positive return for the active pulses the torpedo seeker head could generate. But neither the knuckle nor the decoy was as effective in drawing a torpedo as the metal or propeller noise of the *Manta Ray* would be. The torpedoes would curve gracefully like sharks and immediately head toward the boat. It had been a chance to take. And Brandon still had a couple of other plans to defeat the torpedoes if he had the time and the right luck. Sometimes it was a damn sight better to have luck than a bunch of tactical thinking guiding your actions.

"Control, Sonar. We have additional rapid rotation in the water. Sonar identifies them as two more fifty-three/twenty-seven type Soviet torpedoes."

"Very well," Brandon said.

"XO, Lieutenant Fitzgerald. The Charlie-class submarine only has six forward torpedo tubes, and Naval Intelligence projects they only carry twelve torpedoes. Your thoughts?"

"That is correct, sir. Only four aft torpedo tubes on some variants," Elliot answered.

"He'll have a decoy in at least one of them."

"Doctrine calls for two," Elliot answered.

"Whose? Ours or theirs?"

Elliot did not answer. Silence grew in the control room as everyone waited. For Brandon the urge not to take action was hard.

A faint buzz echoed through the control room as the first wave of Soviet torpedoes zoomed down the starboard side of *Manta Ray*. It sounded like a faint buzz saw.

"Control room, Sonar. Inbound torpedoes passing down starboard side *Manta Ray*. No sign of them going active at this time."

The decoys were working. If the torpedoes went active, they'd hear the pings just before the torpedoes hit.

Brandon tensed, as everyone else did in the control room. He thought if the torpedoes were a mile away, they should be unable to hear them. If closer, they'd know in a minute.

"Thirty seconds to impact," Elliot reported from his position, referring to the *Manta Ray* torpedoes.

Soviet torpedoes traveled faster than the Mark-48s Brandon had fired.

"XO, prepare to fire decoys." If Sonar reported the Soviet torpedoes in a right-hand turn, he would fire the decoys. If not, they were needed for his next attack.

"Aye, sir."

"Ivan has fired four torpedoes, sir. Means he has two left in his bow tubes," Fitzgerald said.

"Also, he has turned right toward our own inbound torpedoes," Elliot added.

"He's masking his props," Brandon said, letting out a deep breath.

A new respect for their skipper filled the control room. Here was a man who had called the Soviet firings a second before he fired. It lessened the fear somewhat, this belief that Brandon was so superior to the Soviet captain that the conclusion was foregone.

"Control room, Sonar. We have additional firings by the Charlie. Faint, believe they are from his aft tubes, possible decoys, only have air-pressure noises of the firing."

"We must be getting close."

"Ten seconds to impact," Elliot reported and then started counting down from ten. Everyone became quiet in the control room, listening to the countdown.

"Control room this is Sonar. We show our torpedoes merging with the target."

Two explosions followed, one almost immediately after the other one.

"Control room, this is Sonar. Soviet torpedoes have passed harmlessly to our stern."

"I think we hit him," Elliot said softly.

Brandon shook his head. He did not have time to think about the hit. As long as those torpedoes that had passed *Manta Ray* had power, they were dangerous. "Sonar, keep an eye on those. They are going to go into a search pattern when they lose contact. We don't want them in our baffles."

The speaker came back on. Chief Davis was in Sonar, while Lieutenant Grant ran the ASW plotting team at battle stations. Brandon would have it no other way, and his confidence in his sonar team was thorough.

"Officer of the Deck, take us onto course zero-three-five. Keep the target off our starboard bow by five degrees. Key is to keep our propellers masked from their sonar."

"Aye, sir. Making my course zero-three-five."

"Sir, forward and aft torpedo tubes are open. Forward tubes three, four, five, and six are loaded with Mark-48 torpedoes. Aft tubes one and two have two torpedoes. Aft tubes three and four are reloaded with two decoys."

"Very well, XO." Brandon turned to the plotting team. "What is the bearing to the target again?"

"THE American has steadied up on a westerly heading, Comrade Captain," Demirchan said from the plotting table that was located near the weapons control station.

"Officer of the Deck, ease your rudder amidships and tell me your course."

"Aye, sir. I am easing my rudder amidships to course one-nine-zero. My speed is eight knots and my depth is one hundred fifty meters."

"Very well." He had the American submarine. What he needed was a refined firing solution. This time he would fire a two-torpedo spread followed by two more and then hold the last two in the bow for the kill when the maneuvers of the evading submarine provided his inept Sonar with more data.

"Sonar reports slight noise from the American submarine," Demirchan said.

"What is their definition of a slight noise?"

"They think he may have opened his aft torpedo doors."

"And he may have not," Bagirli sneered. "Tell Sonar to be more persistent in their analysis." The American might have opened the doors, but in the position where he had the K-321, there was no way the American could have heard them. Bagirli had no way of knowing that Brandon's firing of the two decoys had been misinterpreted by his sonar team. And as the *Manta Ray* eased forward into a sharp right-hand turn, the K-321 sailed toward the false noise signature generated in the water.

Nearly a minute passed, with Bagirli listening to the normal flow of reports and commands within the control room, before the overhead internal communications system speaker squawked.

The voice of Chief Starshina Luzhkov broke the low-level exchanges with a shaking cry that filled the control room: "Control room, Sonar; torpedoes in the water. High-speed revolutions off our starboard bow. Constant bearings at this time. Range is close. I repeat range is close."

"What are the bearings?" Bagirli shouted.

Lepechin grabbed the microphone and relayed the question.

"Give me targeting solution!" he shouted to Demirchan. "Plotting table, what the hell are you doing? I need targeting."

"We are working, sir," Lieutenant Iltchenko replied in a nervous voice.

"I don't have time."

"Control room, this is Sonar, torpedoes bear two-zero-zero degrees. We hold target at one-nine-zero degrees, sir."

Bagirli's thoughts twirled with confusion over the two differing angles being given him. The wide separation between torpedoes and target told him—"It's a decoy!" he shouted. "Ignore the one-nine-zero and concentrate sonar on two-zero-zero. Two-zero-zero degrees is where the American is at." He did not have time to figure out how the American was able to disappear at one-nine-zero and reappear at two-zero-zero. He had torpedoes coming toward the K-321.

Bagirli had to do something.

"Weapons! Fire forward torpedo tubes one and two at the contact at my command."

"Directions, sir."

"I am giving them."

"Fire tubes one and two," Demirchan announced. "Tubes one and two fired electrically. Torpedoes running on one-nine-zero—"

"One-nine-zero? The American is at two-zero-zero. I told you to ignore the one-nine-zero—"

"Sorry, sir."

"Fire forward torpedo tubes three and four on bearing two-zero-zero!"

As on the *Manta Ray*, the K-321 XO lifted the coverings that protected the firing pins from any accidental launch and pushed both of them. The rolling vibration of the torpedoes leaving the boat rocked the control room for a second.

"Sir, forward torpedo room reports torpedoes three and four fired electrically."

"Very well."

"Sir, I recommend evasive action along with deploying the decoys."

Bagirli thought for a moment, trying to reconcile his distrust with the recommendation. He had a moment of epiphany. Everyone on board had the same desire to live as he did, therefore for this action he would have to trust some of what they offered. Only for this action.

Critical seconds passed as he debated this internally before he acknowledged Demirchan's recommendation.

"Weapons, fire decoys one and two. Officer of the Deck, bring the bow dead-on to the inbound torpedoes. Do it quickly. Make noise in the water behind us for the torpedoes. Steady up on two-zero-zero."

"Decoys fired electrically, sir!"

"Very well."

Bagirli recalled the remaining tactical action he had mapped out with himself when the opportunity to sink the American had presented itself earlier. He turned to Demirchan again. "Weapons, reload forward torpedo tubes one and two. XO, have the aft torpedo room refill the decoys immediately."

"Coming steady to course two-zero-zero, sir," Lepechin reported.

"Very well."

"Control room, this is Sonar," came the quieter voice of Chief Starshina Luzhkov. "Inbound torpedoes are showing slight right bearing drift."

The decoys were working, but those American torpedoes were better quality than his 53/27s, even if they were slower. As long as the torpedoes were in passive mode, the decoys and the slight knuckle he had managed to put in the water might draw them past. If he could keep them from detecting the aft noises of the engine rooms which resonate from every submarine, he would take the attack to the Americans.

"Control room, Sonar; one minute to impact."

A minute was a long time in someone's life when it was threatened. Maybe God slows down time for you in those instances, to increase your chance of living. Bagirli smiled. It had been many years since he had thought of God. God was something his parents remembered, but it was something the Party recognized as a fable. The Party was definitely no God, and he had no faith in either of them at this moment.

"Tell the crew to prepare for torpedo hit," Bagirli said.

Lepechin jerked the microphone down from the handset and relayed the warning. All through the boat, time slowed for everyone. The next minute would be the most terrifying in their lives if they lived and the last one if they died. Everything depended on Bagirli having made the right choices.

A deadly quiet settled on the boat. The soft hum along the port side of the K-321 increased in tempo along the skin of the boat, much like the sound of an approaching buzz saw.

"Control room, Sonar," came a whisper from Chief Starshina Luzhkov. "Right bearing drift increasing. The torpedoes are going down the starboard side of the boat."

The intensity of the torpedo noise filled the interior of the K-321, and the torpedoes were so close the crew could track them from near the bow until they were nearly past the stern of the boat. Then the buzz saw sound started to decrease, until . . .

The first torpedo continued aft and exploded near the decoys less than three hundred meters from the stern of the slow-moving K-321. The second explosion followed almost immediately, the warhead set off by the pressure from the first explosion. The second explosion was less than one hundred meters from the K-321.

The explosive might of the two hundred pounds of TNT in a torpedo warhead created a vacuum in the ocean, sending forth a concussive wave of water compressed to a near-solid state for a second, but that second was long enough when it hit the aft section of the K-321. The submarine's starboard propeller twisted and bent, ripping away the triple compartmented seals that protected the internal parts of the shaft from the surrounding water.

The Atlantic is a cold ocean. Currents run northward along the coastlines of the New World, bringing warmth to the British Isles, and then curve southward along the coasts of France, Spain, and eventually western Africa. Gathering warmth again, the currents brush the equator, where they turn westward toward the Caribbean and the never-ending circle begins again. Captured in the center of these strong currents are the cold, seldom-stirred waters of the Atlantic Ocean. With the K-321 at one hundred fifty meters, the added pressure of the water at that depth, combined with the concussion wave, tore through the remaining seals and rushed up along the shaft.

"Sir, Engineering reports damage to the starboard propeller, and they are reporting leaks inside the shaft compartment."

"Shut down starboard propeller," Bagirli said. At this time, no one suspected the enormity of the event.

Bagirli shut his eyes for a moment. The American had gotten off the first shots. Bagirli had fired four torpedoes and none seemed to have hit.

"Sir, orders?" Demirchan asked.

Bagirli said nothing. The American was still out there, and the enemy's sonar would have told them the K-321 was hit.

"Sir?"

He opened his eyes. "Yes, Captain Third Rank Demirchan. I am thinking."

"Sir, may I recommend we depart the area to assess our damage?"

Run? His number two in charge wanted him to run. The American would escape, and the K-321, regardless of how minor the damage, would limp home, to an inglorious welcome. A welcome after he—Bagirli—had once again shown the world that the Americans were to be feared.

"We will not run," Bagirli said softly.

"Sir?"

"I said, we will not run as long as the boat is able to fight!" He turned to the plotting table. "Lieutenant Iltchenko, what is the bearing of the American submarine?"

"Sir, our last bearing was one-nine-zero, sir."

"Ignore one-nine-zero! Has anyone been listening? The American submarine—the enemy—is at two-zero-zero! The one-nine-zero is a decoy, a knuckle; there is nothing at one-nine-zero!"

"Aye, sir," Iltchenko replied. "The bearing to the target is two-zero-zero. He was in a right bearing drift, so his bearing will have eased some in the last minute."

"What do you mean 'was'?"

"Sir, I am sorry, but the explosion has blinded Sonar. We are readjusting the hydrophones and expect to be—"

"Am I surrounded by incompetents?" Bagirli shouted, fists held straight along his side. "The explosion was far aft of us. Far enough that it has hurt, but not killed, us. I need that bearing!"

"Sir," Demirchan interjected, "last bearing was two-zero-zero, sir."

At least he had a bearing and it was the right one. "XO, prepare to fire forward torpedo tubes five and six."

Demirchan opened the protective coverings of the respective tubes.

"Weapons ready, Comrade Captain."

"Very well, XO. Fire forward torpedo tubes five and six."

"Fire five; fire six!" Demirchan announced as he pressed the firing buttons.

A second later, Demirchan added, "Forward torpedo room reports all torpedoes fired electrically. Torpedoes running on bearing two-zero-zero, with three-degree and three-second separation, Captain."

"Very well," Bagirli said. There were other things he needed to do. The engineering spaces.

"Ask Engineering to report condition of the boat to me. I want to know the severity of the damage."

"Very well, Captain," Demirchan said, nodding at Lepechin, who pulled the handset down from its cradle and relayed the request to Engineering.

Demirchan left his position and walked over to the periscope platform.

Bagirli watched his approach, wondering why the officer had left his weapons position.

"Sonar reports it is tracking our torpedoes, Comrade Captain," Iltchenko said. "They are running true—"

"I know they are running true!" Bagirli snarled. "What I need is you tracking the American submarine so we can see our torpedoes merge with it." He turned back to find Demirchan standing beside him.

"Sir, we must leave the area," Demirchan said quietly.

"Why?"

"Sir, we have an engineering casualty. We only have one propeller available. If we lose the other one, then—"

"But we are in a battle, Comrade Demirchan. We are in a battle with the Americans, who will laugh and—"

"Only for this one moment will they laugh, sir. Once we have corrected our engineering casualty, we will return and destroy them."

"We can do it now," Bagirli whispered with an urgent plea. "We can fight."

"Sir, we have depleted our forward torpedoes."

"We have six running."

"Two have missed or we would have heard the explosion by now, sir. If any of the other four hit, we will know."

"We should be reloading the forward torpedo tubes, XO."

"We are reloading them, sir, but torpedoes take more time than decoys."

"We need to see if our weapons hit the target."

"And if they hit, we will know. Your idea of firing those last two torpedoes was brilliant, sir. The Americans will be too busy trying to run from them to fire at us again. We have this one moment of time when we can evade them long enough to fix the K-321."

Bagirli started to object, but realized that what Demirchan was proposing was the correct course of action—as long as they returned if this engagement failed to sink the American. The K-321 had lost its starboard propulsion capability. Probably minor, but . . .

"Sir!" Lepechin shouted from his position near the helmsman. "Engineering reporting flooding in Shaft Alley."

"Shaft Alley" was the term used for the metal casing that surrounded the shafts from the engine that turned the propellers, to the seals at the very end, where the shaft penetrated the boat and attached to the propellers.

"How major?" Bagirli asked. His attention diverted from Demirchan's argument, his reluctance to disengage returned. The XO recommended he flee the fight. It was the right thing to do, but if he did and they failed to return and find the American, then his career was over. His prestige never recoverable. He would be deskbound in Kamchatka or Severomorsk watching ever-younger captains take the pride of the Soviet fleet out to sea.

"They are assessing, sir."

DOWN below, the black gang were testing the pressure in the shaft to ascertain how much flooding was occurring. As they raced along the outside of Shaft Alley, the water pressure increased, pushing against the forward end of the alley, against the seals that protected the engine that turned the shaft.

Water is a heavy element, and the deeper you go in the ocean, the more the weight of all the water above you pushes against the water beneath, increasing its weight.

Lieutenant Commander Mashchenko shouted up to the men above him. Shaft Alley went through this small compartment three meters above the deck. The crew reached the small walkway alongside Shaft Alley via a narrow metal rung ladder welded to the walkway and the deck. "What is the pressure?" he shouted.

He did not hear the reply over the noise coming from the shaft.

"Sir!" one of the engineering chiefs shouted from above. "I think it is still flooding. It means the outer seals are breached."

"How badly?"

"Won't know until we go inside it, sir."

Going inside meant opening Shaft Alley, and once opened, if there was a major casualty, it could flood the boat and quickly send the K-321 to the bottom.

The chief and several starshinas stood near the huge plate bolted to Shaft Alley. It would take minutes to open it, because each bolt had to be unscrewed. If the alley was flooded, they would be unable to put it back in. The first bolt would be shot out like a massive bullet when it reached the last thread.

"Sir, should we open?"

"*Nyet*! Do not open."

Mashchenko scratched his chin for a moment. A drip of water fell on the back of his hand, causing him to look up. Water was condensing on the overhead and along the pipes. The temperature was dropping.

"Don't open, Chief. The alley is flooded. Leave a watch at the watertight door leading to this compartment. Take the rest of the repair party to the number one engine room. Check the seals between Shaft Alley and the turbines."

The chief held up his hand and started down the ladder to where Mashchenko stood. A second later he stood in front of the chief engineer. "I am sorry, I cannot hear you up there, sir. What I hear is the sound of water inside the alley."

Mashchenko repeated his orders. "And regardless of what you find, Chief, reinforce the seals." He watched for a moment until they departed the compartment and then he followed. The watch secured the watertight door behind him.

Mashchenko turned to the young sailor. "Starshina, you know what you are to do," he said. "If you hear water in the compartment, you warn us. Hit the *Boyevaya Chast's* five communications circuit and warn Engineering. You are then to leave this compartment and move to the next one, staying there to be the eyes and ears of the boat. Do you understand?"

The man nodded. "Yes, sir."

"Don't risk your life unnecessarily. Call if you hear anything, and we will send a damage control team if the water breaks through." Mashchenko turned and hurriedly left the area, heading back to the main damage control area for Engineering.

A groaning noise reached his ears as he headed forward. As the chief engineer of the K-321, he knew every little noise, nuance, and peculiarity of his engines. This sound he knew came from the flooding that was contained for now, but not for long. They had no choice but to surface.

SIXTEEN

October 14, 1973—Sunday

"SONAR reports two explosions, sir," Fitzgerald announced.

A cheer went up in the control room.

"Keep it down," Brandon said with a wink. "We still have two torpedoes remaining behind us somewhere." Sonar had reported the first two torpedoes fired by the Soviet Charlie-class as running out of fuel and stopping.

"Probably joined the first two and gone searching off into the Atlantic," Elliot said.

"Let's hope so," Brandon acknowledged and then turned to Fitzgerald. "Give me the status of the boat again."

"Sir, we are on course zero-three-five, depth two hundred feet, and speed is five knots."

"Very well." He turned to Elliot. "XO, have the forward torpedo room prepare to reload expended weapons. What is our present weapons status?" Some would have asked why he was going through the ritual of asking constant repeats of statuses that everyone in the control room knew. Enough Navy wartime experiences had taught him as soon as possible after a combat action, to reestablish a common baseline, a common start, the basics of the boat, in preparation for the next action. In combat, time was very relative, and moments of glee over successful action could be ruined quickly by the enemy.

"Sir, we have Mark-48 torpedoes loaded in forward torpedo tubes three, four, five and six. Tubes one and two are empty. Aft tubes have two Mark-48 torpedoes, in tubes one and two, with two decoys, in tubes three and four."

"Very well, XO." He had four torpedoes left in the forward torpedo tubes. Reloading during combat was a dangerous and many times deadly affair, so he had four torpedoes forward and two aft to fight the Charlie.

"Sir, Sonar reports noise changes coming from the contact's engineering room."

Brandon and Elliot's eyes met. There were a couple of theories of what would happen to a nuclear submarine if it was sunk during combat. One theory was much like every accidental sinking since nuke submarines started patrolling the oceans: the reactors sank to the bottom along with the submarine and its crew. The other much more Armageddon-like theory was that the reactor could melt down, explode, and energize every environmental group in the world.

"Control room, Sonar. We have high-speed rotations off our starboard bow. Close aboard, sir! Close aboard!"

"Weapons, fire decoys three and four! Officer of the Deck, right ten-degree rudder!"

Elliot flipped open the protective covers and pressed one trigger after the other. The soft vibration of decoys firing rolled through the boat.

"Prepare the boat for torpedo hit, Mr. Fitzgerald," Brandon said, his voice calm. "Calm under fire" was how his fitness report from Vietnam read. It didn't mention the strength of his sphincter muscle.

Immediately over the ICS speaker went Fitzgerald's warning to the crew.

"XO, have aft torpedo room reload decoys. Have forward torpedo room load one decoy into tube number one."

"Aye, sir."

Brandon looked at the Christmas Tree panel, checking to see that all the lights were green, thereby revealing the boat was as watertight as it was going to get.

"Torpedo noise increasing in intensity."

The bow of the *Manta Ray* began to respond to the slight rudder turning the submarine angle against the inbound torpedoes. Brandon wanted to mask the propellers and narrow the profile of the *Manta Ray* against the passive seeker heads of the torpedoes.

"Put the noise on the speaker," Brandon said. He wanted to hear the noise as it approached and hopefully be around as it passed. Why hadn't Sonar picked up Ivan firing this second pair of torpedoes?

Behind the *Manta Ray*, the decoys shot off along nearby paths, generating into the water noises that simulated a submarine's. The first Soviet torpedo turned away from its course and headed toward the outermost decoy, hitting it directly.

The explosion shook the *Manta Ray*, rattling the coffee cups secured in one of the desk drawers. The lights blinked off for a fraction of a second and then returned to full glow.

The second torpedo was pushed off course by the explosion, turning it farther to the right. The second decoy lured it slightly, but the explosion had pushed the second decoy one hundred feet beneath the *Manta Ray,* and as its propulsion system continued to function, the decoy ran along the same course as the boat.

Manta Ray masked the propeller noise the torpedo was most likely to lock on, but the decoy beneath the submarine pulled the torpedo down toward it. The second torpedo pushed under the *Manta Ray* and continued downward on the port side of the submarine, where it hit the second decoy a glancing blow. The blow caused the trigger device inside the torpedo to partially activate. The trigger rested a millimeter from the top of the explosive device that would set off the five hundred pounds of Soviet TNT. The blow had not been powerful enough to cause the torpedo to explode. The torpedo continued forward at full speed, heading downward and away, and three seconds later the motion completed what the decoy hit had failed to. The Soviet 53/27 warhead exploded one hundred feet deeper and nearly two hundred feet from the *Manta Ray*.

Within thirty seconds of the first explosion, this one caught the *Manta Ray* and rolled her thirty degrees to starboard. Those not strapped into their seats at their consoles and everyone standing found themselves grabbing hold of something to stop their fall across their compartment. Several busted their heads on metal fixings and bulkheads.

Brandon's feet were swept from beneath him, with only his grip on the overhead pipe keeping him from falling. Elliot tumbled away from the weapons control panel and slammed into the edge of the plotting table. Lieutenant Grant and his plotting team were like bowling pins, falling everywhere around the table. Grant fell on top of Elliot for a moment before scrambling upright, grabbing Elliot, and helping the XO to his feet.

The *Manta Ray* rolled to the left for a moment and then righted itself. The lights flickered for several seconds before returning to their normal intensity.

Lieutenant Commander Fitzgerald was being helped up by the chief of the boat, who had been grabbed by the planesmen as he tumbled forward. A slight gash bled from the forehead of the master chief.

"Damages!" Brandon said.

Fitzgerald pushed the ICS switch down and repeated the question to Engineering Damage Control Central.

Water burst from one of the overhead pipes near the forward watertight door. The COB, Master Chief Hugh Tay, dashed across the compartment to the spurting water and quickly twisted the wheel to shut off the flow of water. Water sprayed his face and uniform.

"Damn," Tay said. "That salt water burns."

Fitzgerald reported the pipe casualty to Damage Control Central.

"Sir, Commander McMahon is gathering the data, but we have some personnel injuries. Doc has already been dispatched.

Reports of some burst pipes, but local crewmembers secured the leaks and rerouted the water. CHENG has dispatched damage assessment teams. His gauges show no major Engineering casualties. You have both reactors, all engines, and ability to maneuver at your discretion."

Around the control room, the buoyant nature only minutes ago had been replaced by the realization of how close everyone had come to joining Davy Jones's locker. Sailors were picking up papers, pens, and pencils from the deck. There was quiet throughout the control room.

"What are your thoughts, XO?"

"Sir, maybe while Ivan is waiting for the noise in the water to lessen so he can see what he has done to us, we can pull away, watch his situation from a distance, and reorient ourselves into a better tactical position."

"We could put another couple of torpedoes in her."

Elliot nodded. "Aye, sir. We still have four torpedoes in the forward torpedo room. If we fire and miss, that will leave us with two. If we disengage and watch her from afar, we can rearm."

Brandon nodded. Sound, tactical advice. He dropped his hand from the pipe and was unsurprised to discover that his palms were sweaty. "Officer of the Deck, give me latest status on the contact."

"Sir, Sonar reports the contact bearing zero-six-three, slowing in speed. Depth unknown."

"He's got to be between one hundred fifty feet and four hundred feet, sir," Elliot offered.

"Seems like a lot of math there, XO," Brandon said.

Elliot continued without comment. "It would put him between the layers, which probably means he has a rough guesstimate on our depth." The last few words tapered off.

"He's more likely nearer the four-hundred-foot marker. Soviet submarines like deeper waters when they travel."

"Navigator," Brandon said to Lieutenant Label. "Give me a course to take us away from the Charlie-class, but put us in position where we are nearer his baffles. If we have to return, I want to be in the better position this time."

Brandon thought about the message from Joint Staff: Seek

out and confront the Soviet submarine that had fired on
Manta Ray. Once located, take whatever action necessary to
ensure the safety of the *Manta Ray* without leaving the control of the area to the Soviet.

It didn't take a rocket scientist to understand the Penta-
gon-ese in the message. Both he and Elliot understood the
words as "Sink the bastard." Whatever happened to the
Nimitz or Halsey or Farragut in the Navy who would speak
plainly?

Both he and Elliot believed there was a growing allure to
the "cover your ass" mentality, competing with the war-
fighting emotions and legacies of the U.S. Navy. This was
probably why Brandon would always be a commander and
retire as a commander. No doubt Admiral Clifton had ham-
mered another nail into his career coffin before the *Manta Ray*
even exited the Keflavik harbor. Oh, well; screw them if they
couldn't take a joke.

Lieutenant Label looked up from his position at the navigation table. "Sir, I recommend coming left to course zero-
two-zero at eight knots, sir. If we remain on the recommended
course at eight knots for thirty minutes, it will open up our
range from the contact. At time twenty thirty, sir, I would
then recommend coming to one-seven-zero. That will put
you off the aft starboard quarter of the contact."

"If the contact is still around at that time," Elliot added.

"Very well, Mr. Label." Brandon turned to Fitzgerald and
relayed the maneuvering orders to the officer of the deck. A
minute later the *Manta Ray* pulled away from the engagement
to open up the distance. Brandon gave a caution to Sonar to
keep watch on the two torpedoes that should be miles behind
them now. He would feel better if he had confidence they had
already run out of fuel.

"SIR, we must surface," Demirchan said to Bagirli. "We have
flooding in the starboard shaft. If it should break through—"

"Control room, this is Sonar. We have regained contact on
the American. He is in a left-hand turn and increasing speed."

"He is running, Captain Third Rank Demirchan. Would you have us leave combat when we have the enemy on the run?"

Demirchan opened his mouth to point out that the American was not damaged, that the American might be doing the humane thing of leaving the K-321 to treat its casualties.

"The American is moving into a more tactical position to fire upon us, Captain Third Rank Demirchan. Do you agree?" Bagirli asked, his voice rising. Every head in the control room turned to the two men standing near the periscope platform.

Demirchan leaned forward and whispered, "Sir, I agree that the American is leaving the area, but we may have a serious casualty that, if we do not surface and try to repair, may sink us."

"That is a load of Siberian crap, XO! Nothing can sink the K-321. It is the pride of the Soviet submarine force."

"Sir, Lieutenant Commander Mashchenko reports the starboard Shaft Alley is flooded. If that is so—" Demirchan replied sharply.

"If it is so, XO, then Shaft Alley will contain the water."

"We do not know if the propeller is still attached or the inner seals will hold."

"I presume Mashchenko is doubling up the damage control protection for the inner seals?"

"Yes, sir, he is—"

"Then what does it matter whether we surface now or we engage our enemy? Send him to the watery grave he so richly deserves. Now, enough of your suggestions and recommendations, XO. Get back to your position."

"Sir, we have no weapons available in the forward torpedo tubes."

"Then, Captain Third Rank Demirchan, I recommend— no, I order—you to have the forward torpedo room crew start an immediate reload of tubes one and two and to notify us when they have completed it. Meanwhile, we still have two weapons in the aft torpedo tubes, don't we?"

"Yes, sir, but once they are fired, we are defenseless."

Bagirli grunted. "Submarines have few defensive weapons other than stealth, and that is what the ocean is for. As long as the K-321 has a torpedo, we will stay in the fight."

Demirchan nodded, "Yes, sir, Comrade Captain. I will execute your orders immediately."

Bagirli watched his number two officer walk briskly back to the weapons console. What were today's officers coming to? Not wanting to fight was anathema to the Russian and Cossack heritage that ran through the blood of the Soviet nation.

MASHCHENKO crawled forward through the narrow space to where he could see the damage for himself. The two members of the damage control team pushed their backs against the bulkhead to let the chief engineer pass. Water seeped around the edges of the seals. He reached out and touched the edges, bringing away moisture, and touched the water to his lips. Salty. It was definitely ocean and not condensation.

He looked at the two men. "Can we put some bracing around the seals?"

The chief starshina who was scrunched up behind Mashchenko answered, "Sir, we can try, but this is a circular fitting. It will take us about an hour to fit the bracing, and that includes having to cut the wood to fit this narrow confine."

"Then get started, Chief. I will call the bridge and see if we can surface to take the water pressure off the seals."

"That would help immensely, sir."

Mashchenko started to scramble backward.

"Sir," the chief said.

Mashchenko stopped. "Yes?"

"I am not sure the seals will last until we can rig a proper brace. The water has already increased in seepage since we have been here."

"That has only been a few minutes." Mashchenko said aloud, his eyes roving along the exposed portion of Shaft Alley. If this should rupture, the K-321 would quickly flood.

"Commander, I do not expect the seals to last much

longer against the water pressure outside. Shaft Alley is completely flooded."

"I will talk to the Captain."

Mashchenko pulled himself backward through the narrow entrance until he felt hands pulling him out and onto the deck of the main engine room.

They had minutes before the seals erupted and this compartment was flooded.

"How bad is it, Commander?" Lieutenant Anchova asked.

Mashchenko sighed. "It is not good, my deputy. This is what I have ordered your on-site damage control team to do." He quickly passed along his orders to Anchova, who under his deputy chief engineer hat also was the damage control assistant, the person responsible for training and leading the damage control teams.

"If the chief believes we are in danger of losing the seals, sir, I have great confidence in his assessment."

"As do I, Lieutenant," Mashchenko said, pushing by the young officer and heading for the ladder. At the bottom rung he turned. "Choma, get every unnecessary person out of this compartment and place a safety and security watch at the entrance up here."

"Yes, sir."

The last thing Mashchenko wanted was to have a mass of people fighting to escape if and when the seals erupted. He had to get to the internal communications system and tell the control room to surface.

Thirty seconds later, Mashchenko entered the main engineering control room where Damage Control Central was located. Here, a starshina chief was keeping track of the efforts to control the flooding.

Several asked how it was, but Mashchenko crossed directly to the internal communications system and pressed the *Boyevaya Chast's* one button for the control room. Lepechin acknowledged.

"CONTROL room, this is Engineering. We have a major problem down here. The Shaft Alley is completely flooded.

You may have noticed the slight tilt of the boat to the right."

Bagirli looked at the key hanging by a piece of string from the bulkhead. The key was leaning right a couple of degrees. The tilt was not so bad as to bring attention to it.

"We have to surface or the inner seals are going to rupture. When they rupture, the water will at a minimum fill main engine room number one."

"Wait one," Lepechin said.

"Sir, I must strongly recommend once again that we surface until we have gotten this casualty under control," Demirchan said.

Bagirli shut his eyes. Was the casualty as bad as Mashchenko said or was the chief engineer part of this conspiracy against him?

"Sir, what should I tell the chief engineer?" Lepechin asked.

Bagirli opened his eyes. "What is the bearing to the American contact?"

"Last bearing on the contact was two-zero-zero, sir, with a continued right bearing drift."

"What do you think the enemy is trying to do, XO?" Bagirli asked.

"Sir, we must surface," Demirchan said, his voice emphatic.

Bagirli nodded. "Commander Lepechin, tell the chief engineer we will surface momentarily."

Demirchan visibly relaxed. "We should do it immediately, sir," he said.

"We have two more torpedoes in the aft tubes, right?"

"Yes, sir."

"Tell aft torpedo room to prepare to fire tubes one and two."

"Sir, do you think that is wise with—"

"Do not ask me if I think an order is wise, XO. It is not wise to run from a battle when you still have the means to fight and to win."

"Sir—"

"Fire aft torpedoes one and two at my command."

Demirchan turned to the weapons control panel.

"Fire one; fire two." The XO lifted the protective covers and pressed the firing buttons for torpedoes one and two in the aft torpedo room.

The slight concussion of the two torpedoes leaving their aft tubes rolled through the control room. But down in Engineering, which was located below and farther aft of the torpedo room, the vibration of the aft torpedoes leaving their tubes was slightly greater—great enough to shake the inner seals of the shaft. The ocean took the opportunity to rip through, sending hundreds of kilograms of metal bursting from its purpose. The two men in the narrow tunnel died instantly. Two more standing at the entrance got caught by the high-pressure flood of metal and salt water. The other three, including Lieutenant Anchova, ran for the ladder even as the water lapped around their knees.

Anchova pushed the two sailors up ahead of him, and by the time he was climbing the ladder, the water was already up to his head. He continued to scramble upward as the rising water chased him.

At the top, he dove through the watertight hatch as water started to pour through it. As he joined the other two sailors, the three of them pushed the watertight door shut, fighting the pressure.

"Stop!" Anchova finally said. "Get through to the next compartment."

In the next compartment, the three were able to secure the watertight door.

"CONTROL room, this is Damage Control Central; the inner seals have blown. We have lost two aft compartments to complete flooding. We are not sure about the Shaft Alley compartment farther aft."

"Surface the boat!" Bagirli shouted. If the Shaft Alley compartment flooded, they would be unable to stay trim. It might even pull the K-321 down.

The *ah-oogle* alarm of the boat surfacing reached every unflooded area of the K-321.

Lepechin started the series of orders to pump pressurized

air into the ballast tanks and push the seawater out, forcing the boat to the surface.

"**CONTROL** room, Sonar; high speed rotation in the water. We have two torpedoes in the water coming our way. Current bearing is zero-four-zero. They have a three-degree left bearing drift."

"Means they're going to pass behind us," Elliot said.

"Means they're going to have a chance to hear our propellers," Brandon replied before turning to Fitzgerald. "Officer of the Deck, right full rudder, steady up on course zero-four-zero."

The boat tilted to starboard as the *Manta Ray* made an emergency turn to right. The new direction would put the bow of the boat toward the torpedoes and help mask the propellers and the engine room noises aft. It seemed to Brandon that he had done this so many times the *Manta Ray* should be able to figure out the necessary maneuvering automatically.

"XO, reload the expended decoy in the aft tube."

"Aye, sir. Current status is we have two decoys in tubes three and four. We still have torpedoes in forward tubes three, four, five, and six and in aft tubes one and two. We also have a decoy in forward tube one."

"Give me a firing solution on the enemy." Brandon had been prepared to leave the area to check his own casualties. He had never sunk a submarine. He was one of those post–World War II submarine commanders who had done a lot of stuff, with the exception of sinking another vessel, much less a submarine.

"Sir, we hold the contact bearing zero-four-five with a slight right and slowing bearing drift."

"Weapons, prepare to fire forward tubes five and six."

There were two reasons Brandon intended to attack. One was the other guy just did not want to call it a day and go away. Never leave the field to the enemy or leave him able to fight another day. The second was his two torpedoes in the water would aid in masking the *Manta Ray* from the two torpedoes inbound.

"Ready to fire at your command, sir. Forward torpedoes in tubes five and six are programmed for zero-four-five."

"Make it zero-five-five for five and zero-five-zero for tube six, XO. I want to catch him fore and aft."

"Control room, Sonar; High speed rotation increasing—slight left bearing drift on both inbounds."

The drift would take the two enemy torpedoes toward the stern of the *Manta Ray*.

A couple of seconds later, Elliot answered, "Solution entered, sir."

"Very well, fire five; fire six."

At the weapons control console Elliot lifted the plastic covers and pressed the two red firing buttons, one after the other. The soft vibration of the torpedoes leaving the tubes rolled through the boat.

"Fire five! Fire six!"

"Control, Sonar; inbound rotations increasing; left bearing drift increasing."

"Forward torpedo room reports torpedoes five and six fired electrically. Everything good in all respects," Elliot added.

"Control, Sonar. We have our torpedoes on sound."

Elliot added, "Torpedoes running on zero-five-zero and zero-five-five."

The two *Manta Ray* torpedoes would continue to separate as they drove farther and farther from the boat.

"CONTROL room, Sonar; we have high-speed rotation closing on our starboard beam; no bearing drift!"

Bagirli looked over at Demirchan.

The K-321 was creating a mass of noise, from the flooding aft, to the clearing of the ballast tanks as the submarine sought the surface. There was little Bagirli could do.

"Fire decoys aft tubes three and four, XO!"

Demirchan flipped up the protective covers and pressed

the firing buttons. The two decoys shot out from the aft torpedo tubes.

"Sir, decoys three and four electrically fired."

One decoy went farther out than the other, drawing the
Manta Ray torpedo farther to the left as the seeker head
detected its passive noise. Then another sound reached the
seeker. It was the sound of the water being pushed from
the baffles of the K-321. In its logic head, baffle noise over-
rode the sound of propellers that made up the basic signature of a decoy. The torpedo immediately veered right, and
this time it was aligned squarely with the center of the aft
half of the K-321.

This first torpedo hit the K-321. The two hundred pounds
of TNT did not explode until the torpedo penetrated the dou-
ble-hull skin of the boat. The explosion split open a long,
wide gash along the skin of the K-321. Water pressure did
the rest, breaking the K-321 into two sections. In the aft section with Lieutenant Commander Mashchenko, the engineers
and the aft torpedo crew died instantly, even as the shattered
remains of this half of the K-321 spiraled toward the bottom
of the Atlantic.

Seawater rushed into the open space, filling it in minutes.
The forward half of the K-321 turned upright, with its bow
pointing to the air one hundred meters above it. The watertight integrity of the doors and hatches held for a couple of
sections before the water began slamming through them as if
they were putty.

Bagirli fell backward, landing on what had been the aft
bulkhead. The fall broke his back, but even before he had an
opportunity to feel the pain, the water tore through the compartment, compressing humanity and squeezing life immediately out of it.

The second torpedo hit the forward remnants of the K-321
and exploded, but in the seconds between the two hits, the
K-321 had already died.

"CONTROL room, this is Sonar," came the somber voice of
Chief Davis. "We have two explosions immediately followed

by the sound of metal crushing, sir. I believe we have sunk the Charlie, sir."

There were no shouts and cheers this time. Regardless of how, for the past four days, the two boats had been maneuvering for the tactical advantage to sink each other, at heart they were all submariners. What had just happened to the crew of the *Manta Ray*'s adversary could easily have happened to them.

"Navigator, make appropriate time entry, at twenty forty-seven hours, that two torpedoes from USS *Manta Ray* hit and sank an unidentified submarine that had fired against it."

"Sir, it was Soviet," Fitzgerald said.

"We think it was Soviet, Mr. Fitzgerald. We don't know for sure. We will leave it to Naval Intelligence to analyze the sonar recordings, and we will leave it to the investigative committee at the Pentagon to reach the conclusion."

What Brandon did not mention was the unwritten order to never put into a logbook anything that indicated a battle between the United States and the Soviets. "Unknown" was better for disclaiming, and when this Middle East war was over and the two superpowers settled back down to the Cold War, they both knew they would still have to reconcile their presence at sea.

"Officer of the Deck, prepare to surface to search for survivors."

Thirty minutes on the surface yielded nothing. The sea had taken the enemy to the bottom. It was dark, even with the searchlight scanning the ocean; the small sea state lapped waves up near the deck of the *Manta Ray*.

Brandon ordered the *Manta Ray* to submerge, and the boat turned back to its base course, heading toward the Spanish Naval base at Rota, where the largest American Navy presence in Europe was located. He still had damages to repair.

Later, Brandon and Elliot sat in the wardroom writing the situation report. Brandon had two days to prepare it, since his communications was down, but it was best done while memory was fresh. They decided that once they were tied up at Rota, Brandon would ask for a car to meet the boat. While

Elliot took care of arranging the repairs so *Manta Ray* could assume its operational area in ensuring open access to the Mediterranean, he and Fitzgerald would go to the Naval Communications Station to arrange the transmission of the top secret message back to Commander Sixth Fleet, Commander-in-Chief U.S. Naval Forces Europe, and the Chief of Naval Operations. Those three bosses in his chain of command could determine further distribution.

SEVENTEEN

GORSHKOV nodded as he put the single sheet of paper on his desk. "So, no news from the K-321 for over a week, Admiral Papanin and Admiral Kagin. We are presuming she is sunk, or had been sunk, or is in such critical condition she is unable to communicate?"

"Yes, sir. She has not responded to any of our communications or orders to do so. Admiral Zegouniov diverted one of his wolf pack to search the operational area where K-321 was last located."

"Do we know what happened to the American submarine the K-321 was shadowing?" Gorshkov asked, drawing out the word "shadowing" for emphasis.

"Yes, sir. It is at their American base in Rota, Spain, undergoing repairs. It has hull damage, its long-wire antenna has been destroyed, and there is some extensive internal damage we are told, but have been unable to verify. It should have gotten under way two days ago for operations off the southern coast of Spain," Papanin replied.

"But it didn't?"

"What our people are picking up in the bars of Rota is

that the damage is more than originally estimated by the skipper. We expect it to sail in the next couple of days."

"And its mission?"

Kagin answered, "To ensure access for any American forces deploying to the Mediterranean."

Gorshkov put his elbows on his deck, raised clasped hands, and then leaned forward to rest his head on them. None of the admirals in the room said anything. After nearly a minute, Gorshkov raised his head and spoke. "Gentlemen, we have to assume the K-321 was lost to hostile action. For the time being, we will call this a probable assumption as we continue to search, but like you, I doubt very much if the K-321 is anything but lost."

Gorshkov took a sip of tea before he continued. "The fact that he had been firing on the Americans and the fact that the suspected American submarine in this action suffered damage is a testament to Captain Second Rank Bagirli's fighting in the best tradition of the Soviet Navy. After this Middle East war is over, we will determine what medal we should award to this hero of the Party and hero of the Soviet Union."

Admiral Papanin and Admiral Kagin stood. "Sir, we agree wholeheartedly. Bagirli will be an inspiration to every Soviet submariner throughout the Navy," Papanin said.

"As well he should," Gorshkov said without standing. "Make sure that a classified message goes forth expressing concern that the Americans may have tracked, attacked, and after a valiant underwater fight, may have either sunk or severely damaged the K-321."

"Aye, Comrade Admiral of the Fleet," Papanin said.

A moment later, the two submarine admirals were out of the door.

Gorshkov's chief of staff entered the office.

"Sir, did it go well?"

"It was as I expected, Captain. It seems the Americans, without provocation, have attacked and sunk one of our submarines, which was operating peacefully and in international waters at the time."

"Sounds good."

Gorshkov shrugged. "It is a tragedy for today's fleet and

for those heroes who have given their lives for our nation. But it is an opportunity to press the Politburo for funds to start to build a carrier force to round out our Navy."

"Yes, sir. I have some proposals here."

"Leave them for me to read." He looked up at the young officer. "Tell me, Viktor, for it will be officers such as you who will take the Navy into the future. These old bones of mine will not always be able to keep up with the technological advances and evolving operational techniques as we continue into the nuclear age. What will you do with such a Navy?"

"Sir?"

"You. What will you do when you wear the epaulets of an admiral and are in a position where you can guide the future of the Navy?"

"I guess, sir, I will be writing beatitudes to those officers such as yourself who were responsible for giving us such a Navy."

Gorshkov laughed. "You are so full of shit, Viktor. If that is what you will do, then we will always be second to the Americans on the high seas, so stop the groveling and tell me. What would you do?"

The officer blushed. "Sir, I would be looking for the technology that might catapult our Navy ahead of the West. Not just the Americans, but I would be worried about the Chinese, the Indians, and the Brazilians."

"Chinese, I understand. The Indians, I understand, but Brazil? It is nothing but a country of partygoers and jungle."

"Yes, sir, that is the public profile. But Brazil has the resources, and eventually will have the technology to develop those resources. When Brazil decides to enter the world stage as a power player, it could become formidable. I would work to develop that relationship while I would strive to limit any growing Chinese Navy force."

Gorshkov thought for a moment and then asked, "So, what is the technology of the future?"

"I don't know, sir, but if we could come up with something that would make the sharing of information easier, it would help develop our ability to fight together. Computers that could be carried—"

"That will be the day. Computers are for eggheads, not for real sailors."

"Yes, sir," the chief of staff said. "Sir, here is your schedule for the day. You have a meeting with the premier for lunch."

Gorshkov nodded as he took the schedule, laid it to the side, and lifted the notebook put on his desk. "And this is the proposal from your team on how to integrate an aircraft carrier arm into the Soviet Navy?"

"It is, sir, and it provides both the positive and negative aspects of building, manning, running, and fighting them. I have tried to keep the cost as low as possible."

"Would the cost stand up to scrutiny?"

"It would depend on who within the Politburo is chosen to decide whether we do this or not."

Gorshkov laid the notebook back on the desk. "I will take care of the Politburo."

He sat there silently when his chief of staff had left the office. Sometimes there must be sacrifice to build the future. Gorshkov knew that to be a true oceangoing superpower Navy, the Soviet Navy needed aircraft carriers. His argument would be that the K-321 would have sunk the Americans if it had had the added value of an aircraft carrier task force to support it.

He lifted his cup, took a sip, grimaced, and put the cold tea down. He pressed for his steward.

"AND that is the story so far, Admiral," Rear Admiral Padron said. "Admiral Rectanus is still overseas, sir, and will get on your calendar to provide more insight as we develop it.

George Ellison nodded. "Everything confirms Commander Brandon's story. We have seen nothing to indicate the Charlie is still around, and everything points to the Soviets mounting a limited search for it.

"I don't understand. If it was one of our submarines, we would have everything we had out hunting for it, and not try to keep it from the public eye either. We would want to know where our sailors are and what happened to them if the story is bad. But everything you are showing me, Tommy, fails to support that premise. The Soviets are not mounting a massive search, even if we don't know where the Charlie is.

"That's not entirely accurate, Admiral," Padron replied. "The Soviets are searching the ocean area where the battle took place. The damage to the *Manta Ray* is consistent with a near explosion. The initial review of the logbooks and the reports by the submariners on your staff should all substantiate what Captain Brandon has put in his reports and in his interviews."

Ellison picked up the two sheets of paper in front of him. "TOP SECRET—Eyes Only" was stamped in brilliant red across the top and bottom of both sheets, with each page numbered as either "1 of 2 pages" or "2 of 2 pages." "The White House will be receiving this wrap-up report after I have forwarded it to Admiral Zumwalt and he has chopped it through Admiral Moorer for the Joint Staff to review." He looked at the clock. It was approaching nine in the morning. "By this afternoon, President Nixon will most likely be reading this with Admiral Moorer standing nearby. Is there anything we are not sure about in this report, Admiral Padron?"

Tommy Padron shook his head. "Not a thing, sir. The one thing that will be a mystery until someone on their side talks is why the lone Soviet Charlie-class, designed to take on aircraft carriers, decided to fight a pitched battle with the one Permit-class that was modified for both surface and subsurface warfare. Goes beyond my comprehension."

"I understand you guys at ONI believe the Soviet Charlie that was sunk was also an anomaly to its class?"

"Yes, sir. It had weapons delivery changes, but we believe this boat was a test platform for designing the new class of submarines the Soviets will roll out of the shipyards in the next decade."

"Is there anything else, Admiral?" Zumwalt asked.

"If I may ask, sir, while we have been putting together the analysis and data into an all-fusion intelligence report, what we have wondered is, how is the crew of the *Manta Ray*?"

"They are doing fine. They had one death on board, but it was unrelated to the action. As for the crew, Rota is still a fine

Navy liberty port and the submariners are having their own fun there. The *Manta Ray* has finished its repairs. I would have released her to continue her mission, but I wanted to make sure we had finished answering any questions the President and others may have had before we sent her into the Strait."

"*Manta Ray* did a good job."

"That she did. The captain handled himself as I would expect any and every Navy officer to when faced with an imminent threat: he took the necessary action to protect his ship and his crew. Most likely they will be released to continue their mission in the next forty-eight hours."

"Thank you, sir; I will tell everyone at ONI. They will be gratified to know."

Ellison waited until the door shut and then pushed the small button on his telephone. A female voice came through the speaker. "Yes, sir."

"Emily, I have a report that needs delivery to Admiral Zumwalt immediately, and I would like a copy retained for my files before it goes."

The door opened and an attractive civilian secretary entered.

"Emily, after you make the copies, get me on Admiral Zumwalt's calendar. I will deliver this one personally."

Emily acknowledged Ellison's request and sashayed out the door, her pleated knee-length skirt bouncing nicely off her legs.

There were benefits to being stationed at the Pentagon.

Tom Clancy's
SPLINTER CELL®

WRITTEN BY DAVID MICHAELS

SPLINTER CELL

OPERATION BARRACUDA

CHECKMATE

FALLOUT

CONVICTION

penguin.com

COMING NEXT MONTH

Readers thought they knew the whole story in
Tom Clancy's Splinter Cell®: Conviction...

They were wrong...

TOM CLANCY'S SPLINTER CELL®
ENDGAME

WRITTEN BY DAVID MICHAELS

Third Echelon operative Sam Fisher knows that several disastrous missions have depleted the ranks of the Splinter Cells. What he doesn't know is that a stunning piece of evidence has been uncovered— pointing to a traitor within their ranks...

Sam is that man.

M521T0809

Don't miss the page-turning suspense, intriguing characters, and unstoppable action that keep readers coming back for more from these bestselling authors...

Tom Clancy
Robin Cook
Patricia Cornwell
Clive Cussler
Dean Koontz
J.D. Robb
John Sandford

Your favorite thrillers and suspense novels come from Berkley.

penguin.com

M14G0907